I0547186

in the silence

Andrew Wooster

Wooster Media Publishing, Haverhill, Massachusetts

Published by Wooster Media Publishing
Haverhill, Massachusetts 01832

Copyright 2019 by Andrew Wooster
Cover Art by: Shelby Watterworth

Grateful acknowledgment is made for the permission to
reprint extracts of "Packed My Things" by Megan Burtt.

All rights reserved. This book, or parts thereof, may not be
reproduced in any form without permission.

Websites:

AndrewWooster.net

ShelbyWatterworth.com

This book is dedicated to Gary Vaynerchuck.
Thank you for making me understand the value of
gratitude, self-awareness, and perspective.

A special thank you to my mom, and nephew
Jonathan, for all their love and support.

One

Anywhere but In-Between

In the face of unchangeable circumstances, the bright find a way to escape, the optimist continues to pray, and those with unwavering righteousness seek ways to repress. It doesn't matter what form of denial you choose. I have the facade of a charmed life.

I attend the prestigious Linden Academy, am co-captain of the varsity basketball team, have an internship at the Mayor's office, and I have a girlfriend more driven and together than I can ever imagine myself being. I have become good at blending these together to create a surface that is rarely questioned by anyone.

Underneath this, though, I battle through periods of depression. It has become clear to me that even when I am balanced, I am still leaning toward isolation. And it only takes a blink for the need to disappear to overtake me.

When this happens, I have no choice but to visit my sister. I drive the six hours it takes to the New York State Hospital, where my sister lives. My parents admitted her when I was twelve and she was weeks away from turning fifteen. They had exhausted all of their options – this was the only explanation I was given. I stood beside her as she changed. As moments became days and days became months. Most of me accepted this was their only recourse. But it makes me wonder what the definition of unconditional love is when those who claim it make a choice to give up on their own daughter. I visit her often. We play checkers or just watch TV. My parents don't know I visit her and my friends don't know I have a sister.

On my last visit, though, I needed to talk. I needed her to listen; to be the sister who organized a carnival for the neighborhood when she was nine; the sister who carried me home when I broke my leg. I wanted to frustratingly push back the last six years and amputate the pain inside me. The idea failed. My thoughts were sputtered by her hollow looks and outbursts of hysterical laughter. Instead, I asked her who she thought was more suicidal, her or me. Without her answering, I said, "I guess it doesn't matter, really. I am the one with access to razor blades."

I laughed blithely at this to dull the effect in case anyone had overheard. In this world, it is far more acceptable to be cruel than to be honest. I kissed her on the forehead, said goodbye, and started the drive home. It has been almost six months since that visit, and I have not seen her since. The feeling in me to visit her again, to see her again, is a string of guilt and regret. The longer I go without seeing her, the less control I have to disobey when the need hits me.

A landscaping job over the summer wasn't enough to keep my mind from thinking, and those thoughts from inducing anxiety and fueling my depression. I don't know how to control the ache that is a constant pressure in me. I want to ignore it, but it has control over me.

My girlfriend, Lily, indulges my lack of sleeping, and my long stares that she tells me are too lost not to unnerve her. I see her pulling herself together, as though nothing is restricting the process. I am not sure if it is lack of will or lack of ability, but I am unable to follow her lead. I find myself isolating more and more. From her. From my friends. I go from school to basketball practice, to jogging aimlessly, increasingly further from home. This is my time to disappear from my world. Lost in the music streaming through my headphones, I find back roads, abandoned parks – anywhere isolated I seek.

When I feel myself running out of breath, when the tinge of wanting to slow down removes itself from its subtle barrier enough for me to become aware of it, I start sprinting. I stride for as long and as fast as I can. A killer is chasing me, the love in me is being burned and I have to find water – the intensity of these runs scares me. But it is necessary. I find that on the edge of exhaustion is the only time I can allow myself to release. Depression is the opposite of release. It is the compilation of hurt, pain, sorrow and despair. I need to be away from everything – all the poison that has become blood, all the angels sent to protect that have since fallen – to cleanse myself, to allow myself to release. I lose myself in these runs, hands on my knees, in complete focus on steadying my breathing. It is in these few minutes of utter exhaustion where I gain the strength to show the world a smile…the strength to pretend things are fine.

My home is a small ranch setup, covered in cheap sliding and broken-down shutters. It is desolated when I find my way back there. My father works his second job from six to midnight, and my mother is out of work at three and sleeping by three twenty. As I arrive, it is still and quiet. I go down the slight hill on the right side to the back entrance that leads to the basement. I unlock the door, step into the short hallway, and then into my room. This space was never meant to be a bedroom. There are no windows, and the walls turn and bend to avoid the furnace and water heater on the other side of them. The pipes and boards creak from overhead, sending jolts of noises through the solitude of the room. I don't really notice that anymore, though. Everything that surrounds, or intrudes, blends into a sense of normalness.

I throw my sweatshirt on the floor, take my t-shirt off, and whip the streaks of sweat from my face with it. I had left my green lava lamp on, and as I collapse onto my bed, that is the only light in the room. I find the remote for my MP3 player in my sheets and continue where I left off on my playlist. I sink into my bed, allowing the music to alter my temperament. The tiredness from the run and general lack of sleep allows my mind to drift and my eyes to close. I am almost asleep when I hear a muffled vibration. I slide to the edge of my bed and reach for my cell phone. It's Josh, so I answer.
"Hey," I say.
"We've got a game at ten," I am told.
"What?"

"Impromptu fun, man. We're gonna break into the gym and have ourselves a game. Shay is coming. Lily should be there, too."

I flip the light on and shudder slightly at the brightness. That was my chance of sleep. The adrenaline of a game was enough that I wouldn't find that space again soon. I had seen Lily briefly at school, but the more conscious I become, the more I want to see her again. I read that the first thing you think of after meditating is your truth. That is who Lily is to me. Shay and Josh complete my circle of friends. My mind has spaces of chaos I disappear into, but Lily, Shay and Josh are the life I have built in opposition to it.

"She hasn't called me." I say, already digging through the pile of clothes on the floor for some playing shorts.

"Well, she's gonna be there. Eric is over at my house now, so pick us both up at nine forty-five, then I will proceed to school you and all the other pathetic losers who wind up on your team."

"You win one game and now you've become all cocky." I respond.

"Whatever." He retorts. "Later."

I throw my cell on the bed and check the time: eight-thirty. I grab the shorts and shirt I had picked out and give them a whiff. They smell rank, so I throw them in the wash and take a shower. The one benefit of having a basement converted into living space is that it was built with its own bathroom. I have thought the space was built as some sort of banishment. I moved in a few months before my sister was sent away.

At nine-thirty, my clothes are still damp, but I put them on and head to Josh's house. Our home gym is also used as a community theater. On one end, there is a three-foot rise onto a stage. This leads to the strange mix of locker, dressing and wardrobe rooms. It creates a pollination of sexes with only signs on the doors to draw an invisible separation line. If you weren't obvious about it, you could get away with pretty much what you wanted to. And most did.

I lull to a stop a few hundred feet before Josh's house. Josh is without question my best friend. On a micro-level, we have each other's back. We see the world in the same way. On a macro-scale, we are different. He has an infrastructure, a stability that returns him home. His parents are evangelical Christians who view me as a non-believer's influence. I do not understand what that means, exactly. I guess when you are instilling something very specific, with no room for doubt, having an independent voice is negative. What might have started out as a slight rebellion has become a friendship unhindered by pretense. Finding someone who is honest with you is rare. Finding someone you can be honest with is even rarer.

My foot is hovering off the break and over the gas when my cell rings.

"Hey," I say.

I hear a release of air, as though she had just inhaled before I answered, and now is breathing out. This had become common lately. I knew who it was without any more detail.

"Quit smoking, Shay. Your teeth are gonna turn yellow and no guy wants a girl with yellow teeth."

She laughs playfully at this.

"You are not supposed to know I am smoking when I call you on the phone. I am calling from a blocked number for a reason, you over attentive prick."

Shay is the only girl I have ever met who can layer the infliction of her voice to both cut you down and turn you in at the same time.

"Besides, since when do guys care about *teeth*?"

At 5'6 with auburn brown hair, deep green eyes, and a body that holds itself more maturely and confidently than a seventeen-year-old should be able to, Shay was right. Any guy looking at her is so awed at all the obvious, her teeth would never be a concern.

"Fine. They couldn't care less about your teeth. So, you showing up tonight?"

"I guess. Josh will be kinda pissed at me if I don't, right?"

"He would get over it."

"I'll be there. What else am I gonna do, sleep?"

"Sleep is for the weak." I tell her.

It had been a summer of sunrises for us. There is a special bond that comes through exhaustion, and Josh, Lily, Shay and I blurred into shades of the same person.

"I am picking up Josh and Eric now, then we're heading over."

"Is Lily coming?" Shay asks, more to test how I answer than curious to know for herself.

"So I've been told. I haven't talked with her since fifth period."

"She called me an hour ago. I didn't pick up and she didn't leave a message."

"I'm sure she'll be there." I say, bored with Shay's game. "So, see you in a little bit?"

There is a long pause. I hear her inhale and exhale; the stuttered breathing of her smoking before she responds. "Yeah. See you in a few." She waits another long pause before saying, "Bye"

"Bye." I click my cell off and put it back in my pocket. I softly press the gas and roll the distance to Josh's house.

I walk up to the door and knock. There is a weird nervousness in me. I have long since given up on the idea that Josh's parents were going to like me, approve of me, or look at me with anything less than disdain. But, somehow, it always bothers me to be around them. That, and also there is some lie Josh had to make up to be allowed to go out this late. Not knowing what it is, I was placed in a teetering situation, where I could get caught saying something that went against his lie. The whole process swirling in my brain is exhausting. It takes his mother less than a minute to answer the door.

"Good evening, Noah. Come in. Josh and Eric are upstairs."

She walks away before I am able to step into the house. I kick off my sneakers and toss them over to the left. I do this just quickly enough so that when she turns around to tell me to, it is already done.

"I remember." I say, smiling. I have learned the hard way not to joke with her. I say what I need to say and move on.

The outside of Josh's house emits wealth, and the inside confirms all the assumptions. It is decorated with such care, it almost annoys me. Everything is settled in its place with no room for revisions. Maybe there are benefits to this type of structure; an understanding of how to function in the world. I didn't see it. I don't live in that kind of world.

When I walk in the room, Josh and Eric's full attention is to the TV as they play a video game. I stand beside them for a moment. Not getting any acknowledgment, I say, "Yo, assholes, let's blow."

Josh looks up at me, glaring.

"If my mom hears you say that, I will get in trouble." Josh informs me.

"And don't think I don't find it amusing that what I do can get you in trouble."

Swearing is strictly forbidden in the house. I know this. But I have a hard time switching how I am depending on the circumstances around me.

"Blame me later. It's time for some ball," I say, leaving the room.

They are behind me quickly and we pile into my car. Josh was riding shotgun, and Eric stretched himself out in the backseat. Leaving the driveway and turning off his street, Josh cracks the window and lights a cigarette. He knows I hate this, but he does it anyway. Outside the presence of his parents, it is as though a shroud has been lifted from him. I understand this rebellion, this need for release. But it comes out selfishly a lot of the time. However, Josh has charm. A charisma that morphs this into an acceptable arrogance. You have to see him gripped in his parent's chokehold and contrast it with him stepping to the shores of freedom in order to understand - and be frightened by the separation in the two.

"Toss that shit out the window." I tell him. He looks at me for a second, annoyed, but it quickly fades to laughter and then to a smirk.

"Can't I even inhale before you start bitching at me?"

"Whatever, man. Could you please not?"

There is a slight anger in this battle for authority. Eric stays silent in the backseat. This isn't for him to throw his cents in. Josh and I have formed an understanding of the need for control, or at least perception of control, the other has to have. Understanding each other this way has enabled a sense of trust.

He takes a drag and then throws the cigarette out the window. He looks at me – expression solely in his eyes. I glance at him and get the sarcastic 'happy?' I expected. I know there is more if I prolong my gaze. If you are able to translate the language of a person most of the time, the depth will scare you. What one keeps in the silence of themselves is often left there for a reason. Outside the barrier of one's mind, their truth is frightening.

I begin to turn back to Josh when I hear a heavy bass version of an R&B song start coming out of my phone. It is my ringtone I chose for Lily. It came right as we started to trust each other with the depths of one another.

"You already know…"

"I wanna fuck you," Lily giggles as she completes the lyric.

I was the one who first played her the album version of the song a few years back, when we first started hanging out. The edited radio version of the song leaves a different taste in your mouth. Her reaction was pure shock. I saw the reveling, or development, of a layer to her. A loss of innocence, a growth in maturity – I was never sure. All I knew was that there was a change.

"I'm en route." I tell her. "You're coming, right?"

"Already here. Evan just undid the lock. There are like five of us here so far. Shay just texted me. She's gonna be here in a minute."

"Cool. I got Josh and Eric with me. See you in like five." I tell her.

"Okay. Love you."

"I love you too."

Lily is my first real relationship. The summer leading into our sophomore year was when we first hooked up. Some kid's uncle had a house in Marblehead, and let him live there for the summer. He threw the wildest parties. There were people having sex on the grass, getting naked, and jumping in the ocean. I don't believe anyone ever left. We all just passed out and woke up partially sunburned the next afternoon.

At one of these parties, I was roaming around the house when I saw her. She was playing a piano – which seemed and looked silly because the stereo music completely drowned out her playing. But maybe that was the reason she was playing. I sat next to her and started playing chopsticks. I looked at her straight in the eyes until she joined in. She was a little uncomfortable at first, a little nervous. I think she liked being in her own world, among the chaos. I was animated. In a space where we couldn't hear each other speak, I had to be funny, charming, with only hand and body language. I made her smile, then laugh. That is when I motioned for us to talk outside. I hadn't planned on spending the night *talking* to anyone. But I started being absorbed by her. When daybreak came, we looked around at all the bodies sprawled out. It looked like a massacre. We laughed at the silliness of it and traded stories of the previous times it was us. In the stillness of the early morning, in the company of each other, intoxication-free, there was a calm, a state of peace. We stripped our clothes off to our underwear and ran into the water. We both dove under water. When we surfaced, we whipped the salt water from our eyes and battled the glare of the rising sun; searching for each other. Her body was shivering when we embraced. I tasted the salt on her lips and pressed past the surface to find the layer beyond that. I was fifteen. I was well acquainted with lust, but this brought me somewhere I had not been.

It was a night that you wanted to leave everything undisturbed. To allow nothing to taint or disrupt the memory. But it also left you craving more. And so, a day later, I called her. A few years later, we are seniors in high school awaiting college acceptance letters, and saying 'I love you' in the place of 'goodbye'. I could never quite place when that phase of the relationship hit us. We never said goodbye anymore. This didn't comfort me and it didn't make me feel suffocated. It made me question it, and dizzy trying to figure out how it should make me feel.

I had known Josh since freshman year, as we both spent a lot of time on the JV bench. But it wasn't until that same summer, at basketball camp, we became friends. A growth spurt and constant practice had done us good and we were named Co-MVPs of the camp. The meeting of Josh and Shay came that fall, the weekend before school started. I was unsure of it. I knew Josh. I knew how he was. Setting him up with a girl was asking for that girl to resent you forever. And being that Shay and Lily were grade school friends, best friends, the opportunity to mix that with Josh was unsettling. Lily did her best to ease my tension regarding the coupling. She told me Shay was the kind of girl who would be enticed by Josh's bad boy, crass persona.

Our high school, Linden Academy, only accepted three hundred students. With this size, it held a school year kick-off retreat. It was explained as a way to set expectations for the year, and for everyone to get to know each other outside of school. Being a small school, establishing lasting friendships is a cornerstone of its prestige. Josh and I arrived early and were told to hang out in the conference room for everyone else to get there. We knew, or at least knew of, most of the other kids, but stayed to ourselves. It wasn't until we saw the basketball court around the back that we woke up. A pick-up game was forming, and we were all in.

Josh and I were known as JV players, which is to say we weren't known. This year's starting five had been predetermined at the end of last year. But a few minutes into the game, it was clear a new reign was beginning. Josh and I had wound up on the same team (the last time that ever happened), and we dominated. It was a game to eleven with the final score being eleven to zero. The more we poured it on, the more Josh started to talk. When you skunk someone, you have all the power to trash talk, and he took full advantage. The second game we were on opposite teams, resulting in a deadlock at ten to ten. At this point, people started filtering out and became our audience. The boredom of hanging around enticed the excitement of the game. With over a hundred people crowding around our small basketball court, the atmosphere changed quickly. There was a buzz I had felt before.

Josh checked the ball to me at the top of the key. I saw him scan through the crowd and breathe in. He did a stutter step to the right which I blocked, but when he did it again, I went to the left. This left me momentarily unbalanced, and Josh drove to the rim. I recovered but was clearly beaten. Just as Josh began to rise to slam home the win, he slowed. I heard him say, "damn". I was able to strip the ball, clear it, and zip a pass to Eric for a game-winning lay-up. The audience roared and my teammates gathered around me. Through the commotion, I looked to find what had distracted Josh. Standing at the edge of the doorway, I saw Lily and Shay.

The cheers died down and we were called by faculty telling us that the meeting was beginning. Josh and I hung back so we would be the last ones in. Waiting for us was Shay and Lily. Lily and I had been together for a few months at this point. I had hung out with Shay a few times, but I hadn't figured out how to feel settled around her. Something about her weaves itself under your skin. Looking at her, I felt guilty. As though she would read thoughts that weren't even there. But even in their absence, she would make them true, she would make them appear.

Lily introduced Josh to Shay. Shay began talking in her way I have learned is manipulating and controlling, but it didn't dent Josh. Instead, he responded with his own version and brought it to a stalemate. Lily and I were sure by the end of the weekend they would be together, but they never even kissed. It almost seemed like they became so wrapped up in having someone to trade barbs and sexual overtures with, that risking losing that was greater than their libido for each other. A couple or not, the two of them began hanging out a lot and became inseparable

We park in front of the gym and head to the side street that runs along the back of the gym, separating it from a baseball and soccer field. I type 161924 into the number lock and open the door. Josh leads, Eric behind him, and I lag in the back. Stepping onto the gym floor, Josh takes his sweatshirt off and does a few stretches. I stretch in the hall then walk in.

There is a three-foot rise at the end of one side of the gym that is made up as a stage for our drama's practices and performances. It comes with an odd mix of locker gyms and dressing rooms. A spoken line of separation only encourages us to cross it.

My eyes scan to the 3 on 3 game being played, making a note of who is there, but my eyes drift up to the stage. There are four or five girls (Lily not among them) dressed up in gowns and heavy makeup, reading from some paperback playbook. On the edge, toes curled around, Shay stands. She is poised, with an unwavering serious, yet vacant look. I take a few steps toward the stage, trying to catch her eye. It is clear her eyes are not searching for something…they are trying to disconnect. She wears a black baby doll shirt and a short leg-clenching jean skirt. Her hair is done up in two ponytails, the left side behind her, the right side hiding part of her face. It gives off a forbidden girl-like quality. Young and innocent looking. But at the same time, holding a darker shade to her. "I'd like to grab those ponytails from behind." Eric comments. I had forgotten he was there.

Josh's response to this is a half-laugh, half-grunt. He glances up at Shay but forces his attention to the game. He calls for the ball, and this ends the game. Getting the ball, Josh squares a good four feet beyond the three-point line and shoots. The ball swishes through the hoop, bounces up to the stage, and rolls to Shay. She grabs and holds it, then waits a beat just until it starts to annoy Josh, before throwing it back to him. She gives him a playful smile, then disappears behind the side curtain. I jog to the other end of the gym as Josh stays on his side and the others shoot to see who will be on our team.

These games always play out the same. At the start, it is strict fun. Pushing each other for position, double dribbling, it was all good. As we went deeper into the game, that part would fade to a more serious game. We play up to 21, but it wasn't until one of us reached 15 that the game really begins.

At the opposite end of the stage, Josh nails a 15-footer, giving his team a two-point lead at 15-13. As the ball is inbounded and we start up the other end, you can feel the switch. In the middle of Alex and Dan crossing, I thread the needle to behind the arch on the right side. This creates more than enough space away from Josh for Eric to pass me the ball and I square and nail a game-tying shot. When I reach half court, my eye catches Lily. She is half exposed, half hidden behind the curtain. She wears a flowing 70's style light green skirt and her hair flows down to the small of her back. Her face is turned down, reading a playbook. Almost as a form of telepathy, she lifts her head slightly and raises her eyes to look at me. She gives me a secret smile. It is these moments, these hidden in plain sight moments, that I cherish the most. It is like an inside joke that is spoken in front of the world, but is only audible to me.

In my lapse of focus on the game, Josh has run past me and cleared a path to the basket. I chase him but have to dodge a beautiful set pick right in front of him. Josh jumps from the left side of the basketball and I am half a step

behind from the right side. For a second, it looks like a game of chicken. But neither of us move. We will worry about the collision after we hit the floor. Hanging in the air, my only concern is stopping him, and his only concern is scoring. The only way I am going to be able to stop the jam is by disrupting it enough so it rolled on the rim long enough for gravity to be on my side. Which is exactly what I do. Using my left hand, I swipe at the ball, loosening it just enough so it didn't go through but bounced on the rim – and then fell off. The rebound is tipped first by Josh, and then me. Dan and Rob crash the boards too, but I finally come away with it. Possessing the ball, I quickly outlet it to Eric and sprint down to the other end. We catch the other team back peddling, and a perfect bounce pass later I throw down a monstrous two-handed jam. There is violence to it as the backboard sways, and the rim snaps back. The girls give hollers of cheers. In a single motion after landing, I jump on the stage and pull Lily to me. As I move her mouth to mine, I whisper 'hi' before kissing her. If you find yourself in a situation where you can increase your pulse alongside someone you love, doing so is never a bad thing. "Don't leave until I see you." I tell her.
"I'll be around somewhere."
"Then I'll come and find you." I kiss her again, and then jump back into the game.

My absence has allowed Josh's team to score rather easily, and the game goes back to being tied. We go back and forth until we are deadlocked at 20 all, with Josh controlling the ball. The rest of the players leave us isolated at the top of the key. He drives to his right, which I block. For a second, I think he is going to pull up for the shot, but he returns to the middle. He does a few moves in an attempt to shake me and finally drives full tilt to the left. Three feet below the foul line, he stops and jumps into a fade away shoot. This is done expertly. There is nothing I can do. I turn around to box him out, if there is a rebound. Everyone else crashes toward the basket, except for Eric who sneaks his way down the other end of the court. Josh's shoot clanks on the back of the rim, spins on the left side of the rim, and falls off directly into Rob's hands. Looking up, he throws a baseball pass to Eric who walks in for an uncontested lay-up to win the game. My team runs to Eric and jumps in victory. By the time we turn around, Josh's team has left for water. When they come back, we shoot for different teams and play again.

The second and third games aren't as close. The teams I am on just click more and we take the next games as well. After the third game, Josh is more than a little annoyed. The fact that it is nearly 1am helps decide that our fun will come to an end. The stage had emptied halfway through the last game with shouts of goodbye. I tell Josh I will meet him outside. Eric says he is going to grab a ride with Reef, which I barely hear as all I care about is finding Lily.

I jump up on the stage and zigzag through the clutter to reach the dressing room. I open the side door and step inside a large, spacious room. The walls are painted a grayish green with black speckles. It gives off a quiet, introspective mood. There are seven lamps spread throughout the room and no overhead lights. Two lamps in the back are on, but the rest of the room is dark. I turn the closest lamp to me on and find Shay face down on the carpet in a dress that is already unzipped.

"Shay?"

"I need alcohol." Her muffled voice whines.

"Alcohol only leads to needing coffee, and you know how much you hate coffee." I tell her.

She lifts her head and rolls slightly so she can see me.

"I'm starting to acquire a taste for it,"

I laugh, which makes her smile.

"Did everyone else already bail?" I ask.

"Lily and Jade are here somewhere. Game over?"

"Yeah," I tell her.

"And who won?"

"We were just having fun."

"Come on. I wanna mark it on the wall in the girl's room, right next to your and Josh's dick measurements." She sits up as she says this, eyes gleaming. She loves this kind of flirty banter.

"My team won, alright? It doesn't matter." I say, trying to dismiss it.

"It matters a little. Or is a little just in Josh's case?"

She stands up, letting the dress drift off her shoulders and fall to her knees. She wears a deep green bra and panties. She arches herself just so, making sure I get the full effect of her figure. This flaunting of herself, this flirting would seem to contradict her friendship with Lily, but this is Shay. If Lily was beside me, holding my hand, she would act the same. My responses, however, differ. Shay knows this. If Lily or Josh, or anyone else is near, I close off. I make some joke or fill the air with thick sarcasm. But alone, I allow the flirtations to hang there and become tension.

She waits for me to speak and I give myself a moment to absorb her.

"It bothers you that you don't know, doesn't it?" I say, like I am casting a bait. "I can look at you and tell that you break into a C, but me? With guys, you have to get close, *really close* to find what kinda coin he has rolled." I say, taking a deliberate step closer to her.

Shay laughs. Placing a hand against the wall, she steps out of her dress. She looks like she is going to move into the distance between us, when Lily appears in the background of her.

"Hey, guys. What we doing?" She asks as she walks to us. Her voice is void of tone.

As she gets close to reaching Shay, she moves slightly to the left, creating a triangle with our positions. I quickly change this by walking to her. I give her a greeting kiss, place my arm around her waist and tug her to me.

"Nothing. I was just looking for you. Let's go. I left Josh outside."

"Don't you want to help Shay find her clothes first?" This is not said with anger or jealousy. It is simply said to show that she is aware.

"She is a big girl. I am sure she can handle it." I give Shay a brief smile before wrapping my arm around Lily. "See you outside." I call back to Shay.

"Fine." She says while we are just still in earshot. "I'll be out in a minute. Right after I find my clothes."

Josh is leaning against my car as Lily and I approach. You can smell his annoyance.

"Finally. I almost broke the window. I gotta get home. The Revival ended at one."

"Was that what you told your parents?"

"It worked. The only way they will let me hang out with the hell-bent sinner is if I am trying to save him."

He pushes me and crackles with laughter. Lily laughs too. I find it funny but can never laugh at these jokes. There is some piece of pride or ego that thinks I should be insulted by this. I'm not. And that somehow bothers me.

I don't need to say anything to break the laughter because Shay comes into view, scurrying her way to us. "I'm here. Where are we off to?"

"Home," Josh says, grabbing the keys from my hand.

"Yeah. Chem test tomorrow. I am gonna try and get a few hours of sleep." Lily says.

"Boring pricks." Shay says with a pout.

"Lily." I say, getting her to face me "Could you drop Josh off? You know me and sleeping."

She looks at me, concerned. To bury yourself in the angst of high school is great, but lately, it has become only acceptable on weekends. Summer is over. Senior year is upon us. She knows I can't put things in tiny little boxes and be fine the way she can, and this worries her. I have begun to have the feeling that she was growing out of her depression just as I am sinking deeper into mine.

"Sure." she says, giving me a hug and then kissing me on the check.

She grabs my face and gives me a hard look in the eyes to make sure I absorb what she is feeling. I look away and nod; she brushes her lips on mine before pressing them into a kiss. She whispers, "I love you."

"I love you too." I echo.

Lily moves to Shay, hugging her.

"Goodnight, my dear."

"Goodnight, sweetie"

"All right, man. Be good." Josh says to me as we clasp hands and lean in for a shoulder hug.

"Later." I tell him.

"Shay, great dramatic reading tonight. We will have to do it again real soon." Josh says to Shay as he begins walking toward Lily's car.

"Definitely," Shay responds, "Maybe next time you will win." She says, gleaming.

Josh glares at me as he walks away. Barely audible, I hear him say "asshole" before fully turning his back to me

"Well," Shay says, "It's just us. Where should we go, what should we do, what should we drink?"

"All important questions." I tell her, "And I could not care less about any of them."

"Okay then." She pauses, thinking. "Van Gogh vodka, Handley Lake, drink and talk till sunrise."

"Till sunrise," I say in agreement. "I'll drive."

We get in my car. My MP3 player is set on shuffle, but I leave a narrow playlist on it so I will always hear a song I want to. Megan Burtt's "Packed My Things" starts playing. It's a song about being restless and searching for someplace to belong. One of the lines that always stood out to me is:

Cause Heaven's only got a place
For folks who really know
That this life's ain't forever
So, I packed my soul to go

I have played the song so much that Shay softly sings along. Handley Lake is a large circle lake, 200 feet away from the highway. It is a place you can disappear in without fear of becoming lost. That summer, it had become our favorite spot. Watching the sun come up over the trees and shimmer off the lake is the most peaceful time of my day. It had gotten so routine that there is a piece of me that feels empty if I don't see it. I had never seen it alone with Shay, though. Josh and/or Lily had always been with us. But that night, it changed. It wasn't as though there was any discomfort between Shay and I. It wasn't as though we needed Josh or Lily to be there. It is just they always had been. This was different. A slight one. But a noticeable one nonetheless. Neither of us spoke of it, but it existed. The sun rose, streaking through the trees and casting light off the lake, with Shay and I fully awake, leaning on each other. We only had a few hours until school, until a Chem test. And neither of us wanted to move.

Two

I've Got to Think to Relax

The Chemistry test is brutal. After reading the first two questions, I have absolutely no idea. I skim the rest of the questions and sigh. I lost the ability to regret or care about failing tests in fifth grade, but on occasion, it still frustrates me. My only hope comes from it being multiple choice. If I really concentrated, I could deduct my way to a seventy. Lily is scanning through her notes as I walk in and she doesn't look up. There are times when my ego or embarrassment over her indifference would make me blow the smoke away and *get* a reaction. I have mellowed on this some, choosing my spots. I don't think you can bury your intensity but you can dull it, or best yet, you can learn how to control it.

My education on this came about a year and a half ago. Lily and I had gone to some party, I don't even remember whose it was or why it was. I walked into a room and found Lily sitting on the floor talking with a group of people. She had ignored me for the entire night. It wasn't that we had a fight or anything, it was simply that, for some reason, her disposition brought her away from me. I faded into the party for a while but it began to anger me and, mixed with alcohol, I had to alter it. I walked to her, bent down beside her, and whispered, "let's grab some beers and get some air." She didn't respond to me, but moments later, she added a comment off of the story this other girl was telling. The slight was so recognizable, I heard a few 'burn' from the others in the room. I rose to my feet and grabbed her hair. I placed my other hand on her back and forced her up. There was physical pain and annoyance as she faced me, but that melted from the intensity that radiated from me.

"Or, option two. We fuck in the bathroom." I tell her.

There was a pin-dropping silence throughout the room. Caught in a silent movie, Lily shifted her eyes to the left and moved her neck inches to catch a glimpse of those around us. Everyone was doing their best wax museum pose. There are many versions told of what happened that night, but the truth is, she took *my* hand and led the way. My act of 'violence' startled most. Josh had to come in and calmed the stirring rumors, saying it was an inside joke and that no one should read too much into anything. It helped, but being high school and all, mine and Lily's reputations became striped with violence and S&M. It became weird for a while. Tales of wild, drunken escapades were rampant in school. The idea of sex in the bathroom had almost become trite. So, why had this one instance gained so much flouter? It was curious to me. Was it our stature? Because of the scale of the audience that witnessed it?

I never try to be anything. I either was or I wasn't. I played basketball and was good at it. That being true, popularity came with it. I never cared about it. It was simply there. So, when it stopped, when smiles became sneers, it had no effect on me. A few 30-point games later, all was forgiven. For Lily, though, it wasn't that simple. On some level, as a guy, the brashness of what occurred heightened my reputation. But Lily was the one who had to handle 95% of the backlash. The following week was student council elections. As an incoming junior, Lily was the clear front-runner for student council president. She had a business-plan with the first hundred days all mapped out. It was so impressive, it translated into her getting a job at the Mayor's office, and her being able to squeeze me in with a two day a week internship there as well. However, high school politics is a popularity contest; not meant necessarily for the best qualified. That incident damaged the perception of Lily's character just enough to allow Jason Miller to pull out the win by a mere three votes.

This devastated her to the point of her crying in the bathroom for three hours after school. All I could do was hold her. This was my fault. I was the one who caused this pain. The guilt almost killed me. But she wanted me to stay with her, so I did. A part of me loved her for that, but a part of me hated her too. She made me stay with her pain. The pain that I caused. I wanted to run away, to disappear into a shit load of Vicodin. That way of 'handling' pain had become a learned behavior for me. When my sister was sent to New York, my parents made sure I was well-equipped with whatever mood-altering drugs I wanted. That was the day I stopped taking any medicine. As hard as it was to see the girl I love with tears in her eyes, with full knowledge I was responsible, somehow not feeling it would have been worse. These days, though, I was beginning to give second thoughts to that idea of feeling.

Lily doesn't see Shay and I when the bell rings. She skates out ahead of us. I dodge my way to her and lightly tug at her shirt, pulling her toward me. She sort of stumbles from a loss of balance briefly before she sees it's me.

"You know, to take a test, you have to make it for the test itself." She smiles and kisses me.

"I was there." I say in defense. "Thanks for noticing and saving me a seat. I can't copy off of you from across the room."

"Really? From my experience, I have found that you have a knack with mirrors."

Shay rolls her eyes. Bored and annoyed at standing beside us.

"Ya. I'm gonna bail. We still doing lunch?" Shay asks.

"Sushi, baby. It's Noah's day to pay."

Josh enters our triangle with a burst and Shay brightens. The game is now fair: two on two.

"My day to pay?" I retort. "You cherry-picking son of a bitch. What, your day never comes up? You call a Leap Year?" I say.

"Hey, I always pay at our 3am breakfasts, do I not? Lunch is your bag." Josh states.

"True enough." I say. "But Sushi? They take twice as long to bring you your food, and they don't even cook it."

"You have no dining class." Shay tells me.

"Don't stop there," Josh tells her. "This kid is void of class. Every aspect of his life is completely classless."

Josh pushes me and we shadow box against each other for a minute.

"At least I take my shoes off for your psychotic mother." I throw at him. He stops for a moment. For all his bitching and rebellion against them, he is still sensitive when someone says something about his parents. Even when it is just a joke. Even when it is me.

A perk of being seniors is being able to have off-campus lunches. However, it is a privilege held on a short string. If you are late for your next class once, you are banned from leaving campus for a month. Do it again and you are barred for the rest of the year.

The warning bell rings, signaling there are three minutes for us to get to our next class. This is where the group splits up. Third period is the only time of day none of us have a class together. It is a period for an elective. Lily and Shay went with the yearbook staff, while Josh – on the behest of his parents – opted for Theology 101. I am not really sure if Josh has a first choice for college. It seems like he would, but his parents have already determined his destination: Oral Roberts University. Taking Theology, they said, would help his creditability. I never got around to filling out the form. When school started, I was informed that I had been placed in an extra study hall. The only good part to this is that Erin Keller is also stuck there. We had been friends in junior high, but since high school began, we had rarely seen each other and until this year, I had not realized she even went to the school. There wasn't a person that I had known before high school that I was friendly with on any level except for her. She reminds me of the difference between intensity and history. Spending thirty consecutive hours with someone gives you glimpses of who they are. But compared to a year's observation, it is meaningless.

We agree to meet in the parking lot at 11:30am for lunch and head off in our different directions. Three steps away from the group, Shay gets approached by Rob. I am out of earshot but his line makes her giggle. Her giggle shivers her body in a fluent motion. This is how she flirts. Her thoughts and feelings are spoken in body language. If she starts to flirt verbally, you have an opening. You better make the most of it because it won't last long. Evan and Eric catch up to Josh, and Lily becomes surrounded by the afterschool yearbook staff. I walk the tunnel-like hallway, alone, to the other end of the building.

I step through the doorway of the library just as the bell rings. They put the elective version of study hall in the library to encourage research and enable the use of computers. Mrs. Nelson is the moderator, but she never speaks. She sits at her desk grading papers or reading some book. There are only three other students here. Two play chess in the corner and Erin is collapsed in a chair; her large orange, ratty plastic bag she uses as a pillow. She is half trying to sleep and half attempting to read her French book. I slide into a chair at the table next to her.

"Hey,"

"Ne pouvez-vous pas me dire essaye-t-vous de dormir?" (Can't you tell I'm trying to sleep?) She says this without looking up or opening her eyes.

"Damn, Erin, you know I'm taking Spanish."

She lifts her head up with difficulty and looks at me, trying to hide a smile.

"Ce n'est pas mon défaut." (That is not my fault.) She says.

"Fine," I say. "Intentaba ser agradable, pero lo olvido." (I was trying to be nice, but forget it.) I tell her.

This makes her laugh so loudly, we get "shushed" by the people playing chess. Mrs. Nelson doesn't give us any reaction.

"Tardé a tres años de español. Podemos comunicar en cualquier lengua quieres." (I took three years of Spanish. We can communicate in whatever language you want.) She tells me, with an edge in her voice.

I look at her blankly for a moment. We are caught almost in a staring contest. I look away and start pulling books out of my bag when I say:

"I guess I neglected to mention that I am not *passing* Spanish, so I really have no idea what you just said."

This gives Erin a giant burst of laughter. To the point, this time, that Mrs. Nelson looks up and the chess players look at us as though they would kill us…if they were not playing chess.

"You are going to get me in trouble." Erin warns me.

"How is it that I have this power to get people in trouble? Am I consequence-free?"

"You are a star athlete. So, as far as trouble in school, yeah you pretty much are." There is no jealousy in Erin's voice. She speaks it simply as a fact.

"Well, shame on me then because I am not taking full advantage of that."

"Well, it is there when you need it." Erin says. She straightens herself and finds her place in her text.

Erin is here on a scholarship like me. Hers is academic, mine athletic. For the first two years, my parents scraped together the money to send me here. I am pretty sure they pulled some equity out of the house to make it possible. When basketball brought me a free ride for my junior year, I saw a weight lift from them. It was unsettling. Before that moment, I was unaware that I was a burden; that I had the ability to affect them. I guess I always thought that my sister had comatose them. It didn't solve all their problems, maybe not even most of them, but it helped somewhat. And that put an importance to basketball that it hadn't held before.

"Hey," Erin says, quickly before diving into her bag. She pulls out a gray piece of paper with black ash-like writing on it. It is a concert flyer.

"They are really good. You should try and make it."

"Who are these guys?"

"Local band."

"What kind of music?"

"The flyer should give you hints,"

"The only thing I get from this flyer is the feeling I need an ashtray or hand sanitizer." I tell her.

"Their emo/punk/rock,"

I put the flyer down and go back to my book.

"I like bands more defined." I say.

She is surprised by my reaction, almost hurt. I was sort of kidding. Sometimes sarcasm is taken as cruelty.

"When are they playing?" I ask, picking the flyer back up.

"Next Friday."

"Well, that answers that question. We are playing South Shore Academy next Friday." I pause. "But maybe I can swing by afterward. What time is their set?"

"Probably not till ten."

"Game will end around then. But I'll come by after. Maybe I can drag some people with me and catch their last song or two. Are they really that good?" I ask.

"Yeah. I think you'll dig them."

"So, what is behind you caring so much?"

She kind of blushes and looks away.

"A girl can't be a fan?" She says in a coy way that reminds me of a minor league version of Shay.

"Oh no, you can be a fan. You can also be a groupie or a…"

"Girlfriend?" I say.

"There's that."

"Just because I may be dating the lead singer does not mean the band isn't good."

"You're right. It also doesn't mean you have to be discreet about it either." I tell her.

"I wasn't. I just don't pontificate about it."

It was subtle, but that was a slight dig at me. My relationship with Lily is public, but it is nothing we promote. Do we shove it in people's faces? I didn't think we did. But, truthfully, it was nothing I ever thought about.

"Fine. I'll be there. Just make sure I'm on the list."

"I can do that. But only for you and Lily. The rest of your entourage or tagalongs will have to shell out the five-buck cover."

"Fair enough." I say. We both go back to our studies, letting the rest of the period go by in silence.

There are packs of kids rushing out of school come eleven-thirty. Josh is joking around with some guys from the basketball team, leaning against his rusty blue hatchback. I scan the rest of the parking lot for Lily or Shay. Not seeing them, I walk over to Josh.

"No, man. It is crazy. Her hobby is sucking his dick." Eric states. For some reason, this is very funny. I must have missed the set up.

"A hobby I mean to make a job." Reef says, obviously being the one Eric was referring to.

"If anyone of you says, 'Yeah…a blow job' I will kick your ass." I announce, stepping into the group.

"Reef was telling tales of his girl. She has this curious obsession of gagging herself. Well…" Josh pauses for effect. "I guess gagging wouldn't apply in Reef's case, but you get where I am going."

The group roars with laughter. Reef's comeback is a head-drooping series of 'yeah, yeah, well's'. I become bored quickly. Outside of basketball or a party, I have concluded I have no use for a lot of people. Most people, maybe. My mood is not that of friendly banter. I scan the parking lot again in a desperate hope of finding Lily. At the end of the last school year, I started getting what I could only understand as anxiety attacks. There did not appear to be any trigger or even warning signs. They just hit. It is a dizzy spell filled with an influx of rage. They have never manifested into anything irreversible and Lily has also been able to calm me down, to talk me off the ledge. She and Josh are the only ones who know about them. Standing beside the banal conversation, I feel one coming. I need Lily.

I finally spot her skipping down the steps leading out of school. Her sundress glides off her body as she prances down the final steps toward me. This is the first chance of the day I have to absorb her. She wears a black choke collar with a heart that is slightly off center. Her dirty blonde hair hangs evenly behind both sides of her shoulders and her makeup is sparse. She smiles like she has caught something in her mind that she replays to keep her happy. It is not pretentious; not fake; not peppy. It is contagious. It makes me smile. The guys move onto another topic, but I don't hear any of it. I walk toward Lily, meeting her halfway.

"Hey," she says when we are about three feet apart.

At first, I don't say anything. I scoop her up and kiss her with a longing I rarely display in an open forum. I have learned to control my intensity, but sometimes when you analyze longing instead of embracing it, you lose the force behind it. I had no control of my tempo here. Feeling her body pressed against mine both raised my blood pressure and calmed my soul. There was no complication. Only love.

"Get a room. Or at least a backseat. You are ten feet from your car. God." Shay says, whipping past us. This comment is tongue in cheek as she is the queen of public affection. Her current boyfriend (for the last five months) is a twenty-three-year college senior. Lily and I have only met him twice, but suffice to say the comment was very hypocritical.

"Are you hungry?" Lily asks me.

"Yeah. But I guess I don't mind sushi. I will just order an orange and spend the time peeling it."

"I wonder why more places don't have fruit on the menu."

"There are Vegan and Vegetarian places that have it. America does not have the culture where ordering fruits and vegetables for appetizers are normal."

"True. It's kind of sad."

"Yes. But if they did, I would think it was weird."

"Yeah. Me too. I think I wish I wouldn't, though." Lily says.

"Well, we can order a bowl of oranges and begin to change ourselves."

She giggles a little. As we walk toward Shay, who is standing impatiently at her car, Lily snuggles into me. Josh sees us and breaks from his group, then starts toward Shay's car too. We arrive at Shay's car about the same time and stand there a beat.

"So, I guess I am driving?" Shay asks, a little put out.

"You are the one with keys in your hand." Josh informs her. "I got shotgun." Josh says, climbing into the car.

"Fine." Shay says, walking over to the driver's side.

I look at Lily and give her a wicked smile.

"Looks like we found our backseat."

She playfully pushes me out of the way and slides into the backseat. I follow her in. Shay blasts some old-school 90's metal as we leave the parking lot.

Josh is the one who introduced us to this sushi bar. It replaced a Chicken Market in the plaza down the street from school the prior year and is the only Japanese place I have ever eaten at. The only taste of sushi I ever had was on the first trip there. That night, I had become violently ill and vowed since that meat, poultry or fish had to be damn near burnt for me to eat it. Lily, though, had become fond of it, and Shay pronounced her love of it weeks before we ate there. So, there I was; eating salad and oranges two to three times a week at a sushi bar.

Josh leads the way as we enter. There is a table in the back left that he has an OCD obsession about. We have left a handful of times because that table was taken. This time, however, it is clear, so we sit down. Josh quickly places an Alaskan Roll order and tea while Lily and Shay look at the menu.

I ask for a bowl of oranges. Josh and Shay aren't paying attention, but Lily looks up from her menu. The waitress – a young girl with no waist at all, probably twenty; the owner's daughter – looks at me, attempting to find a sign that my request is sarcasm. There is none, so she repeats my order back to me.

"A bowl of oranges?" She says, with only the slightest indication of it being a question.

"Yeah. You have them as an add-on. Could you give me, say five, in a salad bowl or something?" I ask

The doubt of my seriousness is replaced by a submission to the oddness of my choice.

"Yes. I will bring them out. Thank you."

She takes my unopened menu and leaves. Lily is still looking at me when I turn to her. She gives me an 'I can't believe you actually did that' look. I shrug.

"I'll share my oranges. You can still order something else." I tell her.

"But doesn't that go against the idea of changing my idea?" She says, cutely recognizing the redundancy of her sentence just as she completes it.

"Yeah, but you don't have to go cold turkey. Rome wasn't built in a day. History wasn't born in a day. Fill in another cliché here." I draw a line in the air with my finger.

"Why should I put off till tomorrow what I can start today?" She asks, folding up her menu.

I smile and give a laugh at the absurdity of what we are doing. I love that she will follow me into the absurdity, and that, even though they sit next to us, Shay and Josh have zero clues of our conversation.

Josh's Alaskan Rolls and tea are brought to the table and Shay orders Yaki Soba Noodles with vegetables and chicken. Josh orders Philly Rolls and asks for lime with his tea. The waitress does the customary bow and leaves. Shay and Josh look around the table almost confused that no one is talking. They were both in the mode to enter a conversation; not start one.

"I didn't get a bow when she left the first time." I say, mock complainingly.

"That's because you threw her with your order." Lily tells me.

"Whatcha order?" Josh inquires.

I sit back in my chair, not sure if I want to discuss it. But then realize that when the oranges show up, there will be no hiding them.

"Oranges." I tell him.

"Orange what?"

"Not orange. Oranges. I got a bowl of oranges."

"Are you serious?" Shay says, underneath a gulp of laughter.

"You can't order a bowl of oranges." Josh says, convinced.

"They have oranges on the menu. I am sure they can handle tossing them in a bowl." I say, a little annoyed, but understanding the humor of it. "The whole event of me ordering them was done with you non-attentive people beside me."

I look directly at Shay when I say "non-attentive". It had become common for Shay to call me over-attentive, so having a situation to throw it back at her is nice.

"I am sharing the bowl with him," Lily informs Shay and Josh. "It occurred to us it is rare in America that fruit is served as an appetizer. And that we even thought it was strange. So, why not take advantage of a place that offers it?"

"You think it is strange because it is strange. Simple as that." Josh tells me.

Before we are able to continue, my bowl of oranges triumphantly arrives. Lily lays out a napkin and I give her an orange. Picking up one myself we begin to peel. Shay and Josh's eyes are fixed on us.

"Okay." I say, breaking the momentary objects Lily and I had become. "Us eating oranges isn't that fascinating. What else is on our minds?" I throw out an open-ended question to spur us in another direction. I had breakfast with Shay at A Coffee Spot that morning. From school, to basketball practice, to a pick-up break in, I had hung out with Josh most of the day before. It wasn't that we ran out of things to say to each other or that we hadn't heard all of each other's stories. It was just we understood and appreciated the comfort of sitting in silence with each other. When Shay's food arrives, she ate. Josh finished first and read his placemat. Lily and I went on peeling and eating our oranges. Once we settled in, we all realized how much we needed a chance to breathe.

School ends uneventfully. Shay and Josh leave for their part-time jobs. Lily heads off to the Mayor's office. The mayor has been trying to organize the grade schools in town to form volunteer fundraiser committees. The more money raised through them, the smaller classes, better programs, and better equipment the schools can have. This seemed fairly simple to me, yet putting it together has been difficult. Lily has been working on it for over a month now. I told her I might stop by later and give her a hand. I needed to take a nap first as I have been up for 38 hours straight. I have reached the point of utter exhaustion; the place where no caffeine can reach. She offers to drive me home, but I decline, saying I will be fine.

I pull into my driveway to find my father's car is there. I check the time: it is not quite four. This is odd and causes me to walk through the front door. My dad works so much these days, I can't even remember the last time I saw him. I walk in to find him and my mom sitting at the dining room table. Cups of coffee are on the table, but they seem to be untouched.

I take my book bag off my shoulder and hold it in front of me. My mom is the first to look up at me and gives me a smile. I look to my dad who I almost don't recognize, being that he is wearing his glasses. They are heavy-looking black-rimmed ones. The frames look old. Not worn, just by the style. As though they were his first pair, and through the years, all that has changed were the lenses. There are papers partially covered by his left arm. I can't tell what they are, just that they are typed. My dad removes his glasses before he looks to me.

I have my father's hazel eyes. That has always been said since the day I was born. I look the most like my mom, but my eyes are from my dad. It's hard to look him in the eyes because I can read him well. When I look in the mirror, whatever I am feeling bleeds out. The same is true with my dad. Whether he wants me to or not, the emotion inside him is never hidden from me. There is sorrow in him; and a tiredness that I can't even claim. They sit there quietly, only giving me a quick look of hello. I don't know how to respond to them. Over the last three or so years, I rarely have.

"What's up?" I ask, as a question, not a greeting.

"Nothing really." My dad tells me, but doesn't follow it up with anything.

"Okay," I say. "Why are you home?"

"I have a doctor's appointment in a little while. I stopped home to say hi to you and your mom. Why don't you grab a snack and take a seat?" He tells me.

"Okay." I say, finding this kind of odd.

I toss my book bag off to the side and retrace my steps back into the kitchen. I pour myself a glass of milk, grab a granola bar, and return to the dining room. Both my parents look as though they haven't moved an inch. I take the head seat. My dad is to my left, my mom to my right. The papers that were under my dad's arm are gone. I see his briefcase in the corner.

"So, how is basketball?" My dad asks. It is a simple question, a friendly, obvious one.

I hold my voice inside for a moment and swallow my impulse answer. This is a mundane question, routine. However, the length of time between the question, and the fact that it was coming from someone who should know the answer without asking, made it hard for me to answer without sarcasm. I guess my contention with it is if you really cared about the answer, you would never have to ask the question.

"Good." I tell him. "Next game is the day after tomorrow. Then we have South Shore next Friday."

"Next Friday? Great. I can make that one." He tells me.

"You are going to come to my game?" I say, without the ability to hide my shock.

"We both are." My mom's words cause my neck to spasm over to her.

"Wow." I say, searching my mind for another word to say. "Wow."

"That's okay, right? That we come?" My mom asks.

"Yeah. Of course. I am just surprised is all. Neither of you have come before. I didn't think you cared." I say, realizing how harsh that might have sounded.

"When your school gave you a scholarship, we should have taken better notice, I am sorry for that." My father says as he reaches into his briefcase and pulls out an open envelope. He slightly twists the edges in his hands before extending it to me. "Clearly, you are rather good." He hands me the envelope.

My eyes dart up to the upper left to see the return address before I pull out the letter. I know what it is before I start reading. Even so, it is still surreal.

The first few lines are just flowery propaganda about how amazing the university is. It isn't until the second paragraph that I am officially asked to join their basketball team and offered a full scholarship. It is a division two school. I knew I was good enough to get a few letters from schools like this. My parents clearly hadn't thought I would get acceptance letters for a few months at the earliest, and they certainly didn't expect any scholarships, especially a full ride. But there is the letter from Albany State University, giving a monetary value to my playing skills. You fill out applications, write essays, and send out money, but I never thought about the responses. To me, it was like sending out a message in a bottle: you get to a point in your life where it is your turn to do it. And so I did. Now I had an answer to what I should do after high school, or at least a choice. I wasn't stuck. I didn't know how I should react. I am excited. But it is the kind of excitement that has this nagging feeling that what has impressed *you* really isn't that impressive, and once outside your bubble, the truth bursts. I didn't care, though. As small and as meaningless as it turns out to be, it was an accomplishment. Mine.

I get back in my car and drive. I drive to the Stadium and see a few pick-up games being played. I know most of the kids there, but it is a vague, distant way so I don't stop. I kind of want to play a game. To prove to myself I am good. To justify what I received. Only, it is the kind of adrenaline I know will dissolve after my first shot. I know I won't be able to sleep, but will collapse if I try and extend any energy.

I decide I want to find Lily. However, it is only five. She has at least a few more hours at work. I want to talk to Lily isolated. I want to tell her about Albany State. I want to be the only one to hear, see and feel her reaction. I could not do that now. The Mayor's office would still be congested. I think for a minute about calling her and having her meet me someplace, but could not indulge in that kind of selfishness. She is going to be working until at least seven. I am promised a call as soon as she is out. I am too antsy to sit on my hands until then, so I head to Entropy Perfumes at the mall where Shay works.

It's a weekday, so I know it will be pretty dead. I walk in a side service entrance, follow the hallway and enter next to Shay's store. I peer in from the corner to make sure she is customer free. She wears a flowing open back metallic top and a jean mini skirt. Her top is a size too small, which only affects the length as it comes down to the top of her skirt's button. Shay's style is an extension of herself. It is thought out, but always embraces any flaws believing in instinct more than reason.

"I would like to try the newest scent. Chop, chop." I say when I get close enough to speak in a normal voice. Shay puts her clipboard down and turns to me.

"Hey. Aren't you supposed to be unconscious by now?"

"Me? Sleep? Surely you jest."

"So what, you came to rub in how you can sleep but don't want to, while I – as exhausted as you – have to work and cannot sleep? You sadistic son of a bitch." She laughs and then yawns.

"I was about to sleep when I got a letter."

"You got a letter?"

"That I did." I hand it to her. She glances at it and then looks up.

"No shit."

"Yeah. Kind of surreal." I say.

"So, you going?"

"I don't know. It's the first letter I've got."

"Makes me want to check my mail. We just kinda tossed all these letters out like messages in a bottle. It feels strange to see you get a response." Shay says.

"Now imagine being the one getting it."

"And a full ride." She giggles. "It will be funny if Josh doesn't get any basketball offers. There is kind of an unspoken jealousy about that with you guys, right?

"Not really. Co-Captains, Co-MVPs. We have never reached a point where there is any cause for jealousy."

"Well, now you might have." She tells me

"Thanks for that shining bit of happiness."

"Don't stress. He kicks ass too. I am sure he will get a few unrequited recruitment letters."

I stay silent for a while. The letter isn't unrequited. I had wrote, called and sent videos of my games. I can't tell Shay that. For that would lead to the question 'why?'. And I did not want to explain that it is because the school is less than an hour from where my sister is.

"What did Lily say?"

"I haven't told her." I say.

"Really? I get to be your first? I am flattered, but a little disappointed at the quickness of it." Shay flashes her sinful smile.

"She is stuck at City Hall for a few more hours. I dare not breach the gates."

"You can hang here if you want. Nothing exciting, though."

"Except simulating conversation and the simulating of maybe more."

Shay's laugh gets caught and becomes a cough.

"You are lucky you have a girlfriend, cause your lines suck."

"Please. If I wasn't joking, I could game you." I tell her.

"Do I look like a girl who falls for game?"

"You look like a girl who wants to, but no one has been able to impress." I tell her.

She mulls this over.

"Could be. But my boyfriend might disagree."

"Your boyfriend should be a year outside of college, and he is picking up high school girls. Do you really want my opinion on that?" This is not contentious; it is tired. A refrain played again and again.

"Your opinion is pious when love is not."

"Yeah, and Nabokov understood love well." Shay says.

"He understood that sometimes love is not rational. Maybe there would be more love in the world if there weren't so many rules choking it."

"Okay. Fine. I will agree with that." I say.

I had found myself in a corner, not being able to articulate why her relationship was unsettling to me. It might be my own possessiveness of her, or that it was a part of her life that I wasn't exposed to. If you are involved with 99% of a person, that 1% can get under your skin. Before I can attempt to shift her logic, an older woman –

probably in her late fifties – walks into the store and approaches Shay. I bow out and head to the food court. It had become an addiction. Whenever I am at the mall, I have to get an Orange Shake. I don't quite understand why. I guess we all have a little OCD in us, and this is mine.

When I reach the stand, I am third in line. Behind the counter is this girl, Rachel something. She is a freshman but I have seen her around school and at our games. She has this blooming quality to her. Looking at her, the analogy of a butterfly half out of its cocoon comes to mind. Half of her is beautiful, but the other half is too young to be thought of that way. When my turn comes, she has my drink all ready. She gives me a pleased-with-herself smile. "Predictability is one of my flaws." I tell her as I hand her the money. I notice she charges me for a small, despite giving me a large.

"Attentiveness is one of mine". Rachel says, waiting for my reaction before giving one herself. I wave a loose smile. Her eyes brighten and I am able to see her back teeth.

"Thanks for the drink." I tell her as I begin to walk away.

"So, Ashley broke her ankle, did you hear?" Rachel's words are strained. As though her desire to speak them out won her fear.

"Ashley West?" I ask, turning back to her.

"Yeah. Just this afternoon."

Ashley West is a junior cheerleader. Josh dated her, or slept with her, or something last year. Right before summer break, I think. I don't know her well.

"So, what does that mean for the squad?" I ask with weary interest as I take a sip of my drink.

"I got bumped up." She says this with controlled enthusiasm.

Hearing this causes me to look at her differently. It caught me off guard. The word 'cheerleader' evokes dirty, flexible thoughts in me. This must have been visible because she blushes and looks away. I feel lust start to swarm me. I have to leave. I have to find Lily. Then I have to sleep. There is weakness in exhaustion and a hunger beginning to stir in me.

"Good for you." I tell her. "I'll see you Friday, then?"

"You will."

I do my best to give her a congratulatory look, and
then walk away. I don't stop and say anything to Shay on
my way out. I jump in my car and race off to Lily. As I am
driving, I text her asking,
"U Out?"
        Her response is quick, saying,
"Soon. 10 minutes."
 "I'll b there in 7." I text back.
"K." She responds.
        The parking lot of City Hall is empty, except for her
car when I arrive. I leave a space between Lily's car and
mine. I wait in the car for a second but am too antsy. I get
out of my car and walk in circles, not wanting to go in but
hopeless to the fact that it might come to that. I am saved
when I see Lily walking out. She locks the door and
saunters her way to me. Her book bag is on her back with
two other bags draped on either shoulder. Her keys are in
her hand as she pops open the truck when she is about
twenty feet from me. I grab the bags from her and throw
them inside.
"What a hellish day. My mind is numb from going over all
this paperwork." She stretches and takes elastic out of her
hair. I close the truck, scoop her up, and push her against
her car. This is done so quickly that she can only react after
she is pinned.
"Well, hello to you, too." She looks me in the eyes,
studying. "You get any sleep?"
"No." Is all I say before I kiss her, yearningly. I nibble on
her ear, move my way down her neck to her collarbone,
then start to peel the top of her shirt. This is when the
euphoria hits a caution flag for Lily as she understands
how deep my aggression is.
"Wait, Noah."
        I stop. I am completely out of myself. Almost
drooling like a dog, hungry to the point of starvation, weak
to the brink of collapsing. Lily understands me better than
anyone. I have been in the state before.
"Not here." She whispers to soothe me. "Get in the car and
I'll drive us to the Cove."
        I don't say anything, but find my way to the
passenger seat. The Cove is not far. It is clearing beside the
river. With heavy rain, the entrance is covered by water,

but most of the time, you can drive right inside it. That is exactly what she does. She backs in so we are facing the river and backs up just far enough to only have the faintest of light stay with us.

"Back seat?" Lily asks, but it isn't really a question. I climb through the space between the passenger and driver's seat; Lily steps out of the car and opens the back door. I prop myself against the door. Lily takes off her sweatshirt, revealing the same sundress she had on in school. She takes the shoe and sock off one foot, steps in with that foot and then does the same with the other. On her hands and knees, Lily inches her way to me. She slides up to me. Placing her hands on my thighs, she is in a perfect upward-facing dog yoga position. She kisses me in a fluttering tension-building way. I sink low until my neck is resting on the door handle. I respond to all her touches and kisses, but my mind starts to fade. I am a light flickering before dying. In a jolt, I become aware that she has stopped, but when I look up to her, I am no longer sure of the time. She isn't looking at me: she is watching me. I know I wouldn't have fallen asleep. I know I didn't. I lift myself a little so my back is resting square against the door.

"What am I going to do with you?" Lily asks, to herself more than to me.

"Hey. I am fine. Tired and stressed is all. I got some good news today, though." I want to filter the mood that had begun to surround us.

"Yeah? What's that?"

"I got into a college. Or University. Albany State."

"New York?"

"Yeah. Got a full basketball scholarship there too."

"Wow. I didn't even know you applied there." She pauses. I see her mind trying to connect dots she doesn't have the information to. "Is this some sort of recruitment thing?"

"Sort of, I guess. I applied there, but you can't apply for a basketball scholarship."

"I didn't apply to any New York schools." She says softly.

"Hey, just because I got in doesn't mean I'm going there. It is still early." I tell her.

"I know. I am just caught off guard. Happy. But surprised."

"And you know what else?"

"There is more?" Lily gasps like a game show contestant.

"My parents are coming to my game on Friday."

"See, now I know you are full of shit."

I laugh.

"And isn't that sad. Me getting into a college is more believable than my parents coming to one of my basketball games." I say.

"Let's focus on the happy." She tells me.

As she kisses me this time, I wake up some. In an awkward twist, I reverse our positions. She wraps her legs around my back and the noises in our heads shut off.

I wake up the next morning before the sun. I find myself on the other side of the back seat with Lily's head on my chest. This immediately makes me try and control my breathing, which only succeeds in increasing the air I inhale. I glance at my watch, finding that it is just after 3am. I had six or so hours of sleep, but could do for a lot more. I have basketball practice in the afternoon, and a poor showing there would only increase how many laps I would have to do. I don't close my eyes, though. I stare out to the stillness of the river. Thoughts rush into my mind, making it spin and swirl. They are nothing concrete, nothing I can grasp and make sense of. Rather, they are a dust cloud polluting my brain. I do my best to empty my head and resign myself to closing my eyes again. I wake again a few hours later to Lily's stirring. She lazily sits up and sees my eyes are open.

"Hey," She says, giving a light smile. "Did you finally sleep?" She laughs. There was once a time both of us barely slept.

"I got eight hours of intermittent sleep. I am almost not tired."

"Good. I like my man pulled together." She yawns and stretches. "You mind if we take off? I need a shower and mouthwash badly." She tells me.

"Yeah. Drop me off at my car?"

"Of course."

We get out of the car and walk around to the front. It is nearly 6am as we drive, and the streets are empty.

"Congratulations." We have been riding in silence, so Lily's words take a second to sink in.

"For what?" I ask.

"Getting into college. I am really proud of you. I am sorry if I didn't act it last night, my head was elsewhere."

"Oh. Yeah. It probably wasn't the best time to blurt it out. It just kinda popped into my mind and then out of my mouth."

"What are we if not random and impulsive?" Lily says.

"Dead." I say.

"Right." She pauses. I look at her face. I see her remembering and then smiling. "Last night was a lot of fun. You completely took my mind away from everything."

"Such was the idea." I tell her.

There is a lightness that overcomes me as I look at her. Being with Lily has taught me that nothing can erase your pain, emptiness, or sorrow, but the right person can alleviate it. I had begun to hold onto the differences between us as a coming rift, but the truth is, they had always been there. That is how we balanced each other. There were times she fell into me and I understood how to comfort her, and there were times I fell into her and she knew how to comfort me. We are each other's counterpoint. It is an amazing thing. It is a blessing to live with. The fear is in losing it.

Three

At The Brink of Everything

I swear there is blood from my lungs climbing up my throat. 'They are called suicides for a reason' I tell myself, inhale, and then sprint back to the foul line. It is almost six; practice was supposed to end at five. Josh is ahead of everyone, running like a track star. He is showing off. If it mattered, I would care, but I know I am getting my 37 minutes no matter how many more suicides he does than me.

"Showers," our coach yells before blowing on his whistle.

I stop in mid-stride. I stretch, and try and get my breathing in control as the rest of the guys head to the locker rooms. Josh looks back as he reaches the outside door of the gym. He knows why I am staying and is not surprised I haven't moved. He doesn't say anything. He pauses and then catches up with the others. I move to half court and stare at the padding on the concrete that is three feet past the backboard. I know I am alone, but look around just in case. I have heard of people sitting on the ledges of buildings, feet dangling over. They don't jump, probably don't want to jump. But they want to bring themselves to the brink so they can feel what it might be like if they did; so they can see if they can fly. My version of that came after practices. I align myself at half court and sprint into the padding on the wall. I crash violently, bounce off the wall and on to the floor. I get up and repeat. I am bruised and dizzy from this, but continue for a good ten minutes. Josh found me knocked out on the floor once. I don't remember it, really. Logic concluded that my head must have banged against the floor and given me a concussion. Josh had this helpless concern for me then. He did not understand what the hell I was doing. It wasn't clear enough to me to explain, so I just said sometimes I need to lose myself. He thought about this and then nodded in acceptance. He needed to lose himself too. He smoked and slept with random girls for the same reason.

I come out of the gym and catch Josh in the hallway. "That was a quick shower."
"I don't dwell." Josh tells me.
"I'm hitting the weights. You down?"
"Dude, I just showered."
"You gotta put in the reps if you wanna impress. What else do you have to do?"
"I can always *find* something to do." He tells me.
"Whatever, man. You gotta spot me. I have first set." I head to the gym, and without looking, I know he is following.

Our gym is a closet of a room with only six machines and a small variety of free weights. I throw a hundred-eighty on the bench press, then lay down on it. I grab the weight and start wielding it before Josh is in position. He stands above me, zoning out.
"Hey, you and Megan wanna come to this club next Friday after our game?" I say without slowing down.
"What's happening there?"
"This band is playing I wanna check out. Five buck cover." I tell him.
"Maybe. I'll talk to her about it." Josh says.
"Good. Maybe we can get Shay's guy down too. You haven't met him, have you?"
"Nah."

There is a bit of Shay being the girl Josh is too nervous to ask out hanging there whenever her boyfriend is brought up. He enjoys taking shots at him to almost a perverse degree. But that is reserved for only when Shay is around. They are acerbic jabs that are designed to get a reaction out of her. They usually work, but her reactions are the disappearing of herself into the mold Josh has crafted for her. She knows what he wants to hear, or what will twist him inside. She will say, "Why do you care who I fuck?" Extending the sound of the '*f*' to emphasize the last word. She slides nearer to him to see who blinks first.

Shay has had three boyfriends this year, and the times in-between it seemed evitable her and Josh were going to hook up. Both of us can claim sexual tension standing beside her, but there were barriers between me and her. With Josh, there were times the welcome gates opened. How far he walked inside has never been revealed, but it has been clear he has always walked out blue.

Josh and I switch places and he lifts the weight, controlled but slower than I was.

"So, I haven't gotten a chance to tell you this yet, but my parents are coming to Friday's game.

Josh sets the weight down and sits up.

"Really?"

Lily has met my parents a few times. I could never see us all having dinner together, and the lack of that taught Lily about the relationship of my parents and I. It was through that prism she saw us. Josh is the only one who has spent enough time observing me around them to fully understand the significance of their showing up to a game. He has seen the child yearning for affection, and the subsequent indifference showered on him. You can tell a lot about someone by how they were raised. Their anger, longing, rebellion can all be traced back to that.

"What prompted this?" He asks.

"I got a scholarship to Albany State. A basketball one. Full ride." I say.

"Holy shit. What conference are they?" He asks.

"I don't know. They are division two."

"Oh." He says, excitement draining from his voice.

"What?"

"No, I am glad you got into a school, but division two? Merrimac College is division two." Josh tells me.

"Is it? That puts a new spin on it."

"I would rather get into a D one school and walk onto the basketball team."

"Yeah, you can afford that." I tell him.

"C'mon, man. Don't play that card."

"It isn't a card. I have no college fund. Forgive me for shuddering at the idea of going a hundred plus grand in debt."

Money is a subject avoided. He is the one with courtside seats to games; whose father drives a $100,000 car. I am the one who wears Salvation Army clothes not as a statement or an attempt to be 'vintage', but because it lessens the bills. His parents consider me classless, and this is a main reason. I hide under the guise of a scholarship to acclaim. What others assume isn't my problem.

"Did Lily even apply to any New York schools?"

"No".

He gives me a 'there's your answer' look, failing to realize that, if that was my answer, I would never have applied there in the first place. Then it hits me that neither him nor Shay applied to any New York schools either. Sometimes, the closer you are to someone, the more your own individuality blurs. The four of us were an example of that. There had been no talk of all of us sitting next to each other on the plane ride to our new school, but a close facsimile was the quiet assumption. My scholarship has disrupted that. It has awakened a conversation regarding it. If this had been the case when I told Lily and Shay, I missed it, but Josh spoke to it.

"Closest I applied to is Rutgers; Shay Syracuse; Lily Penn State. That's a weird thought; to be that separate." Josh says as he resumes pushing the weight.

"But, c'mon," I contend, "isn't it predetermined that you are going to Oral Roberts? The rest of us all applied to Tulsa. That could work, right? Lily applied to a school in London. It doesn't mean I am going to have to get a passport if I want to see her."

"No. You will see her for Christmas at first, maybe spring break. That dwindles down to phones calls, then emails, then Christmas cards with pictures of her kids." Josh's words are stuttered as he passes 15 reps. Breathing heavily, he finishes his thought, then puts the weight down.

"A little bit dramatic and bleak, don't you think? I always thought we transcended the cliché of not being friends outside of high school." Josh moves off the bench and I slide on for another set. He waits until I am pushing up my second rep before responding.

"Yeah, I don't know." He says with a tone of uncertainty and distress I haven't heard before. "And you are right. I am going to Oral Roberts. I don't need a letter to confirm I am getting in. And I don't have a choice no matter what any other letters say. My parents indulged me the money to send them out. And without them, I am shuddering at the thought of going a hundred grand in debt."

Not having money is a burden. I understood that. Josh's parents controlled him with their money. They dangled options and perks in front of him like cat toys. This practice had been going on so long it no longer is 'do what we say and you can have this', it is 'if you don't do what we say, you *can't* have this'. He felt as suffocated as I did. Just for completely different reasons.

We go through the rest of our weight cycle, which takes a little over an hour. We hit the showers and are at our lockers when Josh's cell phone rings. The ringtone is generic. He checks it and then answers.
"Hey, Megan. What's up?"

He looks down and away from me as he speaks. When it is just us, he usually puts it on speaker when girls call. But Megan has lasted longer than any of his previous girls. Over six months. There have been rare instances of her being included in our group. I like her. She is sweet and has the most salacious curve to her back I have ever seen. She is a born-again Christian (which is actually a lie made up to please his parents. The only times she has ever been to church is when she has gone with him.) In a way, she is the perfect girl for Josh to have by his side. She cheers him on at every game, and is skilled at the politics of dealing with his parents. But there is this vapidness about her I haven't been able to shake. Shay has a vanity about her as well, but that only highlights the obvious side of her. Inside, there is a lot more going on. I am not sure there is with Megan. I could be wrong, I probably am. As long as he is happy. How many times do we say that? I often think I have no perspective to give him since my current relationship is all I have known of relationships. But I do think most people who say 'as long as they are happy' say that knowing the person has no idea of what makes them happy. At our age, we are learning bits about ourselves. How presumptuous is it to claim we understand what happy for us is?

I go on a rant about this for a while, and then everyone within earshot tells me to shut up or crosses the distance to be out of earshot. "You think too much." Josh tells me. I tell him that is one of the many reasons I find little sleep.

"Yeah. I am about to bounce from here." Josh says, still on the phone. "I can meet you there in around twenty minutes." Josh throws the last of his things in his duffel bag and then motions for us to leave. "Alright. Bye."

Josh ends the call and throws the strap of his duffel bag over his shoulder. He doesn't offer any information about the phone call, and we walk outside quietly. The parking lot is empty except for Josh's car and my car. We come to his car first. He opens the door and hangs his arms around it.

"I've got to pick Megan up at the tanning salon. Then we're heading to the movies. You wanna call Lily and meet us there?"

"I don't know if she can make it." I say. "Shay and her are working on this yearbook thing. The winter village thing is being set up and they are helping slash taking pictures."

"Okay. You still staying after tomorrow for the test prep?"

"Yeah. Shay too. Lily is gonna have a long night at the Mayor's office, but I told her we'd catch up with her after. The lake is getting kinda cold, so maybe we can just chill at A Coffee Spot or something."

"Sounds good. I'll check you later." Josh climbs in his car and drives off. I wait until he is out of eyesight before I throw my bag in my truck.

As I am getting in my car, I see a few cars start pulling in. Without seeing anyone at first, I know they are from our school's drama club. It seems as though they have carpooled as two cars produce eight people. I recognize six of them with Erin as the centerpiece. They have to walk past my car to get to the gym, so I wait idly for them to do so. Erin takes a step ahead of the group and gives me a smile.

"Hey. Practice all done?" She asks.

"Yeah. It's all yours." I tell her.

Erin walks to me and her group follows her. We say hi to each other and they stand beside me in anticipation of a conversation. Other than Erin, I have never said more than a few words to this group of people. I have no idea what to say, so I push whatever awkwardness I have into indifference and look at Erin. I decide she is the one who is either going to speak or the one who is going to leave. I will just stand here until she forces one of those options.

"Have you ever read Harold Pinter?" Erin asks as though that was a continuation to our non-existent subject, or a ridiculously flawless segway. I am a little unnerved as they all stare at me as though I should not only know who Erin is talking about, but have some sort of expertise in the matter. I search my mind for some answer that doesn't make me seem like some sort of dumb jock. It hits me that there were reasons I did not hang out with this group of people: I did not want to be put in situations where I felt like a moron. The exact situation I find myself in now. I find saving grace in my stalling as I notice one of them carrying a book title, "The Homecoming" by just-my-dumb-luck Harold Pinter.

"Some. Why? Are you doing one of his plays this semester?" My lie is said so smoothly I even believe it.

"We are." Erin says, showing no surprise in her tone, but leaving a glimpse of it in her eyes for me to see before blinking it away. It is a game. She allowed me to see that, briefly. I exhale a little too loudly and listen as she continues. "We will be performing the third and fourth weekend of January. Your tickets are already preordered, right?" She says this teasingly.

"Yup. Right alongside with my Prom tickets." I say, which makes the group laugh. So sure they understand. So locked into the structure of high school. So convinced at the obviousness of me. Hate for them surges in me, quickly manifesting into rage. But – I said what I said as a joke. With the purpose of getting a laugh. The swirl of emotion dies inside me with this realization.

"Well, if you're nice, I might be able to get you a playbill autographed by the cast," Erin jokes. "We have to get in," She adds, too quickly for me to respond. "We may not have to run sprints if we are late, but it is unpleasant nevertheless."

"I wish I had some energy pills to give you guys or something, but I will offer a 'have fun'." I tell them.

I get the laugh I was again trying for, but feel lame. Why did I say that? I am attempting to relate to people I have nothing in common with. They say goodbye and I am stuck leaning against my car.

I have always believed that alone time is a two-way divide: freedom or a feeling of being directionless. Personality, and in my case, mood, determines the choice. I get in my car and start to drive. A list of options of what I could do float in and out of my head. Pick up my prescription at the pharmacy, put in some hours at the Mayor's office, homework, sleep. I have a history paper due the following week that I have been procrastinating on, but that would require the type of focus I know I am currently unable to produce. I settle on stopping by City Hall and the Mayor's office. It is nearing seven o'clock so it is a toss-up if anyone else will be there. I have been given a set of, what I like to call, janitor keys. In reality, all they give me access to is the side building where Lily has a workspace and the windowless office with Lily's name on the front of the door.

It is past seven as I pull into City Hall's parking lot. As I had thought, the parking lot is vacant. City Hall is built on a slight rise. Akin to a talk show host elevating his desk from their guest's chair, so too is City Hall heightened above the level of the other buildings around it. I am sure it looks odd to out-of-towners, but to the locals, it has become a flawless part of the architecture of our city's oldest monument. The time I have spent working there had given me, not a connection, but an awareness of the surroundings of the city. A perception unhindered by a news reporter's opinion or the gossip of gathered but misinformed information. Everything I take in penetrates solely through the transparent lens of my own self. It is a whispered inner debate whether or not this affects me, and to what degree. Currently, I seem to have rested upon being the fly on the wall, without will to be a Samaritan or a civil servant, but also without the strength to leave. I like to think of it as the process where I figure out how I want to define myself. However, there are others (teachers, guidance counselors) who have called it 'indecisiveness' and a 'cop-out'. I tell myself there is no one whose words I respect enough to find their disappointment, disapproval to mean much. I have spent much of the last four years banishing that part of me. Recently, though, I have seen flashes in Lily's eyes. I pray that day never comes.

I unlock a side door and walk into a hallway barely lit with a generator light. This is a path I do not need light to find my way on. I climb up two flights of stairs to the third floor and take a right down the hallway. I flick the light to Lily's office on and glance around. As usual, the place is immaculate. Organization was something I never took seriously. If I understand it, then that is good enough. The room is bigger than you might expect. I say it is a closet, but it is closer to a walk-in closet. A desk, filing cabinet, two chairs and a bookcase fill the room. I sit down at the desk and pull out a folder from the right drawer of the desk. It is labeled, "Fundraising District 2". I always go to this folder first. It is the middle school I went to and that gives me more of a desire to help it.

The further into the process of organizing fundraising committees, the clearer it became what our real task was: making people care. Attempts at stripping away apathy are usually futile. To create a working organism there is a certain dedication needed. Not simply one weekend a month, once a year. But that is what we are trying to accomplish. To put a structure in place. The obvious ideas of having a bake sale and car wash resulted in little cash and left no room for having a sequel. It became clear that a grander vision will have to be found. Lily came up with the idea of marketing apparel. She created test designs (including a school logo), a full range of prices, and a verbal contract to being able to sell them at the town library and other local shops. It was a completely thought out, realized idea. And, just like Lily, no one had any idea of what she was thinking until her reveal after its completion. It turned out really well, becoming a fad at the school. Every kid wore some version. Bumper stickers, mugs, pencils, and pretty much everything else followed. We were able to change the schedule to enable a commerce class where the kids learned about what we were doing and could help out. Kids are much easier to influence and spark. The early success made us understand the culture we wanted to create, from inside the school first, and then beyond. We soon branched out and became like a caravan. We had a presence at every event in the city and even a few in neighboring cities. A little over a month into it, we had a profit of almost $10,000 dollars. We were astonished. The other schools came running to us, wanting a piece. We were very specific from the beginning that this was going to be individual by school. There was no pot, no sharing. However, the success of the first school is what gives us our headache now. We are trying to better all the schools, and even though competition is a good thing, we need to have enough diverse ways of making money so that every school can benefit. Establishing success in one school was supposed to motivate the other five, but instead, it has just made them whiney and jealous. The good that came out of it was the creation of a template. Now the challenge was to parlay it.

The folder has newspaper clippings of events District 2 has been at, along with sticky notes with Lily's comments on them. Things like, "we missed out on the older sister's" and "we needed more people here". I have seen the process where her notes became memos and proposals, enough to decode her shorthand. There is usually a checklist of things that need to be done in the front of the folder, but I don't see it. I flip through the entirety of the folder but there isn't one. I find this odd since Lily's habit has always been to set up the next day's work before she left the office. I give up and put the folder back in the drawer. I turn her computer on, sit back and wait for it to load up.

My cell vibrates, indicating a text message. I pull it out and read it. It is from Lily. "I am seven hours into missing you." I can hear Lily's voice speaking the words as I read them. There is something inherent in the words, 'missing you' that I have always translated into meaning you need them. That there cannot be cause to miss someone if there isn't some need inside you to create it. Her text makes me smile. I had not seen her since lunch and the awareness of time had slipped from me. Glancing at the clock, it stuns me that it is a little past eight. It shouldn't, being I arrived after seven, but in the space of an hour, I had done little to pass the time. The computer brightens and loads her desktop. I go to shut it down again when Lily's background picture loads. It is of Shay, Josh, myself and her. Megan had snapped it the first time she hung with us. It was the week after school ended last year. We had all gone into Boston and wandered all around. It struck us how involved we were with each other and how everyone else we saw was distant and cold. The subways were the best example. That is where the picture was taken. Lily and Shay sat next to each other with me next to Lily and Josh next to Shay. We were caught in a joke that Shay had told, laughing hysterically. The camera phone picture came out great. It looked like an album cover from a European pop band. I stare at it for a minute before I shut down the computer. I wield my phone and send Lily a response: "How long till we remedy that?" I am in my car and out of the parking lot before my phone rings.

"Hey, you," Lily says, a slight rasp in her voice. "I just got out of the Winter Formal meeting. Where are you?"

"I am just leaving City Hall." I tell her.

"You put some time in?" She asks, happily surprised.

"Not as much as you. I just reviewed some clippings. Free-form brainstorming." I tell her. I have become good at phrasing my words to act greater than the actions they are describing. She knows this, but finds amusement in it.

"So, what are you up to now?"

"Nothing, really. You?" I ask.

"I am dropping Shay home because she is being totally lame and doesn't want to hang out past eight." I hear Shay in the background moaning about that comment and wrestling with Lily for the phone. She is the one driving so I know soon I will be talking to Shay.

"Are you popping speed? How the hell are you still awake?" Shay's voice booms through the phone. I don't respond because I can hear giggling in the background as Lily fights to get the phone back. Soon after, the phone blanks out. Three seconds later, it rings again.

"I am sorry 'bout that." Lily starts. "Shay was being immature." I hear Shay scoff. "We are just lucky that no little old ladies were crossing the street." Shay scoffs again and Lily bursts out laughing. "It seems as though Shay needs her beauty rest. Mr. College Stud is coming down this weekend and, being that it has been a few weeks, she needs sleep and time to read Peter Cottontail so she will know how to turn him on." Again, I heard a fit of laughter – this time from both of them.

"Wanna meet at Atomic in like twenty? They are open till midnight. And, truthfully, I can't stay out too late tonight but I do want to see you." She says.

"Yeah. Sounds good. And tell Shay that next time I see her I will slip her some speed so she won't be such a baby about staying up."

Lily laughs and I hear her relay what I said to Shay. I hear her response very clearly.

"Did you hear that?" Lily asks. Before I can answer, Shay commandeers the phone again.

"I said, ASSHOLE."

"Not the first time you've called me that." I say.

"So, Mr. College Stud is coming this weekend?"

"Don't call him that." She tells me.

"Why not? Mister refers to him being male, which I assume he is. College defines where is at educationally. And Stud is a superficial judgment. I am just going with Lily's assessment on that one." There is a pause.

"Sometimes you are tiring." She says. Within a second, Lily is back on the phone.

"You deflated her quickly."

"I used big words and talked fast." I say.

"Yeah. So see you in a few?"

"Definitely." I tell her.

"Cool. I love you."

"I hold love for you too." She clicks the phone off. I switch lanes and ready myself to turn toward Atomic.

The Atomic is a place for hipsters. I did not have a definition of hipsters until I went there. The most current (I can't really say popular) Alt Rock music is always played; they have these vintage couches that are some sort of leather, and crazy random paintings on the walls. Most of its business is college kids, being that there is one a mile away from it. I am not sure why I like it. On the surface, it is the opposite of me, but I guess maybe underneath it is more like me than I will ever admit. Lily likes the bacon, turkey and Swiss club they have, and being open late, it has become one of our spots.

Like I had thought, I arrive first. I order a hot chocolate and find a chair so my back is in the direction Lily will walk.

Lily opens the door so gently that the bells on it do not even move. She has changed her clothes since I last saw her. She wears blue jeans, a white t-shirt with green lettering reading, "Cause/Affect", with a black zip-up sweatshirt. She spots me without me moving and walks over.

"Hey," is her slow, tired greeting. Looking in her eyes, I can see they are bloodshot; circles are forming under them. It hits me how Halloweenish I must look. Before she sits across from me, I take her hand and pull her down to me. We kiss lightly.

"Shay safely tucked in?" I quip.

"Yeah. To be fair, my pace is a car, and lately your pace is a rocket ship." Lily has found a way to criticize me lovingly. "She said she is still coming to the game on Friday. Even with Mr. College Stud." Lily giggles at herself. Her face curled up in a smile is the sweetest, most adorable image to be captured by.

"So, you're still coming too, right?"

"Do you even have to ask?" She says, then pauses. "You don't want me to sit next to your parents, do you?" There is a hint of girlfriend obligation in her voice that defines why I love her. It is a scary, awkward thought, but I know if I ask her to she will.

"Nah. At best, they have an abstract way of looking at parenting. I doubt they will make it beyond halftime." This comforts her. "But do you really want to sit with Shay and...what's the guy's name anyway?" I ask.

"Evan."

"Well, that is a perfect Mr. College Stud type of name. " I say, making her laugh.

"I know, right. And I will probably hang out with Emily and Tess. I am helping them with this school literary magazine thing, so we will probably come straight from there."

"Aren't we ambitious lately." I say.

"Yeah, well some of us have yet to get into college." She kicks me under the table.

Our conversation is our way of calming our breathing. We talk about our day, about everything floating in our minds. The random, the tension, the stress and the fear. We can see weight dropping off the other. I cannot remember when we started having talks like this, but they had become as needed as air and water to me.

"I keep forgetting." I tell her. "After the game on Friday, do you wanna see a band downtown? Erin's boyfriend's band is playing and she wants us to check it out. She said she will even put us on the 'list'.

"Well, if we are on the 'list' then I guess we have to go." She teases. "What kind of music are they?"

"Yeah, I can't really say. She gave me this lengthy description and I think I blacked-out for some of it. Safe to say there will be guitars and maybe a drum."

"Sold. Does this mean you'll dance a little?"

"I will dance a little if you will mosh a little." I tell her.

"I can agree to that. Should I bring out the dance club or grunge clothes?" Her gaze on me is luring.

"Surprise me." I stop. A smirk crawls on my face. "Megan is gonna be there, too."

"You are telling me Shay, Evan, Megan and Josh are all going to be there?" Lily asks.

"Yup. If you put enough factors together, something is going to react." I pause. "But beside that, I really want to put on a show. I try not to care, but I want to prove to my parents that I am good enough to deserve the scholarship I got, and that there will be more to come. You don't get opportunities for validation often and I want to crush it."

She lets the words exist for a moment before responding.

"And you will. I am betting all my money against South Shore. They are gonna lose by thirty." I laugh. "Then after the domination, we will let loose with some drinks and dancing." I give her a look. "And some moshing. I wasn't finished." She says, shaking her head and grinning.

"So, just get through tomorrow and then Friday will be great." I say in a morose tone, but Lily looks at me as though I did. It was a throwaway line.

"I have a feeling that if I ask what that look is for, the answer will require a conversation we are both too tired to have." I say, acknowledging and dismissing it at the same time.

"You're probably right." She says, dully. We lock eyes and hold ourselves there for a moment. I can see she is scared for me, sad for me. I am unsettled by this. It is like we were both drowning, but she was pulled out and now was being forced to watch me – unable to help as I go under. Seeing all this makes me wonder what she sees when she looks at me. It occurs to me that maybe it is something that justifies what lies behind her eyes.

The Big Ben Clock in the corner begins to chime. That is our queue to leave. I look to it and then around the place. We are the only ones who remain.

"Shall we?" I say, getting up.

I take her hand as we walk out. The air outside is noticeably colder with a wetness to it. Lily zips up her sweatshirt and flips up her hood. She had found a parking spot on the right corner from where I had. We cross the street and stop in the space separating them; I block her path to hers and she blocks mine. We still hold hands but allow our arms to extend to almost a stretching point. We look at each other knowing neither wants to be the one to initiate leaving. We both laugh, which causes us to collapse into each other. Our embrace is a resting spot, a safe place to land. Lily tilts her head up to me. In this position, our near-foot height difference is felt. I brush the strands of hair from her face and then cusp the lines of her jaw, pulling her face up to me as I lean toward it. We kiss unabashingly until we hear a shout of, "Get a frickin' room, ya horny crack whores!" We turn to find the voice and recognize James Hart. A guy from our grade. He is all smiles as he walks with his lady on the other side of the street. I give a short wave as Lily takes a step back into the non-existent shadows. I notice the recoil.

"Don't do that. He was just cracking on us." I tell her as I step toward her.

"People twist shit and then the telephone game of gossip starts, and I can't walk down the hallways of school." She is scared rather than embarrassed, angry or hurt. I am taken off guard by this.

"I thought we weren't caring about what others thought?" I ask her.

"The idea was to give them very little to think about."

"Since when? Since when has PDA been an issue? We are damn near king and queen of the school."

"Penetrating tongues after midnight on a street corner goes beyond PDA." She says, sternly.

"Okay. Let's back up. What are you upset about?" I say, trying to bring some rationalization into the fray.

She covers her face with her hands and pulls them down, like she is trying to peel off a layer.

"I don't know. Nothing. It just wigs me out when we are caught in the throws...I just don't want to become a headline again."

A rush of realization hits me and I get memory flashes of the last two years. I could not come up with a single example of someone seeing us make out (besides Josh, Shay, and their current boyfriends/girlfriends) outside a party, club or an obvious social setting. I had never paused to consider it, but it was clear that it was something Lily thinks about and carries around.

"I had no idea that still bothers you." I say, not needing to specify the catalyst of the reaction.

"It is not something I brag about. Most of the time it doesn't."

I want to say, 'What, when there is no correlation to what you are currently doing?' But it sounds harsh in my head, so I know it will come out even harsher if I say it aloud. I also want to ask 'since when are our conversations degraded to what we brag about?' but I stay silent there as well. Lily's eyes are red, but she is not crying. Does she want to? Or are we just both insanely tired and this is being blown out of proportion? My mind wanders but fails to come to a conclusion. Lily is less than three feet away from me, yet I have never felt such a distance between us. It unsettles my core. My confidence is thrown into disarray. It is a moment I feel the greatest need to have some sort of clairvoyant understanding, yet I'm empty. I hang there hovering beside her. Her eyes are down and are becoming increasingly hollow with every second we exist in this dense ether. Abandoned of thought, I let my instincts lead me. I lace my arms around her and hug her as delicately and reassuringly as I can. I wait until I feel her arms move to my back before looking at her.

Her eyes are still red but have been blinked clear. There is courage in her face, but not enough to allow her to speak. I want to tell her that this fear is not some great shame. That I understand. I never want her to experience the pain she went through before. I thought that had already been said. I thought it was obvious enough to not need words. But I know I cannot control the fickle tides of high school gossip. I know any words of comfort I might say will have a tint of lies in them, so how am I to speak? What am I to say?

"We can't control someone else's, or everybody's, perception. It is a waste of energy to try. Making out on a street corner, no matter the time, is not deviant. We already gave them a more scandalous story, right? It might be talked about, but it certainly isn't interesting enough to make the headlines. Randy Eckart getting a hand job from Melanie Spencer during Mrs. Fence's Trig class, now that is a headline." Lily laughs and, in doing so, coughs up the last bit of water from her eyes. Her smile is unwilling, yet uncontrollable.

"There. Nothing cuts deeper than your sorrow, nothing rejuvenates like your smile." I say.

"You're right. I don't know why that hit me like that."

"It's okay if you are okay."

"I am okay."

"Then okay." I confirm.

"But I really gotta get home. Sleep. Parents waiting up. All that and more awaits me."

"Well then, I will not keep you. Text me when you get home?" It has become a ritual when we leave each other that she texts me to let me know she got home alright. It is so routine, she does it even when I don't mention it.

"Of course. Breakfast, 7am, Diner Aces?" She asks. Diner Aces is a place that holds poker and 48 tournaments every weekend. One time over the summer, Josh scored big time to the tune of $800. We played all night and when morning came, we ate breakfast there. It had become a spot of ours since.

"Can I say maybe? The only thing that sounds worse than sleep right now is waking up from sleep once I get there."

"So, you don't like sleeping because you are afraid of waking up? Most people reverse that."

"Yes, Freud. That is why I don't like sleeping, but also why I am a unique kind of guy." I say and give a mock bow.

"I love you. If I wake up in time for breakfast, I'll call you."

"Sounds fair. I love you. Till tomorrow."

"Till tomorrow." I echo.

I follow her most of the way home before she turns off. Every second we are lined up in front of a red light is agony.

My house is covered in blackness as I arrive. The sky is clouded, some kids broke the streetlights with BB guns, and not a single light in my house is lit. I head to the back pathway and push through the unhinged gate. I enter my room, flick off my shoes, strip and crumple upon my bed. I am about to reach for my pillow when my cell rings. It isn't Lily's ring, so a shot of annoyance shivers through me. The pulse of Shay's ringtone comes through. I grab my phone from my pants and answer.

"It is near one, Shay." I tell her.

"And you're telling me that you are sleeping? I would hardly believe that." Shay is way too awake and way too jovial for me in my current state.

"Just got home and, yes, I am trying to sleep. What's up?"

"Okay." She starts. "I didn't want to tell you like this, but what the hell. I am pregnant." She says, reducing her tone.

"What?" I say, waking up.

"It was this random hook up at O'Shea's last month. I don't know what I am gonna do."

"Are you serious? Holy hell, Shay."

"I know." She pauses just long enough for me to get that it's a joke. "I am so screwing with you!" She crackles with laughter.

"I am sure that is funny, but I am exhausted and, surprisingly, would like to get some sleep."

"If you don't want to talk to me, fine."

"If it was anyone else, I would not have even answered the phone." I tell her.

"Really? Not even if it were Lily?" She says, bating me.

"If it were anyone but you, Lily or Josh I would not have answered the phone. Is that clearer?"

"Yeah. But I don't feel quite as special anymore." She says in a pouting voice. I usually love these calls and all the subtext in them, but my eyes and head burn from my lack of sleep.

"I will see you at school, Shay."

"And at that test prep afterwards, right?"

"Yeah. My GPA can't afford to miss it."

"Your GPA? You already got into college. Your GPA means shit now."

"You're right. You talked me out of it. I guess I won't go."

"No, that's not what I meant."

"Hey, you talked yourself into this corner, so now my attendance will remain a mystery until it starts. Goodnight now." I say, hanging up before she responds.

As my phone resets itself, a text message appears from Lily. It reads: "Safely home xoxoxo" After reading it, I shut my phone off, grab my pillow and close my eyes.

When I wake up, I am so groggy that I'm sure I was asleep for less than an hour. I hit the button on my clock on top of my end table. The illuminated time reads, 1:07. It is about what I thought, but then what I actually saw registers with me. It is PM.

If I hurry, I can make my last class, which starts at 2:15pm. I rush into the shower, throw some shampoo in my hair and as it rinses, use it to wash the rest of my body. When I am out of the shower, I grab some mouthwash and spit it on the ground before I get into my car. In my car is when I turn my cell back on. I have ten missed calls and four voicemails. I scroll through my missed calls: Lily, Josh, Lily, Shay, Lily. 'Yeah, yeah', I think. I delete the voicemails without listening to them. People are pissed off I am not there, I get it. I appreciate the heads up, but don't care about the specifics. I will deal with whatever comes my way solely in the moment. To overthink, or think in general, never helps. It only instills stress.

I mingle slightly as I head to my locker, but not with anyone who seems aware that I just arrived. I grab my books and head to class. Civil War is a class I share with Josh only. Shay and Lily are stuck in the Depression. I am glad at this because it will give me more of a chance to get re-acclimated. Walking into class, I feel like a thug as, upon seeing me, the kid sitting next to Josh changes seats. I take the seat anyway.

"Nice of you to join us. You don't answer your phone anymore?" Josh quips.

"I slept in."

"I thought you didn't sleep." Josh says.

"I needed to catch up."

"And?"

"Honestly, I can't feel a difference." I tell him.

Josh laughs and I can tell I have settled back in.

"Prep got cancelled." Josh tells me right before the last bell rings, signaling class is to start.

"What? Why?"

"I don't know the reason. I just know the answer. Shay and I thought we would hang out with the train kids. Chill at the train station. Eric and Rob are slumping there today." Josh tells me.

There is a train station a few blocks away from school. This is mostly reserved for underclass kids whose parents are too busy to drive them. However, Rob and Eric's parents seem to ground them every other week, which did nothing if not strip them from their cars. Josh is far more social with them than I am, and has hung out at the train station with them before. Why he didn't just offer them a ride home was something I never asked. I guess sometimes small things that offset our routine are needed. It confused me why Shay would want to join us. She certainly does not shy away from mingling, but this will be a free form, foreign context. One that I do not associate her with. But then, I realize at the heart of this is Josh, Shay and myself hanging out. Everyone else is just background when we are together.

I open up my textbook and get out my notebook. I hate taking notes to the point that in junior high, I got permission to use a tape recorder to refer to later. Lily and Shay let me study their notes, but without them in the class, I find it hard. Josh is no use. It frustrates me and degrades my intelligence. I am not focused on school generally, but I do really try on the absence of other's notes. Josh has learned this and breaks the conversation when the teacher begins.

School ends and Josh and I hang at our lockers, waiting for Shay. The school empties pretty quickly and we are held at pause. In this vacantness, we have nothing to say and become antsy. Josh texts Shay but does not get a response.

"Why are we walking to the train station anyway? I get hanging there, but why not drive there and leave when the fun is done? Walking there and back just seems stupid." I say, part trying to spark a conversation, part seriously wondering.

"Well, the idea was for us to all walk together." Josh explains. "However, Ms. Shay has ruined that. I say we give her five more minutes and then bail. The train doesn't come till 4, but it is already past three. Give ten minutes to walk there, and we should get going."

Josh has little patience for these types of situations, and it is entirely possible that Shay was either flaking on the idea or already there. Without her answering, it is hard to tell.

"Call Lily." Josh tells me.

"I can't. She is all focused. Her phone is probably not even on." I say, dismissingly.

Josh picks up his bag and I know he is about to take a step to the door when...the scent of Shay reaches us. We are caught in it before she turns the corner and becomes visible to us. She is wearing a dark pink cold shoulder butterfly dress. The only reason I know it is called that is because I was with her when she bought it. It is the kind of dress you find yourself looking up her legs to her thighs as your blood starts to rise before you come to cloth. I can feel Josh tense up and then shake it out. I come to think that love is finding the ability to stifle sexual tension. Josh has no such ability; especially when it comes to Shay.

"Wipe your mouth, you are drooling." I say when Shay is in earshot, but not loud enough for her to hear. Josh glances at me, but is too distracted to retaliate.

"Well, boys, we ready to walk?"

"Been ready. We've been waiting almost twenty minutes." I tell her. She looks at me sternly. It is rare when Shay is not in a playful mood; which causes it to crush your heart when she cries. But I could tell she is teasing. She cannot hide the gleam in her eyes.

"Are you giving me a lecture on punctuality? Mister Absentee. School starts at 8am, not 2pm." Shay bites. It is such an obvious thing to say, I can tell she is less impressed than she normally would be.

"Fair enough. Shall we?"

"Yeah." Shay says, leading the way.

It is two flights of stairs out of the building from where we were. Shay pontificates about the term 'cloud 9' and the relationship it may or may not have with people's inkblot view of cloud formations. It is at once a psychology analysis and an absurdity humor routine. Shay's intelligence really comes out when she is on these rants, but neither of us are paying much attention. A block into our trip, she stops and seems to want us to respond to what she has been talking about. Josh and I look at each other – we have nothing, so Josh puts a spin on what's been scorching his mind.

"So, you thought since we were gonna hang out at a train station you should dress like a tranny..."

Shay cuts him off.

"If you complete that thought, I will cut you!" She says, pushing him, harder than jokingly. "Crass much?"

Josh is being harsh. Her outfit, while seductive, I would not consider slutty. Both of us have seen Shay in slutty clothes, and this was far from it. But that was Josh. There were times when Shay looked so hot that he could not resist commenting negatively about how she looked. I understand why he does this. I think Shay understands, too. But understanding doesn't make it less insulting or annoying.

"You are a real prick sometimes. I am glad Megan is gonna be around this weekend. If you get laid, maybe you'll calm down." It is the first time I had ever heard her speak Megan's name. She has spoken to her, hung with her, but never said her name. The effect of it was piercing. I am not sure if there is such a thing as bringing subtext to the forefront, but that is what she did. Without speaking directly about why Josh, in essence, called her a slut, she makes a chess move. All I can do is watch and all Josh can do is stay silent.

We stay in this triangle for a moment. Shay holds her gaze on Josh, while his is squarely on the flowers in a nearby lawn. She loses the intensity and starts to look around and then at me. Lily is my defense in these situations. When she is not there, I feel like I am the third wheel in an argument between a married couple. And when there is a pause and Shay looks at me, I become the unbeknownst affair guy that she wants to leave with. I don't get caught in it and start walking to the train station. Shay follows and then Josh. By the next block, we are heavy into a conversation about the best dramatic movie of the nineties. Our debate is based on the tiniest details and actually turns into a quote fest. Nothing has been forgotten. I think we have gotten to a place where we understand and accept each other's flaws.

There are probably ten kids waiting as we get to the train station. Eric and Rob are off to one side trying to dribble past each other. We head toward them. When we are about twenty feet away, Eric chucks the ball to Josh who does an around the back over the shoulder globetrotter move, and then passes it back.
"Nice of ya'll to show. You made that hour wait fly by." Rob says with a half-joking annoyance.
"Our lateness is courtesy of Ms. Shay." Josh tells them.
"Well then." Rob says, getting a pass from Eric and then sending it over to me. "All is forgiven." Shay does her best curtsy, evoking a laugh from Eric and Rob. We break into a square, and with Shay starting in the middle, we play keep away. We mockingly go over what would have been covered at our English test prep. The great lessons and insights of American Literature give us ample ammo to joke. We get so hysterical, we damn near keel over. None of the others come over to us and say anything. We weren't trying to be separate, we weren't being exclusionary. There just is a disconnect between us. That broke when a high throw sends me jogging after the ball. It rolls over to the other group. My eyes follow the ball as it is stopped by someone in heels. As she bends down to pick up the ball, my eyes travel up to see Rachel. She bounces the ball back to me.
"Never would have pegged you as the butterfingers kind." She says.
"Yeah, well I guess I am not perfect." I say, giving a short laugh. My eyes are on her face, but become distracted by a strand of her hair. It curls around her neck and then slides down her collarbone, resting at the edge of her cleavage. The length of it is like a trail left in the woods. I know I am going to get burned, but cannot help but follow it. My peak is brief, but when I return to her face, I know I have been found out. She looks at me appalled, and then without blinking, her eyes dissolve the emotion into lust. Girls have done this to me before, but she pulls it off better than most.

I hold up the ball and say, "Thanks." I turn to leave but she doesn't let me.

"With you and Josh playing, I'm surprised you don't have people lining up to be in the middle." I turn back to her. I can tell she chose her words very carefully, using 'people' instead of 'girls' to make it a little more ambiguous. "She is a clever girl." I think to myself. "I will have to remember that."

"The game is harder than it looks. Most can't keep up."

"Oh, you underestimate me? That's okay. I don't mind having to prove myself."

I look at her, not really knowing how to respond. She is overtly being dirty and enticing the hell out of me. It is dangerous. Because I have a girlfriend. Because she is fourteen. I give her a nervous smile and then walk back to the group.

As I throw the ball over to Eric, I hear the train's whistle. It pulls up to the platform, and everyone starts piling in. Eric and Rob say a quick goodbye to us and then shuffle in with the rest. We wait for it to begin pulling away then we cross the parking lot to A Coffee Spot.

Inside, Shay orders an iced hazelnut and a poppy seed bagel. Josh opts for bottled water. I just hang back and don't order anything. I feel restless but too tired to do anything about it. I wasted most of the day sleeping, and now all I want to do is crash on a couch and watch a movie. When I see they have paid, I lead the way out. Two guys our age are outside the door as I push it open, but move aside as myself and Josh pass through. However, when Shay follows us, they squeeze in beside her, pressing up on her. It is a form of non-hand groping. I notice it, but when Shay doesn't say anything, I let it go. We step off the curb and hang there for a moment to decide what to do. Josh looks back and sees one of the guys staring at us through the window.

"Does this kid have a problem?" He says, which causes Shay and I to look toward him and the kid to look away.

"I don't know what I hate more, assholes hitting on me or passive-aggressively leering at me." Shay says.

"What?" Josh says, sensing a reason to be angry.

"Walking out, they pressed up against me. It wasn't much, but it was definitely intentional." Shay can see a rush of anger go to Josh's face. He is nothing if not protective. "It was nothing. Let's get out of here." She says, trying to defuse the situation. We begin walking away but catch them looking at us again. That is all that is needed. Something is going down now. There is no stopping it.

Josh starts barking at them through the window saying, "What you looking at? You got something to say, come out here, and say it." I am sure they can't hear him, but he is animated enough for them to get the drift. One of them is paying, but the other one, the one who was staring, starts to chatter back. These moments when I know a confrontation is near, yet I am given time to think about it, I always get nervous. My violence, I have learned, is mostly impulsive. I hadn't taken the offense to what had happened as Josh had. Shay was okay, that was what mattered.

Shay has stepped back to distance herself almost ten feet from us. She wasn't going to leave but she didn't want to be part of it. I look to her and she gives me a 'I wanted to let it go, but if they want to keep it going, give them what they deserve' look (yes, Shay can convey a lot in a look). In a way, this gives me permission for the inevitable. Which is good, because they were on their way out.
"These fucking cocksuckers better repent or it's gonna be brutal." Josh tells me.

Coming out, the one with a drink puts it on a nearby phone booth as the other approaches us.
"What is your problem?" He says, addressing Josh.
"We weren't the ones leering, jack ass." Josh tells him.
"We weren't leering at you, that's for damn sure." He tells us.
"Walk away. Now." I tell them.
"Or what?" The other one says. The stupidity of this conversation is what finally gets me mad.
"Unless you want to rumble, walk away." I tell them.
"Does it look like we are leaving?" They step to the edge of the curb and we step up to it. We are in a staring match, each wanting the other to make the first move. Then it came.
"Hey, sweet ass, after we take care of your friends, how about a quickie behind the store?" one of them says to Shay. This causes Josh and me to step up onto the curb. Now, on an even level, we are a good three or four inches

taller than they are; a fact never really understood until
then. We can feel them recoil and get a shiver of fear run
through them. It's justified. Josh lands a right to the
stomach of the one closest to him, pushes him up against
the wall, and lands another right to his face. He collapses to
the ground, barely conscious. The other one tries to run off,
but I am quicker. I catch his shirt and turn him around to
me. I land a left to his face and a right to his jaw. He is still
standing, but I am sure I have broken bones. I grab him by
the shoulders and throw him to the ground.

The brawl is quick. But the prelude of yelling has
alerted some attention. I look at Josh. He is staring down at
his opponent – daring him to get up.
"Let's bail." I say, pushing his shoulder slightly. He spits on
the kid and then turns and comes with me. Shay is a little
ahead of us, waiting. On some level of our conscious,
running away would be a sign of fear, so we walk swiftly.
"The police station is just down the street. They'll be here
any minute." She says, worried for us. We get to the train
station and cross the street. As we turn the corner to the
street our school is on, we hear police sirens. Josh lets out a
snicker and I can't help but laugh too.
"Fights where the only thing you hurt is your hand is never
a bad thing." I say to Josh. We pound fists in a moment of
celebration. Shay, however, is not amused.
"Was that completely necessary?" Shay rhetorically asks.
"That is not quite the chivalry rewarded 'thank you' I was
expecting." Josh says, trying to lead Shay to show a little
appreciation.
"That guy threatened to rape you behind the store." I tell
her. "Some would say castration is necessary."

She knows I am right but still feels conflicted. This
isn't the first time Josh or I have bruised someone who was
being inappropriate toward her, but it was the first time in
broad daylight. Environment really changes perception. I
got that, but it still didn't change how I or Josh wanted to
handle the situation. Shay is grateful. In a different
circumstance, with a little alcohol, she probably would be
turned on. As she mulls this over, we can hear an
ambulance in the distance. We reach our cars before she
says anything.

"Thank you. I will bake you cookies later." She says. Not exactly what we had thought, but it is all we get as she drives off.

"I guess she is going home." I say.

"What were we supposed to do?" Josh asks, questioning himself.

"Precisely what we did. She'll get over the shock of it. We really kicked the shit out of them."

"Yeah, we did." He says, a smile returning to his face. "Did you see them when we stepped up on the curb? That was priceless. Dumb pricks thought they were bigger than us!"

"Don't run your mouth if you can't handle being shut up."

"Damn straight."

We hang at our cars for a minute, but both of us realize we should get out of the area. The police will be scanning looking for two guys on foot with at least a general description.

"You up for a movie? I wanna sink in a seat and zone out for a while." I say.

"I dig that. Your place?"

"Sure. Met you there."

I get in my car and drive off with Josh right behind me. For kicks, I take the way that leads past the train station just to see the aftermath of what we did. There are two police cars and an ambulance outside the store. One of the kids is talking to the cop while the other is attended to by the EMT. Josh and I ride past undetected.

My cell starts singing Lily's ringtone. It isn't quite five, but I can guess why she is calling.

"Hey,"

"Are you okay?" She says, with obvious worry.

"Me? Fine. Happy with some go and a little bit of luck." I tell her.

"Seriously."

"Did Shay tattle on me?" I say, in anything but a serious tone.

"She said you and Josh got in a fight."

"Not with each other."

"Yes. I know that detail. Is everything okay?"

"I can handle myself," I state.

"I know that. I just don't want you to wind up in jail or something." She says. I almost laugh. That wasn't ever a real possibility to me.

"Why not? I hear conjugal visits are hot as hell." I rasp to her.

"Whatever." She says in such a way that I think she is going to hang up.

"Don't be mad." I say, starting to explain. "These guys were messing with Shay. One insinuated he was going to rape her. They needed to be knocked down a peg. Or two." I tell her.

"She told me that." She says, weakening her position. "So, you are safe?"

"Yup. Heading home. Josh and I are gonna watch a flick. You wanna come over?"

"I am still at the Mayor's office. Just on a break"

"Ah. I see. Call me when you're done?"

"Of course. Should I bring over some ice for your hands?" She asks, teasingly. I am glad we are past the lecture part.

"Nah. But we could use the ice for other things."

"With Josh there? Hardly."

"Hey, we need someone to hold the camera." I say. She giggles softly. Just the reaction I was going for.

"Yeah, yeah. I'll call you when I get out." She pauses. I can tell something is distracting her. "Love you." Her last words before I hear the click of the conversation ending. I throw the phone on the seat and keep on driving.

I think, most days, the best way to describe me is as a Picasso painting. Twisted and jumbled. Frightening, odd, and random. When I was about eight, I saw a picture of his work called, 'Man with a Cigarette' I latched onto it. It is beautiful if you truly study it. I have often thought that was like me. I don't know what I want Lily's response to be when she hears I broke someone's jaw. I guess I want her to understand my reasons, my intentions. In the moments where you need to stop thinking and just react, your view narrows to see only what is in front of you. From that moment, you want the memory to exist strictly in that context. The death of the truth comes when others try to interpret the big picture. This angers me and I shut down my listening of their words. I do not ever want to get to that place with Lily. I have to find some way of conveying that to her.

Four

Is or Could Be

     I wake up before seven, throw on a concert t-shirt, and a pair of jeans. I pack my jersey, shorts, and everything else I will need for the game tonight. I allow myself a minute to think about the game. About my parents coming. There is no nervousness in me. If anything, I find it hard to get excited. Almost like reverse psychology, my motivation is being stirred away from me. At times, I feel jaded, worn, numb, and indifferent – but never about basketball. The state I am in now, I could not feel stress if it were injected in me.

     I head upstairs and pour myself some orange juice. I hear some shuffling down the hallway and then am amazed by the appearance of my mother. She is dressed in her typical long skirt, blouse and cardigan. I am too caught off guard to speak.

"Good morning." She says with a smile. She seems genuinely happy, which is a state I have not seen her in for quite some time. This lightens me beyond the degree I thought I was burdened. At first, I don't know how to react, but I know I need to test the reality of it.

"So, what has prompted this good mood?" I ask.

"I don't know. I don't think I need a reason." She goes about gathering her lunch and jacket absentmindedly. "I am excited about tonight. It is long overdue that your father and I see you play." She isn't really talking to me when she says this. I hardly believe she realizes she is talking aloud. "We should have come sooner. I can't even imagine. I don't even know…"

     Her voice trails off and leaves my mind to find ways to complete the sentence "…my son; if he is any good; what the atmosphere is like; any of his friends; what he feels." She turns to me, smiles, and kisses me on the cheek before leaving.

I am left alone to finish my orange juice. Despite the influence of faith from Josh, I have no spiritual belief. I cannot say whether or not I agree or disagree. I rarely have those thoughts and they are quickly banished when I do. They only thing I think it is good for is times like these: when you are alone, feeling lonely. It is the demon's prayer hidden under blankets. I don't hang there. I grab an orange and then head out.

I am halfway to school when my cell rings.

"If half the world is blowing kisses in the wind and the other half is pissing in it, do you dare step outside?" Lily starts. She sounds drunk or maybe just giddy from exhaustion. She replaces the consciousness of my mind with a fresh makeup. I am left in a trance and don't say anything.

"Hello? That was a joke, Noah."

"I guess it would depend on who is kissing and who is pissing." I tell her. She laughs in such a way that makes me yearn for the summer. For time to be able to be stopped so I can just exist in the moment.

"Are you nervous about tonight?" Lily asks.

"No. Not at all. It is surprising, really."

"Well, that must be it."

"What?"

"Whatever is swirling inside you is unbalancing you. Your lack of nerves is affecting something else."

"Possibly." I want to say I would feel better if she said she would give me a BJ in the bathroom before the first bell. I don't. "I am five minutes from school. Are you there yet?" I ask.

"Yeah. Shay and I are hanging in the parking lot. Josh went in with some basketball kids. I should know their names, but I don't."

"Probably Kevin and Reef. They're the two bench guys we need tonight." I tell her.

"Game days are so distracting." She says.

"Distracting for some. Focused to others. See you in a bit,"

"Okay."

I throw my phone on the passenger seat, think about stopping to get coffee for Lily and Shay, but drive straight to school.

Lily and Shay are surrounded by people as I enter the parking lot. Shay sits on the hood of her car, legs dangling and swaying. This is her habit when she is bored. Lily is fully engaged in a conversation with the group. She is clearly leading, if not the focus. I slide into a back parking spot and head over to them. My presence is noticed by a few people lingering around, but only acknowledged by Shay. She bends her neck to her right, purposely away from those near her. Her hair falls over the profile of her face. She lets it sit there for a moment before brushing it away and gives me this look that conveys how bored she is, and at the same time, tempts me to say that one word, or do that one thing that brings fire into the dullness. Reaching the car, I go around the other side to where Lily is. I walk slower the closer I get. Her audience kind of straightens themselves when they see me, expecting a pause. Lily, however, is lost in her thoughts. She speaks like a great actor reciting a monologue. I know the words are not rehearsed, but they flow so fluently that it's hard to believe in the purity of their origin. She is talking about global warming and the little things we can do to help decrease it.

I stay behind her, briefly, before wrapping my arms around her waist. She forces the initial annoyance of being interrupted into warmth. I am aware of the subtleties of her, and even as we embrace, the guilt of her instinctual reaction and the hurt of it are felt.

"And that is why we need to ship treadmills to the artic – so the polar bears can build up their endurance." I say, getting a huge laugh. This breaks Lily's seriousness.

"Or we can just teach them how to float on their backs." Lily responds, lightly pushing me. This gets a laugh too, which is enough to get Shay off the car to join us.

"Thoughts, Shay?" I say, putting her on the spot. She doesn't miss a beat.

"Yeah. Live for today because tomorrow there might be an altering climate change that buries us all under water." She says, summing everything up. We could go back and forth with one-liners like these for a while, but the first warning bell for school sounds, disbanding our group. Shay takes off ahead of us, leaving Lily and I to walk in alone. I cusp her hand in mine and we walk into school.

The clichés about athletes being treated differently I find true only on game days. As we walk down the hallway, everywhere we look is covered with signs and banners. The huge section of wall, that usually holds the school's emblem, has been replaced with a collage of newspaper clippings of the last few victories. Teachers and students both say good luck as we pass them. I don't think it is something you ever get used to, but with time, you develop a comfort from it and an understanding of it.

We see Josh already decked out in his jersey as we enter the classroom. Chrissy – a cheerleader – Eric and Rob are around him jabbering away. Josh seems bored, but willing to soak up the ego boost of attention. We could join them but opt for a few empty desks in the corner. Within a minute of this, Josh has switched seats to be next to us. "What's this, you too good to sit next to me?" Josh says.

We are chosen family. I understand why it is easy for me to embrace this, or Shay who lives with her single mother. But Josh and Lily? Their family life is stable. I wonder sometimes what their motivation is. I don't mean that in an untrusting way. I understand my need for our group, for Shay's; just not theirs.
"Alright then." Josh says. He extends his hand and we do our game time ritual handshake. A fist to the wrist, two slaps front, one back, another front and end with a fist bound.
"Did you read the report on South Shore?"
"We've played them twice already this year. I don't need to read about what I already know." I say. Josh looks at me, taken aback. I am not usually brazenly cocky. I say things in jest, with sarcasm. I had said this differently. It hit me by the look on Josh and Lily's face. I thought about it for a second and then shut up the analysis in my head. Whatever was swimming in me was surfacing. I don't understand it but decide to simply allow nature to take its course.
"Alright then. Collins has scored 30+ his last three games. You better play sound good D tonight."
"He won't score in double digits." I say, opening up my textbook. I am not a fan of melodrama and am relieved the class starts seconds after my last sentence.

My last three classes are study hall, history, and economics. I know there will be no consequences if I skip them, so I do. Right versus wrong becomes blurry without consequences. I evoke the thought in Josh and we both bail at lunch. We just kind of leave. Minutes into lunch, Lily texts me asking where I am. My reply is simply: "game day". I know she understands what I mean by this, but her understanding doesn't always mean she won't be pissed off by it. I know she wouldn't have come with us. She would have given a glare of disapproval, so we disappeared without her. We head over to this roast beef place near South Shore to eat, then over to a park to shoot around.

Around four, Josh drops me off in front of South Shore's gym, then drives off to pick up Megan. The surroundings of the gym are unfettered of people. I find the door unlocked and I slip through and into the visitor's locker room. As has become custom at away games, I strip, head to the showers, and let water drain on me. I have come to think of this as my form of meditation. I stay under the water until it changes from hot to warm, or until a melody begins humming from my lips. After my shower, I change into warm-up clothes and head out to the gym.

It is not a large gym. Probably would hold two hundred people if packed. It has an on-top-of-you feel to it. Mostly due to the baloney seating behind both hoops. As I dribble onto the couch, I notice an assistant coach sitting on the home team's bench. Hearing the bounce of the ball, he looks up at me and we exchange "hi's".

I place the ball at mid-court and do a series of vertical jumps that do less to stretch as to reverse the effect of the shower. It accelerates my heart and raises the tempo of my mind. From that, I grab the ball and do a quick pace shooting drill. Always behind the three-point line, I shoot and, hit or miss, I sprint for the rebound, sprint back to the arc and do it again. I knock down the first six before missing the seventh. As I gather the rebound of the seventh, I notice the couch watching me. I have seen him before. He scouted our last two games. He isn't analyzing, though. He is admiring. I am never strictly cocky or insecure; what controls me is what option I choose. Do I ally-op it to myself? Or meekly smile and start shooting fifteen footers? I decide to continue what I am doing and return to the three-point line. I hit the next three before a rebound finds its way to the bench and the coach. He picks it up and weakly throws it to me.

"Where's the rest of your team?" he asks.

"Where's yours?" I joke back.

He laughs and looks back at his notebook. It occurs to me that he is barely thirty. I am about to go back to shooting when he looks back up to me.

"Congratulations on the Albany State scholarship." he says.

I look at him, surprised.

"Are you a scout or a tabloid journalist?" I quip.

"A bit of both, I suppose."

He has rattled me slightly. I can tell he realizes this as his smile grows more and more smug. I check the time. Josh should be back any minute and the rest of the team soon after. I sink one last shot and then head back to the locker rooms.

"See you at tipoff." The coach calls. I nod, and am almost out of earshot when I hear, "Hope your parents get good seats."

How the hell does he know they are coming? I guess in the parameters of my team it was no secret, but I would never suspect a teammate to be an informant. He must have overheard it. That rat bastard. This stirs in me for a minute, but as it penetrates deeper, it is absorbed and I become centered by it. I am a circus performer tonight. Not only is my play under a scope, but the validity of obtaining a scholarship and the honor of my neglectful parents are on the line. This doesn't cause pressure or instill nerves. I have unmitigated confidence. I have owned this team before, and tonight will be no different. I play for the joy of it. For the streetball pickup game. This is my sanctuary.

As I step into the locker rooms, I hear sounds of pleasure in the form of giggles. While the voice is not memorized, logic would conclude it is the voice of Megan. As I pass the showers, I half expect to find her lying prone on the benches. She isn't, though. She is merely leaning against the locker next to Josh, scurrying from attacks of grabby hands.

"You're back." I say, announcing myself.

"And here to kick some South Shore ass!" Josh exclaims in such a way I think he might head butt me.

Megan hangs back, straightening herself. We are currently in the stage where Megan wants us to be close enough that we hug each time we say hello and goodbye; whereas I am not fully comfortable with it. There is no subtext to it. Human contact that is supposed to express intimacy I reserve for those to who I feel intimate with. Megan has yet to reach that plateau. I can't say why she hasn't and I don't know if she will. In the meantime, I allow hugs out of respect to Josh, if nothing else.

She wears a deep purple felt-like skirt that wraps her thighs together. Her shirt is made of thin black wool. It is backless, tying around her waist like a belt, and is tight without being overt about it.

"Hey, Megan," I say.

"Hey," She says in such a friendly tone, I almost think it is fake.

She glides around Josh and wraps her arms around my neck. Josh isn't paying attention to us. He moves over to the corner and starts to stretch out his calves. If I was in a playful mood, I might try and get a reaction out of him. I have enough to sift through currently, though, and I don't want more. Before more can be said, the door crashes open and we hear the rest of the team arrive.

"I guess that's my cue for me to find a seat." Megan says. She kisses Josh and follows the exit signs.

There is hype in the team that is not a product of Josh or me. In fact, I find us to be the most mellow we have been all year. Coach goes over the keys to the game but I am not listening. At this point, I am antsy for the game to begin. When we start heading out of the locker rooms and to the gym, we become intertwined with South Shore. As a mass of people, we enter the gym; parting from there like the red sea. The crowd is 90% South Shore fans, with a few rows sectioned off for us. I find Lily in the aisle of the third row. She appears to be in full discussion mode with Emily and Tess. They are girls I am aware of, but would never say I 'know' them. Their first names and the fact that they work on the yearbook is as far as I go. The team breaks into a layup drill. I participate for a few minutes before I go over to Lily.

"She is full of shit, this one. You know the phrase, 'take it with a grain of salt'? Apply it here." Lily turns to me and, laughing, presses the left side of her body into me. She takes the sarcasm of my dig and translates it into the compliment I was intending.

"You warmed up?" Lily asks.

"Pretty much." I say. I look to Emily and Tess who have been silent since I showed up and, seemingly, have taken a step back. I meant to interrupt, not intrude.

"So, will you ladies be joining us for the after-party?" I say. They look at Lily. Clearly not understanding what I am talking about.

"There is this club show we are going to." Lily explains. They take another beat.

"Are you inviting us?" Emily asks.

"If that is what it takes for you to show up – then yes." I say, a little offset by her asking it like that. This time there is no debate in them.

'Yeah. We'll be there." Tess tells me.

"Awesome. Get comfortable. Our show starts in less than twenty."

I jog back to the court and catch a long rebound. I am a step inside the three-point line as I square to shoot. Before I release, I see my parents enter the gym. There was a mixture of doubt in the anticipation, but seeing them now jolts a rush of emotion in me. The ball drops from my hands and I find myself walking toward them. They see me and wait idly.

My mind floats to the first time I remember playing basketball. I must have been seven or eight and, as a family, we had gone to the park and found a basketball left there. My dad picked it up and made a few shots before sharing. My sister and I could hardly hit the rim with our shots, but my dad made it fun by just dribbling and playing keep-away with my mom. I still have these images of my family together like this in my mind. I can still feel the emotion in the memory. But I consciously erase them from my mind when they surface. When I open my eyes, the contrast from then and now is too stark.

There are no cohesive thoughts in me so I am overjoyed that my father speaks first.

"A lot of people here." He states. This, of course, causes me to look around.

"There are usually about this many people. This is a smaller gym." I explain. So, you should probably find some seats. Tipoff is soon. I suggest the other side. If anyone realizes who you are, you may be razzed on." I can tell they don't understand what I mean. I pause for a minute to figure out how to say it so they will. "To distract me, they will say things to you."

I can tell the basic idea they get, but they have no idea of the potential severity. I guess you have to go through it to understand. Lily and Shay were heckled to such an extent last year that Josh and I were thrown out a few times for our retaliation. My parents walk around to the other side and I rejoin the team, which has huddled near the bench.

The countdown to game time on the scoreboard is under ten minutes. Our couch is saying that we dominated them last time and – even though that was their only loss of the year – that makes them our little bitches. I can't help but agree. I see the clock go under four minutes as we break from our huddle. The starters move to the court as the others find their way to the bench. I am near the foul line when Josh comes over to me.

"It all kosher?" he asks.

"Blessed by a rabbi as recently as an hour ago." I tell him. He smiles.

"All right then. Let's git 'er done." We clasp hands. The rest of our team gathers around us and inner momentum begins to form.

I don't know if any other teams do this, but we tend to have play setup at tipoff. Depending on who controls the tip, a series of picks take place usually ending up with an easy layup. It works to perfection here as the ball is tipped back to me and Josh finds himself alone under the basket. I whip the ball to him, and five seconds into the game, we have already embarrassed the other team. The game stays tight, though. Josh and I end the first half both with fifteen points. But the score is only 39-37. The thing to me that was worse than the score was the fact that we didn't play in control. Neither did South Shore, but I didn't attribute that to anything we did. I lag behind as we head to the locker rooms when I see Erin leaving.

"Hey," I say to stop her. She turns around, embarrassed.

"I am sorry, I gotta bail." She says, apologizing.

"I figured. I got a bunch of people coming after the game, so delay them a little if we aren't there, okay?"

"I'll try."

"C'mon. I know you have some influence."

"Which I will try and use. Now go and figure out how to blow them out in the second half." With that, she leaves, and I turn down the empty hallway that leads to the locker rooms.

When I enter the locker room, I am glad I delayed. The atmosphere is thick with guilt. Everyone is quiet. Almost as an ignition, when I am noticed, the coach starts yelling again.

"Ah. There you are. Is this the example you give to your teammates? We have played like shit. Is this the respect you give to this team and its coaching staff? Here we are designing a way to prevent you from being embarrassed in this second half, and you just saunter in whenever you like."

He stops, looking for a reaction. I look to the team; their heads are hung low. I don't know if I agree with the 'breaking to build them stronger' method, but I have no choice here but to accept it. I mumble a weak 'sorry' and slide onto the bench. Our mistakes are diagramed and corrections emphasized.

Coming out to the court for the second half, the crowd seems to have all become drunk. A cup of water is thrown at me and taunts begin as soon as I am seen. They go from a chant of 'Noah, Noah' to 'Lily is a slut (clap, clap) Lily is a slut', and then as we start to warm up, it changes to 'bastard child, bastard child'. I look to the stand and find my parents. My father remains stoic, but my mother starts to look around nervously. The noise in the gym is deafening. It is the atmosphere I had been anticipating. My eyes find Lily, and upon seeing me, she stands up and starts cheering. Megan is sitting next to her and she stands too. Josh comes up from the side and changes my attention, "Win first, pussy later." He cracks me on the head. "Focus, son."

I am thinking, but I need to clear my mind and react. To just play. South Shore inbounds the ball, and Josh and I fall back in defense. There are times we get to the edge of taking over the game. I shut down their star player. With four minutes left in the game, he has only scored seven points. I have 26. Still, when the time clock goes under a minute, we find ourselves down by five. Josh drills a three to cut it to two when South Shore calls a timeout. The crowd erupts with encouragement, then starts chanting, 'bastard child' again.

"These guys are relentless," I say. Rob is the only one who hears me.

"Shut them up then. Let's take this and celebrate on their floor." Rob impresses. His look is determined. I smile my best 'all right then' smile, and head back out to the floor.

The ball is inbounded and their point guard sets up the play. It turns into an isolation with the kid Josh is guarding. He drives to the hoop, but Josh tips the ball away from him. Their point guard gathers the loose ball and resets. They hold out until the shoot clock is down to the last second before shooting. It clangs off the rim and Reef rips the rebound down. The game clock ticks to less than ten seconds as we bring the ball across mid-court. Josh and I stand on opposite sides. We sprint to the corners of the foul line. Josh stops on a dime, setting a pick. I sprint to the left corner, getting the ball behind the three-point line, and shoot as time expires. The ball feels good out of my hands, the crowd is at bated breath as the ball floats through the air. It hits the inside of the rim, bounces, then rolls out, and back down onto the court. The court is rushed by South Shore. The game is over. We lost. Our coaches quickly usher us off, but I slip away from them. This is easy in the pandemonium. I find my way to the empty hallways of an adjacent building and sit down against the wall. The noise of excitement is dull where I am. Thoughts are being shouted in my head but I don't allow myself to understand their words. There is a way to deny reality to seep into you, or at least a way to delay it. That is what I want.

I stay in the locker rooms after everyone leaves. I want to stay in there long enough so that everyone else has gone. I don't want to hear sounds and images of choking. I don't to be consoled. Disappointment lingers for long enough without other people emphasizing it. I don't want to go through interacting with my parents. I had played good. Great, even. My stat line said that. But that one shot, that last shot, took all the gained success and changed it to unmitigated failure. I have already dressed, but I strip and head back to the showers. I lean my head against the wall and allow the stream of hot water to strike my back. My breathing is rapid, as though I had just run two miles. I try and steady it but am unable to. It occurs to me that anxiety doesn't necessarily hit you while you are anticipating something. It can also affect you in the wake of the event. I believe that is what is happening to me. The slower the thoughts in my mind become, the quicker the pace of my heart. My arms start to twitch. I clench my fist to stop this but it hardly helps. I begin tapping my fists against the tile of the wall. My arms still shake. I punch the wall with my left hand so hard, I crack the tile. Blood drips from my hand, turning the water red before disappearing down the drain. I continue to pound the wall and realize that violence, like exhaustion, is another way to release; but channeled violence. I am no good now. My cheeks are wet and I tell myself it is the water from the shower. I am not crying about losing. I can honestly say there is no clear reason. At the point of release, all the distorted mixture of things repressed start to surface. To analyze these feelings is as pointless as debating the meaning of an inkblot.

I am oblivious to the length of time I stay there. There is red smeared rubble of tile in front of me, with the force of water still flowing. My hands are scraped and scarred. They have been rinsed of immediate signs of injury, but I may have broken a few bones. My head and hands support my weight as I lean against the wall. My breathing has slowed. I feel myself settling back to normal. I rest in a hazy state, half conscious. I am not sure how long he has been standing there, as I am unaware of him until he speaks.

"Kid, what the hell are you doing?" Josh's voice is worry veiled with sarcasm.

I don't jolt to face him. I turn the water off and turn to him. He takes half a step back in an uncertain, unsettled way. I blink and rub my hands over my face. But without paint, I cannot hide. I walk past him in silence. I am at my locker, jeans and shirt on, putting on socks when he joins me.

"I know this probably has nothing do with the loss, but do you mind if I pretend it does to make this easier?" He says this as a joke. As a way to bridge a conversation. I stuff the remainder of stuff in my duffle bag and stand up.

"I have grown to believe that a healthy meltdown is better than a permanent breakdown." I tell him.

"Got it. You drained it from your system. Know, though…"

"If I need to talk, vent, I know. I appreciate it. Just tell me that the parking lot is empty?"

"Yeah. Except for Lily. She made me come back here. She left you a bunch of messages and is really worried about you." My cell is in my bag. I don't dig for it.

"Where is Megan?" I ask.

"At the show. I dropped her off and came back. Her fake ID has probably gotten her pretty well blitzed by now."

"Well then, let's hurry. Sounds like you have fun on tap."

We walk out of the gym and over to our cars. Lily is by mine and walks to us. This is a situation where she should be angry, but she isn't. She is scared. I hate this distinction.

"I am so sorry. I kinda zoned out. I didn't mean to make you wait so long." I say, overcompensating. She wraps her arms around me and looks up with water-glazed eyes.

"Are you okay?" Her voice is soft, yet bursting.

"I am super-fantastic and ready for some moshing." There is a hint of a smile in her eyes, and I think I might be able to salvage the evening.

As we reach the venue, music blares out onto the sidewalk. Lily, Josh and I arrive together and cut our way to the front of the line. As though we have a magic wand, Lily and I cross the rope with just the mention of my name. Josh is left behind for a moment as he has to shell out money. Inside, the lights are so dim, I take Lily's hand so we don't separate. The band is fully geared up and the audience is loving them. On our way to get drinks, we bump into a few people from school but don't stop. It is too loud to talk anyway. I look behind me and see Josh scanning the crowd for Megan. I glance around for a moment to. We seem to notice her at the same time. She is on the side with two guys attempting to talk with her. She is smiling and flirting with the kind of body language that was meant to fuck you up. She has the Shay quality of teasing you to the brink before walking away and making you love it. I hadn't been paying attention to Josh's mood, but I know how he reacts to these types of things. Luckily, Megan sees Josh and breaks away from these guys and goes to him. Confused, they start to follow her, but when she reaches Josh, he kisses her and fondles the length of her back in such a way that her individuality vanishes, replaced by an undeniable unity. It is a depth of connection (and willingness to display that connection) that I have not seen with Megan. Not just with Megan, but ever.

Lily tugs my hand, and attention, back to her as she hands me a drink. It is a clear plastic cup that I down without looking at the liquid. The taste of a Cape Codder coats my throat. It has just enough alcohol for me to taste. Lily sips the same drink and looks at me like she wants me to say something.

"Thanks?" I say. I don't need an expression to know she couldn't hear me. I knew she wouldn't be able to which is why I thought it pointless to say anything in the first place. Then, what she wants arises in me. I bend down to her and move my lips next to her ear. "Thank you." I say. My raised voice is heard as a whisper. I gently bite her earlobe and wrap my arm around her waist.

"These guys aren't bad." I say into her ear. She nods her head in agreement and I realize that no more words are needed.

When their first set ends, the lights come back on and a barrage of people begin heading their way to where Lily and I are standing. We quickly move to the left and dodge our way through the crowd to the now nearly empty stage front. As the people thin out even more, we see Shay standing alone in the middle. Megan and Josh are over on the other side and Shay sees them first. We don't need to see her face to know Shay's face brightened upon seeing them. She does this full body shimmer to position her body and instill a rhythm in her walk. She begins her walk toward Megan and Josh when we catch up to her.

"There you are." Lily says. Shay's attention has been shifted like we hoped. But the confrontation is only delayed as I see Megan edging Josh toward us.

I do not see how it can be considered wrong that Megan wants to join us. She knows that we are Josh's best friends and, besides Josh, we are the people she wants to hang with while she is here. I get that. But I know it will somehow create an angry tension. Evan has gone to get drinks for him and Shay. I can smell the Tequila on her breath and know her tongue is dripping with venom if it is required. Megan is clearly tipsy herself, but she is more passive. She is more apt to run away crying. This would lead to a fight with Josh and Shay, and most likely lead to a fight between Josh and Evan. It could be entertaining but it also could be messy. I await the fate as Josh and Megan reach us.

"Hello!" Megan bubbles. She hugs Lily and Shay before embracing me. Josh offers an encompassing, "hi" to all of us, hanging back a little. There is nothing to spark a conversation here, and as Evan returns, he breaks the silence that was almost becoming uncomfortable.

He hands a drink to Shay, says hi to us, and introduces himself to Megan.

"Sorry, I missed your game." Evan tells Josh and I. "I had to catch a later train here."

"Not a big deal." Josh says. Josh is playing cool, trying to be indifferent. And maybe, in this moment, he is.

"So, what happened? You win?"

"They lost." Shay tells him. She dismisses the importance and ends the interest in the topic

We stand there with nothing to say to each other. There is no celebration in me or Josh. Without the commotion of music, I find myself wanting to disappear. I could disappear with Lily, but existence beyond us is encroaching. My spiral away is interrupted by a tap on the shoulder. I turn to see Erin.

"You came, and you brought a crowd. Very nice." Erin says. Erin is the one person, outside my circle, who can effortlessly remove me from a funk. She stands there in complete joy. Without burden.

"If someone puts me on a list, I am there." Lily jokes.

"What list?" Shay asks.

"Never mind." I say.

"Did you catch most of the set?" Erin asks.

"Lily and I caught the last few songs. They are good." I tell her.

"I heard the beginning." Megan says. "That song, 'sunset snapshot...so I get to keep the belief from leaving' was beautiful." Erin looks at me to explain who Megan is.

"Oh yeah. Erin, this is Megan, Josh's girlfriend. And Evan, Shay's boyfriend."

"I caught onto the associations, but names are helpful. Glad you guys came." Erin says. "I agree. That song is my favorite. The piano is haunting."

"I'm sorry we missed it," Lily says.

"Well then, you are saved. In the back left, they are selling demos. It is track two." Erin promotes. "I gotta go mingle, but thanks again."

Erin leaves as quickly as she appeared. The floor is again becoming crowded so we decide to get some air before the final set starts. I check my watch and find it is past eleven. The night has a swirl in the wind, with thin clouds that distort the starlight. It is kind of eerie and the coldest it has been this year. It is almost February, but I have never felt the need for more than a sweatshirt, although with a gush of wind, my bones are chilled. Megan is the only one who brought a sweater. Lily starts to shiver and Shay wraps herself in Evan. Their only separation comes when Shay tries to light a cigarette. She cannot keep the flame lit long enough. She quickly gets frustrated and begins mumbling swears under her breath. Evan calmly takes the lighter from her but has no success either. Josh is half done with his first smoke, clearly enjoying Shay's struggle. Megan plays this up by kissing Josh and stealing his cigarette with her tongue. He wrestles with her to get it back, pinning her against the wall, breaching her lips with his fingers and removing it. From behind, I wrap my arms around Lily and rub her arms to warm her up. She looks up at me and smiles, collapsing the side of her face into my arm.

"I think I have a blanket in my car." I tell her.

"Thanks. I'm okay, though. If my red lips turn blue then maybe." She says.

For the first time that night, I realize how made up she is. Her lips shine a cherry red and she wears just enough mascara for it to be noticeable. A low rise light green skirt, and a flowing black tank top that is almost longer than her skirt completes her outfit. She is stunning, and I had not paid any attention to it.

"C'mon, hook me up." Shay tells Josh. He is on his second cigarette, and lit one for Megan too.

"You have a lighter." Josh tells her.

"Why do you always have to torture? Why can't you ever just be nice?" Shay pouts, trying to use her sensuality to sway Josh. Megan, who wouldn't with one less drink in her, sees this and pulls Josh away from the group, then kisses him in her best porno fashion. He is obviously taken back, but only hesitates for a split second before indulging. Shay has no cards here. She looks at Evan, then at Lily and I whose attention is rapt to find out what is going to happen.

"Fine," Shay says and walks over to them. She moves behind Josh and reaches in his left pocket (where she saw him put the lighter). She has no regard for their intimacy, and because of this, they break apart.

"What the hell are you doing?" Megan shouts at Shay. Josh is too stunned to do much of anything other than swing his neck around to try and see what she is doing.

"Ah, there it is…Oops, that's not the lighter…There we are." She pulls out the lighter and lights her cigarette. Megan stays a few feet away, appalled at Shay's actions and by the fact that Josh is allowing it. Once lit, she flips the lighter back to Josh, gives a smug smile to Megan, and walks back toward us. Megan takes a step toward Josh.

"What was that? How could you let her do that?" Megan's voice rises in anger.

"I was teasing her by not giving up the lighter. She just called my bluff." Josh reasons.

"'Called my bluff'? That doesn't make any sense. She felt you up in the middle of us making out." Megan is getting madder than I have ever seen her.

"You are reading way too much into this." Josh says, trying to calm her down. "Shay doesn't adhere to personal space sometimes. It doesn't mean she is disrespecting anything."

"C'mon! That is bullshit. You cannot see that was intentionally done as a power play?"

Josh has to think about that. I give Megan credit – she is right. Shay was marking her territory. She has never been that overt about it with Megan around. I guess if there was any bit of insecurity in Megan, it would be because of Shay. Evan seems unaffected. Shay got what she wanted and then came back to him like a self-thrown boomerang. Josh and Megan's conversation gets too quiet for us to hear, and then Megan walks off to her car. Josh follows her, trying to pull her back, but she breaks away and continues walking. She gets inside her car and Josh slides in the passenger seat.

"Why, Shay, why?" I ask her.

"What?" She says, acting overly innocent.

I shake my head and take Lily back inside. Her skin is full of goosebumps. Inside, the lights begin to flash and the band returns to the stage. A steady bass line overtakes the crowd noise.

"I believe I promised you a dance." I tell Lily.

We shuffle our way to the floor and find just enough space. My hands move to her waist, her fingers interlock behind my neck. I close my eyes and let the music drown out the distortion in my head. I begin to wonder what my parents thought of the game and how I was such a pansy for not facing them afterwards. You gain a certain kind of dignity by handling things with class, and I failed in that. I guess there is a piece of me that believes my parents look at me as the last hope for salvation. It is a feeling that has never been justified by any of their words or actions. But maybe it is a pressure I put on myself. I saw the change in my parents when the decision with my sister was enacted. I saw the last bits of joy drain from them and I have lived with the repercussions of that joylessness. I am the one who remains. The only one who could return joy to them...to our family. I want to believe that. I want to hold that hope. But maybe the truth is that the space of something lost cannot be filled by the expanding of what remains. Without my sister, there is no balance to save the fallen. It has been over six months since I have seen her. The need strikes me fast and holds in my heart. I suddenly have to see her.

Lily's hand grazes my cheek and pulls my face back to her. Her eyes search mine. I wish I had a mirror so I could see my face, so I would know what is causing the confusion on hers. It is a look of interruption. A look that only someone who has been allowed to see the depths of you would ever presume to possess. I take her hand in mine and move it away from my face. I turn my head from her and adjust back into the room I am in.

"Where did you go?" Lily says as the song ends.

"My mind is just clouded. Sorry."

Another song starts up and Lily leads me outside. The air is even colder than before. Exhaling, I can see my breath. Lily's voice is quiet, but her body language demands me to explain.

"My mind is cluttered. I didn't mean to ruin our dance."

"You didn't ruin our dance. That isn't the point." Lily says as though what I said was a cop-out.

"I don't know what I should say." I tell her.

"What's wrong? I know it isn't the basketball game."

"If I knew what was wrong I would be in the process of fixing it." I say. "And this game had a few layers that could have fucked me up. It wasn't just a loss. It wasn't just *me* losing it. It had this symbolic meaning. Or at least could have." I say angrily, but turn away almost as an apology afterwards.

"Then let me help you untangle what's inside you." These words are not offered as a plea, but somehow, they sound that way to me. To want to understand a person is one thing, to ask to understand them is the polar opposite.

"I just need to clear my head. I am sure I will feel more coherent tomorrow." I pause. "If I take off, could you catch a ride with Shay?"

She looks at me for a long beat, and then to the entrance.

"I don't know if I can find her. Or if she is even still here." Lily looks around nervously. I can tell she is not doing this to appease me, but rather looking for other options for rides.

"Look, I am not going to strand you. That worried look on your face is enough to give me a panic attack." I move to her and put my arm around her.

"Well, you're freaking me out. You're not talking to me. Sometimes I think you are going to just abandon everything and take off."

I have no reassurance for her, so I stay quiet. Why did Josh leave? Why did Shay have to be bitchy? My strongest feelings of needing to be alone are stifled when I know I will be leaving someone lonely. As I hold Lily, I feel her shaking. I wonder if it is just because of the cold.

I pull out my cell and see that Josh left a message. I tell this to Lily and dial in to listen to my voicemail. "Sorry I had to bail. I would explain, but you were there. We got the weekend to crash so I will call ya sometime tomorrow. Later." I hang up my cell.

"Nothing new. We saw why he took off." I tell Lily. Lily knows how Shay is. But I wonder what goes through her mind when she sees her sabotage the night like she did. "Could you call Shay?" I ask.

"Yeah," she says, awkwardly fumbling for her phone. With each unanswered ring, tension mounts. She finally closes her phone and shrugs her shoulders. It is done in a way of submitting; of showing vulnerability. She releases all control and placed the outcome squarely on me.

The decision here is ridiculous. It isn't about me wanting to bail and Lily wanting to stay. It is me wanting to leave without her. The weight of this distinction I am sure neither of us can grasp. I should drive her to her car, or bring her home. But I cannot break the stubbornness of not wanting to. I know Lily understands how simple all this should be; that there should be no hesitation or complication in it. But there is a stubbornness in her too. She could just allow me a moment of selfish reclusiveness (much the same way she allowed Shay a bit of bitchiness), but I know the infection in me has been shown to her. At varying levels, the black hole that my sister creates Lily has seen; even though it has never been named. She knows the symptoms of me spiraling.

"I am sure if we go back inside we could find Erin, and I am sure she will give you a ride." I tell her.

"I don't want a ride from Erin," Lily says. I look at her slightly indignant. "Don't look at me like I am being difficult. She is with the band. It will be past two before they get outta here. This is crazy! I am too exhausted to play tug-of-war. Something is fucking up your head, I get that. You wanna keep it wrapped up inside of you, I understand. Josh is gone. Shay is god knows where. I am not walking home. At least be man enough to give me a ride home before you go clear your head." Lily's voice rises with anger and crashes with condescension. She is rarely like this, and even rarer is it directed at me. It stuns me for a moment.

I turn away from her and take a few steps forward. I turn back to her and ask for her phone. She hands it to me. Lily stays back, watching. I open Uber. She is bewildered. "What was that?" She asks. "Did you just get me an Uber?" She is in so much disbelief that she cannot find rage. I hand her phone back to her.
"Yes. They'll be here in ten minutes. I know this isn't completely cool, but it is my best idea. I have to take off."

Offering a 'sorry' is trite, so I don't. I cross the street to my car. As I drive out, I pass Lily. She stands unmoved outside the club. I know she will be okay, though. She is a lot stronger than I am. But I know she wishes I was stronger for her. It is a void that usually doesn't reflect, but when it does, it's impossible to ignore. I have no idea how to fix this, and such is the reason I do not like facing it. As I turn on the highway, a dusting of snow begins to fall. Snowflakes hit my windshield, melt to water and then evaporate from the heat blown on them.

Five

I'm Not Sick, But I am Not Well

I first remember my sister getting sick a week before I turned ten. Even to this day, I don't have a grasp on what night terrors are. The cause, meaning, all that shit. The root of why she was sobbing hysterically meant little to me. I only wanted to rip it out of her. To rid her of the pain. I was helpless in this. Understanding how helpless I was merely increased the need. I don't know if that was the start, or just the progression, but she stayed in the hospital for over a week. I was only allowed to see her through the small window on the door of her room. Her face was always turned away. I was never sure if she was sleeping or sedated. When I got older, I realized there is little difference.

On the day she was released, I was waiting in the hallway with our mom as dad pushed her out in a wheelchair. Her demeanor was too exhausted to show much emotion, but upon seeing me, she gave me a small smile. She was the big sister. She had always taken care of me. But from that smile, I was granted equal standing. There was something in her not having the strength to give me reassurance that forced me to obtain the strength myself and to hold onto that strength for her in case she collapsed again. Back then, I had no basis to understand the weight of this.

The next two years were a constant back and forth between hospitals. My mother quit her job to take care of my sister, and I was bought a bike so I would not need a ride anywhere. I heard whispered arguments and tearful restless nights. But I suppose it was assumed that I wouldn't understand, and it was hard enough to go through, let alone trying to explain it to someone who couldn't understand it anyway. But the illusion that this was something within my grasp was needed. I was left to isolate. I rarely saw my sister awake, so a kind of disconnection began to form. I created my own reality of what was happening and I played it out in my head every day. I would write down dialogues between my sister and me, and my parents and me. All the answers I wanted came from the altering tones of the voices in my head. This was the transition to the life I know today. The four of us shut down.

I distinctly remember the Spring before my eleventh birthday. I came home from school to find my mother eating cereal alone in the dining room, and my dad reading by himself in his den. It wasn't the separation that affected me (even though the happiest moments I can remember are the when the four of us were together). It was the sense of removal that saturated the air. They both had so many layers of barriers that getting close to them was impossible. This shook me. Even if it was thought of as unpleasant or difficult, the option of talking with my parents had always been there. In that moment, I became aware that this was no longer true. My comfort when life hurt, confused or drained me had always been my sister. My older sister. My second mother. I had lost that recourse as well. I know many people grow up quicker than they should; in an environment that they shouldn't have to endure. I am not unique. Underneath the guise of a stable family going through a crisis, parts of me weakened and died. Some grew back in some reincarnated form, changing who I was, and changing who I was on course to become.

I turn off the main strip and down a narrow road that leads to the hospital. I left a little before 1am. I glance at the clock to find it is nearly seven. There aren't specific visiting hours, but it seems too early to show up. Besides, I am starving. I pull into a truck stop diner to eat. My legs ache when I step out. A six-hour journey will do that to you. Especially after a game. I had put my phone on vibrate and ignored it through the trip. Walking into the diner, I check my phone. There are no voicemails, but seven text messages. None from Lily, though. Shay wrote, 'you are being an asshole'. I am sure the other texts are pretty much the same, so I don't look at them. Sometimes, the ones you love distract you from what you need. Maybe I am going to disappear. Maybe when the need to disappear hits you, the pain it would cause others becomes secondary. I don't really know what I think will occur when I see my sister. There is no revelation that can come of it. If she is able to say my name, I will consider it a win. I just need to see her. And whatever solace or sorrow that brings is what I am after. It is a weird feeling that should be written into a parable: I don't know what I need, but I know where I need to go to find out.

The diner's house omelet is one with feta cheese, spinach, and chopped up sausage, I decide on that. An old 50's song starts to play from the jukebox, and despite the contrast of people, the atmosphere is welcoming. I sip my orange juice and stretch my neck.

"You look too young to be hauling a ridge." It takes me a second to realize the waitress is talking to me.

"Nah." Is all I come up with.

"So, is it my turn to ask the cliché, 'what are you doing in these parts?' question?" She asks. Her attention on me is a little awkward.

"Um…" I stutter a little, trying to figure out how I want to say it. "I'm visiting my sister. She doesn't live far from here."

"Where are you from?"

"Boston."

"Boston? That's quite the drive. Maybe you should think about being a truck driver." She laughs at her joke and is then called away for a refill of coffee before I get a chance to respond.

I watch her for a minute. Her banter snapped me out of my mind. She snapped me back. A sense of my surroundings comes to me, and the reality of a six-hour, all night, drive sets in. I allow myself to only briefly remember leaving Lily alone, shivering on the sidewalk. It is not something I am running away from (well, I guess I did literally, but figuratively, I'm not). I will face it. But not now. I have a strict focus.

The waitress returns with a new glass of OJ. I look up at her, noticing her nametag.

"So, if most waitresses use false names on their nametags, why even bother with them?" I ask. She ponders this for a moment with almost a giddy glee of having something to think about. At best, I was merely trying for a laugh. "They have to call us something. Better to not let them be creative." She says.

"Fair point. I will just stick to calling you Betsey then."

"So, your sister isn't joining you for breakfast?" Her question is innocent enough, but I recoil. It isn't something that I am self-aware of at first, but from her reaction, I can tell I must have. I don't talk about my sister. I have to be careful here because I know it is a flood gate. If I open it up, I don't know if I will be able to stop.

While I am trapped in my inner struggle, she slips away. I have taken more of her time than she should have allowed. I understand this. But, somehow, her absence bothers me. I had recoiled, but that can only happen why you first unfold. I am away from my world. From my girl and friends. That being true, I am also close to a part of me that they are not aware of. Maybe I see this as the complete picture of myself. There are things unknown, but nothing held back, nothing hidden.

She drops my omelet in front of me and vanishes before I can look up from it. I try to bury the forming desire of her company. I guess on some level I know I am not a loner, but that theory has never been tested. My little bouts of isolation have hardly been convincing to the fact. I have left before, but this time, I removed myself. It wasn't a progression of events, it was a sudden jerk brought on by a piercing change to the temperament of my mood. I don't know what awaits me when I return home. There is not much doubt that eventuality will allow everything to mend, but that 2% of uncertainty curls inside of me. Loneliness, insecurity creeps in. I can't turn back. I can't return home. But I don't know if I am strong enough to continue. There is this pressing fear growing in me. A nervousness that shouldn't exist. This is my sister; my blood; my oldest friend. But everything has changed. I have no idea what I will feel, think, say when I see her, and I have less of an idea of her reaction. It is like returning to a memorized landscape, only to find it in disrepair. Overrun by weeds and dead grass. It is haunting because in the midst of the view, all you can think about is the beauty that once was, and the hopelessness of what it has become.

I lose myself in my head again; to analyze, to become paranoid. I am not stable enough to do this, but I have little control. I finish my omelet and OJ, then find that the check has been placed in front of me. The bill is just over ten, but I throw down a twenty. I slide off the stool and head for the door.

"So, you think you'll swing by for dinner?" Betsey's voice is loud but somehow directed. She is talking to me. I turn to her without a thought of how to answer such a simple question.

"I guess I'll see. I have no idea what time that could be." I say.

"You are lucky we are open 24/7 then." She tells me.

I give a short-lived smile and exit. It is after eight now. It is cold but sunny and without wind. I lean against my car and watch the slow stream of traffic. I allow myself to drift. Meditation, to me, is losing your outer conscience for inner consciousness. I replay the last twenty-four hours in my head, in some sort of aerial psychoanalytical way. Josh is right – I was an asshole. I free myself from guilt by concluding that Lily knows that I have shit in me. That something is off tilt. Maybe this is part of the attraction, but I tell myself it is part of the acceptance of being with me.

The road heads into a patch of businesses. Katz Residential Hospital sits back a few hundred yards from a strip mall. It is an odd shaped rectangle-ish building, made of brick and concrete. For the length of it, there are few windows; all equipped with steel bars. There are no signs indicating what the building is. It is in plain sight but does its best to fade into the background; to hold firmly to the indifference of those who would pass by. To this end, all parking is done in the rear of the building, showing itself only to the woods behind it. I pull around and park next to the door. The facility normally has a staff of ten on days and less at night, and holds around thirty patients. Visitors are few, and sedation prevents any dust-ups.

I have not been here in quite a while. Over six months. But everything seems so familiar. Nothing about it seems changed. Life here seems to stop time. As I breathe in the isolated air, I feel at peace from the consistency of the place.

I ring the bell at the front door and wait. The door is open fairly quickly and a nurse I know, but cannot recall her name, answers. She remembers me, though.

"Noah. Nice to see you, dear." She is a woman in her late fifties with unkempt brown hair. Glasses dangle in front of her from a band around her neck.

"Thank you." I say, trying to buy time to read her nametag. She isn't wearing one. Why would she be?

"Margaret. It's okay. It has been a little bit since we have seen you."

"I know. I think early summer was the last time."

I have been here enough to hold some rapport with the nurses. They know I play basketball and that I work at the Mayor's office. But what I have told them is offset by other information they are privy to. The fact that my sister is in a mental hospital; that my parents banished her here, leaving her forgotten. That her brother can only share a few hours every few months. If knowing this doesn't shade their feelings and opinions about me, it certainly shades my feelings and opinions on how they should regard me. They are all older women who read romance novels while sitting in a rocking chair as they supervise the zombie-like residents. Like I said, this isn't a place where people come to get better: it is a place people are put when all hope is gone.

"Your sister is with the others in the activity room." Margaret tells me.

"Thanks, Margaret," I say as I walk past her.

The activity room consists of a few couches, chairs, a TV set, a table, and boxes of games piled in a corner. I find my sister sitting in the far corner on the edge of a couch, hands carefully folded on her lap. I stare around the room for a moment and take her in. She is a little less than three years older than me, which makes her almost twenty-one. Most are dressed in robes, but she wears jeans and a t-shirt. It is an old t-shirt from the first concert our parents took us to. It was the week of her birthday and dad told her that he had asked them to play their song, 'Jessica', in honor of her birthday. She laughed with disbelief, but was young enough to not completely dismiss the idea. Her face is downcast. Her hair dangles past her shoulders, hiding her profile. She is much the same as I remember. Standing in the space that allows me this view, I hate myself for not coming back sooner. Before I step toward her, though, I mentally lower my expectations. The landscape of illusion is pretty, but never holds up against reality.

As I walk across the room, I am observed but not interacted with. There are glances, not stares. Such a fleeting thought you would rather be ignored. I sit down on the couch beside her. She does not move. If it wasn't for a steady, slow inhaling, I would think she wasn't alive. I try to say something but the ability to speak fails me. I clear my throat, and force the words out of me.
"Hey, Jess. It's Noah. Your brother."

She raises her head as though it took an incredible amount of effort, and turns it to me. She waits a second, squinting her eyes, as though I wasn't quite in focus. Then a calm remembrance comes to her and a smile graces her face.
"Noah. My brother. You came to visit." She leans over and hugs me. There have been moments like this before, where she appears to have a much better comprehension of her situation than she should. Maybe that is the most tortured part: that there still remains a place underneath the disease, even if it is distant.
"I did. How have you been?" I ask, hoping her state will last at least a little while.
"Ducky." She says, indicating sarcasm by surveying the room. I laugh.
"So, I hear they have checkers here. You up for a game?" I speak slowly and clearly. Jess seems as though she has been battered by the will of something stronger than her own. Her disease is the equivalent of years of abuse. The doctors submitted to its defeat, my parents had as well, so had my sister. I stand alone on the island of hope. I tell myself this is the reason for the moments of clarity in her.

Jessica moves over to the lone table in the room and I dig through the cardboard boxes of games. I set up the board; she is red and I am black. As we always have been. We play the first few moves in silence. She has never been mute through any stages of her disease. But coherent is another story. We play through a couple of games and she always asks to play more. I begin to settle in and start to think that maybe the angst I have about my sister may be born out of guilt. I have had over five years to process this into acceptance, but have never allowed closure to come. I sit with her and play checkers for almost two hours. The nurses come in and take everyone out for lunch, but leave us. I don't have to ask. They know my routine and permit us to have it. I have often wanted to ask them about the families of others, but never have. The youngest I have seen is probably at least twenty years older than Jess. It does not matter here, though. Age – like time – seems to simply not apply. They are all the same. The atmosphere of this is freeing at first. There are no worries, no cares. Nothing is hurried or judged. Nor demanded or…felt.

A nurse comes in with a cup of water and three pills for my sister. Jess takes the cup and pills without looking at the nurse. I want to ask what they are. I almost think the pills were forcing her in a comatose state. Couldn't she just stop taking the meds and wake up? This sounds like such a simple solution, only, I know it wouldn't be true. Her medication was stopped, changed and started to an extent that alleviated any doubt towards its necessity. She had become a danger to herself. And her seizures are so strong that, without preventing them, she would probably die. The nurse gives me a short smile, then walks out. A little while later, the other patients return from lunch. I have never observed them really. Casually, yes. But I gave myself time to see their details. There were three women in their fifties who all sat together in their own little group. They didn't talk much, but whenever one of them did, the others would laugh hysterically. It was amusing to watch. They would be blankly staring out into the distance, turn to each other, speak a few words, laugh, and then return to staring. A few others pace around the room; dragging their slippers along the floor. Most, though, just sit idly. Like statues.

When Jess turned ten, my parents threw her a surprise party. All her friends from school, ballet and the neighborhood came. Our rented room burst with probably over fifty people. She soaked up the attention. She was the perfect host. And as thin as her attention was spread, she made sure to include me, to make sure I was a part of everything. I wasn't shy, really. It was just when things got too hectic, too crowded, too chaotic, I would retreat into a space I felt safe. Jess also allowed me to escape from there. I felt safe when I was with her.

Margaret, the nurse from the front door, comes over and tells me they left sandwiches out for Jess and I whenever we were hungry. We finish our sixth game and then Margaret leads us to the dining room.
"If you need anything, we are always around. We try to be flies on the wall but we are always near." Margaret says to me before leaving. I hadn't thought about it, but the nurses didn't seem to be around much. I guess to preserve sanity they need to find a pocket of their own. I got that. The longer I stayed here, the more restricting it became. I suppose jail can seem peaceful at first, but then cabin fever creeps up and the itch of stimulus crashes in. As we finish our sandwiches, I know I need to leave soon.
"Jess, I need to get back soon." I say, careful to omit the word 'home'. She looks at me and the joy of my company translates from her gaze. Maybe this means something to her too? We share a moment where, I don't want to say acceptance, but a certain peace comes to me. I walk her back to the activity room, then hover at the entrance. Jess takes a step in and turns to face me. The doorway is an awkward separation, so I also take a step in. We lightly embrace, and I kiss her on the forehead. There is a sadness in me that I can tell she doesn't see or share. This somehow increases it in me, but makes it easier to walk away.

I follow the hallway back to the entrance, say goodbye to Margaret, and exit.

My first trip up here, I spoke with the nurses at length about my sister's condition and the medicine she was taking. I wrote everything down, as though a few hours on the internet was going to give me a Ph.D. But I had to try and understand. I had asked my parents the same questions, but was ignored. I demanded the answers from my parents, but they literally push me aside and leave the room. The elephant was taking up the entire room. It got to a point where we just ceased to be in the same room as each other. By the age of thirteen, I had a bike, a paper route, and had learned how to make scrambled eggs. I had independence in the most negative form of the word.

Now, almost four years from my first visit, my understanding is not much better. My mind switches back to when I was eleven, before everything, and I have no choice but to be back in her company. My parents, in ways, are more dead to me than she is. When I see her and look her in the eyes, I can see the distance between then and now, and I am able to travel backward. I am able to live in a happy, complete version of myself. The walk from the front door to my car is the return to the reality of the present. I have a migraine when I sit down. My vision is blurred. I stay there, hands on the side of my face to balance the spinning for a good five minutes before I can refocus.

Maybe I did need to open up about it to Lily. Stuffing it inside is only hurting both of us. But revealing things in conversation is one thing; bringing up the most intimate details of yourself in a stark non-sequitur way is another. I have to come clean, though. I have dug a hole that can only be filled by laying the cards on the table. As I drive off, I make a pact with myself to stop letting things linger.

I glance at the time and am shocked that it is almost 4pm. That places really does remove time from your thoughts. It has been less than 24 hours since I have seen, touched, or spoken to Lily – but it seems like forever. When I am in my little town, she calms the torment in me. But here, here it is subsiding by itself. The netherworld that my parents live in, the expectations of basketball and school are my chains. Distance equals freedom. But is it real, and does it last? I have no answer. All I know is how I feel. There is a clam in me that I do not think I have ever felt. I bite my tongue to focus my thoughts. There is anger for Lily in me. She was supposed to understand why I needed to leave. She wasn't supposed to bestow guilt and alienation because of it. And Josh and Shay weren't supposed to take her side. They weren't supposed to blame me or call me an asshole.

I breathe through these emotions, knowing that in this moment they mean nothing. It may be deflecting responsibility. I may be cruel, unfeeling. But it occurs to me the burdens of a person are caused mainly by their surroundings; by what they allow around them. There is chemical imbalance depression, and then there is depression brought on by stress and a lack of hope.

I am of the mindset to let the wind dictate my direction for a while.

I am lost in thought when my cell rings. It is Josh. "Whatup?" I say, casual as hell.

"Kid, where are you?" Josh's voice is more annoyed than concerned.

"I am in New York." I have lost the will or strength to lie.

"What the hell are you in New York for?"

"I will tell you later."

"When are you coming back?"

"I don't know."

He waits for me to expound but I don't. I can picture his facial expressions as he tries to think of a way to pull more information from me.

"Lily is hurt." He says.

This throws me. I knew he was going to bring up Lily, but I thought he would say 'pissed' or something. But hurt?

"I kinda got that from her silence." I quip, deflecting how that hit me.

"You overdramatic bastard. Why would she call you? *You* are the one that just took off."

"To be fair, you just took off first."

I hear him laughing and the distance that had accumulated over the last 15 hours fades away.

"Fine. I took off. But you disappeared. I just called it a night."

"It was a little more dramatic than you simply deciding to 'call it a night.' I was fairly messed up in the head, I will give you that, but I was still amused."

"Yeah. What's the girl's version of a pissing contest?" Josh asks. I laugh.

"Being bitchy?" I offer.

"Yeah. I don't know what Shay's deal is."

"Yeah, you do." I tell him.

"What?"

"It is the same as yours. Neither one of you can stand it when the other has a boyfriend/girlfriend?"

"What? Why would you say that?" He pulls back defensively.

"Do I really need to explain it?" Silence. "Fine. If you need it laid out for you, I will when I get back."

"So, you are coming back?"

"Was that really even a real doubt?" I ask.

"Yeah. If you put the analysis on you, something you will see is that you kept drifting further away. That's what hurts, what scares Lily – all of us. There is almost this feeling that one of these times you aren't coming back."

One of the weirdest moments you can have is to hear the thoughts in your head spoken by someone else. Like the reciting of a poem written during isolation – carried by a bard throughout the lands, then read in front of you as though you were not the author. Are my feelings that transparent? Are the words and actions that others witness dissected? (Well, 'others' being only Shay, Lily and Josh.) The comfort of their understanding has always been the crux of our relationship. But it had never before occurred to me that residue of me lingered when I left, when I disappeared. That there could be some profound absence in them, beyond concern, worry or even hurt, when I had the instinct or the impulse to leave.

I become aware that I have been pacing the empty floor of the diner. I exit it and begin to pace aimlessly outside.

"That's a little much to talk about on the phone, wouldn't you say?"

"I didn't mean it to spark a heart to heart. It just seemed like the right time to say it."

"Fair enough. My drive back is a good six hours and I still don't know when I am starting back. So...I don't know. I guess I will see you sometime tomorrow. And don't be surprised when I am not in school."

"I kinda figured that. You need to call Lily, though.

"I'll talk to her when I see her." I say.

"That's not good enough, man. This is deeper than anything before. Even if she doesn't answer, just leave a message saying you will talk to her tomorrow or something."

"I will call her on my way back. The shit in my head merits more than words over the phone. I need to look at her when I speak."

"I hear that."

"Okay. I will see you sometime." I say.

"Later, man."

I hang up the phone and exhale.

I put my car in drive and have turned on the road back to the highway when I hear my phone again. I don't want to talk to anyone, but the bass version of a song is recognizable – it's Lily.

"Hi," I say. "Hey," Lily's voice is soft and unsure. "I wanted to make sure you are okay." This isn't some guilt trip reversal she is playing. It is genuine.

"I'm fine. On my way back." I tell her.

"Where are you?"

"New York." I say. Leaving space to say more, but I don't.

"Did you talk with someone at Albany State?"

That would make sense. It would be a logical thing for me to be doing in New York, but I know she doesn't think that's why I am here. If it was logical, I wouldn't have just taken off.

"Not exactly. It is a layered story. Can we talk about it when I get back?"

"Yeah."

"I'm sorry I just took off. Did you get home okay?"

"That's a complicated answer." She says.

"Right. I will call you when I am back."

"Okay." She hangs up before I can say anything else.

I am living in two worlds and they interfere with each other. There is only one way to solve this. I have to tell Lily about my sister.

Six

Forgiveness is a Slow Dance

It is after two am when I arrive at my house. As predicted, it is completely dark. Void of movement, feeling, or life. I park at the far corner of our horseshoe-shaped driveway and head around to the back basement entrance. I turn the lava lamp in my room on and crash on my bed. I lie there for a while, zoning out, looking at the dancing light on the ceiling. I stretch my body to its maximum extension, twist and crack my back, and then pull my blanket around me. The bumps and cracks in the road are supposed to be there to add character and texture to the experiences. But all they do for me is disallow sleep. I no longer even try until I am exhausted, burned out. I have been awake for thirty-eight hours, nearly two days. As I close my eyes, I fight against the jitteriness of letting the control of consciousness go.

I wake feeling rested, but in my windowless cave, I am unaware of the time. I strip my clothes, shower, dress and walk upstairs for some OJ. I pour my drink when I hear talking in the next room. I look to the clock on the oven and find it is actually after five. My parents are home. I would normally ignore this and head out the other way, but I don't. They may have buried the existence of their daughter, and my aim is not to judge that. I simply want them to know that I haven't. That part of me calls out for her and remembers what it was like when we were a family, a functional, middle class, happy family.

I step into the dining room to my parents sitting at the table. Dad holds a coffee halfway to his mouth and mom sits next to him leaning in to read the paper that rests in front of him. They both hear me come in and look up. Their smile is weak, a required smile of parents mimicking what they read in a parenting book when the pee strip first turned blue.

"Hello," My dad says. "How was school?" He is oblivious. It is funny, really. I hold back the laugh and hold in the resolve to stay.

"I didn't go."

Their look is one of confusion. Not one of 'what do you mean you didn't go to school?' More of, 'that's not what you were supposed to say.' I wait for them to figure out what they want to say.

"What do you mean? Why didn't you?" My mom asks.

To have a conversation, sometimes you need an opening. You need the person to ask the right question that allows you to answer in the way you want. This is the first time I have ever had that chance with my parents. I can't ignore it.

"I went to New York."

"What's in New York?" My dad asks.

"Jessica." I say

There is dead quiet. It has literally been years since we have talked about Jess. I was too young to protest when she first went away, and since the decision was sealed, all evidence of her has been removed. Her old bedroom now a den, the rare family photos on the wall are just of the three of us. The nearest extended family lives three hours away, so interaction with them over the last seven years has been very minimal. They stay still for a few moments before stirring. It is almost like it took that time for what I said to sink beneath their skin. My dad fidgets in his chair, clears his throat, and looks at me. His eyes aren't clear. They seem like they are lined with water. Like he has pushed his eyelids out to stop tears from falling, but the water build-up has glazed his eyes. I don't know if this can truly be called emotion, but it is the closest thing to it I have seen in him for as long as I can remember. I am far too jaded to believe this conversation is going to restore anything, but it may be a start.

"You went to see Jess?" He stutters out her name.

"Yeah. I drove up there Saturday night and spent some time with her on Sunday."

My mom still has not adjusted to the subject. She remains still, leaning back in her chair with the occasional wrinkle in her face that is quickly stuffed back inward.
"And they let you see her? Did you talk to her?" Dad asks, kind of baffled.
"Of course they did. Most of the nurses know me." This information is a revelation to my father. He has barely processed the fact that I saw Jessica, now I am adding that this wasn't a one-shot deal.
"How many times have you gone up there?"
"I don't know exactly. At least twice a year for the last three years."
My mom reacts to this. She is astonished. Flustered, she rises from her chair, takes a step away, only to sit back down again. Her movements halt my dad from responding. He watches her unravel her stoic veneer. I am unsure of how I should react and/or continue. I settle on playing the role of a psychiatrist. Listening and waiting for them to be ready to continue.
"You are lying. You only got a car last year." My mom states.
"There is a train that stops hardly two miles away from Katz." I tell her.
"So, at fourteen, you were walking two miles alone in New York?"
"The most dangerous aspect about that part of New York is being run over by a moose. And once you've met one or two, they just become a part of its charm." I tell them.
"Where did you get the money for the train tickets?" she asks, accusingly.
"Newspaper route. Stray cans. Birthday money." I tell her.
My mother stirs in this for a while. It is clear she is deflecting who I was seeing with how I got there and if I stole the money.
"Did you talk to her?" My dad returns to his prior question.
"Yeah. Somewhat. She is pretty medicated, but I think she still knows when I am there. Look, I guess I should have told you I was going. Hell, even asked you to take me. But the first time I went up there…I had not seen her in close to three years. My sister. She was taken away and I was left without her. I was ten. How was I supposed to comprehend what was happening to her? What it meant

bringing her there?" These are rhetorical questions, and as such, they don't try and answer them. "I went up there and they let me see her. I honestly have no idea what the visitor protocol is there, that had nothing to do with it. It wasn't like I was going to be denied. I think they saw a child of fourteen who just took an eight-hour train ride and then walked a half an hour to find his sister. I didn't understand it then, but there is desperation in that. I was a stuttering boy. They took me to her room. We looked at each other for a minute like when you come out of a movie cinema and your eyes have to adjust back into sunlight, but then it hit her and she knew me. She hugged me, and for the next five minutes straight, we cried. Her coherency didn't last. It bended out and I was left with a shell with vacant eyes and a babbling voice." I pause for a second to look at my parents. Their hands grasp each other's and their cheeks are stained by tears. Yet I can tell they want me to continue. "I pleaded with the nurses to do something, give her something to bring her back. I was angry and hysterical, but they were calm. They explained it wasn't that simple. All the whispered words and scattered letters from doctors, all the pieces I began putting together. I left that day with a new understanding and knowing that I had to go back as much as I could. I had created a choice for myself, and I wasn't going to discard her or abandon her. The emptiness I felt without her outweighed the pain of seeing her sedated. And I know there are times, maybe minutes, maybe only seconds, when her eyes adjust and she sees me there. The smile, the atom of joy that reaches her because of it is more than enough to keep me going back."

There is blame and guilt dripping from my words. No matter what way I said it, this would be true here. The unearthing of it in my parents is unsettling. I feel no sadness in my reveling, but feel a slight anger. Their denial of my sister, their unwillingness to enlighten me of what was going on, had become resentment. I look at them now crying their backed-up tears and wonder if they had ever given thought to all the nights I cried, not understanding why. And when I understood, the tears were still confused. The isolation of my pain manifested in depression, anger, drugs, alcohol binges. All the clichés. I had all the warning signs. But they saw nothing. Jessica wasn't the only one they abandoned. They abandoned me as well. And that was without cause. I grew up and figured myself out. I learned to handle things in a way only I determined. I needed to open up to them about visiting Jess. They needed to know how they had forsaken us. That what they did affected us. Even if they understood it in the dark recesses of their mind, I needed them to see it transparently. That isn't why I started talking, but seeing them now, I know that is what facilitated the burden in me.

They don't speak, nor look at me. I stand over them, blocking their only exit, stone-faced as they cry. This is the definition of victory that Hollywood has sold us. There should be a pulse of confidence and assurance stringing through me. There isn't. My sister had said, right when she started getting sick, that 'part of growing up is untangling how the world is explained to us.' There is not a truer example of that than this moment. The notion that our parents are the ones to teach you, guide you, mold you, are false. They birth the template and they allow nature to take its course. I realize this is not universal. Lily and Josh's parents, for better or worse, are still crafting their children. But for me, that ended when I was ten. Old enough to remember what it was like but too young to dictate any change.

I wait for a few minutes, thinking that eventually they will offer some sort of worded response to me. I am not shocked when none comes. I know that the relationship I have with my parents will return to status quo, and that the conversation we just had will only remain a memory between the ether and me.

I am in my car driving when I call Lily. It goes to voicemail, which most likely means she is at the Mayor's office. I don't leave a message. I know she will see I called and get back to me when she can. The act of me calling means I am home. After the monologue I had with my parents, I am ready to tell her, to explain about Jess. And pissed off or hurt, I know she won't shut me out. My second call is to Josh.

"Hey, man. I take it you're back?"

"That I am." I say. "Where are you?"

"Home. Where do you want to meet?" I imagine that is one of the luxuries of growing up: that your home is somewhere you can have important, meaningful conversations.

"I don't know. Where do kids go these days?" I joke.

"Well, it is almost March in New England, so that narrows it down. A Coffee Spot?"

"Which one?"

"On Lafayette Square." He says.

"Okay. Give me like ten."

"Sounds good. See ya then." His phone clicks off. I throw mine down on the passenger's seat and head over to Lafayette Square.

I get to A Coffee Spot ahead of Josh. I don't like coffee much, so I order a French Vanilla. I am not hungry, but get a chocolate chip muffin to pick at as well. I find a table in the corner and sit down. As I do, Josh enters. He gives me a short wave before ordering, then he joins me.

"Return of the grievous angel." He says as we clasp hands. "Welcome back, son."

"Thanks. I didn't mean to just disappear...well, actually, that is exactly what I meant to do. I just didn't mean it as a slight." I tell him.

"I get that. No slight to me. But then you didn't leave me freezing on the sidewalk, rideless."

"Is that what all this is about? That one fact?" I ask.

"First, don't minimalize that. You disappearing is on one tier, and you abandoning Lily is on another. That is what this is about."

I take a sip of my coffee and ponder what he said.

"I know I screwed up."

"Okay then. There is more to it than just that." Josh says.

"I called Lily but she didn't answer. She must be working. I'll catch up with her later." My mind begins to drift before lighting up. "So, you have a story or two to tell. What's up with you and Megan?"

Josh shakes his head before saying anything. "It is a migraine. She flipped out."

"You don't have to tell me – I was there."

"Yeah. It was a scene. I don't know if it was jealousy, infringement or what." A sly smirk appears on his face. "It wasn't all bad, though. There were a few perks. She jacked me up like I was a devil." Josh tells me.

I have heard tales of Josh's conquests. In a way, we have compared notes, but his praise of the experience and, by degree Megan, is astonishing.

"So, all has been forgiven?"

"I don't know. She wants some power play apology from Shay." I laugh. That won't happen. "I tried to talk with Shay about it but she was…well, Shay-like. There is no need for an apology in her eyes. It is part of our dynamic, you know?"

"Oh, I understand. It seems Megan wants to know how far under your skin she is; if she means more to you than Shay." I tell him.

"If that is her aim, it is a ridiculous question. They are completely different. Shay is one of my best friends and Megan is my girl."

"Maybe that is the point. Maybe Megan wants you to consider her your best friend AND your girl. Maybe there is no separation in those to her." I say.

"Hence my migraine," He says.

"Yeah," I say. "Well, she is in a relationship with you. What has it been, almost seven months?"

"Eight at the end of next week."

"Time flies. I have no advice then. I barely remember the last girl before Lily." I say.

"I do. Danielle Gloss. End of freshman year. Cute red-head with full lips and no ass." He laughs hard at that. "Her mom worked nights so you practically lived at her house. I remember you called me once from the laundry mat cleaning her mom's sheets." He has to stop because his laughter is choking him up. "Oh, man, that was priceless."

"Clearly you are forgetting the disgusting reason why I was there." I say.

"Oh, I remember. I never said I wasn't crass."

We both break into laughter. The situation was absurd, and we are immature enough to howl at it.

"Did she move or something? I never see her around school." I say.

"She's still there. Seventy pounds heavier and fully freckled."

"Really? That's a shame. She was a sweet girl."

"Just because someone lets you throw it in them, it doesn't make them sweet." Josh says.

"She let me crash at her place." I offer.

"Noah, she was a bitch. That whole summer she went around calling you inchy."

"Damn. I must have blocked that out. How could I not remember that?"

"I made sure you didn't hear it much. Come fall, you were with Lily and she had gained thirty pounds. She had nothing to say after that." Josh says.

"Ain't that some shit." It is weird to pause for a minute and think about how it was, who we knew before Shay and Lily.

"Yeah. You may be a relationship guy now but you got some notches on your belt first." Josh tells me.

"I guess I did."

"Sometimes I wonder about the pros and cons of being in a relationship."

"You have been with her long enough now for me to ask this question: do you love her?"

Josh shifts back and forth. He knows this should be an easy answer, but there is a lot of hesitation in him.

"I don't know. What is love? Where are my examples of love in the world?"

"Your parents are still together." I say.

"Staying together and loving each other aren't the same. I guess they are still in love, or some version of love. There is this idealistic picture of love that is full and vibrant that we are made to believe in. It is a jigsaw puzzle we never find all the pieces to."

I want to offer myself and Lily as an example but know that, under the current circumstances, I will be walking into trouble. Outside of Lily, I understand his point, though. But I also think that isn't what he is, or has been, looking for. It has been lust fulfillment and monotony-quenching. A girl or two has been hurt by this, has wanted it to be love, but overall, high school is a part of the ocean that has a concentrated amount of fish, and with such, loneliness never festers.

"I have an affinity for her." Josh continues. "But I don't think it is love. I am not bored with her, though. I am still enticed by her, drawn to her."

"Even before she lit you up?"

"Yeah. It is deeper than sex...it's just...I don't know, missing something."

"She doesn't fit." I tell him.

"What?"

"With Lily, Shay and me. She doesn't fit. Shay is too much of a free spirit to be trusted by Megan. She felt you up with Megan and her boyfriend watching. That shit turns her on. And the three of us have this little world that maybe she doesn't understand. Or maybe she does, but knows she isn't a part of it so she wants to bring you out of it."

"I guess there comes a point where choices have to be made." Josh says.

The decisions that are hanging in Josh's mind have nothing to do with Lily or me. The impediment between Josh and Megan is strictly Shay. Even with that being the case, should he choose against Shay? The fallout would reach Lily and me, and possibly dismantle the group. It is something I had never given serious thought to. We had become so seamless that it would almost be impossible not to take it for granted. I see the torture in Josh's eyes as he mulls this over. There is no piece of wisdom I can give him.

"I got your back either way." I tell him.

Josh sips his coffee and finds something outside to look at before turning back to me.

"What was your first thought when you met Shay?" Josh asks.

"Why does Lily's best friend have to be so damn sexy. I had only known Lily for maybe two weeks. It was crazy. Shay doesn't back down either. There is no control in her. I spent half the night thinking it was heading toward a three-way." I tell him.

"Wouldn't that be a time."

"Messed with my mind. She takes some getting used to."

"And then you tried to set me up with her."

"Lily wanted to. I was skeptical." I say.

"Yeah. That never panned out." Josh says, looking out the window. I see a little opening.

"Why didn't it? It seemed like it was going to a couple of times." I ask.

"It almost did a couple of times. Brink blinks just make you crave the view."

He drinks some of his coffee and sits back. There is a sadness in him. Is it regret? Longing? I am sure he doesn't even know. I want to find a way to mention New York, my sister, but the mood doesn't seem correct.

"You know me and Lily – we give each other long leaches. Remember that party last year where Lily got drunk and Jacob Reardon had his hands up the back of her shirt undoing her bra? What was that? And I am not saying I was cool with it, but hell, it didn't mean anything. It becomes part of the canvas." I tell him.

"And if I didn't happen to see them, it could have been more."

"That is how I look at this. I realize I have some deserved atonement ahead of me. I get it. But with trust comes understanding, right?"

Josh allows this to settle the discussion for a minute. Lily may be the sister figure, but I am his best friend. A brother of choice, not of blood, and somehow that makes the bond even greater. His anger at me is almost more to keep me in line so I don't cause hurt to myself. He, more than anyone else, knows how destroyed I would be if Lily and I ever ended.

"I had your back, though. I went house on Jacob. His black eye lasted a month." Josh says, proudly.

"That you did. That was a wild time." I hold back for a minute. "I will talk to her. Don't think I won't. I have bouts of being an asshole but I am sane now."

"I know that. It's all just confusing enough with the Shay/Megan thing, this was unexpected."

"Sorry to add to your migraine." I offer.

We both get another round of coffee and talk some more. I had missed a basketball practice and coach wasn't happy. It is amazing how many people put up with me. There is the side that says I missed the game-winning shot and therefore lost the game, and the other that says without my thirty points we would have been blown out. Coach will make me run some extra sprints to save face, but in the end, I know he will be cool. He knows I don't need a pep talk or a heart to heart. My teammates might be a little harder to ease over. I am a leader of the team, me and Josh, and my bailing and then missing practices is not being a leader. I know there are a few who are jealous of me and will try and make this an example of why I am not as good as people think. As I think. They will try and tear me down a few notches. I know once the game begins, I zone out and live only within those lines. I will have to earn their respect back and I have all the confidence I will.

Josh tells me more about his attempt to talk with Shay on Sunday. He was at church until four, but then he met her at the ice skating rink. In junior high, she was top five in the state. An ankle injury at thirteen changed all that and she hasn't competed since. She still visits the rink and watches the junior division practices. If you see her there, with the stillness of her watching the girls skate, you get the clearest picture of who she is. Of what is in her heart. It is not, however, the best place to garner an apology. Apparently, the conversation was quick. Josh chatted about randomness at first, but found no segway. So, when he brought it up, Shay dismissed it. When he continued to press, she blew up at him calling his relationship with Megan a sham. She called herself 'a flirty temptress' who plays the game to alleviate boredom and to get what she wants. If she thought Josh was seriously offended, she might give it some thought, but not when it comes from his 'tart of the month.' Say what you will about her attitude, but that last line is hysterical.

Halfway through my second muffin and third cup of coffee, Lily sends me a text message. "I'm out. Wanna meet up?" I notice it is after eight already. I text back, "Atomic in 20?". "K" her response. I turn to Josh.
"Gotta face the music." I tell him.
"It'll be cool." He tells me as we get up.
"Here's hoping." I tip my cup before dumping it in the trash.

It is black outside. The sky is full of clouds with no light allowed through. I can feel the moisture in the air and hope the rain holds off for at least a few more hours. From our starting point, I know Lily will get there before me. It is hard to gauge my mood. I don't grovel well. I guess it will depend on how Lily acts toward me. Fights can be smoothed over simply by looking in each other's eyes. There is a certain understanding that is conveyed there. But Josh had warned this was going to take more than merely stating all apologizes and kissing the sorrow into forgiveness.

I spot Lily's car as I pull into a space. The surroundings are more crowded than I like. Lily stands just off the curb to the left of Atomic's entrance. She is wearing jeans, a white collar shirt with a royal blue sweater over it and her black-rimmed glasses. She doesn't look like a high school girl; she looks like a graduate student. That hot intellectual chick you would meet in Manhattan. Her hair is parted to the sides and flows evenly down the sides of her face. There is no emotion in her body. She is not impatient, annoyed or bored. She is purely waiting. As I cross the street, her eyes find me. There is a hint of relief that is swiftly replaced by a sort of disconnected resolve.

"We gotta get inside before it starts raining." I say as I embrace her. Her arms lamely wrap around my back. I can feel her withholding herself.

"It is March, Noah. It's not going to rain, it's going to snow." Her tone is razor-sharp. She leads the way into the café and pauses upon entering.

"Find a seat and I will get us some drinks." I say.

"Green tea for me." Lily says before turning away.

If she is trying to be unattached, she is doing a hell of an impressive job. I know what she drinks. I can gauge her desires without having to look at her. As I order our drinks, I begin to unravel her mood. It is a mixture of hurt and pride. She doesn't deserve to be treated like she was. I don't deserve her. As much of a history that we have together, sometimes an action can cancel everything out.

I join Lily at the side table she has chosen. She takes her cup and sips it slowly. She finds every other spot to look at except for me. I need an opening. A starting point. I need something to ease into us talking.

"I'm going to quit working at the Mayor's office." I say.

"What?" She asks, surprised and confused.

"It's not for me. I did it so I could spend time with you, but we are going in different directions when we are there. I need to find something different."

"Okay." She says, unsure. "I thought you believed in what we are doing."

"It's not that I don't believe in it. I don't know how to put it. I guess it is about the level of conviction. It is about the positive impact I am having on it and how it is affecting me."

"I wasn't expecting that, but it is your choice." She says this dismissively. "Just don't not show up. Tell them. Give them some notice."

There is a shift when you are talking to Lily the person, and Lily the professional. The expectations she has are greater. The capacity for bullshit is zero and the room for second chances is narrow. That is the way she is addressing me. It is my fault for indulging that side, but I see I have fallen in that arena. I must climb out.

"Did you enjoy the concert the other day?"

Lily stares at me, a raw rage perching on her lips. "Is that a joke?" She accuses.

"No. I was just…" She cuts me off.

"Some bit of sarcasm? Because being deserted in the freezing cold at 1am by your boyfriend is not amusing. It is evil. It is deserving of hate and reproach. Is that why we are here? To be trivial about it?"

"No. I didn't mean it like that. I know what I did was an asshole move."

"I never doubted your comprehension of that. That is hardly the point."

Her anger is attaching itself to me so quickly it is hard for me to find words to respond.

"I am sorry. A million times over. I shouldn't have left. My head just went a little crazy and I had to disappear. I don't know how to explain it."

"I don't want an explanation."

"Then what do you want? What can I say or do?"

"It isn't about reasons anymore, Noah. It is about trusting you. It is about knowing I matter to you."

"I veer off, I know I do. But you are my home. You know that. You know me better than anyone. You know the details with the benefit of an outer perspective. You matter the most to me. No other girl, no one else." I tell her.

"I could care less about some random girl all over you. That isn't the part of trust I am talking about. I worry about you. I worry that there are demons that take control of you." She stops and contemplates her next words. "I think you need to think about medication." Lily says.

"What?"

"You have depression. That is why you have to disappear. That is why you don't have control of it."

"I don't think any depression I have will be alleviated by medicine. Some things you just have to sort through. You have to figure out the dark places inside yourself." I tell her.

"I agree with you, to a degree. But, Noah, what is going on with you is beyond that now."

What is she labeling me? I had thought she was going to be angry with me, not claim that I was mentally unstable. There is no emotion in her. She is not talking to me. I am not her boyfriend of almost three years. I am not the guy she lost her virginity to. I am not the one who held her when her parents almost split up. I am not the one who saved her when some random guy was about to molest her up against a wall. All of that has been stripped away. Her eyes hold no remembrance of it. They hold only a clinical diagnosis of why I was how I am. As she said, reasons no longer matter. Understanding me no longer mattered. She only wanted to 'fix' me. I look at her, dumbfounded.

"This isn't concern." I tell her. "You know me. I have bouts, but I snap back. I am here. I am coherent. I love you."

There is a layer that she peels away before speaking. I can see the Lily I know hiding in the depths of her. She is captured inside but granted a window.

"I know you love me, Noah. And I love you. But maybe at seventeen that doesn't mean anything. Or at least the meaning is in flux. Maybe we are too messed up to truly be connected."

"What does that mean?"

"I don't know what it means."

She looks away briefly out the window, then to her drink, and then back to me. For the first time, I see sadness in her. A hopeless sadness. One seemingly brought on by the last resort conclusion of our – of me – being too messed up for her to trust.

"Well, with that said, there is nothing left to say now." I stand up to leave.

"Noah, don't…"

There is a strain in her voice so I turn back and face her. There are tears in her eyes that she blinks into a stream on her face.

"I am not saying...I just want you to be okay." She says.
"I know I hurt you. I get that. I am not trying to just snap
my fingers and expect everything to be great again. I guess
we need time to work through it, you know?" Lily shakes
her head unconvincingly. "I'll see you in school tomorrow."
"Okay." Is all she says before I leave.

   Outside, the snow has started to fall. There is a thin
layer covering the street already. I brush off my car with
my hand and climb in. I am halfway down the street when
my cell phone is out and I'm dialing Shay's number. I need
a serious amount of alcohol and I do not want to be alone.
It takes a few rings before she answers.
"Well, look who is calling. Is it my birthday or something?"
"Can we cut the sarcasm, please? I am back. Yes, I went
away, but no I didn't have some sort of mental break."
"That's not what I said." She says, pulling back.
"It's what Lily said." I tell her.
"What?"
"According to her, I need to be medicated."
'That's a bit dramatic.'
"Thank you. So, what are you doing?" I say while fumbling
for my wallet. "I am about to get blitzed. I have done way
too much thinking over the last few days and need to just
lose everything in my mind."
"Perfect. My mom is out of town. Come over and crash on
the couch. I am down for some wine."
"See, now it is good to be home." I tell her.
"Lily needs some time to forgive you is all. Don't take
whatever she said too hard." Shay says.
"Not going to think about it anymore. I'll grab some booze
and head over. I should be there in half an hour."
"Sounds good. See ya soon." Her phone clicks off.

   I think about calling Josh to see if he wants to join
us, but don't. It will be less complicated without him. I am
not in the mood for complicated things. Maybe Josh was
right in believing things are black and white. Or maybe at
least *some* things are black and white.

   The road is getting pretty slick, covered in snow and
all. I get stuck behind this old man driving about ten miles
per hour. I am antsy and impatient and hardly able to enjoy
this inconvenience. It is snowing and the man is in his
nineties, so I know I have few options. If I honk my horn,

he is likely to have a heart attack. If I swerve to go around, I am likely to slide into a ditch or face a head-on collision. I am not on a main road or anything, but it certainly isn't a back road. Attempting to pass him in the other lane would be tricky, especially in these conditions. I hold tight, grinding my teeth for the few more blocks to my turn.

I head to Westgate Liquors. It is a rat hole of a place. There are always these drunks around the sidewalk, smoking. And they aren't middle age drunks either. They are old – in their sixties and seventies. Their old, wrinkly faces, smoke-stained teeth and their wretched booze breath is a cautionary tale if ever there was one. But it was the easiest place to score alcohol. They rarely carded you, and if they did, there were more than enough people loitering who would be willing to buy for you. So willing there is almost a bidding war to do it. As I drive in front of the place, I only see two people outside. They are bundled in heavy coats and wool hats. It is freezing outside but they look as though they are sweating.

"It's snowing, kid." The old man says to me. "Where's your coat?" it hadn't occurred to me that I wasn't wearing one. I still have my long sleeve Fear No Art shirt on. I shrug. "Got one in the car if I need it." I don't linger for more conversation. I walk straight in and give the guy behind the counter a slight head nod before heading toward the back where they keep the wine. I find Dove white wine, Shay's favorite, and grab two bottles. I pause and think about it, then grab another one. On my way to the front, I also pick up a bottle of whiskey.

I place the four bottles on the counter. The guy rings them up and puts them in two bags before looking at me. "I'm gonna need to see some ID." The guy is barely thirty. He has a slight beard that doesn't seem like it is from not shaving this morning, but rather from an inability to grow a proper beard. He looks at me smugly. It isn't as though he isn't going to sell me the stuff; he just wants to pull a power trip. I hate pricks like this. Without saying anything, I remove my ID from my wallet and slide it over the counter to him. He glances at it and then at me. Unconvinced, he pulls out a scanner and does a real thorough job trying to find something fake about it. He isn't going to. One of the perks I pulled off by working at the Mayor's office is getting in with people at DMV. It might not be accurate but it sure as hell is legit.

The guy gives it the twice over and then hands it back to me.

"That'll be $65." He says. I throw down the exact change, grab my bags and take off.

When I get outside, the sidewalk is empty. It has noticeably gotten colder and the snow a lot heavier. I put the bags in my back seat and take a second to look around. It is kind of a crumby strip mall and the liquor store is all that remains open. I look over the empty parking lot, watching the snow fall to the level of the hanging lights. There is no wind, which makes the snowflakes dancing all that more interesting to watch. Even without wind, their fall is not straight. They float and shift, slow down, and speed up. It is a design all of their own. The sight of this is beautiful to me. It drains out some of the shit swirling in my head. I stand there watching this for a good ten minutes before driving off. It is almost ten and I begin to get anxious about getting to Shay's.

Although Shay is a flirty temptress – by her own admission – she is also a diehard loyal friend. I know full well that as soon as she hung up the phone with me, she called Lily to tell her I was coming over. And her description would not be vague. She would tell Lily I was going to crash on her couch and that her mom wasn't home. She would inform Lily that I said I was going to get blitzed and that she was going to be drinking with me. In Lily's mind, this was probably a good thing. At least I would be in some safe haven. I wouldn't be wandering somewhere.

Shay's house is a small ranch setup. It is one floor and maybe six rooms. Her mother had gotten it in the divorce when Shay was around five. It had been in her father's family, but he didn't contest her getting it. He just wanted to get out and away as quickly as possible. He was a serious asshole. He has popped back into Shay's life a handful of times since. The people around us really can screw our heads up.

The door isn't locked, so I walk right in and lock it behind me. The house is mostly dark. I hear music coming from the living room.

"Shay?" I say as an echo.

"In here." She says. The phrase, 'in here' is usually meant as a simple undetermined direction people have come to say. But with Shay, her words are very rarely random. She uses this in a coy, 'come and find me' manner.

She is curled up on the couch when I reach the living room. The three lamps she has on creates a light haze more than illumination. Shay unravels herself when she sees me.

"Hey," She says, getting up and walking toward me. "It's good to see you." She hugs me and smiles. She is wearing black boxer shorts and a ruby red wife beater.

"I was only gone two days." I say, degrading the importance.

"Should time be the cause of me missing you or can we begin to miss someone from the tiniest bit of separation?"

I grin and cannot hold back a laugh. "I missed you too, Shay."

"Good. Now, what have you brought?" She digs in the bags and places the bottles on the table in front of the chair and couch that fill her living room. "Dove, my favorite." She does a little curtsey thank you. "I will go get a corkscrew."

As she does this, I take my shoes off and crash on the chair. I am not tired physically but feel mentally exhausted. I am glad I came over here. Shay can be conflict-driven, but she can also be the most chill person. And that is her mood now. I need to just exist and laugh a little. To stop all the introspection and remember some happy times.

"I didn't think we were going to need glasses." She says, handing me the corkscrew and taking a seat on the couch. I move over next to her and take one of the wine bottles.

"I bought the personal sized bottles so there is no need for glasses."

"So nice of them to make personal size a liter these days." She jokes.

"Nice indeed." I say, handing her the bottle I just opened. I open the bottle of whiskey next and have taken a gulp before Shay finishes her first sip.

"Wow. You aren't fooling around, huh?" Shay says.

"Absolutely not." I tell her. "Afraid you can't keep up?"

"Do you remember the first time we drank together?" Shay asks. "You thought I was some sort of prissy, can't hold her liquor girl and we drank to a stalemate before we both passed out." She starts cracking up before she can finish her sentence. That was an insane fall night, the first time the four of us spent at Handley Lake. It was September but you could have mistaken it for mid-July. We played 'I never' with bottles of vodka. Lily quit ten minutes in and Josh lost interest quickly. Shay and I finished our bottles and kept going with Lily and Josh's. Once those were gone, we dug out the secret reserve: a bottle of whiskey Shay had stolen from her mom. We took turns downing that, casting off the original game to see who can stay conscious the longest. When that bottle was done, we called it a tie and then we both passed out.

"First of all," I start. "I never thought you were prissy. There is many an adjective, but prissy sure isn't one of them." I start laughing as I remember. "And, of course, I remember that. Well, I guess it is amazing that I remember that. That was the worst hangover I think I've ever had." Shay cracks up even harder from that.

"Me too! My head completely *throbbed* for two days! I swore off alcohol."

"Yeah and that lasted what…"

"Till the next time we saw a bottle." We say in unison. That damn near puts us on the floor laughing. I gather myself to take a few more swigs of whiskey, and Shay starts pounding down the wine.

My mind flares to Evan and Megan, but I don't want to bring them up. Shay might be thinking about Lily, but I know she isn't going to get into it tonight. Shay probably has the best grip on situations. She can pin the cause of something pretty good if you ask her to. But I am not going to. Not now. Not tonight. I catch myself thinking, so I drink more whiskey and open another bottle of wine. Shay has finished up her bottle, so I open the last wine bottle too. Shay puts on her favorite CD and we sort of lean back away from each other, drifting. We speak in short sentences that aren't invitations to conversations, rather they are random thoughts that appear in our heads. I catch myself closing my eyes, then look over to Shay. Her arm dangles over the couch. The wine bottle has dropped to the floor. The little remaining glides back and forth the side of the tipping bottle, like a wave trapped in a pool. I finish what is left in mine and ease it to the floor. I curl myself into the back of the couch and fall asleep.

I wake up the next morning to the sound of the shower. I stretch and check the time: six-thirty. I head into the kitchen and slightly shudder at the fact there is no orange juice. It is my coffee. My start to the day. I settle for an orange on the counter and sit back down on the couch. Shay comes in soon after. She is dressed for school but isn't done getting ready. Her hair is still damp and falls in every direction. Her face is makeup free. She has a black pencil skirt and a red shirt with black stitching along the seams. The girl has style, I have to admit.

"Morning." She says.

"Morning."

"There are towels in the bathroom whenever you want to take your shower."

"I'm good, thanks."

"Noah, you need a shower. There is nothing charismatic about being rank."

"Okay. I will accept that. But even if I felt compelled to take a shower, I have no clean clothes." I tell her.

"Not a problem. Evan left some clothes here I can give you. They might be a little bit big on you, he is pretty jacked, but they will do." She teases.

"Yeah. I will have to do a few pushups before I put them on."

"There you go. That is the motivation I like to hear. I'll go get them."

I head to the bathroom and strip off my shirt. I cup water in my hands and splash my face. It is cold and feels good. I look up and see my eyes have fairly deep black circles around them, almost like I have black eyes. I splash more water on my face, but that doesn't wash them away. Shay comes in and hands me Evan's clothes.

"Hey, what's up with my eyes?" I ask her.

"Popped blood vessel, you got in a fight, or maybe it is because you never sleep. I bet that has something to do with it."

"Do I always look like this?"

"No...sometimes you look ugly." She teases. "Now, get your vain ass in the shower. I wanna leave in like twenty minutes. Wanna just take my car?"

"Sure." She leaves and closes the door. I strip off the rest of my clothes and get in the shower.

Evan's jeans and t-shirt actually fit me pretty well. On the way to school, Shay stops at A Coffee Place, and we each get a flatbread sandwich, and I get some orange juice. Arriving at school, the parking lot is pretty full but we find a spot at the end. As we get out the car, the first bell rings and all the kids start to scatter inside. Josh sees us, though. He is talking to Rob and Reef, who both give us a big wave and then take off before we reach them. We barely say hi to Josh before Shay is pulled away by Emily Jackson, a blonde sophomore who idolizes her. Josh waits until they are out of earshot before asking, "So, how was the talk?" Josh asks.

"Sickening." I tell him. "It is going to take time before we congeal again."

"I told ya she took this pretty hard."

"I know. We'll get beyond it."

The second bell rings, giving us three minutes to get to class. We are halfway up the steps when my cell rings. I pull it out in motion and then stop.

"It's my father." I say, which stops Josh who is a little ahead of me. "Hello?" I say, thinking he dialed my number by mistake.

"Noah...we got a call from Waterbury. It's your grandmother. She died last night." He stops waiting for me to respond. I don't. "Your mom and I are heading down tonight. The funeral is the day after tomorrow. If you want to come, we will get you a room at our hotel." Silence again. "So, just let me know." He finishes.

"Yeah, no," I stammer. "I will be there."

"Okay. I will have them leave a key at the desk when you get down." He hangs up as do I. Numbness runs through my spine, my mouth goes dry. I look to Josh who is waiting, curious as hell.

"I am so not going to school."

Seven

The Life of a Funeral

I have said it before – my family isn't close. I have not seen my grandfather in over two years, and even that was brief. He stopped on his way to some convention or something. I wasn't told about this at all and just happened to walk in as he was leaving. I don't want to say there was no emotion in him, or that our relationship is simply indifferent. I think it is mainly that we never had time to grow any attachment. Even when I was younger, when Jess was around, my grandparents were off in their world and we were in ours. Birthdays and Christmases were the only times my grandparents showed up. I understand how to live in limbo but am ill-acquainted with dealing with absolutes. With endings. My grandparents weren't there, but it was understood where they were. And now, my grandmother wasn't. The reality of that hasn't quite sunk in. I am not sure what I feel about it. It is something else thrown in the stew of my mind. I know I have to go down to the funeral and say goodbye, to have that feeling of goodbye.

Josh insists on coming with me. A phone call to his parents, a text to Megan and a stop at our houses for clothes, and we are good to go. I call Lily but get her voicemail. Of course it goes to voicemail…she is in class. I have a reason for disappearing this time. A legit reason that I can explain to her. I fear, though, that this will make things worse between us. Even a slight cut can be deadly when old wounds are still flowing. I leave her a quick message stating why I am not at school and where I will be for the next day or so. Being able to tell her that Josh is coming along gives my actions some credibility. She should understand.

It is more than a two-hour drive to the funeral home, to the town my father grew up in. The place where his two brothers and their families still live. My dad is the baby of the family, and from what I remember, he was picked on and belittled by his older siblings. In this kind of situation, there is a weird loyalty I feel toward him – someone who I go back and forth hating. This is enemy country for the both of us. A battle we both feel compelled to subject ourselves to. Is it an act of love, or respect for my grandmother and his mother? I think it is more an act of respect for the idea of it. This is the proper thing: to mourn the loss of family. Even when there is distance and turmoil, at the end, they are remembered and mourned for.

An hour into our drive, Josh gets a call.

"It's Shay. I'll put it on speaker." He answers the phone and extends it in-between us.

"Hey, Shay."

"Josh, where are you?"

"Why do you ask a question you already know the answer to?"

"Damn, Josh. I am trying to *verify* where you are. Is that better?"

"A little." Josh is clearly enjoying having this control. "I am on my way to Connecticut."

"Is Noah with you?"

"Why don't you ask him?" Josh tells her. There is a pause as Shay realizes she is on speaker.

"You know I hate it when you put me on speaker." Shay complains.

"And don't think that's the reason I do it," Josh jokes.

"I take it Lily got my message." I chime in. There is a pause. We can hear the sucking inhalation and the exhale; the stuttered breathing Shay has when she is smoking. "Are you smoking in the girl's room, Shay? That's getting to be quite the bad habit if you need a fix before lunch."

Her response is measured. Her thoughts carefully crafted, fed through a filter, and then revealed.

"You left a very succinct message." Shay tells me. "How is anyone supposed to be mad at you for going to your grandmother's funeral?" She doesn't say this as sarcasm, but rather with the inflection that what I did was somehow unfair. That I had covered up my selfishness with an untouchable excuse.

"So, Lily is pissed?" I ask.

"C'mon, Noah. It is not about being pissed. Or hurt. It is about you descending."

Josh quickly ends the call. He does this before the anger has a chance to rise in me. He knew that would trigger it. Shay knew it too. I guess in her mind it needed to be said. The connotation is that I am heading to a place away from them. That I am changing into something they do not like. It is sort of like when Josh jokes that I am going to hell. That I am a sinner beyond reproach. But with Josh, I do not believe in his condemnation. With Shay – in this instance – I guess maybe I do.

At that moment, Josh turns his phone off and I follow his idea. We turn the radio on and keep the conversation minimal. The funeral home is right off the highway, so finding it is easy. It is depressing to see it vacant. Tomorrow, the parking lot will be full. All these people I barely know will be milling about. The street traffic will be delayed and the scent of flowers will be overwhelming. But now, the building is lifeless, void of emotion. We pass it and find the hotel my dad set me up in. We check in and drop our bags in the room before heading to where everyone is gathering.

The function room in the hotel is oddly ornate, with high ceilings, dangling chandlers, and polished wood floors. It is offsetting to see this side of my family: the rich side. I knew my grandparents had some money, but it seems as though everyone here bathes in diamonds. I am wearing clean black cargo pants with a nice dress shirt, but am seriously outclassed by the tailor cut suits that surround me. Josh blends. He has dress pants, a shirt and tie. I see my parents sitting at a table to the middle of the left side corner. I wanted to come. To show some sort of condolence to a mass of people that know me by name at best, by affiliation at worst. I had not thought things through enough to understand what the events would entail, and that sitting with my parents would be part of it. Thank god Josh is with me. This isn't isolation. This isn't disappearing.

This is walking into a room of faked affinity and phony interest. Josh and I are standing at the entrance when I turn to him and move inward. He follows my gaze to my parents and walks with me there.

My parents are listening to a guy with a very full, yet groomed beard as Josh and I sit down to the empty seats next to them.

"Who knew hell would come with hor d'oeuvres." I say as a joke, but I can't hide the truth of the feeling.

"See, I just never thought you had any family because you never mention them. But here they are."

"Yeah. All strung out in pearls."

'That's better than being strung out from other things." Josh laughs. I just nod in agreement.

We turn away from the table and glance around the room. I know there has to be a few people I remember if I see them. Our entrance had not disturbed the flow of the room. We walked through the middle of it, bumping elbows with people but no one even said 'excuse me'. If I had not seen my parents, I would have thought this wasn't the correct room. I stay idle for a minute, waiting for my parents to turn their attention to me. When they don't, I feel more stupid than surprised.

My eye catches a line of yellow that settles a few tables away from us. My attention is drawn to look up. A girl my age stands talking to someone. I am not sure if the image of her is more striking because of the lack of color in the room; everyone else is dressed in black. She wears a marigold dress. It could be contributed to the dullness around us, I am not sure.

"Dude, who is that?" Josh says, voicing the same awe I had.

"I don't know. I thought I had made it clear I have no idea who any of these people are."

"You gotta find out. Go be social. You are the grandson. You have the most direct reason to be here. Everyone here should know who you are."

"I would bet they do – we are a very indifferent family." Almost on queue after I say that, a man, who I vaguely realize is my uncle, approaches us.

"Noah, you came!" He is happy to see me. He is also drunk.

"Uncle James, how are you?" This is a stupid question to ask at a gathering formed by the death of a relative, but I can't think of anything else to say.

"My mother died, Noah! Who the hell good could I be? Without sounding ungracious, at least?"

Uncle James is a Human Resource manager for some drug company. He is the shortest of the three brothers, but makes the most money and has a fashion sense that makes you doubt his heterosexuality.

"So, how long has it been? A good five years I'd say."

"Yeah. It has been a while." I agree. "Have you seen grandpa?"

"Yeah." He turns to the crowd and scans it. "There he is, second table on the other side of the room." I follow his direction and find my grandpa rigidly sitting surrounded by people.

"Isn't he popular?" I quip, not meaning it to be said aloud. My uncle looks at me sternly for a moment before bursting out in laughter.

"The funny thing is, he hates this attention. He really hates it. Who the hell are half of these people anyway, you know?" My uncle grabs a drink off the table and downs it. "That's why I came over here. Chris' and my family are here, well not the kids, but our wives. But beside you and your parents, who else needs to be here?"

It is a fair question. One that I thought was only tripping inside my head. There is an inherent predisposition of being close to family that has always eluded me. It is not as though I am devoid of the desire to be. When my sister got sick, it went from separation to isolation. I had no choice, and they made no effort to see me. In my mind, it was simply the way it was. I have learned not to regret what I have been denied.

Josh sort of pokes me. He sees the opening.

"Hey, by the way, who is that girl in the yellow dress?" Uncle James deliberates for a minute.

"She's the Halprin's granddaughter. The Halprin's are neighbors of your grandparents. I hear she is some sort of junior tennis pro. And that is what I am talking about: why the hell would she want to come to this?"

A short look at Josh and I know he has the same thought as I do. She has come to interject verve into the dismal. A bit of eye candy for the grieving. A girl has to have a certain disposition to want to be in this type of situation.

I see my grandfather excuse himself from the group that surrounded him, then leave the room. I tell Josh I am going to hit the bathroom and follow him. I was fourteen the last time I spoke to my grandfather. I was barely five-foot-three and a hundred pounds. I am now six-foot-three and a hundred and ninety pounds. Will he even recognize me? It takes me a minute to recall his first name. He is grandpa – that is all I need, but that somehow falls short of the context I need to speak to him. I catch up to him outside. He stands on the line where grass becomes a sidewalk. He seems at peace in his solitude. That is the reason he is here. To take a breath away from the chaos of the room. I am less than three feet away from him when I speak.

"Grandpa?"

From this distance, I see he is smoking. He takes another drag on his cigarette before shifting his body to look back at me. He observes me for a minute before addressing me.

"Noah? Is that you?" He turns completely toward me and walks up to me. He takes a half-step close enough to me as though he was going to hug me, before settling on an arm's length space. "My god, you are all grown up." He extends his hand and I shake it. He takes another drag on his cigarette, and pulls out his pack. "Would you like one?" He offers.

"No, thanks. I don't smoke." I tell him.

"Good. Don't start. It leads nowhere good." He pauses and takes another drag.

"Suppose it helps, though, to relax you."

"Maybe it did once. Now, it only holds me hostage. Your grandmother hated me smoking. She almost forced me to quit three times. But I never did." I let his words about his wife float a good distance away before responding.

"I am sorry about her passing." I am so unsure of what to say. I feel as though I have offended him. But when I look to his face, his expression hasn't changed.

"Me too." That is all he says. We stand there, side by side, my mind is filled with thoughts but no clarity to speak them.

"So, you have turned into quite the athlete I hear."

I don't know how to react to this, at first. His knowing that I play basketball is not the surprising part. The fact that he and my parents had a conversation about me in general is something so absent from what I had considered a possibility, it unbalances me.

"Pretty good, I guess."

"Good enough to get a scholarship. Albany State makes sense. You were always close to your sister, it fits that you would want to be near her."

I can't really handle Jessica being brought in the conversation. Two long shivers course through me. I pull my eyes tight without shutting them. It occurs to me that anyone that knows me, or knows of me, in that room would also know of my sister. This is my family. Even if it is not discussed, it is still known. I gather myself and look back to my grandfather. I can't read his look but I know it has changed since I looked at him last. I feel shriveled standing beside him. I have to say something. I have to overcome the barriers of what I keep inside me.

"Yeah." Is all I can give. I feel slightly reclaimed but remain still.

My grandfather takes one last deep drag before putting his cigarette out on the sidewalk. There is a strength in him that I envy. He is unshaken dealing with the death of his wife. From all these people wanting his attention during his grief. I want to ask him if he internalizes it or has found some way of processing it. Before I can –

"I better get back and attend to my guests." My grandfather tells me. He starts to leave and gets ten feet away before turning back to me. "It was good talking with you." This is said with the kind of sincerity that did not need the sentiment to be echoed to make it valid. I say nothing; I stay still. I wait until he has disappeared back into the hotel before I follow him.

I linger at the edge of the function room, giving myself a moment to survey the room. My parents haven't moved and are blissfully engaged in conversation. From this distance, they appear happy, peaceful. We try and build up our lives, but sometimes, they are built up without our direction or control. We become lost in the architecture which holds us in. Sometimes we all need a respite, an escape. Watching my parents now, I begin to doubt the mantra, "it gets better". The older you get, the harder it becomes to loosen life's grip.

My eyes wander and I find Josh. He has found an opening and has his mouth inches away from the ear of the marigold beauty. She laughs and smiles. Bites her lower lip and pushes him slightly. Josh has a way. In less than twenty minutes, he has this girl eating out of his hand. He spots me watching him and comes over. The girl looks over to me, put out, wanting to know the cause of this interruption. I turn my head, hopefully before she can read my face.

"Hey, man, you bailed on me." Josh says.

"Sorry. Got some air with my grandfather."

"And?"

"And nothing. There is no story to tell." I say.

"Fine. An antidote than."

"He smokes."

"That's better. I know that isn't your only thought on talking to someone who you haven't see in what–?"

"Three years." I tell him.

"Yeah."

"Probably right. Haven't processed it yet."

"That's fair." Josh says.

"Besides, you seem to be the one purporting intrigue."

Josh gives one of his proud of himself smiles.

"Her name is Emily. A senior. Boyfriendless since the summer." Josh tells me.

"Wasteful in a place where the median age is fifty-five."

"Then there is us. And you already had your indiscretion."

Josh speaks with a hyped up, horny tone. I know he did not even consider him saying that would bother me. I blink the words away.

"Not to be a cockblocker, but we are sharing a room. And if I do need a grieving process, it is not going to involve hearing how hard you can make a girl cum."

Josh laughs wildly at this. I had said it as a half-joke, but find myself glad he took it solely as one.
"We have spent enough time in close enough proximity for you to have a good idea anyway." He says, laughing, "And, of course, Megan might object to any play or foreplay away from her."

Josh pulls out his phone and starts typing. When he finishes, he hands me the phone. It reads:

> *Megan, I am sorry. We have to break up. There is this beautiful girl wearing a marigold dress that I really want to fuck, but will feel bad if we don't break up first.*

"You're such an asshole." I say, giving him back the phone.
"That covers it, right?"
"Erase the message."
"What are we without our impulses?"

He waits for me to answer. I don't.
"Dead."
"This isn't the time to quote Shay." I tell him.
"I am gonna do it." He turns his body away from me and looks back with a wide, devious smile. I take a swipe at the phone but he is quicker. I step toward him, and with a second attempt, I grab it and twist it out of his hand. I go to erase it the message when I see it has been sent.
"It was sent." I tell him.
"What?" He takes the phone back and stirs with anxiousness. "Shit, man, I was just goofing around." A sorrow that turns to melancholy, and then reflectiveness, courses through his body. "That kinda sucks."
"Blame me. Immature joke." I say.

Emily, the marigold beauty, has waited idly long enough and starts walking toward us. Maybe every funeral needs a dash of beauty to help invoke life.
"I could just let it go and see where this leads." Josh tells me just as Emily gets within earshot.

She enters our space with the ease of someone with the ability to walk through walks. With the self-confidence that no barriers could restrict her. She looks at us as individuals, without favoritism. Neither of us speak but that does not distract her.

"Hi, I'm Emily." She says to me. She holds her arm out to me and waits.

"I'm Noah." I go to take her hand, but she pulls it back.

"Are you Phyllis' grandson?" She asks. I hesitate a little.

"Yeah."

She embraces me tightly, yet moves her body fluidly against me.

"I am so sorry for your loss. We all loved her."

I am taken aback. By someone telling me that I lost something, and by someone saying that they loved the object of that loss. I am unsure how to respond.

"Emily works at the hospital. She took care of your grandma." Josh explains.

"I volunteer." She says this in a tone protesting the compliment. "I have lived next to your grandparents my entire life." Emily tells me.

I nod. I am not sure if I had settled into the environment, or if after a certain amount of time in a situation, your mind offers clarity by default. My eyes drift back across the room. I am the only grandchild here. My uncles are here with their wives who are drunk and drinking. My grandfather holds court with a mass of people around him. He seems bored but accommodating. It occurs to me that he is the only one with any real cause to mourn. He just lost his wife. They had been together for forty years. I think of the connection I have with Lily and that has only been developing for less than three years. I can't comprehend the idea of spending forty years with someone. You can throw words around like, "Forever", "Always" or "As long as we live", but I consider those to be kind of abstract. Maybe it is better that way, though. Maybe time is meant to be understood only when looking back. I think back to the last few weeks. I have an understanding of what a dick I have been. Only I have been rationalizing it. Justifying it. Having to justify something is denying the truth of it. You do it because you can't accept the truth. And until you can, nothing changes.

My attention switches back to Josh and Emily. Josh seems like he could tell I had disappeared and is holding a conversation with one person and one shell. Emily doesn't seem to realize. She laughs and smiles at Josh. I have seen many girls behave this way in front of him; swoon at his charm. But Emily is too beautiful to need flattery to impress Josh. Maybe that is the game she is playing. If only for a few days we can fit into any mold. Maybe that is the release some people need.

"You up for it?" Josh asks. I steady my focus and look at him.

"What?"

"It's only ten. You up for some pool?" Josh asks.

As I look at him, it is easy to tell what he wants my answer to be.

"Nah. I'm beat. I'm gonna crash soon."

"Are you sure?" Emily reaches out and grasps right above my elbow. She presses and pulls just enough for me to realize what she is doing. In this moment, I see that Josh hasn't secured her yet. A newer, clearer reason why she is here presents itself to me. The longer it stays in my mind, that more sense it makes. She wants to feel. To have the sorrow and anger climax and feel some sort of purge. Her eyes are searching mine. With all the interest she has shown Josh, she still holds all the control. He wants her and she knows it. It is obvious she wants someone too. The part that had been missing is that she is indifferent to who satisfies that want. I can only imagine how relieved she is that Josh and I are here. The other options in this room would require alcohol and ED meds.

"Yeah, I'm sure. You have fun." I tell them.

"Okay. We're out then. Call me if you need anything."

"Thanks. I'll be fine."

Emily hugs me in a 'this is your last chance' kind of way. I have to shift my hips.

"I'll see you tomorrow." She tells me before leaving. The bond her words held are a little unsettling to me. In this setting, though, I suppose they are accurate.

With Josh and Emily gone, I look back into the room. I stare at all the people, my family, and a sense of emptiness begins to fill me. My mind plays tricks on me, giving me resentment that I don't have a functional family. Now I am being taunted by that notion. Here is my family, functioning. And I am on the outskirts. It was easier to believe in an unattached family than the now appearing truth that they are attached, just not to me.

Before my mind twists itself back into the will of being medicated, I leave. I head up to my room and sit on the edge of my bed, staring at the carpet, taking sips from a bottle of water. I try and work up the courage to call Lily. I don't know what I want to say to her or what I want her to say to me. I just want to hear her voice. If I listen closely, I can hear everything is going to be alright. I finally pull out my phone and dial her number.

"Yeah?" Shay answers.

"Fuck me." I say, frustratingly.

"Not likely." Shay says.

I inhale and try to relax. If Shay is in a mood, there could be riddles and hoops to get through.

"Put Lily on. Please?"

"She doesn't want to talk to you."

I grit my teeth.

"Did she say that?"

"I am paraphrasing."

"C'mon, Shay. I know it's fun to torture me. I've been a jackass. I get that. I just want to talk to her."

"That's the thing. What you want doesn't matter."

"Are you choosing sides now?" I ask, wary of her answer. There is a long pause. I caught her off guard. Then,

"Hi," Lily says. My nerves flare up again.

"Lily." Is all I can manage. The word trails off and leaves silence.

"I am sorry to hear about your grandmother. I wish I could have met her."

"Yeah. It's been weird to be down here. I am so removed from family that I feel out of place. An abstract painting in a gallery of portraits."

"At least Josh is with you." I laugh. "What?"

"I am sure Josh's intentions were pure, but he has become distracted."

"Meaning?"

"He is hooking up with this blonde girl who was my grandma's neighbor." I tell her.

"What?" There is no hiding her surprise.

"Yeah."

"What about Megan?" She asks.

"They sorta broke up."

"What?!" She repeats. "When?"

"Something like an hour ago." I tell her.

I hear her relaying this to Shay.

"You guys are quite a pair." She says, full of judgement.

"I am sorry for bailing. Again."

"Yeah. You're doing that a lot lately." She says.

"I'm not sure why, but I felt a need to come here. But I did. I hadn't seen her in years. I haven't seen any of these people in years. If at all." I tell her.

"Noah, I understand you needing to go to your grandmother's funeral. Your apology makes me seem heartless." She says.

"No, of course I don't think that." I stop. I know what I want to ask, but am not sure how to phrase it without sounding too vulnerable. "Then why are you mad at me?"

Her sigh is audible. I wish I could see her face, so I could interrupt her thoughts. I hear Shay say something in the background but can't make out the words. I wait for what feels like an hour.

"Lily?"

"I am here." Her voice is somber. "I was thinking." Another pause. "Because you went with Josh." Lily says.

"What?" I say, confused.

"To Connecticut. You didn't even give me a chance. You were gone before I knew it. I realize that the four of us are almost interchangeable, but I thought there was a distinction."

"There is." I tell her. "Of course there is. Josh was with me when my dad called and he insisted on coming. I didn't choose him over you. I didn't choose anything."

"No. You reacted. You didn't consider anything. In that moment of impulse, you thought of nothing. You used to think of me." Lily tells me.

Her words pinball in my mind. The harshness in what it means, and the truth that she knew was unwavering. I sit comatose.

"I have been unraveling. I know this. But, Lily, you are always in my mind. I called you." I say this in defense.

"That made it worse. It was a petty bullshit call to cover yourself when you miss a curfew." She is losing her sadness and anger is creeping in.

"Lily, you know that's not what I meant by it."

"That doesn't change what it was." She says.

"I suppose not." I say, defeated.

There is another long pause. I check to see if she disconnected the call. She hasn't. I think I should.

"I didn't want to say that over the phone. I know you are dealing with a lot."

"Yeah." Is all I can say at first. "I will be back tomorrow night. We can talk then."

"How late?" Lily asks.

"Not sure, eight or nine."

"That's too late."

"Oh." I stutter.

"Sometime Wednesday." Lily says.

"Yeah. Okay. Sure."

"All right. Bye." I hear a quick beep before the call goes dead.

Left in the stillness of the room, the depth of the conversation begins to soak in me. I cannot remember the last time Lily used 'bye' to end a conversation with me. I know I analyze to the point of exhaustion, but the details, what the word choice is, what is not said, is how we decode subtext. I search the room for a mini bar but don't find one. I think for a split second about calling Josh. I know he is occupied, though. I change into sweats and a t-shirt; put my sneakers on and head to the elevator.

When I get outside, I turn left and start to walk. After a block, I start to jog. By the third block, I am in full run. The further I run, the faster I go. I turn right and catch one last glance at the hotel. I am lost in my surroundings and feel all the better for it. If there are any thoughts in me, they are buried deep in my subconscious. Let it work itself out there, let them unwind there.

The night is cold. I run for a while before I develop a sweat, and longer still before that sweat starts dripping in my eyes. I wipe it away with my wrist and keep running. I stride long and quick. I feel my breathing get heavy but I don't slow down. This is what I have been waiting for. I run until my throat clenches up. I stop and hurl in the street. I cannot stop it. I throw up everything I had eaten and wrenched at the pain of my body searching for more. I spin away from the street and collapse on a lawn. I work to control my breath and still feel nauseous. I lie on my back and put my hands over my head. It takes a few minutes for me to start feeling normal again. I stand up and walk in a long, uneven circle. I look around and find a street sign. I Google a map back to the hotel and start back.

It is almost two when I arrive at the hotel. On my way to the elevator, I pass the hotel bar. A sign on the door says, 'closed', but I can see someone inside. On second glance, I can make out who it is. It's my dad. He sits at the bar, alone. A bottle of whiskey on the counter beside him. I test the door and it opens easily. I walk in tentatively and sit down beside him. He turns to me before I am settled.

"Noah. Can't sleep either?"

"Yeah." I say. Not sure if he is drunk. It was a simple thing to say, yet seemed out of place coming from him.

He looks me over.

"You're soaked." He observes.

"I went for a run."

He looks me over again. It is the sort of concentration directed toward me I can't remember having. "Feel better?"

I think about it for a second.

"I do."

He nods and takes another sip.

"Where is your friend?" He asks.

"Enjoying the spoils." I tell him.

"What does that mean?"

'Well," I hesitate. "The simplest answer is that he is playing pool with a girl from the gathering."

"Emily?" He says.

"You know her?"

"Of her. She was kind of hard to miss, wasn't she?" I can't help but agree. "Think what you want of me, but I am not blind. And you went for a run because of," He squints his eyes. "Lily. Right? That's her name?"

"Yeah. That's her."

"Right." He nods his head in agreement with himself.

From behind the counter, he pulls out an empty glass and pours whiskey in it and slides it to me.

"Is it worse to let your child drink, or deny him it in situations such as this?" I don't think he said it as a question, expecting an answer. But as I take a sip, he is still looking at me. I swallow and compose myself.

"It is best to know which will help the child the most." I tell him, taking another sip. A wide smile comes across his face. "That sounds right." He says. I am not sure if he is smiling because he is proud of himself for making what he perceives as the correct option, or because he was pleased with my insight.

He goes back to his drink and me to mine. I finish just ahead of him and he quickly grabs the bottle to refill us, but I stop him.

"Not for me. I am going to try and rest." He nods his understanding. I stand up and head for the door. I stop at the doorframe and look back at my dad. The words, "It was nice talking with you," are on the tip of my tongue, but I don't speak them. I go to the elevator and then to my room.

When I get to my room, I find Josh asleep. I check the time and find it is after 3am. I would have been surprised if he had slept over at Emily's place. There is physical intimacy and emotional intimacy. It is much easier to be slutty with physical intimacy.

I go into the bathroom and put the water to the shower on. I strip off my clothes and wait for the water to heat up. Stepping in, I stand directly under the nozzle and allow the water to fall through me. It relaxes my exhaustion to the point where I catch myself drifting off. I shut off the shower, put some clean boxers on and slide into bed. As I do, I hear Josh turn over.

"Where have you been?" Josh asks.

"That sounds accusing."

"It's almost four."

"I couldn't sleep. I went for a run. Are you done with your devil's business?" I ask him.

"Left her under an hour ago."

My eyes are closed, mind half asleep.

"And?" I say in the midst of a yawn.

"Good times." He turns over and pulls the covers up. I wait for him to elaborate, but he doesn't. I am too tired to ask for more. I close my eyes and go to sleep.

I wake the next day to Josh still sleeping. I check the time – it's almost eleven. The service starts at noon. I lie prone on my bed and stretch the length of my body, then sit up and swing my legs off the side. I sit there slouched, trying to find the will to stand up. I don't. I grab my phone from the night table and find a new text message from Shay.

"Save some strength for when you get home. You are going to need it." It reads.

"Nice way to wake up." I say to myself, standing. I open the shades. Outside, there is a line of cars. My parents and grandfather are at the head of them, giving instructions. I was not requested to be with them. It was never implied with the option of coming down here. But looking at them, I feel I should be. My place is with them. Only, I am not. I am watching them from a window wondering why I am not standing beside them.

I get my duffel bag, throw it on the bed and pull out a pair of cargo pants and a button-up shirt. This is as dressed up as I get.

"Hey, Josh, wake up. We have to leave soon."

Josh slightly lifts his head as he hears this, but it takes him a minute to sit up.

"Damn I am still tired." His voice is strained as he starts to wake up. "What time is it?"

"Eleven. We have to be there at noon." My pants are on and I start to button my shirt up. Josh stands.

"Do you think Emily will be there?" I stare at him, amused.

"She didn't tell you last night?" I ask.

"Somehow, it wasn't mentioned."

"Actually, it was, and she is. Blood wasn't flowing to your memory, I guess."

"Yeah. My memory was filled with other details. I'm gonna take a shower." He takes his bag and goes to the bathroom. "Give me fifteen minutes."

I finish getting ready and sit on the edge of the bed. I debate whether or not I should reply to Shay's text. I have nothing to say and no way to express that. I put the phone in my pocket and collect my things. Josh comes out of the bathroom fully dressed, bag in hand.

"All set."

We leave the room, check out of the hotel and head to the funeral home. The parking lot is full when we get there, so we find a spot on a side street. It is just noon, but walking in, I feel late. It is a medium sized room, filled with people. I see the coffin and a big picture of my grandma at the front. In the first row, my uncles, parents and grandfather sit. Again, I think I should be there with them. I don't think I would be able to walk to them if the room was empty. In front of all these people, I know I can't. I hang to the back.

"There she is." Josh whispers to me. I follow his gaze and see Emily walking toward us. Today, she has chosen a black dress over marigold. As I watch her, it occurs to me that she doesn't need anything extra to bring her attention. It would come to her no matter what she is wearing. She passes Josh and centers herself to me.

"Hey," Josh says, slightly put out. She turns to him but coyly doesn't look at him.

"Noah." is all she says before hugging me. She looks me in the eyes. Hers are full of water. They overflow bringing streaks of water down her face. There is pain in her. A pain caused by a sadness I know I should be feeling. As she wipes the tears from her cheek, I try to focus on the sorrow in me. I try to show that sorrow, but I have nothing. She looks at me as she chokes back her tears, confused.

"Sorry." I say. "I am full of sand." I tell her, which confuses her more.

"Are there any seats left?" Josh asks, addressing Emily. She looks at him, not sure how to shake what I said.

"No. I don't want to sit. I just want to stand here." I tell them.

"Okay." Josh says, leaning against the wall. I do the same. Emily wiggles her way in-between us.

The Pastor is the first one who talks. He reads some Bible verse and says something about a better place. My grandfather is the only other person to speak. There are no songs. At the end, I make sure we are out before the crowd. Josh lingers behind me. I hear Emily say goodbye to me but I don't say anything back. I reach the car and lean against the door. I see Josh and Emily talking. Even from where I am standing, it looks awkward. Josh tries to be engaged but Emily stands there indifferent. He goes to kiss her but she turns away, so he gets her cheek. As he walks toward me, he looks distressed.

"So, you get her number?"

"Yeah," He says glumly."

"And this isn't happy?"

"I don't know." He says. "I am having fucker's remorse."

He says this with a straight face but I burst out laughing.

"What?"

"I can't believe you just said that. That was one of the stupidest, yet funniest things you have ever said." Josh thinks on it and smiles.

"Fine. You knew what I meant though."

"I guessed what you were feeling before I asked."

"Three-hour drive is a long way to drive for a booty call."

"And Megan?"

"It might be repairable."

"Doesn't sound like you want that."

"I guess we'll see. What's the agenda now?"

"I want to wait for it to clear out, then say goodbye to my grandfather and parents. Then we hit the road."

"All right. I'm gonna crash in the car."

"Okay. I'll just be a few minutes." Josh climbs in the car and I head back to the funeral home.

Walking in again, I only see scattered people. It takes me a minute but I find my parents and grandfather in a side room. I step to the edge of the room and wait for them to notice me. My mom sees me first and their talking stops. Their bodies roll into a line as they face me. I am nerved by this and it takes me a few seconds to regain myself.

"I am going to head home. I just wanted to say goodbye." I say, stepping into the room. My grandfather walks to me with his hand stretched out.

"Thank you for coming. It means a lot." I shake his hand and he pats my shoulder. My parents don't say anything.

"Okay." I nod. "Bye."

"Goodbye, Noah." My grandfather says. I turn and leave.

My head is cloudy as I reach the car. I get in the driver's side and pull out on the road. That was awkward. Not just the goodbye, but the last two days. Family is a strange sort of mirror to yourself. You can see how your pieces have been arranged in someone else, and what the picture looks like.

"So, you glad you went?" Josh asks as we get on the highway.

"Yeah. It was good to be here. Jess would have liked it. She loved the family getting together."

"Who?" Josh's question has no intensity in it, but my face flushes with panic. My mind races with ways of taking back what I said. I have nothing. Josh can sense my anxiousness.

"Noah, who is Jess?" I look at him, mute. I don't want to have this conversation. I never wanted to have this conversation.

Eight

The Trick is to Keep Breathing

The next morning, my phone wakes me. It's Josh. He tells me he is leaving his house and should be at mine in fifteen minutes. I sit up in bed and stay there. I had explained everything to Josh. About Jess. About why she was in the hospital. About why I never talked about it. His face did not change expression as I talked. He allowed me to process it how I needed to. I was lost in my explanation, unaware of how it was translating. I told him that no one else knows. Not Lily. Not Shay. And that I had to be the one to tell them. I told him I didn't want to hide from it anymore, but I had to be the one to say it. He said he understood. I trust him with my life but I am uneasy trusting him with this.

I take a quick shower, pack a bag for basketball practice, and walk up to the kitchen. My parents still aren't home. I didn't really expect them to be. I pour myself some orange juice and a bowl of cereal. I feel rested and apathetically happy. Then Lily appears in my mind. I understand my actions over the last few months have consequences that require penance. But they also require forgiveness and acceptance of my offer of contrition. I need the right space to tell her about Jess. In all the anger and hurt Lily has toward me, explaining myself through a lens of clarity should heal it. She said she was scared for me because the way I was behaving wasn't making sense. Now it will.

Josh pulls up to my house, driving my car. Regardless, I get in the passenger's seat. We have hardly pulled away from the curb when he starts.

"That trip shit on a lot of things." Josh tells me.

"What?"

"Megan called me this morning. Five am."

I think to myself, this is the start of everything settling. Me and Lily, Josh and Megan.

"So, why'd you answer?"

"Because I didn't at one or three or the dozen text messages she sent me over the last thirty-six hours. I had to face it. Awake or not."

"And?" I ask.

"I told her it was a twisted joke you played. That I didn't even realize until this morning it was sent."

"I can handle being the asshole on this one. I owe you a few."

"Yeah. I don't think she believed me. We're gonna hang out tomorrow and she is gonna try and read if I am full of bullshit or not."

As he says this, you can feel that he has already resigned himself to the belief that he is full of bullshit.

"So, what's your play?" I ask.

"Live and let die, I guess. I like her a lot, I do. But that feeling doesn't make me less horny when a girl like Emily gets in my sightline." I want to have insight here. I want to have answers. A complete and sound comprehension. But I am lost. I have no ideas.

"If Emily lived closer, choices would be easier." He says.

"If you are concerned about having options, that's crazy."

"It's the quality of options. Besides Megan – around here?" He pauses. I can't tell if he is thinking of choices or trying to figure out how to word what he wants to say. "There is only one other girl…" His voice trails off. It hits me that he is going to say that the other girl is Shay. I cannot have that conversation with him. Not now. Not less than five minutes from school. Not with all the other shit I have to deal with. I hit my MindLost mix and turn up the volume. Josh instinctively turns it up even more. He doesn't want to talk about this either.

When we get to school, the atmosphere around us changes. Halfway to the school's entrance, we are swarmed. I am showered with concern, pity and condolences. Even the teachers come up to me and say how sorry they are to hear about my grandmother. They tell me not to worry about the work I missed. That I have a clean slate as of today. That's one worry off my mind before the bell rings. When it does, everyone scurries and shuffles inside. Josh is ahead of me, joined by a few guys from the basketball team. I hang back for a minute. It takes me longer than I had hoped to be able to walk up the stairs to school. When I reach the top of the stairs, I see Shay off to the side, smoking. We are the only ones still outside.

"Hey," I say. Shay just stares at me. I wait for her to. "No welcome home?"

"You just had one. I am surprised they didn't make you a goddamn banner." There is a bite in her words that I rarely hear directed at me. I can collapse into the tone she wants to have for this conversation if I need to.

"We haven't gone inside yet. There still might be." I kid. She is not amused. I am more surprised than angry at her mood. "Why the hell are you mad at me? Many might, but I don't get you."

Shay inhales her cigarette, tosses it to the ground, and takes a few steps to me.

"Lily is tearing her soul apart trying to understand and help you. That is why I am mad at you. I understand there is a storm in you, but it has gotten out of control."

"I am going to talk with Lily. Everything will be fine." I tell her.

"Good luck with that."

"What does that mean?"

"Lily isn't here." Shay informs me.

"What?" Lily never misses school.

"Not here, sick." Shay tells me right before the second bell rings. She walks to the school entrance. I don't know what to say so I just shout out the first thing that comes to my mind.

"So now she is the one hiding from our problems?" Shay opens the door and stops. She looks square at me; her eyes flare with some mix of anger and sorrow.

"Fuck you." She lets the door slam behind her.

My mind feels dizzy as I follow her. Inside, the halls are empty. Josh and Rob are in my first class, the whole school pretty much just welcomed me back, but a sense of loneliness comes to me. I begin to feel a need for Lily. I must fix this and stop the cracks from forming again.

I am two doors away from my class when I feel a hand on my shoulder. I turn and find Rachel. Her hair is in ponytails resting on a tight fitting white sweatshirt. If it is possible to dress coyly, she has perfected it. She has initiated this conversation, but stands waiting for me to speak first. I just look at her for what feels like five minutes before I snap out of it. Her expression has not changed. She is a canvas waiting to be allowed to show color.

"Hey, Rachel." I start. "You late too?" She holds up a piece of paper.

"Hall pass. I saw you and wanted to say hi, and welcome back and all that." She giggles to herself. "So, hi. And welcome back." I can't help smiling when I look at her. She always seems to be a step away from flirting with me, and I can't quite grasp her intentions. It stirs me in a way that I am helpless not to smile.

"Thanks. Good to be back."

She doesn't say anything. She smiles and gives me a little wave goodbye. As she walks away, my eyes drift along her body. My palms itch and I tell myself this girl cannot only be fourteen. I lose myself in my thoughts of her for a moment. When I flashback, an image of Lily flows through me. It holds itself there. Anxiety climbs in me. Three years of memories are conveyed in a snapshot my mind holds clear. I have a better grasp of all the wrongs I have done to Lily than Shay, than Josh, maybe even than Lily. It is stored in me. It is a weight in me. I have thought that I only need Lily to forgive me, but maybe I need to forgive myself a little too. Rachel gave me a glimpse of what it is like away from my burdens. But I want to process them, not remove myself from where they are.

I call Lily at lunch but it goes straight to voicemail. I call the Mayor's office and ask for her, but am told she will not be in today. It will be after dinner time when I get out of basketball practice, so I decide to go to Lily's house straight from there. Unannounced. She has to know I would if she did not return my calls. I shower, shave and put on clean clothes in the locker rooms and then head over. I am a block away when I get a text from Lily. I pull over and read it. She tells me to meet her at Atomic. I text her back to say I will be there in ten minutes.

Truth is best told in a burst. Without time to think about it. Secrets are hidden to protect you. To scab a wound. I cannot just start the conversation by telling her about Jessica. I cannot just bleed out the words. And it is not that I don't think she will understand, or use my vulnerability against me. I lack the ability to. My heart has too many doors with too many locks to allow me to speak with honesty about Jess. The process of opening them needs to be coaxed. I hope Lily will let me work my way into it.

I park in a lot a few streets away from the Atomic, shut off the car and pause. The sky has become covered by gray clouds and I can hear echoes of thunder. I try to straighten out my thoughts and try to come up with what to say to Lily. I have everything arranged like bullet points, but an explanation in that form seems so contrived that I hate myself for using that reasoning. I decide to start my story from why I left after the concert. The beginning point for perspective is there. The details will fill the spaces. My sister is a part of me and sometimes that dictates that I disappear. Sometimes it consumes me and I do not have control over myself. It is a secret that has been molded by scar tissue. It is the tiniest little box that covers my heart and it has stayed there undisturbed until now.

Walking in, I instinctively shift to the right. Lily is sitting in our booth. She is early and has a cup of coffee grasped in both hands. Black, one equal, one sugar. Her head is tilted down. Strains of hair lightly cover her eyes. I hold my spot, only, she doesn't look at me. I had thoughts of getting a drink, but that idea is drained from me as I look at her now. I sit down across from her. She still doesn't look up.

"I don't know how to ask for forgiveness. I know I don't deserve it." I pause, hoping she will say something. She doesn't. "But is forgiveness ever deserved? Isn't its nature fully reliant on the mercy of another?"

Lily raises her head and looks back at me. Her eyes hold no emotion. The only way I can interrupt this is for me to continue.

"I know you want an explanation. I know you want reasons. It's not because I am an asshole or that I am trying to hurt you, or that I love you any less than I always have."
"Noah, stop." Lily's tone paralyzes my tongue. "I am so tired of this. We have been on the verge of a fight for three months now, but we have kept quiet and that has exhausted me." She says to me.
"I am not here to fight, Lily. I am here to start and fill in what my actions have emptied."
"You have such pretty words. Such pretty, hollow words." She says this softly. I almost believe she doesn't know she spoke them audibly.
I have nothing to respond to that. I am helpless, hanging on her silence, waiting for her. She takes a sip of her coffee. Her hands tremble slightly as she places the cup down.
"Noah, you have been my only for so long. I no longer understand how to exist outside of us. And that scares me because you have chosen to disappear. To abandon me. To exclude me. I see the struggle in you. I do. But I know you don't see mine. And that blindness strips away my belief in you."
She pauses now, looking at me for some sort of response. Some sort of fight. I sit across from her, comatose. "I love you, Noah. I haven't been able to shut that off. Not yet. But maybe at seventeen we don't know what that is supposed to mean. Maybe the concept is still evolving. I just know it's not enough. Not anymore."
I sway on the pendulum of utter numbness and hysterical sadness. I imagine Lily spending the last week plastering her face in anticipation of being this still now. My minds darts through the last three months of memories, highlighting all the wrongs against Lily I have committed. I think of Jessica and know if she is the one I am choosing over Lily, I cannot hate myself for that. Lily is not stoic looking at me now. I feel weakness in me as I try and speak.
"So where do we go from here?" I ask, finally capturing Lily's gaze.
"We can't be together anymore. I don't like who I am becoming with you, and I don't like who you are around me anymore. We need a change before we resent each

other. You have been my best friend. I don't want to get to a point where I lose all of you."

I don't think I am controlling my movements as I stand up. I have nothing I can say here. If that is where she wants to bring it to, I have no response. I move her hair away from her face and kiss her goodbye.

When I find myself home, I text Josh which prompts him to call me. I don't remember ever saying the words, "breakup", but we talk as though he knows. He asks me if I told her about my sister. I tell him I hadn't. I can tell he is still sorting through the importance of my sister to me. Maybe the simple explanation of her existence would have brought more questions, and resentment for me having it as a secret. I don't know. Maybe it wouldn't have mattered. I guess it doesn't matter now anyway.

I don't find consciousness until study hall the next day. My mind snaps back to the mundane chess playing, indifferent teacher and Erin's isolation that has accompanied this classroom all year. I am relieved at the lack of effect my presence or absence has here. I stretch in my chair, and for lack of anything better, I grab my backpack and pull out a notebook. I begin to scribble. I can't draw, so I make shapes and lines. Some connect, some intersect, and some lay off to the side with no relation to the others. A song floats through my head. I begin to write the lyrics down, over my scribbling. I stare at them. Then read them. The melody hums in my head. I am lost in the song when Erin appears over my shoulder.

"That's an odd sentiment for the center of the news of the day." She says. I look at her and kind of laugh.

"Social media fucks with my moping. Can't a guy get a twenty-four-hour reprieve?" I say.

"I don't know what time zone your head has been at, but it has been a week." Erin tells me.

"Last night was a week ago?" I say, before I can stop myself.

"Yes, it was."

I pull out my phone and check the date. April 10th stared back at me.

"April 10th," I say, mostly to myself. "It's almost my birthday."

"Wow. You really have been out of it."

"What?"

"I worry about you sometimes. You are unaware of the most publicized event of the year. If the buzz is any indication, it is going to be bigger than prom." Erin tells me.

"Clue me in, please."

"You are having a birthday party at Grant Function Hall on Friday. Josh has been pied-pipering the shit out of it."

Josh and I had talked a lot about what we should do when we turned eighteen. Sky diving, road trip, strip clubs. But none of that sounded appealing anymore. Nothing did, except whiskey.

"I guess it's nice to be thought of." I say, putting the notebook back in my bag. Erin doesn't say anything. She returns to her seat. I look over to her but she does not look at me again. When the bell rings, I catch up to her in the hall.

"Hey," She stops and turns to me. "I hope you can make it on Friday. You and your boyfriend." I search my mind for his name but I come up blank.

"His name is David. And we broke up a couple of weeks ago."

"Oh." I say, surprised.

"It wasn't on my timeline." She says with more bite than I hope she meant.

"Then you and whoever you want to bring." She observes me like she may have believed only half of what I said.

"Okay. I will come." She tells me before walking away.

"Good." I say in her direction. Without turning around, she gives me a wave.

As I head to my locker, I see Shay, and my core stiffens. She looks at me; her eyes sedated. I have no memory of seeing her since me and Lily. The air has changed between us. Looking at her now, she is filtered differently in my mind. I don't know how to interpret my feelings. We are about to pass each other when I stop – she doesn't. My reaction is slow. I don't stop her before she is past me, so I reach behind and pull her back. She does not resist. She allows me to. She retreats to my position, looking away, her head down with the weight of shame. At least that is what I want to believe. I realize my hand is still gripping her arm, so I let go. This stalemate between us lasts for less than thirty seconds, but I feel we are being watched. I glance around to divert the stares but can tell they return as soon as I look back to Shay.

"We need to talk." I finally say. She doesn't look, doesn't say anything. She nods slightly and steps away.

"Hanley at eight." she says, walking away. I nod in agreement even with her back to me. Before she turns the corner out of view, Lily meets her from the other side. They say a few words that I can't hear. Lily looks down the hall to me. I don't see her now. I only see the image I left, sitting down, eyes not looking at me. I try and smile at her now, but the detachment in her face doesn't allow me to. The bell rings and I find my way to my last class.

I hang back after school to allow people to fill out. I don't want to hear any noise. It is close to four when I walk out. The parking lot is empty except for mine and Josh's cars. I see him leaning against my car, perfectly content in waiting.

"There he is." He says as I approach.

"You have nothing better to do than wait around for a drunken soul?" I ask.

"No one else was going to." He jabs.

"On the contrary. My birthday is gonna be the second coming of Madi Gras."

"Is it? We best stock up on beads then. A couple of single guys like us could really clean up." I allow myself to laugh. He must have told me about Megan. I have no memory of it though.

"Can't wait." I say, opening up my truck and tossing my book bag inside.

"How has Lily been the last few days?" I ask him.

"Don't do that."

His reaction is quick.

"What?"

"Don't ask that." He says.

"Why?"

"Because, how do I answer that?" I shake my head, becoming a little annoyed.

"Shit, Josh, you are making this too complicated. An overview, not the transcript."

Josh thinks for a minute.

"All right. She has been pretty much like you the last few days."

"And how have I been?"

"Hazed over. Barely conscious. This is the first time you have brought her up. I almost thought you didn't want to."

"Is that even a question?"

"It has become one. You accepted the breakup. You haven't spoken with her since."

"Because she won't let me." I protest.

"From all accounts, you haven't tried." This hangs on me and becomes the weight of misery. "I'm not trying to be an asshole – you wanted to know."

"Like you said, I have been barely conscious."

  I take this in and pretend to be engaged in checking my tire pressure. I am not strong enough to handle what is swirling in my head but I am capable of repressing it. I can stuff it in a chamber deep inside for it to decay; no longer needing a resolution. My mind folds itself and I look back to Josh.

"So, details about this party of mine."

"Rented out Grant's for Friday. Kate and Belle said they would decorate. Grant said as long as we lock up, and trash any evidence of alcohol, we can stay till whenever. Kenny has some DJ equipment and promised not to play any bullshit."

"Wow. Well planned, sir."

"Don't get me wrong. This is a brave new world for me too. I just know we are too young to let our failures linger."

  Talking with Josh, the last few days come back to me. Megan didn't give Josh much of a chance to repent before breaking up with him. It might have been more of an ego bruise than hurt, but it was a deeper bruise than I remember Josh having before. Whatever this party was going to open up for us, we were both in need of some warmth.

"I've got to get back home to eat and change. I am meeting Shay at eight." I tell him.

"You're meeting up with Shay? Just the two of you?"

"Yes. And please don't say that so scandalously. We're friends. Still. It is a little confusing at the moment. That's why we need to talk." I say.

"No, I get it. Things need to be reformed." He gives me a shoulder hug. "Call me for whatever."

"Yeah. You too." He gets into his car, blares some music and drives. I get in my car and do the same.

I am three fourths down the path at Hanley Lake when I see Shay. She leans against our deformed tree that has fit us so well. The spot fits just enough in a clearing so the moonlight allows us to see just enough. She wears her sweatshirt hood pulled over her head, strands of hair making tiny escapes along the edges. She is wrapped up in a blanket, idle. I can see the coldness of the night as she breathes, but then realize she holds a cigarette by her side. I stay at this distance for a minute, looking at her. I am paralyzed by the thought of what she means to me now. All the scaffolding is gone. I wait for her to notice me, she doesn't. I walk the remaining distance between us and set my bag down. She looks up and gives a crooked smile in my direction.

"It's getting too cold to come here." She tells me.

I pull out a pillow and blanket from my bag and find a space near her to sit.

"What's life without a little numb now and again?" I try and come off funny. Ironic, even. With this audience, though, I fail.

Shay brings the cigarette to her lips, looks at me as she inhales, then faces straight ahead while blowing the smoke out the side of her mouth, away from me. I pull out a bottle of Vodka and am about to present it when Shay's phone beeps. She pulls it out of her sweatshirt, mutters her anger and stuffs it back.

"Give me that." She grabs the bottle of Vodka, opens it and swigs. She hands me back the bottle as she shivers from the sting of the drink. She wipes her mouth with the sleeve of her sweatshirt and takes another drag. I take a sip myself and wait for her to say something. She doesn't.

"Was that Lily?" I ask. She glares at me.

"No. Don't be so fucking self-involved."

"Wow. Can I ask who it was then? Or are you just going to say, 'Don't fucking pry'?" She looks at me, annoyed.

"Why did I come here?" She starts to stand up.

"Hold up. Calm down, alright? I am sorry. It wasn't the right time for a joke." She stares down at me for a beat. Her eyes trying to hold anger, but the water creeping in them betrays it.

"It was a sarcastic crack. I am not in the mood." She sits down again. "It was Evan. It is not working out very well."

"Did you guys break up?"

She rolls her eyes.

"All the cool kids are doing it. I didn't want to be left out."

"What happened?"

"What happened with you and Lily?"

"I am still trying to figure that one out."

"Would you like me to explain it for you?"

"Would you like me to explain why you and Evan didn't work?"

Her reply is grabbing the Vodka and downing some more. When she hands it back, I do the same.

"I don't really care. I know he didn't love me. I was mostly sure I didn't love him. But it's senior year. I wanted to go to Prom. I wanted to have something to be bittersweet about leaving in the fall."

"C'mon, Shay. You act like you won't get a date over the next five months. I know you were with Evan for a while, but don't think you will wake up lonely tomorrow. Because you won't."

I think about Josh as I say this. I think about myself. Maybe there is another side. You just need to figure out how to get there.

"I want it to mean something. To have a story. To have some scars from where we dragged it because we refused to leave it behind."

"You are talking to the wrong person about that. Having a story, having scars doesn't transcend shit. It only amplifies the ending."

Her eyes search my face, I think for sympathy or compassion, but I have none. I could squeeze out some empathy but I don't have the will. I suppose that's what we always did. We analyzed and comforted when we were too tired to think anymore. When the emotion became too heavy to allow us to function. This is how we behaved. But I couldn't now. I couldn't fall back into the same shell we had always been in. I could not look at Shay as my girlfriend's best friend who had become like my hot step-sister, who I repressed any impure thought that strayed too

far. She isn't that now. We have a story. We have scars.
Maybe it is the Vodka or the imbalance of my emotional
state, but I stay silent. I stay this way even when I hear her
talking to me. I zone out and all the moments I have had
with Shay flash through my memory. I finally feel Shay hit
me.

"Wake up." I shake out of it, take another drink and focus
myself.

"Sorry." I look at her discerningly. Quiet. I fidget with my
bag to distract myself from looking at Shay.

"Did you tell Lily we were hanging out tonight?" I ask.

"Yes." Shay says.

"What did she say?"

"You know her as well as I do. You know what she said.
What has she always said?"

"Have fun?" I say.

"See?"

"But it can't be that simple."

"It is." She tells me.

"I don't understand that."

"Things are different now, yes. But just because you broke
up doesn't mean Lily has fundamentally changed."

I look at her and feel my eyes grow heavy.

"I have." I tell her.

Quiet. I am unsure how long the chasm of time has
been when I look back to Shay, but it must have been
extended. She looks at me with some mix of feeling scared
and intrigued. She shakes out of it when our eyes connect.

"Lily and Josh have hung a few times since the break-up.
What did you say to him?"

"He didn't ask." I tell her.

"Oh."

"He told me afterwards. It was no big deal."

"Exactly. This is the same." She says.

"No, it's not."

"How's that?"

I stare at her for a moment and then put away my
reply.

"Forget it. Never mind. You're right." I say.

She lets this sit for a minute.

"How is this different from Lily and Josh hanging out?"
Shay asks.

"Josh and Lily's relationship has always been different than ours has."

"Yeah. You said that. Explain, please."

I can't tell if she really doesn't understand or if she simply wants me to say it aloud.

"Because I know Josh won't sleep with Lily." I say. Her face is stunned, completely blank. She recovers and looks at me, quizzically.

"Is that supposed to mean you think I would sleep with you?" She asks.

"That wasn't a definitive statement. I meant, simply, there has been a different tension between you and I than ever existed between Lily and Josh. But when I was with Lily, there always was a wall between that. Now there isn't."

I don't look at what I said as an arrogant statement. I look at it as plain, simple truth. The expression on Shay's face is one of the confusion of a girl that has never been directly hit on. But Shay has. She has seen the spectrum of types and ways boys and men have to proposition. She enjoys the attention, the game. She likes to tease and toy. I know her too well to believe this reaction. She turns to me when she composes herself.

"Is that what you wanted to talk to me about? When we can fuck?" She says.

I am taken back slightly by the viciousness in her tone. Her body is tense, defensive. There is no fear, though. She hasn't moved an inch. She actually is leaning slightly toward me. This isn't what I want. I didn't want to fight; I didn't want to sleep with her. I said it…I guess I said it because it was spinning in my head, and if Shay and I can remain friends, it needed to be spoken.

"That is hardly what I meant. I wanted the ether around us to be aware of it is all. I am sorry it came out so overt. I wanted to talk so we could settle us. I don't want it to be like this. Awkward and uncomfortable. I don't want what is going on with me and Lily to affect us."

"That's pretty naïve, Noah."

"Fine, it is. Then I mean I want us to find a way to exist alongside the wreckage. I just lost the girl I love, I don't want to lose another one of my best friends."

Shay pulls her hood down and shakes her hair out. She grabs another drink and looks off to the side. My eyes stay on her, waiting for her to return.

"Lily and I aren't a package deal. She knows we are close friends and doesn't want us to dissolve on her account. And you would do good to remember that she lost her love too. Say what you want about who broke up with who and all the reasons it should or shouldn't have happened. The fact is, she is just as heartbroken." Hearing Shay tell me that doesn't make me feel any better. I thought it would.

"I know I have been self-pitying of late. I am trying to get it out of my system."

"Good. No one likes a moper." She smiles her full Shay smile at me and grabs the Vodka. "You aren't going to wake up lonely tomorrow either. We need your charismatic self for Friday."

"My birthday? You coming?"

"I will make an appearance. Josh seems to have put together a rager."

"Yeah. Eighteen only comes once, right?" I say.

Shay pulls out her phone and stands again.

"It's almost nine. I gotta bail."

"Since when is 'almost nine' our curfew?"

"Noah, it is freezing and I want to be conscious for school tomorrow. At some point, we have to get past what used to be poetic and realize frostbite is not our friend. I will see you at school. Don't stay too much longer."

She gives my foot a tap with hers as she walks by. I watch her walk out of sight before packing up and standing. It is cold. On my way back to my car, I feel myself yawning. Maybe you can shake a stupor.

Nine

"Eighteen"

A few years ago, my father turned forty. I think it is the last proper meal my parents and I had together. At the end, my mother brought out a cake with four candles for my father to blow out. He inhaled and blew them out with a sig. Later, he mumbled something about how birthdays make him become bitter. I don't think he realized he had said this out loud. Or maybe he did. He just didn't realize I was sitting next to him.

Josh has arranged everything for the party. All I have to do is exist in the environment. Enjoy the moment. Allow myself to soak in the attention and all the happiness that can be distilled from it. Josh told me to expect at least a hundred kids. Grant's Function Hall doesn't hold much more than that, so it is fair to say the place will be bursting. I want something here, I just cannot place what that is. Josh and Shay both told me what I needed was separation. I needed a new beginning. It has been three weeks since I talked to Lily. How do you move on? This wouldn't be diving in. This would be recognizing I have been circling the pool. If I like the water, what is the harm in swimming?

Driving into Grant's, I can hear the sirens of dance music and the illumination of strobe lights from the parking lot. It is pretty full, but I find a space to park toward the back. The function hall is a rectangular building that stretches about fifty yards back. We have had basketball banquets here and had gotten to know Grant pretty well. Him letting us use the space wasn't surprising. For dancing and drinking, it was perfect.

As I walk in, I see a dance floor has already been formed in the middle. I am not noticed. I slide along the

side of the wall, looking for Josh. I spot him at the other end
of the room. There is a table next to him with a keg.
"Hey. You showed!" Reef says before clasping my hand.
"We thought you might have disappeared again." Reef
laughs and takes another drink. I don't let my look become
a glare, but he annoys me. He usually does.
"Here," Josh passes me an opened bottle of beer and toasts,
"To cigarettes, lottery tickets and strip clubs." We take a
sip and I turn around to assess the crowd.
"Anyone interesting show up yet?" I ask.
"That depends." Josh tells me.
"On?"
"Who you want to be here."

A dance song blows through the speakers and all
the people along the edges of those dancing now join. Reef
slides in as well. Josh waits for me to also join. When I
don't, he gives me an encouraging slap on the back and
joins everyone. I stay back and observe for a minute. I look
through the crowd and a few girls catch my eye. They are
friends of Lily. They work on the yearbook, or some event
committee or something. One with red hair, Paige, pulls my
focus to her. She wears this silver shirt. I watch her twirl
and twist her body, and I am turned on. I down my beer as
the song changes to another up-tempo song. Paige doesn't
miss a beat and connects to the rhythm. I know she is Lily's
friend and am held back by this. I second guess my will.
But why does that matter? It shouldn't. It doesn't. I pour
myself a shot of Vodka, down it, and go to her.

I walk in the chaos of all the moving bodies and
straight over to where Paige is dancing. I start dancing near
her. Her eyes open a little wider when she turns and sees
me.
"Noah. Hi."
"Hey," Our voices are barely audible over the music.
"Happy birthday." She leans into me to make sure I hear.
She hugs me. She isn't unhappy to see me. To dance with
me. "This is quite the party." She says.
"Yeah." I look around at the decorations. "I am glad you
came."

Paige withdraws slightly and I wonder if she can
hear the aggression in my voice. I am beginning to realize

what I want here. She holds her hands in one another and stares at them tentatively.

"Do you need a drink?" I ask.

"Not now. I've already had a few."

I have hung out with Paige numerous times. Seeing her outside of school is almost normal. Can she sense a difference in my intentions now? Does she understand all the closed doors are now open? A new song starts. An older slow jam that I can't quite remember the name of. I take her hands and move her to me.

"Let's dance." I tell her. I can only hear her respond by reading her lips as her hands reposition themselves on my shoulders.

As we dance, Paige keeps a six-inch rule in effect. Our bodies stay separated, but my hands touch the skin of the small of her back and drift along the circumference of her side. I look in my head for something to start a conversation with her. I know the outline of Paige, no real details, so I have limited beginnings. I know what I want here, and what it is going to take to get there.

"You take photos for the yearbook, right?"

"I do."

"When did you get into that?" She straightens herself. A look of surprise hits her eyes before she starts to think.

"Oh, a while. My grandmother gave me an old Polaroid camera for my tenth birthday; I have been hooked ever since."

"Cool." This allows her body to relax and graze mine.

"I actually just got accepted into the Boston School of Photography."

"That's amazing. Congratulations."

"Thanks. I'm pretty excited." Our bodies press into each other. I can feel a little exhale of breath as Paige collapses into me.

We don't talk; we just let the music sway our bodies. My hands brush aside the hair from her neck. I lean in and say something about a picture I remember her taking last year. I can feel her body shiver at the compliment. My lips brush the side of her neck. I press my lips softly on her skin and linger there. Paige tilts her head back slightly.

"You are a dangerous person to wear jeans around, I am in pain here." I say to her.

She giggles in just the way I hoped she would. I cup the side of her cheek and look into her eyes for some sort of acceptance. When I see it, I kiss her lips. She kisses back. Her hand wraps around my neck, pulling me even closer. The taste of her seeps in and increases my hunger. In a sharp transition, the song ends and a fast-paced one starts. In the change of cadence, us, together, becomes obvious. Paige steps back and looks at me. A stain of being horrified ripples across her face and she backs away.

"I can't. I'm sorry." She heads through the people and leaves the building. I cannot hear anyone say anything through the blare of the music, but I catch a few looks as I go after her.

Paige is at her car when I get outside. She stumbles through her pockets to find her key.

"Hey. What are you doing?" She looks at me and pulls out her key. "C'mon. You don't have to leave. This is crazy."

"I am sorry, Noah. I am not trying to ruin your birthday. But I can't."

"Can't kiss me? You can, you did."

"I can't do this to Lily. She is a friend. A good friend. This would hurt her." Anger swells in me as she says Lily's name. My first instinct is to be territorial still when Lily's name is brought up. In any context, but especially here. Using it as a reason to guilt me, using it against my actions. "Lily broke up with me almost a month ago. Her choice. Not mine. I have grieved, and for that I died. But now I am eighteen. Reborn. Ready for a life full of new experiences. For fun. For beauty. Why is it wrong?" Paige wavers. I feel the debate in her.

"No. Noah. It is wrong because it is so much more complicated than that. The next person you date, sleep with or whatever, she will be center-framed in the consciousness of the school. This school is obsessed with basketball and you are the star. You and Lily were king and queen. There isn't enough time left in the year for people to forget that. Anyone that is with you will be Anne Boylan."

"I don't know who that is."

"That is not important. Maybe in a year if we meet randomly walking down Newbury Street, maybe then, because god knows I want to." Paige stops there and looks at me. I want to say this is because she is debating what she is going to do. Maybe she is waiting for me to make her choice for her. Kiss her. Throw her on the hood of her car. But I don't. I want the taste of skin, but her hesitation makes me understand what I want the most: I want to feel wanted. "I don't want to lose Lily as a friend. Not like this. I am sorry." With that, she gets in her car and drives away. I hardly hear her last words. She is out of the parking lot and down the street before I feel enough to think about moving.

     The music behind me dulls and all I hear are whispers in my head. They are never loud enough for me to hear, causing me to strain to make some sense of the murmurs. My intentions were clear there. I wanted to sleep with Paige. I wanted to forget all the reasons why I shouldn't. Because, now, those reasons aren't there. Lily leaving me alone made me feel lonely, yes. It also left me feeling damaged. That no penance could save me, make me worthy for anyone else. And now I find that others may want me, but there is a wall preventing them.

     A voice starts to become clear through the din. I turn around and see Erin walking toward me.

"You okay? That was quite the lost stare you had going."

"Yeah. Fine. Nothing like a good lost stare, right?" Erin laughs. I didn't realize what I had said was a joke until she did. I am glad she helped me understand it was. "You came."

"You invited."

"I did. You meeting anyone?"

"I will know people inside. Don't worry, you won't have to talk to me all night."

"That's not what I meant. All my friends are outside." Erin doesn't need to look around to know we are alone.

"Josh is running things, so I know he must be inside. Where is Shay?"

"I don't know. She will show. She likes to make people wait and make an entrance."

"So, there you go. I am guessing everyone on the basketball team, cheerleaders, most juniors and seniors are in there. You have plenty of friends to choose from."

"Sure." I say, dismissing her premise. "I meant like a date or anything."

"Maybe. Sorta. Kinda. Not there yet. We are getting closer though."

"And who is this kinda sorta guy?"

"His name is Brian. He is a senior and spends most of his time working on the yearbook."

"A little boring after a musician, isn't it?"

"He is creative in a way that doesn't involve so many late nights and cigarette smoke. As long as you have passion about something, it is exciting. And he understands his passion, which makes it more focused, more directed at what he is passionate about."

"You are hoping that some of it will be directed toward you."

"I don't believe in hope."

"You don't?"

"No. I believe in making things happen."

"Huh. That takes the pressure off when you are out of hope."

"That is one, if not horribly depressing, way of looking at it. What about you? Date prospects in there?"

"Probably not. I thought I had, but she left claiming the next person I am with will be Anne Boylan, which I didn't understand." Erin laughs.

"That is an interesting reference. I think she means the votes have been cast and you are the one who wronged Lily. If you move on first, or maybe at all, the girl who is with you will be breaking the sisterhood code."

"Do you believe that?"

"Yeah. I can see that happening."

"So, what can I do?"

"Well, you can find someone who doesn't care if they are, find someone not at this school, or wait till college and you will be able to do whatever then."

"College is like five months away. I will implode before then."

Erin laughs.

"Then the easiest way is to find someone at a different school. Next away game, flirt with some of the girls. I don't know. Do what guys do."

"The problem is, I am hella rusty. Three years tied to a girl will do that."

"It isn't that hard. You are a cute guy. Just start talking and roll with it." I start walking to the party and Erin follows.

"You make it sound easy."

'Some girls are."

I laugh.

"That's great, but is there any substance in them?"

"Find out and worry about that later. You are not looking for a soul mate, right?"

"I don't know. You are right. That isn't my first thought."

"Okay. Be true to your intentions. That is all anyone can ask." We reach the door.

"Do you want to find Brian, or grab a drink?" I ask.

"I think I will look for Brian first. Find me for a drink later, though."

"Will do."

We split ways and I lose sight of her in the dancing bodies. I head back to the drinks table and accept a handful of shouts of 'happy birthday'. There is an open, half-full bottle of vodka on the table so I grab it and start drinking. Josh has found a pocket in the corner to dance with a girl. I can't be sure who it is, but the girl looks like Mary something. An unnatural blonde sophomore whose family I know goes to Josh's church. Like all good religious girls, she was caught kissing another girl in the bathroom at school earlier this year. Her parents forced a suspension on her. When she came back, she barely spoke. At that point, I lost all consciousness of her. Now, though, the consequence has been forgotten and she is doing what teenage hormones will make you do. I sip my vodka and look around. Erin is right. Everyone here understands what everyone will think if they are with me. What is the point of being here? Let everyone have fun in my name. I don't need to suffer through it. As I accept the decision to leave, someone grabs the bottle of vodka away from me.

"Hog." Shay says with a smile. She buries a sip and hands the bottle back to me. "So, what is going down at this exciting event?"

"Boozing and dry humping as far as I can tell."

"Well, if it is only dry humping, they aren't doing it right. Damn amateurs." Shay scoffs. I laugh.

"It's good you are here then."

"Usually is." She tells me. "Here," From behind her, she lifts up a medium-sized item wrapped in tissue paper. "Happy birthday."

"C'mon, Shay. I don't need a present." I tell her.

"Doesn't matter what you need or want. It is what you will have." I take it from her.

"Thank you." Shay does a little curtsy. I unwrap the paper and pull out a picture frame. It is a picture I don't remember ever seeing or ever being taken. It is a picture of Josh, Shay and I. We are much younger. It must have been taken in sophomore year. There is a note attached to the side that reads, "We will never be this young again. Happy '18th' Birthday. Love, Shay."

"Thank you, Shay, this is the perfect present." We hug in a perfect sister/brother hug that lingers just a little too long when –

"Get a room." We turn to see Reef grabbing a drink. My expression is blank.

"I was kidding. C'mon." Reef explains. I look at Shay and her eyes drill a hole of hate into Reef. He grabs a second beer and leaves without saying another word.

"That guy is such an asshole." Shay says in disgust.

"Yeah. Most of the time." I agree. "So, this is kind of a one-dimensional party. It is either dance or dance. And I guess drink."

"And who have you been dancing with?' Shay asks.

"I have chosen to drink and hang outside. I had one dance with Paige, but she left hating herself for it."

"That was fast. It usually takes me at least two dances before I hate myself." She tells me.

"Cute. Apparently, I am a scandal, and the next girl to be with me is betraying the sisterhood code."

"Yeah. I see that."

"I wish I told that to someone who couldn't see it." I say.

"I know it sucks. Lily is my best friend in the world, so I understand that idea. Paige and her are pretty good friends too. You need to find someone outside of her circle and see what happens."

"That actually makes perfect sense."

"Don't be too happy by it. I told her the same thing." This stings me at first, then I shake my head in understanding.

"It is wise advice. It would make everything simpler if we just got back together."

"Noah, don't start." Shay says.

"I am just saying."

"I know, but don't. Not now, not here. Not anymore."

I pull in what she says and let it absorb in me. I glance around the room again but every pretty girl I see connects back to Lily.

"She cast a pretty wide net. Everyone here knows her well."

"Yeah," She says, opening a beer. "The senior class will be hard to find someone."

Josh comes out of the crowd.

"Hey, Noah, you gotta get in there. Craziness is going down."

"I saw some of it in the corner. Was that Mary?" There is no shame in Josh's response.

"It was. That girl has a long tongue. It is rather amazing."

"How long are we talking? Longer than your dick?" Shay asks.

"Wouldn't you like to know."

Shay huffs and takes another drink.

"She has a friend that wants to meet you." Josh tells me.

"Who?"

"This girl she grew up with in Andover. She goes to Sarah Lawrence."

"Have you seen her? What does she look like?"

"I saw a picture. She isn't here yet but should be soon. She's cute."

"You don't sound convinced." I tell him.

"It was a picture. I can't be selling it hard by a picture. She looks cute. It is of them bowling or something stupid. She wasn't dressed all sexy, so I don't know."

"If someone is trying to set someone up with their friend, they are going to pull out the best picture they have. If you can't tell by that, it isn't a good sign." Shay councils.

"C'mon, what do you have to lose?"

"What do you have to gain?" I ask him.

"A fuck, and the happiness of your best friend."

"You need to separate those two a little more." I tell him.

"You know what I meant. And I already told you about her tongue. Do I need to be more explicit?"

"No. Please don't." Shay begs.

"Fine. Let me just put this in my car and I will meet her. Then we will see. That's all I can give."

"That is all I need."

I move to the edges and walk out of the building. I open my car and put the picture in the backseat. Paige left. What did I care who this girl is? I don't think it matters who the girl is tonight.

As I walk back, a car drives in and out comes four girls. I stop and watch as they walk closer to me. I can't quite place who they are. One of them steps ahead of the rest.

"Hey, Noah." She says. Rachel. I remember.

"Hey,"

"I know we weren't officially invited. Is it okay if we join?" She is wearing black jeans and a white shirt with strings to tighten it at the sides. It isn't the light. It isn't my mood. I have thought this before: she is hot. All the information falls into my memory. She is only fourteen. A freshman. I freeze the forming desire.

"My party is your party. If anyone gives you a hard time and asks, the password is 'sugar'." I tell them. They giggle.

"Sugar. Got it. Thank you."

"You came to my birthday. Thank you."

"Happy birthday." Rachel says, and it is echoed by the girls behind her. I nod and we start walking to the entrance. When we reach the door, I open it for them. Rachel is the last one to walk in before me. She passes just a little closer than the other girls. Barely inside, she stops and looks to me.

"I would love to dance later. I won't be hard to find." She smiles and disappears inside. I pause at the door and sort out how I feel about her saying that, and how I want to feel, and which one will win out. I walk inside and go back to where I left Josh and Shay.

Shay has found her way into the center of a group of people. I look over to them and she smiles as though she was waiting for me to return before she could fully be in this other space. I look around for Josh and find him back in his sordid corner with Mary. I walk to them, interrupted along the way by a chorus of happy birthday wishes and idle chatter. If I am meant to be the host here, I fail miserably. I know everyone, have hung out with most outside of school, but isn't there a difference between knowing someone, being friendly with them, and actually being friends? I suppose if there is, it vanishes when they are invited to your birthday party.

I reach Josh and Mary and find a brown-haired girl to the side of them. She is the picture of a dimly lit image a drunken artist would want to paint. She falls short of pretty but has an earnestness to her that allows me not to turn around.

"Noah, this is Caroline." I give the expected, "Hey," She smiles, and says "hi". Brilliant.

That is all the introductions we get before Mary and Josh find a spot against the wall, shaded by people dancing around them. Caroline does not compel me here. She stands with such a nervous insecurity, I know I don't have to try. Josh might have used me to get to Mary, but Mary served this girl up. Whatever I want from this girl, she will give, not just willingly, but thankfully. So, this is how my 18th birthday turns out, I tell myself. A pawn of a girl and a cheap night of sex. But maybe a cheap night of sex will clear my head.

"Wanna get a drink?" I ask her. She nods yes and follows me. I pour her a cup of vodka and ice and do the same for myself. She sips it with both hands on the cup and I start to think she has never had alcohol before. I debate if I should ask her to dance. I know there is an office type room in the back with a desk and couch. There is plenty of space for whatever we wanted to do. I move beside her and slide my arm around her waist. I down my cup of vodka and resign myself. I start to lean closer to her when my cell vibrates in my pocket. I pull away and check my text. It's from Lily. I quickly tell Caroline I have to go outside to make a call.

My jeans and t-shirt are no resistance to the April cold. My body shivers but my mind is too preoccupied to care. I type in a handful of different responses only to delete them. I reread the message and try to focus on all the things I want to say to Lily. The appropriate time has lapsed and relapsed and lost the perspective that allows my thoughts to make any sense. I dial her number. I need to hear her voice. I need her to say my name, then I will know what to say. When it gets to the fifth ring, my nerves flare up. When it rings for a sixth time, Lily answers.

"Hey, Noah." Her voice is sweet, yet has a different tenor than I remembered. It is like listening to your favorite song on vinyl for the first time. You recognize it but something is different.

"Lily. It is good to hear your voice. It has been a while."

"It has. How is your party?" She asks.

"Empty. Insipid. Lonely."

"Oh. I am sorry to hear that."

"I don't know how to do this, Lily." I tell her.

"Do what?"

"Miss you. Be without you." I say.

"Let's not start that."

"I want you back. There are so many things I need to explain to you. I have no self. I have who I am with you and the vacant shell of a soul without you."

"You are drunk." She says.

"Probably a little." I stop and wait for her to say something. She doesn't. "You know me. As simple, as innocent as your text message might have been, you knew I would over analyze and call you. So, save me the headache. What was the subtext in it? Why did you send it?"

"Can it be as straight forward as it is your birthday?"

"No. It can't." I tell her.

"I know a lot has changed." She stops. "I know I changed a lot of things. But we had talked about what our 18th birthdays were going to be like for the last year. We had so much fun coming up with ideas. The sillier, the crazier, the better. We were going to go to Niagara Falls. Or take a plane to California to see the Steinbeck museum. And now it is your birthday, and everyone is at your party. Everyone except me." I want her to say this with sadness, but there is none. It is said with an emotion that numbs me: acceptance.

I stumble backward in my mind. All the honesty in my heart on the tip on my tongue is swallowed into a cloud. I stand up and press my spine against the edge of the building. Again, I want her to speak. To bring more context to what she said. What it meant. But she doesn't.

"It was an open invitation. You could have come." I tell her.

"No, I couldn't. Because that would take away from you. It would have been about us. And we both are moving on. I hope we can be friends again at some point, but it is too soon."

"Fair enough, I guess. It probably will be a shit storm if you showed up and we weren't together. So, we should get back together and you come down." I say this as matter-of-factly as I can.

"Noah."

"Lily, I love you. Don't prevent me from being able to love you."

"We are no good for each other. Not anymore. You need to run away, and I don't want to be holding you back or trying to fix you. You don't deserve that. And I don't deserve being caught in the middle. My wishing you a happy birthday was a piece of nostalgia. I needed to say it, and even to hear your voice too. You meant too much for too long for me not to. And maybe selfishly I did it for me, for closure." She goes quiet. She attempts a few times to begin again before finally being able to. "I have a date this week, and I wanted to put to bed all the ghosts I still have lingering over you. I want you to move on too. We are both single. We need to understand that."

I cringe at every word of her last sentence. Whatever basin of hope I had left for us getting back together is drained like a vampire who just enjoys the sensation of sucking. I say nothing. There is nothing to say.

"So, goodbye." Lily says. "I guess I will see you around." The call drops without a sound indicating it is disconnecting. It just disappears. Like orange peels sinking in the ocean, you never knew it ever existed.

I push the phone back in my pocket and stay there, slouched over. As the fog lifts from my mind, I remember Caroline, my only option. I wonder how long ago I left her. It seems like two minutes, but when I check my phone, it has been close to an hour. Is she even still inside? Am I too desperate right now for it to even matter? I have sleeping pills at my house. I can take a few of them and wake up in the morning, see Shay and Josh and figure out the rest of my life then. I lean away from the building and head to my car. The parking is thinned out now. Only a handful of cars remain. I still hear the music inside but I don't want to be here anymore. I don't want to be anywhere anymore.

I have gone less than ten feet when I hear a voice behind me.

"It's a little cold to be out here. Alone." I don't turn around.

"It will be warmer in my car."

"It's not time to leave. We haven't danced yet."

I stop and turn around. Rachel stands a step or two outside the doorframe of the side exit where I had left. Something changes in me looking at her. Maybe I don't need to be fixed. I don't need a savior. I need to be believed in. I walk to her.

"I thought I was supposed to find you?"

"You were."

"And you found me."

"You can only play coy for so long before you just go after what you want." Rachel says.

I am beside her. Close enough to smell the cherry blossom shampoo of her hair. She looks up at me all of maybe 5'4, her eyes wide but completely sure. My fingertips tingle.

"How old are you?" I ask with the last thread holding up my walls. Needing that one more piece taken away.

"Fifteen. My birthday was in November." She explains as though the few months will make up the three-year difference between us.

"Fifteen. Wow." I back off slightly. Only noticeable if you were paying acute attention. Rachel is.

"Is age measured by experience? By maturity? They say girls mature three years faster than guys. I have traveled to Italy and France, and seen a lot more than you might think."

"I am sure that is true. None of that will matter to anyone in there."

"I don't care what anyone in there thinks. Only what you think." She tells me.

"What I think." I say.

"It's just a dance. A harmless dance."

I observe her.

"You are too hot for it to be just a dance." I tell her.

"Thank you." She says, blushing in an attempt to be modest. Only, she isn't. She must be a queen in her world. A world where she has overachieved to the point of making it as a varsity cheerleader as a freshman. To the point where she stands next to me unabashedly making me see her, consider her, want her. Standing beside her, the dread and insecurity drips away from me, like a cleansing. "It's a dance until it's not. I think we are both able to decide what we want to happen after that."

This is the act of moving on. This ends me and Lily. We are already over, have been for almost a month, but…this will evaporate the lingering residue. I have been stumbling inside myself. I can blink my eyes, clear my mind, and follow the direction my will leads me toward. I am hesitating because of her age. The perception is that it would be dirty, but who am I to decide what sips into her soul? She waits, looking at me almost humored.

"What?" I ask.

"Nothing. I just thought I would be the nervous one."

"Don't mistake indecisiveness with nervousness." I tell her.

"Wow. Ouch."

"I didn't mean it like that. My head is blurry today." I tell her.

She moves so her body brushes against mine. She arches her neck up so her eyes have a straight path to mine. "Don't overthink this. Find me if you want to dance." She walks back inside. It takes me a beat to hurdle the last bit of hesitation I have, and I dart inside to follow her.

I look around but don't see Rachel. Josh and Mary are still pretty much exactly where they were before, up against the wall making out; there is no sign of Caroline. Not seeing Rachel, I to start to walk further in.

"Getting colder." Rachel stands behind me, smiling as I turn to her. "Getting warmer." I walk to her and take her hand. "Found me." She says as I lead her away from the wall to our own little niche of the dance floor.

A new song starts playing and Rachel instantly falls into its rhythm. My hands are on her hips and she responds to my every movement as though it was choreographed. She presses into me in a delicate, feathery way. I go hard and she does not back away. She teases her body to the edge and then backs away as though she is enticing it to grow and reach her. It almost obliges when the song changes and slows. Rachel interlocks her arms around my neck and looks at me. My eyes slide down from her face to her collarbone to her cleavage vibrating as she sways. My gaze holds on a pendent Rachel wears around her neck. It is two circle halves that don't quite connect with an emerald in the middle.

"It's pretty, isn't it?" Rachel asks. I hadn't noticed she was standing still, watching me look at her.

"It is. Does the symbol have any meaning?"

"I'm not sure if it was designed with any meaning, no. It was my grandmother's. She always said, "We are always finding ourselves because we are always changing." That's what it reminds me of. That's what it means to me." Rachel says the last few words, realizing the vulnerability in them. She looks at me for a reaction. I am completely sold in this moment. There is no need for concern in her. She lifts it off her chest and twists it a little; like a child playing with her hair. I reach under the necklace and cusp it and her hand. I sense her body tense for a brief second. If you weren't paying acute attention to her, you would have missed it.

"Very beautiful." I say, looking at her, giving the compliment a vague placement. I place the necklace back on her chest, allowing my fingers to brush her collarbone before sliding them away from the necklace. There is no leaning in as I kiss her. I descend to her mouth, embracing her lips like they were some sort of remedy to a long-ago ailment. Her lips are soft and taste like cherries. Guilt-free, damn near encouraged. Our kissing intensifies to the point where we are pulling at each other's clothes. We separate for a minute to catch our breath. There is no doubt in Rachel's eyes.

I look around but no one seems to have noticed us. Except for Josh. I see him walking toward me.

"Hey, man, we've got to talk for a second." He pulls me off to the side.

"Be right back." I tell Rachel. I see Mary off to the other side, waiting for Josh.

Josh makes sure we are out of earshot of both Mary and Rachel before he stops. He is not pleased, that much is sure. He flashes with anger.

"What are you doing?" He asks, accusingly.

"I was dancing. Kissing a pretty girl. Enjoying myself."

"You screwed me over with Caroline. Mary is pissed." I look over to Mary.

"She is still here, why do you care?"

Josh calms his anger.

"It made things more difficult. You're right, it doesn't really matter. Except, it led you here."

"What does that mean?" I ask.

"What are you doing with a freshman?"

"It is pretty simple. Rachel is a cool girl, and sexy as hell. I am doing what any guy would do in my place."

"Think. She is fourteen. You are now eighteen. That is statutory rape." This stirs me, I almost let it get to me.

"She's fifteen. That is just some technical bullshit." I tell him. He looks at me like I am making the choice to fall into hell.

"I know we, I, have done some blurry morality shit. But this is going too far. This is perverse."

"Why? Because I am doing it? All the days I was in a relationship and you were single, I never judged you once. Not when you slept with Janice's mother while you were dating her. Not when you knew Katie and Beth had too much to drink. Never." I say.

"I appreciate that. Always. But I hoped you would have stopped me if I was about to go too far. And Beth and Katie had sobered up before anything really happened."

"And what about Mary? She is maybe eight months older than Rachel. How is that so different?" Josh has no answer. But I can tell he is not convinced. "You are overreacting here. If this was yesterday, would you even care?" He thinks on this. He isn't fully convinced but leaves it alone and takes off with Mary. I return to Rachel.

The music is still playing, but there are less than fifteen people left. Rachel holds her arms behind her in a posture of waiting. I think for a moment of what has led me here. To what has led Rachel here. This isn't an accident. She designed the pattern for this opening. Whatever my instinct here is, her reaction is thought out.

"Did your friends bail on you?" I ask her.

"No. I told them they could leave. I can get a ride if/when I need one." She pauses. "Josh didn't seem too happy over there. Is everything okay?"

"Yeah. Just giving me advice mixed with judgment."

"Should I ask about what, or do I already know?" My look to her answers her question. "Okay. But he left." She tells me.

"I can be convincing when I want to be."

"What did you say to him?" She asks.

"I promised I would not take advantage or do anything that this impressionable, naïve young girl did not want."

"Naïve and impressionable, huh?"

"To Josh, that comes standard in every fifteen-year-old." I tell her. She steps closer to me.

"And what do you think?"

"I disagree." Rachel reaches her hand in my jeans and dances her thumb around the button. She brushes her lips on mine before kissing hard, penetrating. She releases and says, "Good."

We stumble our way backward and into the corner office room. I don't think anyone sees us, I don't care if they do. I am unrestricted by thoughts of consequence; by thoughts of tomorrow; by thoughts of any kind. Desire and instinct. That is all the synapses in my brain allow to function. And it feels good. Rachel feels good.

Ten

Effect of Options

The next morning, I wake up alone. I had thought Rachel was asleep before I was. I hadn't thought about the morning. About the aftermath. Waking up, I feel as if my burdens are on a different frequency. My response to what is swirling in my head has a different texture. And to be honest, the speed of the swirl has lessened as well. I notice a clock on the wall as I put my clothes back on and tie my shoes. It is a little after seven. I walk through the function hall and find it remarkably clear. I allow myself to breathe in the remaining air from last night. In the emptiness of the room, I can appreciate everyone showing up in my name. Stepping outside, my mind wanders to Rachel. She is the first girl I have slept with other than Lily in three years. I caught myself kissing spots I knew turned Lily on. I found the uniqueness of Rachel, and she found uniqueness in me. I thought I had nothing left hidden, but she discovered new places. I go home and pretty much sleep through the weekend.

On Monday morning, I get breakfast. I don't call Shay or Josh. I haven't talked to either since Friday. I feel the distance but I am not overtaken by it. It occurs to me, though, I think this is the longest I haven't talked with at least one of Lily, Josh or Shay in over three years. I feel a void in me from this but I also feel the enzymes of my mind processing it. Maybe I have been mistaking withdrawal as need.

I find a back corner to eat my egg sandwich and drink my orange juice at A Coffee Spot by the train station. My mind is filled with memories of Friday night. I needed that release. I am a step further away from Lily now. And Rachel certainly wasn't what Caroline would have been.

She is different than what Paige would have been. How would I have felt today if it had been either of them? I have no expectations now. I understand the options here. It could end up being a one-time thing or it could be more. The amazing thing is that my mind isn't spinning trying to figure it out.

A few minutes after I start eating, the train arrives. A dozen kids or so get off and start walking the few blocks to school. It is interesting seeing them from this distance. There are three distinct groups, only briefly giving any recognition to each other. Separating from one of the packs, I see Rachel turn toward where I am. I see her wave off her group of friends. I don't change positions. I watch as she enters, orders her coffee, and leaves. She is very exact with her time. She doesn't look around, doesn't stand idle. She has her phone out and texting, or IMing away, with the intensity of having to explain in word bytes a novella of a story. Her hair is tightly pulled back into a ponytail and she wears a pair of jeans that look older than she is with a sweatshirt at least a size too big. For those few minutes, I am able to observe her with a different sort of attention than if she had been aware of me. I never had an overview perspective of her. Our interactions had been fleeting glances before Friday night. And Friday night happened under a tint of light that colored it with everything but clarity.

She is a step or two off the curb outside when I get up and follow her. Her pace is slow; one hand holding her coffee, the other her phone, backpack slung over her shoulder. I stay behind her for a bit until I realize I am being a creeper, so I just go up to her.

"Hey," I say, breaking in. She looks up from her phone and stops. Her expression is of tired happiness. She smiles but it is broken up by a yawn. "Not much sleep, huh? That's my life. I have gotten used to it."

"I am a couple of hours behind." She pauses. "I didn't mean to just vanish on Friday. I was living in a lie covered by a lie. My parents called me out on it and I had to get home. My friend, Julie, gave me a ride."

"I understand. You being gone was a little offsetting. I don't even have your phone number."

"What's your phone number? I will text you mine." She tells me.

"857-555-5747"

"All right. Sent." She slides her phone into her pocket and takes a sip of her coffee.

"Here, let me take this for you." I take her backpack, which must have weighed over thirty pounds, off her shoulder and put it over mine. She has the look of someone who has never had their books carried for them and isn't quite sure how to react to it.

"Thanks." Her eyes dart up to mine, away and then back again. I know what she is thinking and I can tell she wants me to bring it up.

I lean in a little closer and whisper, "Friday was amazing."

"Yeah. It was." She says with instinct quickness.

"I am sorry it got you in trouble with your parents. Are you grounded or anything?"

"No." She shakes her head. "My parents are full of school spirit. They want me involved as much as I can be. Staying out at a party till three am is almost accepted. My punishments are more of the guilt trip variety."

"I understand." I pause. We have crossed the train tracks and turned down the street to school before I say anything else. "Rachel, can I ask you a kinda embarrassing question?"

"Sure."

"What's your last name?" Rachel laughs. I don't know how to interrupt this. It is out of regret for sleeping with someone who doesn't know her name, or simple way to break away some tension.

"It is Tea, like the drink, not the thing you hit off of in golf."

"Good. I hate golf." I tell her. She giggles.

"It must be a little strange for you. I never thought of that part of it. You are known in school. Everyone knows you. They have printed profiles of you in the newspaper like you are a member of a boyband or something. I know your favorite color is blue and your favorite books are science-fiction. I guess, though, I am a little bit of a blank slate to you."

"I am a little ashamed to admit it. We knew each other only a little until Friday."

"What do you want to know?" She asks.

"I don't know. I didn't prepare a Q&A." I am caught off guard and it takes me a minute to get myself together.
"Have you been dating anyone?"
"No. I had a serious boyfriend over the summer, but only had a few dates since." She tells me.
"When did you break up?"
"September."
"Does he go to our school?" I ask.
"Yes. He is a sophomore. You wouldn't know him. He's not into sports, mostly drawing."
Everything I am asking is to gain an understanding of what the options are here. She is untied, available, willing.
"I guess you know my relationship ended a few weeks ago." I say.
"The news of that has made its way around school." She says, impressed by my reach instead of worried about the lack of privacy that creates.
"It is over. I am over it. But I am still on the mend from it if that makes any sense." I tell her.
"I think so." She says, head down looking away.
"You turned away. What are you thinking?" She looks up at me and stops. The school is just around the next corner.
"I have no right to have any thoughts on your relationship with Lily or how you feel about it now that it is over. I want you, Noah. I think I made that subtly clear over the last few months and abundantly clear last night. I get we all have hang-ups at some degree, but what matters is if and how they affect us. I don't want to be the rebound girl. If last night was a one-time thing that is fine."
"I didn't say that."
"It was in your hesitation. In how you said what you did. Look, I don't want to be this clingy, ultimatum girl. That's not who I am or who I am going to be."
She stands unwavering. She knows her exact position here. Like she said, it has been thought out over months. I am playing catch up from behind. I am attracted to this girl, yes. But now I am becoming intrigued. She is a new mystery, a new challenge. She is new and that feels good. It is not restarting anything as much as awakening different pieces of me.

"I did hesitate. I need to tread slowly. I can't rush into anything." Rachel gives a grin. "And, yes, I see how that is contradictory given the other night. If we are to get to a place where it means something, it needs to happen organically."

"I agree."

"So, we start off with say breakfast tomorrow? I have practice after school and then, eventually, I need to get some more sleep."

"Breakfast sounds good. I have practice too. A shower and sleep need to happen as soon after that as possible." She tells me.

"Okay then. It's a date."

"It's a date." She concurs.

With Lily, there was an infrastructure built that controlled, on some level, the ecstasy and fallout of any given situation. There was predictability, a safety net of sorts. With Rachel, I am an explorer, chartering my own map as I go. Across the street from school, Rachel stops.

"Can I have my backpack, please?" She asks.

"I got it. We are pretty much here."

"I know. We shouldn't walk in together. There are already a few rumors about Friday night. If we walk in together with you carrying my backpack, it will light a fire. Until we are figured out some, I don't want to go through that. You could probably duck it, but it would label me a groupie. That's a hard stain to wash out."

I lift the backpack off my shoulder and hand it to her. It's what Paige had said and Shay agreed with: there is a price to pay to be with me. A consequence that I, for some reason, am excluded from. I have been shallow at how I thought Rachel looked at me. I am a senior, a basketball player. The reasons for her liking me had stopped there. I had closed up any other reasons that someone could come up with. Maybe Rachel sees me in ultraviolet. Maybe she sees more than I do.

"I am sure we will bump into each other. We practice pretty much next to each other."

"We do." I say. She smiles, turns to take a sip of her coffee and crosses the street. I wait until I see her enter the school before I follow her.

As I walk through the halls, I am swarmed by people. My party was a success and they all want to let me know about all the fun they had. I try to keep moving but with every group that dissipates, a new one forms. I am used to this in a way. I certainly don't think I am very social. That hasn't prevented me from being popular. As much as I know all these people, I don't consider any of them friends. Lily and Shay are social. Josh is social. Am I viewed that way by proximity? I say all that and I find myself living in the element. I act excited to hear the stories, the drunken craziness. The hookups. More than a few. I get one or two questions that ask how I enjoyed it. I deflect, which is easy when the interest in the answer is slight, and say I danced a little, drank a little. A few people make some comments about me and Paige, but nothing seems to stick. At least not while I am within earshot. I reach my locker, grab my books and head for my first class. I stand at the doorframe and examine who is in the room in full scope. Josh sits in one corner, and Shay, Lily and Paige sit in the opposite one.

Josh doesn't say anything at first. He takes me in. "I smell sex and candy." He tells me when I find a desk next to him. I feel the ears bend of those around us minding their own business.
"Talk at lunch. I need a cheeseburger today." I tell him.
"Sold."

At lunch, I walk out to find Shay waiting for me with Josh. What used to be normal suddenly becomes odd. As I approach them, Josh picks this up.
"I had plans with Shay first, but she said you can join."
"How nice of you." I say mockingly.
"I made him promise me two favors." She tells me.
"I don't dare ask."
"Don't worry, I won't ask him to give them to me when we are with you." She says.

I question what has been happening when I haven't been there. It isn't tension between them. It is fully exposed, fully realized. I was expecting to have the news of the day.
"What's up with you two?" I ask, prying.
"Nothing. We're just messing with you." Josh tries to defuse my suspicion. "C'mon." He and Shay get in the car, I follow. Just out of the parking lot, Shay turns to me.

"There is one bit of news." She teases.

"Okay."

"I broke up with Evan."

"You are happy about it?" I ask.

"I don't know about that."

"You are." I tell her.

"I am not sulking. Lunch with my two best guy friends, how is a girl supposed to be sad?" Shay says.

"We are a car full of singles. Freedom has a dopamine effect." Josh says.

We reach the restaurant with our orders in when Josh addresses me.

"So, Noah, what's your story?" Shay puts her phone down and looks at us.

"Noah has a story?" She is surprised and interested as hell. Looking at us, she can tell what it is about. "A canoodling story? Tell us! My attention is all yours." She puts her elbows on the table and her head between her hands. I roll my eyes at her. Josh knows the answer to his question. He wants me to say it. He wants the details of it. He wants Shay to hear it.

"I hooked up with a girl on Friday." I say. Josh sits back in his chair like it was a confession. Shay's eyes perk up even more.

"Now, wait. When you say 'hooked up', do you mean slept with?"

"Yes,"

"Who is it? Josh, is it that girl you were trying to set him up with so Mary would blow you?"

"Crass much?" Josh complains.

"Shut up. You know what I mean."

"I do not believe it was. Mary sucked me off in spite of Noah."

"Crass much?" Shay says, glaring at Josh before they both laugh.

"It wasn't Caroline. It was this girl, Rachel."

"Who is Rachel?" Shay asks.

"Rachel Tea." I tell her.

"Who is that? She doesn't go to our school?" Shay asks.

"She goes to our school." Josh informs her. "She is a freshman."

"A freshman?" Shay scrunches up her nose. "What is she, fourteen?"

"Fifteen." I tell them. They stay quiet for a long beat. "Don't say anything to anybody. I don't know where it's going to go."

"Are you thinking about dating this girl?" Shay asks.

"Maybe. I don't know. Why? Would that be bad?"

"I don't know. Can't say." She tries to figure out her sentence before speaking. "I will tell you, though, Paige poured her heart out to Lily. Told her you danced and you tried to get in her pants. That is going to get around school quick," She warns.

"Well, it is partly true. I guess all of it is true. I have been well educated of the wildfire that will ensue if I started dating someone at school. That doesn't mean I have to be celibate."

"No, it doesn't," Josh agrees. "Just be smart about it. This girl is young. Make sure she can handle it. Not just that, make sure she wants to. Starry eyes make bad decisions."

"Can Mary handle it?" I ask Josh.

"Fine. We messed around. But I am not looking to be in a relationship with her. There is a difference."

"I know you don't think you have options, but you do." Shay tells me. "Don't just react."

"Reacting made me feel the best I have in at least a month." I tell them.

I hadn't considered anyone. Paige was there. Caroline was there. And Rachel stood in front of me until I noticed. Until I acted. Maybe the field did have possibilities. I am supposed to sow some oats here. I am supposed to have some fun. There is a morality play that is performed in my head. It causes the guilt, the regret and hollowness I feel when I am controlled by it. That is not freedom. That is restriction. That is what becomes of our burdens. It wasn't like that in the beginning with Lily. But expectations grew the longer we were together, and that eventually manifested into burdens. We couldn't just exist. On Friday night, I simply existed with Rachel. I allowed desire, instinct, and will to control my actions. That is freedom. Listening to Shay and Josh, their words are an undertow trying to drag me back into the box of guilt and regret. That is not how they live their lives. I just never understood that is how they thought I wanted to live mine. Or that they thought that is how I should live mine. There isn't some sort of grand design in front of me. No breadcrumbs, no yellow brick road. There is an empty landscape all around me.

"I didn't mean to get heavy on you, guys. Like you said with Paige, if this gets out then I want you to know the truth. I want you to hear it from me." I pause. "I talked with Lily on Friday night. She told me she had a date over the weekend and made it clear we were over. I wanted to feel something, you know?"

They nod an understanding as our food arrives. The conversation changes to a breakdown of reading for English class. It touches on prom and our upcoming basketball game before we get back to school. Lily and I pass each other in the hallway. She doesn't avoid me but doesn't speak either. I look back to her and watch for a second as she walks away from me.

Josh and I blow off last period to hit weights before practice. We stop at our lockers before heading to the gym. "So, I know you have your own storyline going on, but I wanted to let you know that Shay and I hung out a lot this weekend." I can't tell if Josh says this as a statement or a confession.

"What does that mean?" I ask.

"I don't know. It is different. Before, there was you and Lily to hold us at bay. If we got together, then that might have disrupted the group. But now...that isn't there."

"What do you want?"

"That isn't a simple question. What do you want with Rachel?" He asks.

"I want it to be simple. I don't want to analyze to the point of degrading or finding reasons not to. I just want to be happy." I say.

"So, that makes the question: would I be happy with Shay as my girlfriend?"

"I have been around the tension enough to know there is something between you two. You need to want to do the work that comes after the lay, as good as that might be. You need to want to build something beyond that."

"That crazy separation between lust and love, huh? That is a bigger question than I have the answer to. I guess if I just slept with someone, I barely knew I could enjoy the fun part and sort through the details later."

We reach the entrance of the gym. It is empty except for the far corner where part of the cheerleader squad is. Three girls in their practice outfits and ponytails are in full discussion mode.

Turning back to Josh, I see Rachel twenty feet away, coming toward us. Josh grabs a ball from the rack, dribbles inside the three-point line and shoots. I take a step toward Rachel. She wears her practice outfit too: spandex shorts with the word "Eagles" written in gold along the waist and a blue sports bra. My mind flashes to Friday. The taste of her skin as her body heat radiated. My memory is focused and stabilized. She walks up to me and slows, but doesn't stop.
"Sorry. I have to get to practice. See you tomorrow for breakfast." She doesn't say this as a whisper or as a secret. It is for everyone to know, but only for us to understand. There is a little gleam in her eyes, giving me a hint at the wonderment inside her.

As she passes me, I find myself staring. There is a confidence and acceptance in her. Above all else, a calm. If people stared at her or if they didn't, she remained the same. It makes me believe that no matter what effect I will have on her, I will never unbalance her core.

Eleven

Everything in its Right Place

I am meeting Rachel for breakfast at 7am, but when I show up at quarter to, she is already there. She has found a table in the middle of the restaurant. Her back is to me as I walk in. As I pass into her view, I place my hand on her shoulder. I leave it there just long enough so she doesn't get up and so she can feel the presence of it. We had talked normally yesterday. We found out about each other and I want it to be the same now. I want there to be more than sexual subtext here, but that is such an easy fallback. Looking at her, I can see the stumbling of her thoughts behind her eyes, as though they are colliding in confusion and regrouping in desperation. But that doesn't capture it. When I let all other thoughts escape my mind, I still slept with this girl. And it was amazing. The problem lies when you cannot release your thoughts and have a conversation with someone. I am bramble. Do you want to know that is who I am? Do you want to hear why Lily left me? Do you want to know that I will crawl away when you are sleeping, and you will never have any reasons why? You will never understand why I cannot tell why I left. I am always leaving. Or maybe I am never here. This is my shadow. My doppelganger.

I hear Rachel say something, but the haze in my mind does not let me understand it. I ask her to repeat herself. When I come to, I see the waitress in front of us. "Do you want to get some coffee?"
"I don't drink coffee, really. Maybe some orange juice."

Rachel orders coffee. We don't speak for a moment. "Like you said, let's start at the beginning. Tell me about your family. Do you have any brothers or sisters?" She asks. I hold back and turn away. Did Lily ever ask me this question? She must have. How did I answer it then? I know what I didn't say. "Are you okay, Noah?" Rachel pulls me back. She looks at me, her eyes growing wider with every beat I don't answer.

"Fine." I tell her. "It is a little complicated. I don't really talk about my family." I stop to take a breath. I have gotten to a place where I can have this conversation. I talked about Jessica with my parents. I told Josh. I can tell her too. I take a breath in. "I have a sister." I feel myself holding my breath and exhale. I have turned away from Rachel to such a degree, my back is almost to her. Realizing this, I face her again. She is twisted, like someone trying to figure out how to put a jigsaw puzzle together when they first dump out the pieces.

"You seem jittery. Are you sure you don't drink coffee?" She offers this as a joke. I exhale again, allowing a laugh at the end.

"It just isn't something I talk about much."

"Your sister?"

"Yeah. My family in general, I guess."

"I'm sorry. I didn't mean to bring up something uncomfortable."

Her words float to me and find a place in the center of me. I look at her. I had just told her the atom bomb I hold inside.

"I don't want it to be something I am uncomfortable with." I explain. "The people I hang out with know me so well, they no longer ask any questions. They know who I have chosen to become." I pause. I search Rachel's eyes the tiniest reason I should stop. I don't see any. "She lives at Katz Mental Hospital in New York."

I have overcome the impediment here. I spoke out loud that I have a sister. I told her where she lives and I want to control the tide of the floodgates, but I don't want to prevent them.

"My sister was placed in an asylum when I was eleven. She was diagnosed with Schizophrenia."

Rachel looks at me, searching for bullshit, to make sure it wasn't a line from a callous liar.

"I am sorry to hear that. I understand how it feels to be separated from a sibling."

Rachel waits a long minute, studying me.

"I had a baby brother, but my mom had a miscarriage." She tells me. Water breeds in her eyes. She blinks them but this is ineffective and has to wipe them clear.

"I am sorry."

"I guess if I have any secrets I don't talk about, it's that." A laugh gets caught in her throat and then bursts out with the water in her eyes. She smiles in a new way at me. I had seen her peppy smile, her smitten smile, and her blissful smile. This was a level beyond that. It was a smile born from a connection, born from an understanding. It unsettles me. Showing me this reveals a vulnerability that I am not quite sure I want the responsibility of seeing.

My phone starts to vibrate, breaking the moment. I pull out my phone and read a text.

"Is something wrong?" Rachel asks. I stare at my phone and reread the text before my eyes glaze over and I am merely reciting it in my mind. "Noah, what's wrong?" Rachel squeezes my arm. I look at her with distress and try to get my head right.

"That was Josh. Just some surprising news." She waits for me to continue. "You should know too. Lily is dating Reef. Apparently, they will be going to prom together."

"Oh." She speaks softly.

She doesn't say, 'why does that matter? You have me now', and I mentally thank her for that. What are we? It doesn't matter what you want to call it when your actions paint a specific picture. I was moving on, but that somehow seems different from having moved on, and that's what Lily has done.

"School is going to be a bit of an earthquake today, isn't it?"

"Probably." I tell her. "And I have a math test." She laughs.

"And practice." She reminds me.

"That's the easy part. I just need to make it until then."

We get our food and have an easy conversation while we eat. Music, movies, books. She tells me about seeing the Louvre museum in Paris. The more we talk, the more my focus on her expands. The more I want to know. In so many ways, she is a silhouette to me. But ink was starting to be drawn over the outline.

When we reach school, we cross the street together. Walking up the steps, Rachel slides away to a few girls in her grade. I stop and look back. She smiles and mouths, 'Go'.

Inside, I head to my locker. I open it and pull out the books for my first two classes. I head down the hall where there is a water fountain a few doors before my first class. I take a drink and taste the rusty, barely cold water. It leaves a metal feel to my tongue, so I lick the roof of my mouth trying to alter it but it doesn't help. When I turn around, I see Lily and Reef hovering at the entrance of our classroom. They are being playful with each other. My instinct is to break it up, to protect Lily. Only, that is no longer my place. She isn't fighting this, she is engaging in it. She is bringing it deeper in. They are in the room enough so that if you did not have my exact angle, you would have a hard time catching them. So, there I stood, in a private peep show. It didn't eat away at my happiness, it eats away at all my emotions, leaving cells that no longer have the ability to reproduce. I can almost feel myself wilting. I had been warned. I understood the concept, but to see it on display there is a realness that cannot be imagined. They start to kiss. It is no simple kiss. No first time, I am not quite sure, people could see, kiss. It is a reckless kiss. A hungry kiss. A nothing else means anything except our kiss, kiss.

I am unable to bend my knee, and am forced to lean my head down to try and coerce my legs to move. I feel a hand on my forearm that slides its way to my hand. I look to it and find Rachel standing next to me. Her eyes are still as they look in mine. She wants me to know she is there, but wants me to determine the rest. I look behind Rachel, Lily and Reef are still making out. When I look back to Rachel, she is looking at them too. I interlock my fingers with her and squeeze her hand, still without saying anything. From the side of my eye, I see Shay rushing down the hallway toward us. I know the look on her face; I know her mind by the way her lips quiver. I ready myself to stifle anything that might hurt Rachel. I am too fractured to allow Shay to go off. As Shay reaches us, she comes into view of our angle of Lily and Reef. I hear Shay softly say, 'oh' and she gives me an 'I'm sorry' look. Rachel observes and records this interaction. The bell rings, signaling three minutes until classes begin. The halls scatter and the room with Reef and Lily fills with kids. They have separated and sit at opposite sides of the room. Rachel pulls her hand away from mine and shifts to the side.

"I'll see you around." She says. I nod. She leaves her fingertips on mine until my gaze finds her eyes. She allows this to absorb for a moment and then walks away. I watch her until she turns the corner. When I turn back, Shay is still there.

"Are you okay?"

"I probably will be."

"Did Josh text you about…that."

"I didn't know they would be making out in front of me, in school, no. But I knew they were dating, yes."

"Lily didn't do that on purpose. She didn't know you would see that."

"That is the point, Shay. When you do things in public, you are stating that you do not care who sees."

I walk into the classroom without Shay. I hear Josh behind me say something to Shay and then to me. I don't answer. I find the seat in the most middle point and sit down. Josh soon finds a seat next to me.

"You got my text, right?"

"Yup."

"I wanted to talk to you about it but you wouldn't answer your phone."

"I realize. Thanks for the heads up." I pause. "Did you or Shay say anything to her about me over the last few days?" I don't mean to speak unclearly, but I don't want to be blunt about it without people around. I know I won't need to spell it out for Josh.

"No. I certainly haven't. As far as I know, neither has Shay."

I nod.

"Good."

Shay has already made plans to have lunch with Lily and almost apologizes for it. I tell her not to think about it and tell Josh to go with them. I lie that I have to speak with Mr. Richards, my history teacher, about a late paper. I can see the guilt in them as they agree. They are not choosing sides. It isn't like that with us.

As I enter the cafeteria for lunch, I get a strange sensation. I haven't been here at all this year. I have a bout of nostalgia. I grab a tray and get in the food line. I am noticed, and a handful of people have bite-size conversations with me while even more say 'hi' or 'good to see you'. I get a slice of pizza, a bag of chips and a soda and then survey the room. Lunch is split up into three time slots, but there are a mix of grades in each. I find who I was looking for and go to the table. A boy is the first one to notice me.

"Hey, Noah." I smile and say hi back. The table's attention is fully on me in that complete submission of control kind of way. Her head cranes back and Rachel looks up at me, surprised, unsure.

"Can I sit with you?" I say, directed at the guy who, so far, is the only one to speak to me.

"Sure. Grab a chair. Rachel, push over, make some room."

"Thanks." I say, sitting down next to her.

There are the same two girls Rachel was with at my party. When they look at me, I can tell they know most of, if not all of, what has gone on with Rachel and I. They are leery of me. I am the senior sitting at the freshman table. I am the one out of place. I am the one invading their space. I am the one who could hurt their friend. I register this. I want to tell them I understand all this and that I am playing my hand to see where it goes. I introduce myself to the group and this leads them to all introduce themselves to me. With me, we are a group of six. I take a bite of my pizza and they all stay silent.

"I didn't mean to stop your conversation. Keep talking."

"We weren't talking about anything super interesting." Natalie, Rachel's friend, tells me. "Just geeking out a little."

"About what?" I ask.

"A lot of things. Do you have a geek side?" Natalie asks me. Rachel has hardly looked up since I sat down. She looks over to Natalie as she asks this and I can't tell if she doesn't want me here or if she is embarrassed by the others at the table.

"I don't have much of a geek side. Except one thing." I pause for effect. "I have a stuffed blue creature that wears a white hat." The table explodes in laughter, me along with them. Rachel looks up at me with a warm smile.

"You don't." She tells me.

"Rachel is obsessed with them." Natalie informs me.

"I didn't know that." I tell Rachel, putting my hands up in defense.

"You must have known somehow." She pushes me in mock disgust. "And I am not obsessed. I am fond of them." I laugh.

"I even have the techno version of the theme song on my phone." I explain, pulling it out. "Listen." I let it play for a minute before stopping it. "See?"

"That is going to be stuck in my head all day now." She says, playfully annoyed.

"Which one do you have?" Caitlynn asks, Rachel's other friend.

"Sneezy."

"Rachel even named her cat Azreal." Derek tells me.

"I have an orange female cat. It just made sense."

"But Azreal is male."

"Not in the original comics." Rachel tells me.

"Don't test her. Like we said, she is obsessed." Caitlynn says. Rachel looks at me sort of bashfully.

"I guess I kind of am."

We laugh.

"So, Noah, this is the first time I have seen you at lunch." The other guy, Jeff, says. I can feel Rachel tense up. She glares at him and the others look elsewhere.

"Yeah. First time this year. Seniors are allowed to get food off campus during lunch, so I have been doing that. If I had known what kind of food was being served this year, I would have been here sooner." I say, holding up my pizza. I get the smatter of giggles I was looking for.

Jeff and Derek are boring as hell. They are my impression of fourteen-year-olds. They are carless which leads to stories of walking around the mall and biking to the comic book store. Their opinions are not based on experience or anything they have read. They are conditioned by cartoons. Their references make Natalie and Caitlynn laugh. This is their level as well. I laugh sometimes. Sheer stupidity is funny sometimes, but it makes me feel as though I am walking backward. Maybe this was me three years ago. I am not grown. I have plenty of immaturity and stupidity in me, it just wasn't in this vein. Even knowing what I know, seeing Rachel in a separate space, she never seemed her age. Her body, her confidence. And this morning, her experiences, her stories. But the more I sit here, the more the only sane conclusion to reach was that all was a mirage. A built-up image based on a superficial appearance and bought culture. My fogged-out mind blurred the reality of her. She silently eats as the others talk and I join her in the silence. I want to seclude myself somewhere with someone. I can ignore the noise, but complete separation is a must sometimes. To be with me, a requirement is a slight disappearance of a piece of you. That is what I would take from Rachel. Not her innocence. I would not corrupt her. I would change her.

The bell rings, ending lunch. We get up and throw our trash away, then say brief goodbyes and we go our own ways. As we reach the edge of the café, I hear Rachel say "Hey" to me. I stop and turn to her and take her in full length. I would tell anyone who caught me looking at her that it is not leering if she enjoys it. It is simply the recognition of beauty. God, I can't make up my mind.

She walks up to me.
"Sorry that they were a little juvenile. I don't want you to judge me in the context of them."
"I try not to judge people." I tell her. She exhales, as though I am making this harder for her.
"Fine. I don't want you to have a negative opinion of me in the context of them."
"I don't know you well enough to have an opin-"
She stops me.
"No. Bullshit. At this point, we both have an opinion of each other. Don't do that."

The room is pretty much empty and both of us are going to be late for our next class. Standing there, I can tell she doesn't care. She doesn't come across as confrontational but rather a needing to be understood. To clarify something that has been misconstrued. What would she think of me if we hung out with Josh and Shay? Would she understand our little world?
"My opinion of you is altered seeing you with your friends. How can it not be? I don't know you well enough to have a chiseled-out opinion. It is still very fluent and I hope you don't think you have me all figured out. Isn't there fun in existing in the mystery?" She almost blushes.
"There is."

My phone beeps and I read the text. It's from Josh telling me Reef was at lunch with them. It was supposed to be just Lily but he tagged along. He wanted me to know before it hit the rumor mill. When I look up from reading, there is no expectation in Rachel that I tell her what it said. "It appears the news about Lily's new boyfriend is going to hit the fan soon."

Rachel softly says, 'oh', and tilts her head down. She doesn't move, but the way she stands conveys that she is uncomfortable.

"Maybe Josh and Shay could hang out with us. Maybe that would dull some of the reaction. Change the narrative." She says.

"I can't have you do that. You are the only one who would have knives thrown at them."

"I don't care about that."

"I can't have all of us hang out. It won't work."

Rachel curls her lips into a ball and furrows her eyebrows. At first, she looks cute and I almost laugh at the sight, but soon, a wave of anger grips her pores and crafts a terror. She looks me in the eyes, with an anger, and it chills me. She allows the look to linger before she starts to walk away.

"Hey, don't be angry." I call after her. She turns around and speaks very deliberately at me.

"You don't owe me anything because we slept together. I have wanted that before you looked at me. And no matter what, I won't regret it. But we are getting to a point where it either is or it isn't. I see the debate in you. I can deal with that right now. But when you hesitate when I suggest we hang out with your friends, it makes me think you are ashamed of me and I will not be with someone with that opinion of me."

I am taken aback. My mind keeps thinking that Rachel isn't real. That she is an object I slept with, that I am programed to feel guilty about because of her age. But she keeps adding shades to the silhouette and I continue to align myself to intersect with her. I cannot see any flaws in her logic that, at this point, it either is or it isn't. When I take away everything else, all the restrictions, all the impediments, and base what I want to do solely on how I feel when I look at her, I have a pure clarity.

"You are right." I tell her. "I want to be with you. I worry about the backlash. It scares me. But if you want to be with me, even with all the baggage, I am in. I will talk with Josh and Shay and see when we can hang." Rachel smiles and hugs me. I tell her I will try and set something up for tomorrow.

I find Josh whistling when I reach my locker. Not a melody, just random spurts of whistle. I look at him for a moment, trying to decode the joke, but he is lost in his own world.

"Why so cheery?" I ask him. He stops and looks at me. He tries to cover up his smile but it only brings more attention to it.

"I am not, really." He tells me.

"You are acting like you found the prize in your cereal this morning."

'Well, metaphorically, that is kind of true."

"Okay. More detail."

Before he can begin, Reef walks by us. He struts like he was dragging his dick on the floor. I am transfixed for a moment as he walks toward a bubble of people. When it opens, I see Lily in the middle. I see them embrace. He cups his hand on the back of her neck and pulls her up to him. The bubble closes, blinding my view. A shiver runs through me and I suppress the urge to dent my locker.

"Is that pain or anger in you?" Josh asks.

"Why does that matter?"

"It changes how we can dissolve it." He tells me.

"Mostly anger. I understand we are dislocated, I don't get why she is displaying it so flamboyantly."

"I think it is a defense mechanism. I don't think she wants to come across as–"

"A bitch." I say, cutting him off.

"I was going to say bitter."

"Whatever it is, it's annoying." I tell him.

"So, get Rachel out here, slam her against a locker and stick your tongue down her throat. Fight fire with fire if it bothers you."

"Tempting, but I am trying to handle this with more maturity than a ten-year-old."

"Why? Isn't Rachel like ten?" He waits for me to look at him before bursting into laughter.

"You can't say shit like that around her, Josh. Seriously."
"I know. I won't. I am sure I will be amazed by this girl."

Rachel wants Josh and Shay to like her. To see us as a couple. I know she feels that their acceptance will validate her to me. That, in some way, the four of us need to bond as friends. Only, that will never happen. When I am with her, I am in a separate, different place. Somewhere I do not have anything to look back on, to analyze or regret. She is my clean slate and I know I have already stained it. But she is my field in the rye.

My phone vibrates with a text message. It is from Shay. It says, "Meet me at Jade's after school. Just U & Me." I reply with "sure" and put the phone back in my pocket.
"Shay just asked me to hang after school."
"I need to talk to you about her." He shifts his body as his mind struggles to structure his words. "We kind of shared a moment last night."
"Okay." I hesitate. I know what it means. This has happened before. Except, it was always simply stated. Josh is choosing his words too carefully for it not to be more. "What does that mean?"
"We made out a little and…" He stops, looks around him, no one is in earshot. "My fingers may have gone south."
"You fingered–" Josh hushes me. I didn't realize I was shouting. "You fingered Shay?" I ask, an octave above a whisper.

Josh can't hide how happy he is while telling me this. How proud of himself he is. It is like a child climbing a tree and getting to that branch where the height finally starts to scare him. Then the day arrives, he overcomes that fear and climbs higher. They want to tell everyone about the view they had. This is Josh. Only, he knows he cannot tell anyone. Except me. I was wrapped up in Shay avoiding me, of how she was going to act having dinner with Rachel, but this trumps everything.
"We have to talk more about this later, outside of school." I tell him. "This is too crazy to not understand all the details."
"It was wild." He agrees.
"How did you leave it, though? You get to that point, how does the story end?"

Josh shifts from side to side. I can tell he wants a better answer.

"How it always has ended. One of us pulls back, in this instance, it was Shay. She was like, "This is weird, we are friends." Blah, blah, blah. We always knew the probability if we ever got together is that we would flame out in a month. And that would affect the four of us. But you and Lily already shattered what the four of us were, so why should that stop us now?"

"Thanks."

"It's not a bad thing. If I knew that you guys breaking up would remove the obstacles to me hooking up with Shay, I would have encouraged it years ago." I glare at him. "I am joking, but you know what I mean."

I know exactly what he means. That doesn't preclude me knowing how it will turn out. Their views of relationships are the same. Which is to say neither have ever taken them seriously. They have fun and disregard. The difference here is that it has felt like they have been in a relationship for the last three years. They have slept in the same bed with a board separating them. Everything has changed. Josh is right, the obstacles aren't there anymore. There is nothing to notice if you damage wreckage.

Twelve

Where The Beginning Is

They are called suicides for a reason I tell myself as the urge to throw up reaches the back of my tongue. Josh strides with me, maybe a step ahead. The rest of the team has fallen behind. Coach has run practice thirty minutes over today. He is pushing us for the final two games. Our focus of late has not been great; or rather Josh and my focus; or really just my focus. Coach blows his whistle and ends practice. Some guys collapse on the court in relief. I put my hands behind my head and work to catch my breath. I take off my sweat-soaked shirt and grab a towel from the bench to clear my eyes of perspiration.

A side door of the gym opens and the cheerleaders file in from outside. This gets a reaction from the team as shouts of flirtation echo through the gym. Rachel is with four girls at the back of the pack. Her eyes look up to find me, but she doesn't move toward me. The knowledge that we are dating has been circulating through school since the second half of the day. It seems to be considered a rumor still. Lily and Reef were the thunder. Lily moving on first was the headline; they chose to make it very public. Rachel and my relationship has been crafted more delicately. Maybe that is a way of coating my indecision. Of rationalizing my doubt. There is a weight off me now with Lily and Reef outed. In some sort of backwards way, me being with another girl was cheating on Lily. That the perception would be that I was cheating on her.

I walk to Rachel, and when I am within ten feet when my point of direction is noticed, their talking quiets. They become a semi-circle that I approach the opening of. They are trying to make it awkward for me, trying to corner me into making some sort of declaration of my intention.

Rachel has been careful of how she was answers questions about us. She tells them we have been "talking" and leaves it at that. If pressed, she responds with, "We will have to see if it goes anywhere." I have come to realize that Rachel is the master at handling questions with a maturity that eliminates second-guessing of her answers. I can play that game too. I can be direct and ambiguous at the same time. I say hi to Rachel, only looking at her. I wait until she says hi back before I glance around the group and offer an impersonal "Hi ladies". From that, they all disperse leaving looks to Rachel to make sure she is okay if they leave. I wait for them to be out of earshot before I laugh.

"That was very high school."

"Yeah. It kind of comes with the environment." Rachel has a huge smile as she pokes at me.

"Fair enough."

"Do you know what your nickname is?" She asks.

"I have a nickname?"

"You do. They call you Wolf."

"That isn't the worst name, I guess. I don't think I have ever seen you in red. That's the point, right? That makes you Riding Hood?"

"That seems to be the inference."

"So, they think I will metaphorically eat you?"

"I like when you eat me." Rachel bends and leans toward me. Her eyes change into sexpot without blinking. The rasp in her voice comes out like my Boston accent with certain words. I am dizzy by the switch and the hunger in me because of it. I float and memories flash in my mind. This girl, this girl...

"That is a dangerous thing to say to me. I am prone to blackouts. I don't have much control when I allow myself to let go." I say.

"I understood that after the first night."

"I suppose you did."

"Don't worry, don't even think about them. They have this little sister concern for me, but it is mostly jealousy. You are kind of a big deal around here." She tells me.

"Me? I am the one who gets to date a cheerleader."

She laughs. "So, we are meeting Josh and Shay tomorrow?"

"Josh is in. I will talk to Shay about it later on."

"Noah, can I ask you a girl question?"

"All your questions are girl questions."

"No, I mean a "girly" question." Rachel clarifies.

"Always."

"Will Shay and Josh like me?" There is a tepidness to her that is contrary to what I know about her.

"Of course." I tell her.

"Do they like Lily's boyfriend?" To get to the place where Rachel says Lily's name and it doesn't sting me would be a blessed day.

"I haven't really talked to them about it recently, but I don't think they do."

"Why?" Rachel asks.

"Because he is a prick." I say with too much anger. Rachel recoils a little. "Before they got together, that was the opinion. They don't know you except for what I have told them. And I have only glowed." I get the smile and the unraveling I was hoping for. "They will like you because I like you. And when they get to know you, they will like you because of you. I need to shower." I tell her.

I start to move away but become aware of how I walked away. I don't want there to be any apathy in our parting, so I turn back to her. She looks up at me, surprised. The gym is mostly empty at this point, but I know I can confirm the whispers. I know I can crossover and create a vibrancy to the vague. I kiss her, with a slowness, with tenderness, with a deliberateness to show this wasn't simply an act of passion, it was a choice. A thought out choice. As we release, I leave my eyes in hers until I can tell she is smiling without seeing her mouth. I watch her walk away before turning to the locker room.

I do not think it is possible to erase the three years Lily and I shared. At this point, it makes up too much of my conscious life. I think that is what Lily tried to do, at first. Now, she has decided the easier option is to distort it. How deep was our love if it can be replaced two months later? If it can be disregarded with such ease. And I have a new girl under my wings just as she has Reef. I look at her actions, understanding I am being hypercritical. I slept with Rachel before her first date with Reef. I allowed our goodbye to settle and become reality. I was her first boyfriend, as she was my first girlfriend. We knew each other in the context of each other. Now, we are separately walking through this new environment; how am I supposed to form expectations? Expectations break the beauty of subtlety. I need to allow nature to take its course.

I make sure I find Rachel after school. She is walking with three other girls, two of who I know. I say hi to the group and am given their attention immediately. Rachel somehow stands next to me without being near me. Maybe Josh is right. Maybe I should throw her against a locker. When I say our relationship is public, all that has meant is that people have seen us leave together, hang out together; that the answer has never been denial when the question has been asked. I don't want a shadow relationship. I don't want to be half in with Rachel. She deserves more than that. Public displays do not have to be throwing it in people's faces. When we are alone, I allow my instincts to steer, I need to function that way around people too.

I take her wrist and pull her so she faces me. I wrap my arms around her and lift her arms up. They reach my neck and she interlocks her fingers. I press into her with the hovering presence of a feather before I feel her body collapse into mine. The entire moment hardly lasts for five seconds, but looking at Rachel now, I see a new dimension. Wanting someone, having someone, and then you come to the security of being able to hold onto someone. I was ready to no longer be in the shadows.

The girls around us slightly tilt backwards, as though they got too close to the actors during a stage play. They are fascinated but uncomfortable by it. Nothing in our actions had been explicit, yet there is almost a seeable mist caused by the tension between Rachel and me. We hold in this pattern for a minute, filling it with small talk before the other girls leave. As they walk away, I turn to Rachel.

"I wanted to let you know I am meeting Shay. We haven't really talked for the last few days and we need to talk some things out before tomorrow. I don't want it to be complicated."

"I guess with Shay and Lily being best friends it only makes sense she would have a little bit of hate for me."

"I'm sure she doesn't hate you."

"No, it makes sense. If the situation was reversed, I would feel the same."

I let that settle. I want Shay and Rachel to get along. But I don't need them to. The four of us were a group, but there were brush strokes of individuality underneath that. If we peel away the paint, we would find that understanding of each other again. The understanding of me now includes Rachel. I really don't know how Shay will respond to that. She seems to be okay with Reef, so it can't be harder than that.

I kiss Rachel before I leave. It is a burst, a quick kiss. It articulates better than my words. There is no one in the parking lot as I leave. I was already late and Shay had texted me twice. We weren't going to be able to talk about everything. But that was true beforehand. A sidebar was never going to accomplish absolution. I had tried at Hanley Lake, and during my birthday, I thought we found a place beyond. There is a difference between being separated and being involved separately. There is a development of sides forming. This can't be stopped. I don't want it to be stopped. I am building my fair share. I just want the neutral areas clearly mapped out.

Shay has finished her food before I reach the table. I sit down, a waitress takes my drink order, and I look at Shay. She tries hard to push down her thoughts away from her face, but fails.

"I don't like it feeling weird between us." I tell her.

"It's not weird. It's just different."

"Until it isn't different, it is going to feel weird to me." I say.

She shrugs as though it is only my problem. She isn't going to help.

"So, what was with the human shield with you and Lily this morning?" I ask her.

"It appeared more dramatic than it was supposed to."

"Okay. What was the point of it?"

"I am not going to justify how she feels." Shay says, dismissing my concern.

"But you are willing to be an associate of it?"

Shay looks at me, eyes clear. They are eyes of conclusion. Unwavering. All the questioning, all the doubt, all the confusion rattling around my mind burns to ash looking at her. My opinion did not matter here.

"Lily is my best friend. I am standing by her. It is not the same thing as choosing sides." She tells me.

"She has decided to mock what we were, repeatedly. Tried to humiliate and disrespect me. By standing by her, you are choosing sides."

"Noah, you and Lily are over. What you were is over. Her acting differently with Reef than she did with you is not being disrespectful or insensitive. It is her living her life. And don't forget, you slept with Rachel before she was ever with Reef."

'Does she know that?" I ask.

"No. But you do. And that should temper your indignation."

I understand what Shay is saying. I do. It makes the kind of logical sense I did not want to hear. I know every inch of what has changed. I have written a dissertation in my head on it and have not wanted to believe it. It is some elaborate science fiction. It is my struggle to believe in God. No matter how close to the edge it is, I never allow the debate to end. There is something painful to me about resolution.

Shay is leaning back in her seat as I look at her. The hardness in her softens a bit. She is my friend too. We have been as close the last three years as her and Lily. I know it is different and, in a way, can never be equal. But I know it is not meaningless.

"So, where does that leave us?" I ask her.

Shay exhales, as though she was holding in smoke from a cigarette. There is an insincere reflection in her pause. She waited to talk to me until she had everything worked out. This is the second half of the conversation. I have no doubt this is scripted too.

"I guess that depends on you." She tells me. "Can you accept me sticking by Lily? Can you understand that? In this chaos, I don't want to lose you. We walked with each other through high school. There was no separation between us throughout that time but what can we be now?"

Shay and I aren't like her and Josh. We could last. We could carve a slit in the fold and feed off each other until the aftermath is worn off. There has always been a stain where a parent's affection should be in us that Lily and Josh never had. Shay found excuses in college boyfriends when she needed to run away. I wasn't that smart. Or maybe I was never that brave. I left with a reason to return. Something pulling me back. Shay left and came back only when she wanted to.

"These aren't many choices." I tell her. "With you standing by Lily, and you and Josh crossing into an inferno."

Her face goes quiet for a minute.

"What did he tell you?" Shay asks.

"Enough."

"Noah, that doesn't answer the question."

"Hey, I tried to set you guys up almost four years ago. How could I possibly be mad if you got together?"

"We aren't going to get together."

"Get together, friends with benefits whatever the kids are calling it these days." I say.

"Noah, no. Josh and I…I just can't. I have been tempted. You know that. There have been moments but I just can't."

"Is there any rationale behind that?" I ask.

"It would mean too much for it not to amount to anything. And it wouldn't amount to anything. One of us would get bored with the other and we would end up hating each other. I can stand us fading away, becoming indifferent. That would preserve the memory. I cannot stand us hooking up for a few months and hating each other for the rest of our lives."

I feel saturated in sadness as she finishes. This is Lily and my fate.

"I understand that." I tell her. I don't think Josh does though. He is still licking his fingers from last night."

Shay puts her face in her hands, trying to cover her reaction to what I said. It is still there when she looks at me. "I will have a talk with him then. And what about us?"

A friendship with Shay at best would have seams in it, and probably be at arms lengths for a while. I can't remember having halfway friends. It was the four of us and then mild interactions with acquaintances. With people who could come and go without making any difference. I cannot imagine Shay not making a difference. But I don't know how to trust if she isn't all in.

"Can we feel our way through it?" I begin. "We can still hang out. Us and Josh too. When it comes to Reef and Rachel, we tread delicately and see how it goes."
"Yeah. We can try that."
"Can we try dinner with Josh, Rachel and me tomorrow?"
        I am looking for a quick answer. I don't get one.
"You're paying, right?" She asks with a smile.
"If you are coming." I tell her. "That sounded unintentionally dirty." Shay laughs and stands up.
"C'mon, I gotta get to work." She tells me.
        As we walk out, I put my arms around her and pull her close. She folds into me. I am still a safe place to land for her. As long as that is true, I know we can make it through anything.
"We are going to be okay." I whisper to her. She smiles and slightly nods her head, agreeing, before we turn away from each and walk to our cars.
        The next day goes by quickly. I don't remember most of it, I sort of went through the motions. Like driving down a road you have driven on a million times, your mind fades off and you arrive at your destination having lost time. Straight from last period, I head to the gym for our last practice before our last game tomorrow. I can hear giggling as I enter the hallway to our locker rooms. The girl's locker room is a hundred feet beyond ours down the hallway. There is a bend to the hallway, but it doesn't take me long to see the source of the noise. Reef has Lily pushed up against the wall. I stay at the same pace as I approach them. I am almost beside them before they notice. Reef glares at me for interrupting. Lily doesn't make eye contact and positions herself behind Reef. I can't read what she is feeling. My desire for it to be shame is too strong. I stop and look at them. It is a staring contest of sorts between myself and Reef. Neither one of us says a word or moves. What am I going to do here? I am not going to fight him. I am not going to curse them out. I just want them to feel as awkward as possible.
        From the other end of the hallway, a group of girls walk out. Lily and Reef turn to them, opening up my view. Rachel is among them. As my eyes catch her, I can tell she sees the landscape of the situation. She takes a step forward, toward us, before stopping.

"Hey, Rachel. I will see you after practice." I tilt my head to her and go into the locker room. I heard her voice say, "Okay". She has handled all this bullshit pretty well. I told her there would be a lot of it. She said she didn't care and that she could handle it, which is proving true.

The school, as a whole, may have a divided opinion on me and Lily, but the basketball team is clearly one-sided; I have full support. That leaves Reef firmly on the outskirts of anyone wanting to interact with him during practice. It becomes so obvious that, at one point, Coach stops practice and yells at us about it. This doesn't do any good. It only embarrasses Reef and separates him further from the team. The happiness I feel by everyone having my back makes me laugh. I never want to leave. I have control here. All this gets into Reef's head and he winds up finishing practice on the bench. He is the first to shower and leave the locker room after practice.

Josh and I lead the team out of the locker room and to the parking lot. There are close to fifty people hanging around. The basketball team and the cheerleading squad with boyfriends and girlfriends all hover around each other. I find Shay and Lily in a group of six, including Reef. I begin to think that no matter the victories I have in the bubble of the gym, outside, here, I am the loser. I am somehow inferior. These thoughts flicker in my mind until I see Rachel. She is changed out of her cheerleader outfit and into a pair of jeans and a sweater that fits her form so acutely, it appears almost as a second skin. She is surrounded by a group of maybe ten, mostly other cheerleaders. She holds court. She commands this audience and has its full attention. I don't know this side of Rachel. I know the love-struck kitten, the sweet girl who will hold my hand when it is shaking, and the girl who will go against her own desire to challenge me not to take her for granted. This is the charismatic Rachel. I take it in and commit it to memory.

Josh and I reach my car; he is parked next to it. I glance over to Lily's group and catch Shay looking up. She smiles a weak, quick smile and bends her eyes back inside the circle. Josh notices.

"Don't even look over there, man. At this point, it isn't worth it."

"She isn't going to hang out with us tonight, is she?" I ask.

I had been illiterate to all the subtext the last few weeks, but enlightening was finally reaching me. Shay is fading me out. To her, that is how you preserve all the good memories. And there is still a part of her that needed me. She didn't choose any of this. Her choice is following the landslide instead of defying it. You can grow out of the need for a brother, or whatever I was/am. Her next boyfriend will act as a replacement. I can see she understands that now. All the little things will begin to mean something different. I know this is true because it has started to happen to me.

"I am guessing not." He tells me.

"So, the three of us?"

"Of course." He says and pauses. "We need to figure out the other side sometime."

Josh needs to check in with his parents before meeting us for dinner. As he leaves, I toss my duffel bag in the backseat of my car and look over to Rachel. She is popular. She has that light in her. I am popular by default but Rachel is popular by design. Because being outgoing and engaging is who she is. I start to walk over to her when she sees me. She quickly punctuates her part of the conversation and exits the group. I see all their eyes follow her trajectory and find me. Most give a giggle of understanding. Some briefly glare with anger for me taking her away.

"Hey," She says, reaching me.

"You didn't have to leave. I was going to come over."

"I know you don't really enjoy groups, so why should you have to?"

"That's not completely true. I may act it sometimes, but I am not anti-social."

"I never said you were. We can go over if you want to." She turns and starts walking.

"That's okay." She stops and walks back to me, smiling. "I like you by yourself." I tell her. Rachel does a mock survey around us. It had thinned out a little but there were still at least thirty people about; people who we interacted with daily.

"Maybe by myself, but we certainly aren't alone." She tells me.

"That part doesn't matter."

I put my hand under her chin and lift her to me as I bend down to her. As we kiss, my body moves hers to the side of the car. My hands go the base of her back. I pull her to me with equal force, pushing her against the car. She doesn't respond with the same intensity as me, at first. I feel her give in to me. She claws at me, probingly. It only takes a minute for the commentary to begin. Shouts of, "Get a room", "There you go, Noah." start echoing around us. As we release and I take a step back from Rachel, a chorus of applause happens. Rachel is not embarrassed in the least. She grins widely. I almost think she is going to take a bow. I find myself enjoying the audience too. Not everything has to be a scandal.

"They seem to approve, at least." I say.

"They see us together now."

"They knew we were together."

"There is a difference between hearing something and seeing something. When you see it, you believe it. Now they believe we are together." She says.

"And that matters to you?"

"Yes. Shouldn't it?" She asks.

I didn't know. I hadn't thought about it, and I told her that.

"Our first night, I knew you wanted me. But I thought maybe that was because I was there. That you wanted someone and I was there. And now I don't know if it means anything."

"I wanted you because you were the hottest girl there. In that moment, I saw it as the only benefit to the breakup, that I could look at you and kiss you. I didn't know what it was. I didn't know you. Now I do and I stay because I want to. Because I want you. The world can know. I apparently have a very active media feed."

I laugh. Rachel soaks up the attention. People have been giving her a lot of attention her whole life, I imagine. She is like Shay in that way. Lily recoiled to PDA outside of a two-second-long kiss. She would never allow me to push her against a car with all these people around. Shay, on the other hand, would push the guy against the car if he wasn't game enough to do it on his own. I have thought of Rachel as a younger Shay. Maybe I am more right than I thought.

"I can be a little animalistic and I have been told I should control it." I tell her.

"Not by me." Her eyes dare me to rip off her clothes and take her on the hood of my car. I want to. Goddamn, I want to.

"Sugar."

"What?" Rachel asks.

"Ground rules. If I ever go too far, if you ever want me to stop, say sugar and I will." I can tell she is enticed.

"Okay."

"We are cancelling dinner." I tell her. She nods and reaches for me as best she can as I still have her pinned. "We need to get out of here before we get expelled or arrested. Get in the car." I tell her as I let go.

There is no hesitation as she almost runs to the passenger's seat. I am just as quick to get in. Driving out of the parking lot, I see Shay and Lily watching us leave. Lily had moved on, Shay was moving on. And so had I. I have every reason, every right to be happy. I have the right not to feel cluttered inside.

Thirteen

The Warmth Inside

Kissing her, there is nothing to me but the moment. All my burdens molt away when I am inside her. We tangle, and untangle, trying to reach a little deeper inward. The world is blocked out, all our thoughts are numb, and we simply feel each other, locked in a consuming pleasure. I move up her neck and kiss her cheekbone. Her head tilts back and her hair covers her face. I place my hand on the back of her neck and pull her in toward me. With my other hand, I wipe the hair away from her face and lean in to kiss her.

My instincts grind still and then start pushing me backward. Staring at me with blissful eyes is Lily. I blink my eyes and refocus my mind, but looking out again, a naked Lily lays beside me. She has a hand on my back and the other on my face. She wraps her thighs around my legs and pulls herself into the space I created. Her eyes never leave mine. My body rises to meet her. I have no control over this, but I hold my face away from hers. I am lost here. This isn't where I was. This isn't who I was giving myself to.

Lily's smile is inviting. She could hold herself here on the verge for as long as it took me before I gave in. She knows I will give in. This disposition weakens me. I shiver at my inability to leave and utter confusion on how this came to be. Lily cups my lips with hers and kisses me with suction so they will never part. When she releases, and the residue feels the coldness of the air, I am helpless. I climb on top of her, spreading her legs with my hand. This is what it was supposed to be all along. The memory of how I got here doesn't matter. What is important is that I am here.

My mind is blank as I close my eyes. I exhale and reach out for Lily. I find nothing. I feel like it takes me an hour to open my eyes, and with every passing second, I am further away from where I was. As I reach consciousness, the reality of the dream enters my mind. I wake beside a sleeping Rachel. The sheet down to her stretched out elbow. I look at her and feel slightly guilty about what my sub-conscience created.

Rachel's face is peaceful as she sleeps. In her stillness, I can look at her face and see her age. But I will never be able to look at her as fifteen. The memories I have coded in my mind hold her as a creature with the will and experience to match my own. Someone who equals whatever I have to offer. God crafted a body that was no longer waiting to be formed, but one with holy prowess. This was just the second time we slept together. There wasn't anything ordinary in it. It was discovery, fresh, wild and free. I replay it all in my head. I remember being able to feel how her breathing changed when I took off her bra, and how my body reacted when she unbuttoned and took off my pants. She rolled half on top of me before she fell asleep.

I stayed awake until, mid-sleep, she turned over, huddled, just off of me. Looking at her now, it occurs to me that in the three years of being with Lily, she only stayed at my house maybe five times. She abided by her 1pm curfew to escape staying at my house. However, when staying at Handley Lake or all of us staying at Shay's, there was never a second thought. But she never wanted to stay at my house, in my room, in my bed with me. When I asked her why, there was never a direct answer. She would never tell me.

Rachel asked me if I wanted her to leave. Her wide eyes looked over to me and I saw one last hurdle to be overcome. I pulled her to me, kissed her and told her I wanted her with me. The question was not said out of insecurity. It was to find out where the boundaries were. There is no balance to what we have. I am either receding or tentative, and Rachel pushes and turns, trying to find a way in-between the cracks in my walls. But, tonight, when we were alone – not just alone but isolated with each other – we existed without the distractions that cloud the air around us. At my party, I sort of blacked out. I submitted to the carnal urging. It wasn't so much as a choice as exhaustion and pain allowing instincts to lead. Last night happened in full, clear consciousness. I want her here. When I look at her sleeping, I smile. But I know I am not fully unwrapped from Lily, and even less sure if I want to be wrapped in someone else. If I can trust that. If I can trust myself in it.

Rachel's legs bend up and I see her eyes flutter open. I see her mind focus on her surroundings as she remembers where she is. She tilts her head up toward me, but the rest of her body stays still. The lamp on my nightstand provides a glow slightly above dim. I watch as she becomes more awake; her eyes don't leave my face until a yawn breaks her hold. Neither of us speak for a few moments. The small talk is the hardest. I can discuss big ideas and analyze concepts. I can ask all the right probing questions to get to know someone. That is somehow ingrained in me. But waking up with a girl in the morning, a girl who you are still in that figuring out stage with, a girl who is replacing someone I love, or loved…or…

Rachel sits up, puts a pillow behind her back, and shifts to face me. There is no awkwardness in her. It is nervousness. I can sense this but I just can't say anything. In my head, I am having five conversations, but I look blankly at Rachel. Not getting any response, she gets out of bed, reaches in her bag, and pulls out a pair jeans and a t-shirt. As she begins to put her shirt on, I finally find my voice.

"I have a shower down here." I tell her.

"And he speaks." She doesn't say this with any anger, more as if notating the date and time.

"I didn't want to lose our staring contest. I am not used to waking up with someone in bed with me."

"Says the guy who was in a three-year relationship."

"It's not bullshit." I tell her.

"Okay."

"Where are you going?"

"School." Rachel tells me.

"It's not even six."

I don't know how to read her. I am used to being around people I can read. Whatever was in her mind while she was sleeping kept her smiling. Now, awoken, her brow furrows and tightens. Her body tenses with stress. I want to observe her so I can understand, only, it is not happening behind glass. It is happening in front of me. It is happening because of me. I need to stop thinking of her as a stranger or as someone passing through, filling a temporary hole inside me. That isn't fair to her, and it isn't how I want to think of her. I shouldn't have to keep reminding myself of why I like her, want her, am developing a need for her, but I do. I tell myself it is the normal process in the evolution of a relationship. Except, I know shit about relationships. I know Lily. I know how she reacts and how to respond to her. I know how to read her. Or at least I did. There has been both a chaotic quickness and a stubborn slowness to Rachel and me. It has been three weeks since my birthday. We have been a couple for close to two weeks, publicly known as a couple for less than a week. We shouldn't have it all figured out. There are bumps and bruises to come and I just have to learn how not to be scared of them.

I get out of bed and go to Rachel. Her shirt is on and she starts to zip up her jeans, when I stop her. I place my hands on hers and push down. Her jeans loosen and fall down to her hips. She looks at me, her pride and will contracting.
"I don't have all the right words to say. My mind is never going to be completely clear. I adore it when you look at me as something special, but know the reality has a few layers of faults. I want you here. Everything else will find its place in time. Do you have the patience to wait?"

I can feel her body tremble. As she nods her head as if to say yes, I kiss her. We are going to need every minute we have before school.

Rachel had told her parents she was sleeping over her friend, Natalie's, but that she would check in before school. This leads me to dropping her off two blocks from her house so Natalie can bring her home. They have the routine down pretty well. As I watch them drive off, my phone rings. Josh wants to meet up before school. He speaks in short clips of sentences. I tell him to meet me at A Coffee Spot so we can walk to school from there.
"I just wanted us to talk and try to remove some of the chaos the last few months have been." He starts.

"That's going to be hard seeing as though we are walking into the chaos." I tell him. We are a few blocks from school before Josh tells me the reason he wants to talk.

"I asked Shay to prom." He blurts. I don't have to look at him or ask any questions. I know how this went. "She said no. She said it would ruin the friendship. I told her my asking and her turning me down might ruin the friendship, so we might as well give it shot."

"Wow. What did she say to that?"

"She said, "You are right. It might" and walked away."

We don't stop walking but we definitely slow down. Josh is injured by this. It is like waiting all Christmas to open the shiniest present only to find it is an empty box. He should have known, though. It was always going to be an empty box with Shay. At least he knows for certain now. It is strange. I have seen Shay regret decisions with such carelessness, it is almost sociopathic. I have stood beside Shay's fire and I know Josh has walked with it. They make sense, in a weird illogical way. But still an undeniable sense. Shay can state all the reasons she wants. None of them convince me.

There is no loneliness in Josh now. It is more of a finality. The end of a pursuit. It is what I have had inside me for almost the last three months. It can carve you up if you let it, and I did. Josh isn't like that. He won't be able to blink it clean, but give him a few days and he will erase the scent with someone else's.

"I also got into college." He tells me with a sort of melancholy that shouldn't be allowed to surround an accomplishment. "I am going to Oral Roberts."

He told me he was going to Oral Roberts the first week I meet him. He said it with such desire that I said, 'And I am going to be a starter at Louisville.' This was my equivalent. When I met his parents, I knew it wasn't so much a desire, it was a programed reality. When you are a kid, a large part of your destiny is predetermined. College is the crossroads, our first chance to make our own decision. Only, the eighteen years proceeding it still brainwashes us. Josh's independent choice here would break himself away from his family. He might hate the idea of Tulsa, but what he would lose if he didn't go would be far worse.

"At least it has 'oral' in the name, that must be a good indicator." I joke.

"Yeah." He brushes off what I said. "Do you know about Oklahoma State or Tulsa yet?"

I didn't. I had received five school letters over the last few months but hadn't opened any of them. I knew where I wanted to go and I didn't want options clouding my mind on the subject. I tell Josh I am going to Albany State, the first time I say those words out loud. I explain to him how close it is to where my sister is. How I felt I couldn't not have access if I needed to see her.

"Did you ever tell Lily about her?" He asks.

"No. I wanted to, I planned to. She broke up with me before I said anything. No reason to tell her now."

"What about Shay?"

"No. I can't explain it to her now either. It will just twist things more. You know. Rachel knows, that's enough for me now."

We walk the rest of the way to school silently. It settles in me what us going to different colleges mean. What it means that I never told Lily and Shay about Jess. There is a stiff melancholy that hangs on us. I search my mind for something that will make Josh smile. Anything that will induce a little happiness. We start to talk about last year when we played Winchester. That was the first game Megan came to and the first night they hooked up. We won by twenty-three, and we toyed with them all of the second half. It is a happy memory for us both, one that can exist as a memory but us still being okay with it. Don't look back with anger or sorrow. But get to a place where you can look back.

It is our final game of the year, a home game. It is also the final game Josh and I will play in high school. Everyone in school is buzzing about it the entire day. I go through the day simply as a basketball player. There is no other context. I only see Lily and Shay in passing or in class. Josh and I get back to the space where basketball is all that matters. That was the crux of our friendship for the first six months. Nothing was complicated then and nothing has to be complicated now.

I find Rachel after school. The game doesn't start for two hours, but we only have half an hour before we need to get ready. She is with Natalie when I reach her on the steps of the school's entrance.

"Hey. Did you get home okay?" I ask.

"You get Natalie out in the open space of two blocks and she is an excellent driver." Rachel says.

I extend my arm to pull her over to me, but she moves to me before I do. We kiss. I look back over to Natalie.

"Thank you, Natalie. I don't want Rachel's parents to hate me."

"They are huge basketball fans, Noah. My dad had your picture from last year when you scored thirty versus North Shore on our refrigerator for a solid month. He would be a hypocrite to say he didn't want me to date you." Rachel informs me.

"It may be different if he knew you were screwing." Rachel and I both look at Natalie. "Hey, I am on your side, I'm just saying."

I don't want Natalie to be right, but she is. I never had the sex talk with my parents. They knew I was dating Lily, so maybe they just figured. Maybe they never thought about it or cared. Lily's parents cared. I am sure they had suspicions before, but it wasn't until the beginning of last school year that her mother confronted her about it. It had been a beautiful August night and Lily and I had slept at Handley Lake. We spent the night talking about the future. Lily wanted to work at a magazine. Not a Literary one, not a fashion one. She didn't know what kind. She wanted to be in the environment. I explained magazines were dying, and she responded with an hour's long plan on how she would set it up online. We hardly even kissed that night. Lily forgot to tell her mother where she was. I had left my phone in the car and hers had died. Shay didn't think quickly enough when Lily's mother called her. So, come the morning when I dropped Lily home, her mother saw me in the car and had steadfast conclusions. I don't want to go through that with Rachel.

"They are coming tonight." Rachel tells me. "We should be cautious, Natalie is right." I mockingly take two giant steps backward.

"Like this?"

"Yeah," Rachel says. "Observe the ten-foot rule".

Natalie tells us she is going to get some food before the game. As she leaves, we walk down the steps and circle around to the gym's entrance. I lace my fingers in Rachel's and tell her it is acceptable PDA. When we turn the corner on the pathway to the gym, we find a large group clumped together, blocking our way. The group must be at least fifteen or twenty people. I scan through them quickly. I know them, of course. They are all seniors. Shay stands in the middle, cigarette between her fingers. She is not involved in any of the conversations going on around her, yet she still stands out as the center of the group. I stop. "Noah, we will say hi as we pass. We don't have to linger." Rachel tells me.

I grip her hand a little tighter. I stay half a step ahead of her. We are noticed pretty quickly. I am greeted with high-fives from the guys and Rachel gets a few hugs from the girls. They are excited to see us, interested to see us. I haven't felt this way since Lily and I broke up. Rachel holds court like a queen. Shay stays in the shadows for a moment, observing. When she finishes her cigarette, she walks in the circle again, then hovers around us like a bee choosing a flower. I can't be fully engaged in a conversation in this space, my attention is pulled to Shay, waiting for her to become the focal point. Waiting for her disrupt the mood.

"Noah." Shay begins, "How is it being eighteen? So much freedom, yet restrictions from what you used to be able to do."

I regard her slightly. I know the diagram of Shay's traps, but anyone could see what she was doing here. There is one string hanging from the seam of Rachel and my relationship. Is she really going to call it out, in the open, in front of Rachel?

"Are you asking me to buy you more cigarettes? I have told you what those will do to your teeth." I don't want to challenge Shay, but I want to advise her not to walk to the edge here. We can both attack one another's weak spots.

"I haven't been carded for a cigarette since I was fourteen. Do you know what statutory means? It is a word that is placed over consensual to create a legal barrier. It narrows your dating pool, but protects children from being charmed by lust."

Her eyes do not leave Rachel as she finishes her sentence. The crowd goes quiet. Shay stands there smug. Rachel's face is blank, devoid of spirit. This isn't a venue or an argument I can win by trading jabs. I could bring up how Evan was twenty-two when she was sixteen. Only, she would spin it into her being a victim. She isn't trying to tear down Rachel. She isn't trying to tear me down. She is trying to tear down the "us" of Rachel and me. A few people awkwardly leave as the tension builds in the silence. I look over to Rachel. She has regained her poise.

"Glass house, Shay."

"I didn't say that as judgment, Noah. You want to be with a little cheerleader groupie, that's fine. I just thought you had better taste is all. Some of us evolve, and some of us devolve."

I hear Rachel exhale and inhale with a dulled, yet stifling violence. Her eyes are less than a glare looking at Shay. This is my place to defend Rachel. This is my place to protect her. But there is no elegant way of articulating when you are put in a position to justify. I don't have a strategy here. Rachel does, though. She walks away. Not with an anger, she turns and walks at a normal pace, understanding all eyes are on her as she leaves. I follow her, catching up to her a few feet away from the gym's entrance. I touch her shoulder and she turns to me. The group behind has moved on and we hear a loud round of laughter coming from them.

"Are you okay?" I ask.

"I have gotten a lot of shit since the rumors of us started. People know they aren't rumors now and I am sure that is not the last time I will be called "a cheerleader groupie.""

"You never told people me were ragging on you."

"I can handle it. My eyes were open going in. I have a quick metabolism to process things."

"You don't have to do that alone."

"I guess I knew that. It is nice to hear you say it, though."

She gives me a kiss before entering the gym. I stand facing the direction she left for a moment, thinking. I understand Shay's bravado, but I cannot allow it here. I walk back to the group, which now has become less than ten people. I find a crack in the circle and step into them. I find Shay and am about to let her know she crossed a line –

only, I see Lily standing next to her. And beside Lily stands Reef. I become so uncomfortable that I almost lose my balance and fall. I look hard at Shay who calmly doesn't back down. There is no longer a safety net if we fight, and I am unsure if I can allow myself to call it that...yet.

"Almost game time, Noah. You ready?" Reef asks, smirking. He is talking down to me, trying to embarrass me. I normally would tear him down. I am stronger, wittier and a far better basketball player than he is. He doesn't get to take shots at my confidence. Except, he is with my ex-girlfriend, arm around her waist. He gloats with every breath about how he is with the queen of the school. The girl I had. The girl I lost. My rage only serves to prove his point. I turn and walk to the gym. Away from them.

When I get to the locker room, Josh is the only one there. He has his jersey on and is lacing up his sneakers. "Change quickly." he tells me, "I want to loosen up before too many people get here."

I open my locker, not responding to him.

"What's up? Clear your eyes." He tells me. "What's wrong?"

I explain to him the scene outside with Shay and Rachel, and then with Reef. My energy is restored as I can see he is completely on my side.

"Fuck them." He tells me. "We go out there and play our asses off and win. After that, we can sort through all of this. And Reef is dead to us. He is going to be invisible in this game. C'mon." Josh tells me.

He leads the way out of the locker room and into the gym. It is already half full as we enter. Josh and I get scattered applause walking in. Rachel is warming up with the other cheerleaders as I go over to her.

"Did your parents make it yet?" I ask.

"Yeah." She scans the crowd for a minute and finds them. I look in that direction. They wave to her, all smiles. They see me looking at them as well and wave toward me. I instinctually wave back and then look back to Rachel.

"They know about us, right?"

"They do." She says.

"And those are genuine smiles? Your dad isn't smiling because he is thinking about the crowbar he has in his trunk?" I ask. Rachel laughs.

"I told you – they love basketball. They are so proud of me for dating you." She rolls her eyes a little. "Probably *too* proud." She laughs.

"And what would they think if I kissed you right now?" I ask.

"If we win then I am a good luck charm, and if we lose, I distracted our best player."

"They really are fans, huh?"

"I told you."

"I guess we will have to win then." I tell her before kissing her. There are few hollers from the crowd. I ignore them. The scoreboard sounds, signaling ten minutes before tipoff. Coach starts yelling at me to huddle up.

"Have fun tonight." I tell Rachel before jogging over.

The game is a lot closer than anyone could have thought. With just over three minutes left, they are ahead by one with the ball. Reef is up with the guy with the ball. He stops his penetration and makes him pick up his dribble. He frantically looks for someone to pass to. The player I am defending circles around and frees himself with a pick. Greg doesn't switch to him, leaving him wide open behind the three-point line. I see this and sprint toward him. The guy Reef is defending has no choice but to bounce pass it to him. He is a little slow, or I am a little too quick, but I am able to swipe it away just as it was reaching his fingertips. The place erupts as I head to mid-court with the ball. There is one defender back, and Reef is sprinting down the court to the right. I wait until the defender commits to me and throw a pass to Reef in stride. He elevates both hands on the ball over his head. He reaches the rim and stops there. The force of the ball colliding with the rim causes it to ricochet back to the direction Reef had come. No one else had followed the play, so it is a race between me and the defender. I get there a step ahead, grab the ball, pivot, and start back to the basket. The defender can't stop himself and crashes into the stand. I have a straight line to the basket, with Reef standing underneath it. This time, I don't pass. I explode to the rim and jam it with as much force as I can. We go up by one. The other team calls for a timeout.

The defender limps to the bench, probably with a twisted ankle. My team gathers around, the crowd rises to its feet. A chant of "Noah" echoes through the gym. Coach yells at us, letting us know there is still plenty of time left. I look at Josh and we nod our understanding of what each other is thinking. I look over to Rachel. She doesn't see me. She is soaking up the energy she is enticing. It didn't matter how much time was left. Not anymore. The other team doesn't make another shot. With time running out, I drain a three to make it a ten-point victory. The crowd rushes the court. I find Rachel and tell her I will see her outside when it dies down. I didn't want to get mobbed. I am in the weight room as the rest of the team gets to the locker room. Coach makes a speech of what a great game it was. "Noah, where are you?" Coach asks. I walk into the locker room. "Hell of a game." He passes me the game ball. The team claps and I give a mock bow.

We hit the showers and change. Josh and I are the last ones there. Reef walks past us and mumbles, "That was a shitty pass." I look at him but don't say anything. Josh isn't that passive.

"What?"

Reef stops and turns to us.

"Nothing." Reef says.

"That's right. Get the hell out of here." Josh tells him.

He does, stopping at the doorway and mumbles, "I am still fucking your girl." Josh instantly pops off the bench.

"Let it go. It's not worth it." I say. Josh concedes.

There is a kaleidoscope of emotions dancing in my head. I exhale deeply, trying to control my breathing. I hear Josh ask me if I am okay before I start to unload on my locker. I pound it three times and let out a scream. I look to Josh with water in my eyes, if not tears on my cheeks. I hold no shame.

"Sprints?" I ask Josh.

"Sure."

We go back to the gym, to the baseline, and sprint end to end. Once, twice, ten times. Josh matches my intensity. We run for over twenty minutes. When I notice the clock, it is after 10:30pm. He goes back to the locker rooms, showers and changes. Heading out, I check my phone. I had missed two text messages and three calls from Rachel. I was supposed to be her ride home and had completely forgotten. There are only a few cars left in the parking lot. A few people hover by Josh's car and mine. As we get closer, I see Lily and Shay waiting for us.

I stop and look to Josh for an explanation about why they were there. He doesn't have an answer.

"I am not going to start anything. I just want to get home." I tell Josh.

"Understand. I will follow your lead."

I walk straight to the driver's side door, unlock it and am about to get it when I hear Lily.

"Are you just going to run away again?"

I look up slightly, don't say anything, and open the door. Lily forces it closed and pulls my arm to her. Her eyes are fire. A blue fire.

"Your plan to get back at me is to outcast Reef now, is that it?"

I stare back at her, trying to decode.

"And you are here to defend him?"

"He doesn't deserve to be put in the middle of this."

"I didn't put him in the middle of anything. He did. Or you did. Whoever did, I had no part of it."

"You are the storm, Noah. Okay? Whatever spun up is because of you."

"Thank you for thinking I am the center of everything, but I hardly give myself that much credit. Just because your boyfriend can't jump for shit and almost cost us the game, don't lay that at my feet."

Lily moves a little away and then steps forward. The water in her eyes purifies with anger, almost hatred.

"Why must you piss on everything? You pissed on me for years; you piss on Reef, on our relationship. Why won't you leave me the hell alone?"

"What are you talking about? I have barely spoken to you since you broke up with me. Yeah. You broke up with me. And I have left you alone. Clearly enough to start fucking some low-rate replicate of me."

"And what about you and your statutory rape girl? No one else but a freshman would look at you, huh?"

"What is the point of this? You are mad at me for Reef feeling bad he sucked tonight? You are mad because I didn't treat you well. I am a horrible person. Miserable. Hell has reserved room 666 for me already. I understand this. I am sorry for ever being in your hair. Alright? I know you have a book of reasons to hate me and I can't change that. I am not trying to anymore. If we could exist as friends that would be cool but I guess right now that isn't meant to be either." I finish. Lily just shakes her head and turns away. She is a few feet away, her head turned when I hear her say something. I can't be sure but I think she says, "I don't hate you."

Shay and Josh had moved off to the side while Lily and I spoke. They separate now. Josh comes to me, Shay toward Lily. Shay gives me a half-smile as she walks to Lily.

"You okay?"

"Wow." Is all I say.

"That was kind of an ambush."

"I really want to kick Reef's ass. Just bloody him up a little."

"You were right before, he is not worth it." Josh tells me.

"Maybe not but the overall result of doing it might be." I say.

I see a shadow in the streetlight as someone walks out into the light.

"Rachel? I thought you got a ride home?" I go to her.

"I was going to. Someone was on the way to pick me up but I heard you come out so I cancelled them. Then, you know, I didn't want to interrupt. I can call them back, you probably want to be alone." She reaches for her phone quickly.

"Hey. No. I will take you home." Her smile is quiet.

"Okay." She moves to the car and gets in the passenger's seat.

"Alright. I am getting home too. See you tomorrow."

"All right."

Josh walks to his car and I get in mine. Rachel is huddled into herself.

"What's wrong?" I ask as I start up the car.

"Nothing." She says.

"I am sorry I was so late coming out and not letting you know. As I am sure you heard, I piss on people sometimes."

We exit the parking lot and reach the stop sign at the end of the street.

"I don't want to be someone you piss on." Rachel says this with the heart wretchedness of a child. I put the car in park and look at her. She has never looked her age before. Not really. I suppose we never allow ourselves to look our ages. I have never thought of her as young before. Now, right now, she looks like a frightened ten-year-old who just wants to be home, in her bed, under the covers. Am I the evil one here? Taking advantage of a girl who had a crush on a senior? She seems so mature, but now I see the innocence, the inexperience lying underneath.

"And I don't want to." I tell her. I know this is hollow. It is simply words. This doesn't mean anything to her.

"Can you just take me home, please?" She asks. I need to say more. I need her not to feel this way.

"You are different to me than Lily." I begin. "We started out differently. I was different when we started dating than I was when I started dating Lily. Whatever that means, however that affects things, I don't know. But I need you to understand that."

"Everyone still calls Lily the love of your life. I hear it every day. That I am the rebound girl. The cheerleader groupie."

"I can't compare three years with two months. I cannot articulate the big picture of us." I stop. Rachel's nerves have stopped shaking. It still isn't enough, though. "But I can say this. Lily doesn't know about Jessica."

"Your sister?" Rachel asks. I nod. "She doesn't know you have a sister?"

"Only you and Josh know."

"Shay doesn't either?"

"No." This takes her back for a minute.

"Why did you tell me and not them?"

"I don't know. That is one of the differences. I felt I could tell you." I can visibly see the anxiety vaporize from her.

I put the car in drive and head for her house. We ride in silence for a while. It is a calming quiet. I didn't hurt her but she was hurt because of me. I weigh what that means in my mind before looking over to her. The mold of her face has returned to confidence and any sign of vulnerability is absent. This hurdle isn't some fight. It cannot be smoothed over with simple forgiveness. It brings us to the point of clarity, of understanding. It gives us the perspective of who we are, both individually and as a couple. The decision now is if we can accept it or not. If what we have developed the last two months is worth all the noise. Looking at her now, I have no doubt in my answer. I wish she would tell me hers.

Fourteen

Is it Ever Really Over?

It is 4am when I wake up and go for a run. I am not taken in by the darkness. It is simply a part of the environment, like the concrete and street signs. My body is on automatic as I run. My mind is hiding away in the attic, chipping away toward the bedrock of everything unresolved. I haven't seen my sister in over four months – since Rachel and I first got together. Should I bring her with me? Is that something too heavy to ask of someone? The one part of me that I am afraid of people knowing about, of judging me on, is something apart from me as an individual. I am fractured because she is broken. Why is this, though? Am I ashamed? I don't think that is quite it. Thinking about it, I come to this conclusion: Jessica becoming sick, being admitted to the hospital, was the end of my childhood. It tore me to pieces and threw those pieces in a whirlwind. I have collected enough of them to be functional. But they have never fit back exactly right. I guess I have never gotten to a place where I know myself away from her.

Bringing Rachel into that turmoil seems destructive. To our relationship, to an innocence in her she might not even realize is still there. It would be better to leave her alone on the street in falling snow. But if Rachel and I are going to last beyond high school, beyond my graduating, this cannot be hanging over our heads. I will have to ask her to come to New York with me. Those are my options.

When I dropped Rachel off, I agreed to meet her parents. This was something that had to be prearranged because I found myself incapable of being in a position where it had a chance of happening organically. I owe Rachel a lot, and meeting her parents is at the top of the list. It was real from the first night with us, it just took me a while to realize it. Everyone at school now understands, so that only leaves her parents. I am not a natural at this. I have to think out every word. I was never close to Lily's parents. I don't think they ever accepted me, they merely put up with me and only allowed it because Lily was happy with me. She was better with me. Not because of me, but with me. It may have been how hopeless I was at points that fueled her ambitions, or it may have been me excelling at basketball that pushed her into finding something she could excel at too. Her parents saw my influence but never trusted it. I guess a parent's responsibility is to see all the reasons to doubt it will work, just as it is the one connecting with another to see the potential not displayed.

After I agreed to dinner with Rachel's parents, I spent the rest of the night in full belief we had just broken up. It is that cliff hanger conclusion after the commercial break. I graduate high school in less than a month and am off to college. It's not as though I care about hooking up with college girls or all the craziness I don't want to be restricted from. I have spent the last seven years with abject freedom from parental rules. It holds no mystery to me, only a haze of loneliness. But I see how people change now. Rachel is in bloom and is still blooming. I won't be the townie boyfriend, but I won't be the star athlete either. I don't know what I am outside of a gym, and more scarily, I don't know how to find out. Rachel, like Lily, needs a counterpart. I haven't been made for that.

When I woke up, I had a text message on my phone from Shay. I didn't want to read it at first as I wasn't in the mood for snarky remarks that early. But I couldn't ignore it. I finally read it:

"This is the struggle with her about you."

It wasn't an apology. I think it was meant to defuse. I don't feel angry about last night. Lily and I broke up over three months ago and Shay and I have been falling apart at varying rates since. It has been a long goodbye held in denial until now. Shay and I cannot be what we were. It had built in bounties and purpose beyond each other. We can't play games and dance around innuendos without outside consequences. It is too much of a wildcard. We would end up exactly the same way her and Josh would. Except, I wouldn't be the one who becomes bored. I also wouldn't be the one who would lose their best friend. We were very much individual pieces, but fit together to form something separate. The environment or who was or wasn't there did not matter, the gravity was always consistent. Now, in relation to each other, we are floating.

I didn't respond to her text. I grabbed a pair of shorts, put my sneakers on and started running. I don't know what time it is, but the sun starts to rise enough to blind me. I stop running and give myself a second to catch my breath. I am far from at peace, but I am at ease. I can head home now. I can face the day.

As I drive into the school parking lot, I notice Josh in mid-conversation with a group of around six. I am not surprised. If Josh gets to school early, you will usually find him in this circumstance. I walk over and am surprised to find Rachel and her friend, Natalie, are part of the group. Rachel is at the other end of the make-shift circle when Josh realizes I am next to him.

"Good. Noah, you remember that time at Six Flags when we went on that sucking thing?" He asks. I tell him I do.

Josh had been telling the story of a trip we took last summer. There was this ride we didn't have any understanding of before we went on it. We walked into this big circle-shaped room completely carpeted and stood there for a minute looking for the interesting part. This kid, maybe seven, tells us to stand against the wall. We did. The door locks and the walls start to move and the floor sinks out from underneath us. Before we could try to prevent it, we are sucked up against the wall. I won't say I was scared – there was no time for fear to formulate in my mind before I was plastered against the wall.

Josh tells the story with the wide-eyed excitement we had when we experienced it. It was like climbing into a carousel to look at the pretty horse, and then been surprised when it starts to move. Josh and I play it up, jabbing back and forth of who was more scared, of who almost threw up and why neither of us have gone back on the ride since. Our audience eats it up and we laugh throughout. It feels good. As it winds down, Josh addresses Rachel.

"If you can get him back on it, be sure not to wear sandals. That poor seven year old's sandals flew off her feet and crashed against the wall opposite her. We didn't hear her cry but when the ride stopped, her face was wet with tears."

I look directly at Rachel as he says this, and her eyes stay with mine. I am not worried about what she will say, there is no angst. I am curious. It is an itchy palms curiosity. "I've never been on that ride. But the surprise is ruined. Why should I go on it now?" Her question is posed solely to me.

"The surprise flavors the experience, but so does anticipation. It would be worth it if we went." Her eyes are gleaming as I finish. I walk over and kiss her.

The bell rings, telling us to get to class, so the group disperses. Rachel, me, Josh and Natalie hang back a little and walk in together.

Our walk from the parking lot to the steps of the school and inside isn't long. Even walking slowly, we make it in less than three minutes. This is plenty of time for Josh, the master of small windows. He is all into Natalie. He manipulates reasons to touch her hair and her forearm. She giggles and smiles, overcome by the attention. She may have an understanding of how boys play games, but this seems out of her depth. I look at Rachel to see if there is concern in her face, but there isn't. I look at Josh and Natalie through the lens of Josh's history of intentions and am suspicious. Rachel looks at Natalie and Josh and sees the innocence in attraction. This confuses me. This sort of attraction marks the end of innocence, doesn't it? It is a full dissolve into a landscape void of innocence.

We separate inside, our classes in different directions. I kiss Rachel and, for the first time, it feels normal. It is not as though it has happened so much it has become routine, or that the act has become mundane. There was just comfortability to it. All the doubt, tentativeness and fear in me feels settled. Rachel smiles, maybe reading my face, maybe just feeling a difference too. She kisses me again before walking away. I stand there for a moment, watching her.

"It's a solid view, but get hard on your own time. We've got class." Josh says, breaking my gaze. As I turn and follow him, I try and think ugly thoughts. It is amazing the lack of control you have when you allow yourself to feel settled and relaxed.

At lunch, Josh decides to go to the cafeteria with me. Josh and I get a few slices of semi-warm pizza and a bottle of water before I look around to find Rachel. When I come to her, she is already staring at me. Her eyes are wide and anticipating. I think she must have been watching me the whole time. There had been no talk of us having lunch together. Except for one time, it never happened in school. This wasn't on purpose. It was me not thinking things through and not understanding that maybe it was the appropriate thing to do. The boyfriend thing to do.

The table sits eight and only six were already there, making it simple for Josh and me to join. As we approach, chairs shift, opening a spot next to Rachel, which I take, and a spot next to that where Josh sits. Natalie is conveniently positioned next to Josh. It is the same group as before, only the dynamic has changed. The last time, there was an air of confusion about why I had chosen to join them. Now, it was known why I was there, and with Josh also there, we kind of took over. This didn't seem to bother the girls. In fact, they seemed to love it. The guys, however, were less enamored. The six of them had been friends since the fifth grade. It was clear, on the guy's side at least, that they had thoughts of it not staying strictly platonic.

When I asked Rachel about them, she told me the older they had got, the prettier the girls became and how unconfident and awkward the guys had become because of it. She said they weren't as close as brothers to her, more like cousins you see a lot. The changes in appearance did cause a divide in them. There was a sexual tension that only went in one direction. When Rachel and I got together, they were upset, but it had grown to a point they couldn't really believe they had a chance with her.

Now, though, with Josh flirting with Natalie, their bedrock of possibilities was cracking. It is better to be in the proximity of what you are attracted to than not be, but when it comes up zero, it is never fun. Josh and I engage with them as much as we can, but the seams in Rachel, Josh, Natalie and I tighten. Natalie and Rachel feed off each other in the same way Josh and I do. The freedom to the rift is something I have not felt for the entire year and having it here is exhilarating.

The bell sounds the end of lunch. Rachel and I get up and throw away our trash. It takes Josh and Natalie a minute to do the same.

"Are you okay with them?" I ask Rachel.

"Is she smiling?"

"Yes."

"Then I am okay with it." She tells me.

I told her I wasn't concerned about now. The beginning is the reason there is a middle and an end. It also entices. I tell her Josh is a great guy but he has never been a good or faithful boyfriend.

"Natalie has been to enough parties that Josh has also been at to understand how he is. Not to make it sound creepy, but she almost has a shrine to him on the inside door of her closet."

I ask her where she keeps her shrine to me. I get the shove and adamant denial of having one that I was hoping for. Having knowledge of this is something Josh would exploit, except the nature of it is so submissive, it is almost unexploitable. When Josh and I walk back to class, I ask him about Natalie.

"So, are you messing with this girl or with me?" I ask Josh.

"What?"

"With Natalie." I say.

"You don't think she is pretty?"

"Whether she is pretty or not wasn't the question."

"No, but it is the answer. The chick is cute. So I flirt. You are with her best friend. If it works out, it makes sense." He tells me.

I see his point. I fear his point. If he and Natalie start going out, it would form a group. It would position itself the way Lily, Shay, Josh and I were. With the difference of us being two couples – the way we should have been with Lily and Shay. Rachel and I had been a little hideaway for me. I don't know if I want to share it, even with Josh.

I stay late after school for a makeup English test. Walking through the halls, there is a calm to the emptiness. I make a wide turn that leads to the main entrance when I see someone in the corner of my eye. I stop and look over to my left. Lily is there, shrived against the side of a locker, barely in view. Even from my distance of nearly twenty feet, I can see tears streaked on her face. I am disarmed by this image. The solitude of us alone in the hallway shatters my nerves. I am paralyzed. I cannot walk away or towards her. I stay locked like this until she lifts her head and sees me. She is startled at first. I almost see embarrassment in her. She straightens herself, wipes her face with her hand and tries to smile at me.

"Hey," Her voice is weak.

As I look at her, it as though a shroud has been lifted from her. As though I blinked and my eyes are seeing clearly in a new dimension of light. I step slowly to her so I can take her in and test her response to me. She is wearing stone-wash jeans, slim fit, that she had bought over the summer. I was with her. We spent over an hour in the store with her trying to explain the different cuts of jeans to me. It was an excuse by me for her to have to try them all on. I could tell she knew what I was doing, but played along anyway. At the time, the jeans were probably a size or two too small, although no one would complain about seeing her in them. Now, they were worn-in and fit a little loosely. She is also wearing her silver snowflake earrings her mother bought her when she first had her ears pierced at twelve. I hadn't seen her wear them in a while.

The closer I walk to her, the more she unravels. I stop when I am about five feet from her. She leans against the concrete wall, slightly arching her lower back upward. She moves her hair away from her face, it falls back half covering her left eye. She moves it again, tucking it behind her ear. I have gotten to this point. She isn't yelling at me, or making out with another guy in front of me. I am unsure of my feelings. Thoughts of Rachel climb in my head and are pushed out by something I cannot identify. I want to wait for Lily to speak but I cannot keep myself steady in this silence.

"Are you okay?" I ask in the most calming tone I can.

"No. Not really. I will be." She tries to sound assured, but falls short.

"Can I ask what's wrong?"

"Do you really want to know?" Her small voice asks.

The fact that I had asked doesn't invalidate Lily's question. My mind is flooded with reasons for why she is upset. Given my imagination, the options that latch on disturb me. Is she pregnant? Have an STD? These are possibilities, but don't make sense given the context of how I found her, huddled up alone.

"If you want to tell me." I say, moving a few inches closer to her.

She looks at me clean in the eyes for a moment, searching for a reason not to trust me. To not allow herself to open up to me. She finds none.

"Reef just broke up with me." Lily tells me, punctuating it with a noise that is a hybrid of laughter and sobbing.

"Oh." Is all I can say for a minute.

I don't want that to be the reason she is upset. We had stood apart when we were both single, and when she alone had a boyfriend, or we both were involved. But never like this. Never with Lily single and me being the one to have a girlfriend. The way Lily looks at me now, I feel guilty for being the one holding the restrictions. I tell her we should get some air, so we exit through a side door that leads to the back of the school by the soccer field. The sun is hot and bright. We walk down closer to the parking lot to find a shaded spot. We glance around at our surroundings, finding we are alone, before turning to each other. I am not uncomfortable standing beside Lily. I am not compelled to leave, but I find it hard to have coherency of what to say.

"Define 'just'." I finally ask.

"Ten minutes before you got there." She stops. I give her the space to keep going. "Apparently, he wants to be single before summer, so I guess he wants to line up some summer flings." She laughs, but you can tell it is derived from hurt.

Lily is not built for this. She wasn't made to be discarded. There is nothing in her that deserves that. She doesn't hold herself with self-pity. It is more anger and disappointment in herself. The shame of, 'I should have known better.'

"I am sorry." I tell her.

"I don't want you to be sorry about it."

"What does that mean?"

"I don't know." She tells me. "It isn't clear. It is not like I want you to be happy I am hurt. I just don't want you to be sorry–"

I cut her off.

"That you're single?" I say this as a statement rather than a question. As a completion to her sentence.

Lily nods her head slightly, enough for me to take it as agreeing to what I said. I turn away from her and repress the urge to punch the brick wall behind me. I clench my fists and fight against my adrenaline. Lily holds her position patiently for the ten seconds it takes me to recompose. This wasn't supposed to happen. Lily had been erased as an option.

"I am not single, Lily." I say, still facing away from her.

"I know."

"This is the longest we have stood beside each other in over three months." I say, turning back to her.

"I know that, Noah." Her face and eyes are still, but I see her hands twitching a little. A sign of nervousness under her reserve of calm.

"And you were kind of a bitch to me last night." I can tell she didn't expect my honesty here. Her eyes dour at me for an instant before she blinks it away.

"I am sorry. I know I made a scene." She pauses. "I know I shouldn't have." I look at her without the will of holding anything against her.

"All is forgiven." I tell her. "Does Shay know about you and Reef?"

"I texted her. We are meeting up later."

Reef is probably out spreading the gospel that he is single. There is no trickle of information. There is a bang, and within three seconds, everyone knows. Everyone, including Rachel.

"I should go." I say, turning and walking away.

"Noah, wait." I take two more steps before I stop and turn back to her.

For the first time, I see confliction in her. It is faded by her confliction that she is right, but still undeniably there. She walks to me until we are only an arm's length apart. Her look is aimed to paralyze me; I have no will to move.

"What do you want from me?" I ask. Lily shifts from foot to foot, looks away and then back to me.

"I know it is not as easy as saying I want you back. I realize there are steep hurdles to that. But is it too much to ask that we start being friends again?"

I want to tell her that I do not know how to be friends with her. That she and Shay tried really hard to bury the possibility of that. I am tempted by the thought of everything going back to the way it was, but I am equally pushed to the freedom of being out from under that history. How can I not feel attracted to her, though? Lily is the only one I have ever chosen to attach my heart to. A girl I fantasied about before we got together, and who I continued to fantasize about when we were together. I thought she was my soulmate. But that was before. Most of what was there is still there as I look at her now. It is what is missing, what was forcefully gutted, that has created the divide we are standing on other sides of now.

"I am not the easy fallback because you are feeling unwanted." I tell her. "Anything beyond what we are to each other now is more complicated than we can imagine."

"I am just trying to be honest with you, Noah. I don't have anything against Rachel." It stings hearing Lily use Rachel's name. As it did when Rachel first used Lily's.

The longer I stay in Lily's presence, with all the windows opening, the more what Rachel means to me detaches. I stop my mind from floating and focus on a mental image of Rachel. She is a girl who took me away from my misery when Lily broke up with me. The girl who radiated the path out of my year-long depression. I never did anything to earn her affection, yet it is always there. I can't stay here and let her be devalued.

"I can't do this now, Lily. I am having dinner with Rachel's parents; I can't have my mind clogged up."

"With her parents? Is it really that serious?" There isn't pleading in her voice, but certainly a strain of trying to find out how hard this is going to be.

"Yeah. It kinda is."

"Kinda is?"

"It is. No qualifiers." I tell her. She retreats a little after that. Maybe she is just feeling displaced and I was the first thing that made sense to try and cling to.

"I should get going." Lily announces. "If I am too late, Shay will get worried."

She walks past me with a jolt. Not slowing down or turning back to me. I start to jog after her when my phone rings. I stop and pull the phone out of my pocket. I see Lily turn and face me while walking backwards from the parking lot. Her look dares me to not answer the phone. It is already in my hand, so I slide it unlocked, expecting to see Rachel's number. I don't. The call is from my father. "Hello?"

"Noah. This is your father. I need you to come home."

"Why?"

"Please just come home."

"I can't." I tell him. His insistence annoys me slightly, but this is the first time I can remember he has ever asked me to come home. "What's going on?"

"It's Jessica." Hearing her name from his voice chills me. All of a sudden, I want to be home. Whatever it is, I don't want to hear it over the phone. "She passed away."

I mumble a reply and put the phone back in my pocket. The effect of numbness sweeps over me like a downpour. I might have blacked out or lost time because, the next thing I remember, Lily is next to me, holding me up. I hear her ask me if I am all right, or if she should call an ambulance, but I am unable to respond.

I am finally able to steady my breathing. I take a few steps to test my balance. I am still woozy and stop. I see Lily out of the corner of my eye. She is frightened. I inhale deeply, holding it in before unleashing a scream that extends beyond the core of me. I break down in tears before shutting it all away. Lily sees my composure and looks relieved.

"Who was that? Are you okay?" Lily asks.

I look at her as my mind tries to force my body to move.

"My sister died."

Fifteen

The Death of My Sister

All of Lily's words are whispers that a wind blows away from me. I am conscious just enough to understand how close to comatose I am. I hear myself ask Lily to call Josh for me. She does. I make it to the steps of the school, sit down and wait. Lily stops asking me questions and waiting for replies. She stands off the curb of the sidewalk in the parking lot. She is a shell of who she was ten minutes ago when she was unearthing the buried emotions to hide her loneliness. She stands there, fidgeting; uncertain of every thought and instinct. I want to snap out of it. I want to exhale and realize I have been hanging on a fence for a long time waiting for this to happen. I wanted my sister to get better, to be the person she was before. But if that wasn't a choice, if that wasn't going to happen, there was only one other conclusion. I knew that. It is something you never can be ready for.

Shay arrives before Josh. I hadn't seen Lily call her, but it makes sense that she did. She goes to Lily. They are far enough away that I cannot hear what they say to each other. I am observed as though they are debating whether they should call an ambulance or leave me. After a couple of minutes, Shay ascends the stairs to me. There is a look of concern, but more potent is her anger. She sizes me up for a minute to see how much of it she can use.

"Are you okay?"

"Will be." I say. Shay waits for more. I don't say anything else.

"You have a sister?" Shay asks. My eyes go cold and I am pierced with a shiver of what I am about to say.

"She died. I had a sister." I tell her.

"And she lived in New York?" Shay asks. They have connected the dots, or at least some of them. I am not going to give a timeline or a history. Not now. I know Lily and Shay hearing I have a sister affects the perception, the memory, of the last four years. I just can't talk about it now.

Josh arrives before more questions are asked. I get up and say goodbye to Shay, and walk down the stairs. Before I get in Josh's car, I look to Lily. Her arms are folded over her chest and she looks like she has been crying. I regain myself enough to be able to walk over to her and give her a hug. Her body shakes slightly. I look her in the eyes. She blinks the water out of hers and looks into mine. "I am sorry I never told you. It is a long, hard story to tell. I loved you as much as I understood how to when we were together. I know that wasn't enough." I walk back to Josh's car and we drive away.

I don't tell Josh where I want to go, but I can tell by the route he takes that he understands I want to go home. There is no commentary from him on my sister or how I found myself alone with Lily after school. And I am thankful for that. We stay quiet for the entire ride. My body begins to adapt to the new wave of tension crashing and reforming in me. There is no balance to anything I have ever thought or believed. I had separated a piece of myself and left it with Jessica. Now, it has returned as a specter forcing its way into me. It scatters me, demanding I am rearranged to find space for it.

Josh pulls up to my house and puts the car in park. I look over to him.

"Thanks." I say.

"Yeah." I cannot complete the movement to open the door.

"If you need anything, let me know." Josh tells me. I nod that I understand and exit the car.

My parents are sitting at the dining room table as I enter. They don't move except to look up at me. I sit at the empty chair at the head of the table and wait for one of them to speak. I am caught in this moment for what feels like hours. The three of us blankly stare at each other, not speaking. There is no room for anger toward them now. No room for regret of what I could have done. The last seven years had exhausted that from me. There is only emptiness from the realization that she is gone.

My mom speaks first. She tells a story of when Jessica was ten and I was seven. We had this family outing where we took a boat ride to have lunch on this island. The boat was supposed to come back in two hours, but ended up being over an hour late. Jess got really nervous we were going to have to swim back, especially because I wasn't a strong enough swimmer to make it. My mom laughs as she talks, her eyes glisten with tears, yet there is happiness in the memory. My parents tried to assure her the boat was just running late, but she was convinced he wasn't coming back. She was nearly halfway done making a makeshift raft when the boat showed up. Out of embarrassment or anger at the boat driver (probably both), she didn't speak to anyone for the rest of the day.

That was the starting off point for us taking turns in telling family stories. Each adding details to the other's story. We remembered and reflected in a way I never had before with my parents. There were no awkward pauses, no thoughts held back. There was a lot of happiness I had forgotten about.

It is past nine when my dad starts to yawn. He breaks from the table and briefly goes over the logistics of the next few days. The plan was to head down to Connecticut the day after tomorrow. Which means I have to go to school in the morning. I head to my room, crash on my bed, and stare up at the ceiling. I begin to decompress. As soon as I close my eyes, I am asleep.

I am in the middle of rolling over when a flash of thought pulls me awake. Rachel. I had completely forgotten about dinner with her parents. I didn't show. I didn't call. I just wasn't there. I reach for my phone and find two missed calls and a text from her. I check the time, 3am, and write her a text.

"I am so sorry about tonight. I will explain tomorrow." I send it and exhale. Less than a minute later, I feel the phone vibrate in my hand. Rachel replies.

"I talked with Josh and he told me what happened." I hate texting when you cannot tell the tone of what is being written. My text must have woken her up. Her text wasn't thought out, it was simply stated. I feel selfish here thinking that my sister dying should hold more weight than me missing dinner with Rachel's parents, and there is no conflict in me that it shouldn't be. To Rachel, though, they may be equal. I am not sure how to resolve that.

Rachel texts again.

"I am sorry to hear about your sister. Let me know if I can do anything." The words are generic, but when coming from someone who is not generic, it is comforting. I sit up and call her. The phone doesn't complete its first ring before Rachel answers.

"Hi, Noah." Her voice is soft and has a little rasp. I can tell she is still half asleep.

"I know it's late. Should we just talk tomorrow?" I offer.

"This is fine. I am glad you called."

Now, in this moment, I do not know what to say. I don't want to talk about Jessica and I don't want to apologize for missing dinner with her parents. I do want to talk to her, though, and hear her voice. I want to know she is not angry at something I feel I need no forgiveness on. We exist for a long moment while she waits for me to speak.

"I guess I don't have much to say." I say, giving up thinking of something.

"Will you be at school tomorrow?"

"Tomorrow I will. Then I will be gone for a few days."

There is another pause. Dead air. I wish I could see what she was doing. How she was waiting. Is she distracted by other thoughts, focused on something in her room. Or even while waiting, do I have her full attention?

"Can we plan on breakfast tomorrow?" Rachel asks.

"Yeah. Should we invite Josh and Natalie? Help that along?" I say. I want to fill the spaces with as many stories as I can to dull the interest in mine.

"I'd rather it just be us. Tomorrow at least." The more awake she gets, the more there is hidden underneath her words. "It's their decision to make."

"I thought you wanted them to get together?"

"I want Natalie to be happy. And when that runs out, I will be there to help her find something else that will."

Is Rachel not happy? Is that what she is saying? We only mean to each other how we perceive the other. It is what held me back with Rachel at first. The biggest obstacle I had to overcome. I never felt a change in her reaction toward me. We had become more settled. We had the ability to recall a memory and have it bring a smile to our face. I am the boy she sought and got. A senior. The captain of the basketball team. It has always been enough to dull the black spots of me. But I know Rachel has looked close enough to see the full picture. What am I really offering her? The sex is great, so there is that. Relationships have lasted on less. I have pieces scattered in me, but no outline to give me form. Any identity I had was lost at sea when Lily broke up with me, when basketball ended, when my sister died. I am back at zero. I am not falling. I am not balancing on a tightrope. I am floating through the absence of gravity.

"Wanna say seven for breakfast? Should I pick you up?" I ask.

"Seven is good, but I will get a ride. If my parents saw you they would want to meet you, it would become a thing. I know you don't want that." She says. She is right, but I somehow feel I am failing her.

"I do want to meet your parents." I tell her. "I know it is important to you."

"It is important to me." Is all she says. I hang on, waiting for more, but there is nothing.

"See you in a few hours." I laugh a little, attempting at levity. Rachel does not step into the space.

"Okay." Her line drops. I leave the phone by my ear for a moment as though an echo will reach me. As though my mind is still processing a missing sentence.

I lay back down. My eyes stay awake. My mind is not thinking, it is caught in the blankness of my stare. My alarm wakes me at 6am, only, I never really fell back asleep. I take what is supposed to be a quick shower that lasts twenty minutes. I throw on a pair of jeans and an old concert t-shirt, then head out. I arrive at our breakfast spot a few minutes early, but Rachel is already there. I see her through the window, her head is bent down looking at a menu. I pull myself out of view and hesitate before going in. Rachel has become more than an enviable ending. We never have had a fight – barely an argument. I had been slow to unravel, but never created false expectations. Until last night. The reasons shade it, but I cannot prevent it from existing. There is no guilt in me. Walking into A Coffee Spot will show me Rachel's reaction. Whether she wants me to give more when I have no more to give.

I walk in and sit down across from her. As she looks up to me, I see a somberness that I hope is purely exhaustion. I have had this look most of the last year and one has always been masking the other. I have never seen Rachel without light in her eyes. I do not see a difference between causing it and allowing it here.

"I ordered you an OJ. It should be here in a minute." She tells me. She picks up her coffee with both hands and takes a sip.

"Thanks." I say and wait for her to put the cup down. "I should have called you yesterday."

"I know how big a part of you your sister was. I understand losing any other thoughts. I am glad you called me when you did. I would have come by, but Josh thought you needed some time."

Josh was right. I want her comfort and her help to break the formation of tears being created inside me, but last night I had no balance to understand that.

"I explained to my parents everything and they wanted me to let you know that you are in their thoughts."

I had thought Rachel would be pissed at me. She says she understands the barrier between relationships and family. Until a relationship becomes family, there are times of isolation. I can't tell if this is her belief or her forming conclusions of my behavior based on what I have said to her. It succeeds in relieving me of the last bit of denial that Jessica is gone. A shiver pierces the bottom of my spine and runs to my shoulders. I turn away and tightly hold my eyes shut. I don't cry. I allow a few bursts. But I wasn't going to allow it here.

I succeed in repressing the swirl and look back up at Rachel. Her eyes hold a vacancy to them, only, the longer I look at her, I can see emotion pushing forward. We hold here for a minute.

"Did you already order some food?" I ask.

"No." Is all she says.

I take a sip of my orange juice and clear my head. When I look back at Rachel, it is clear her eyes have never left me. I am long past thinking of her age as a separation between us. That I have the upper hand because of it. But I have thought that she wanted me more. She chased me. She waited around for me to get to the same place as her. And from that place, I began taking pieces from her. The need for her presence began to climb under my skin. I don't think I was aware of that until looking at her now. My throat gets a dry tickle as I am finally able to read her thoughts.

She had told me she had three boyfriends before me. She had lost her virginity to the third, who she broke up with a month into this school year. She had said it wasn't that she stopped caring for him, she still had feelings for all her exes. Their relationship had gotten to a place where there was nothing new to be learned. Everything started repeating itself. They hadn't heard all the other's stories, it was her reactions to them, even the new and interesting that started to repeat. Her stimulus to them evaporated and they became background noise. White paint on the walls. The memory of this hits me now, even when I gave it little thought at the time. She had said that after her last break up is when she started to crush on me. We had passed in the halls, her wires were tripped, and she knew I was the next guy she wanted.

This was pillow talk one night when we both woke up at 3am with no desire to move or go back to sleep. It was an insight into her that I collected but never put to use. I enjoyed the surface so much, I neglected to look deeper. Rachel aimed to see through my surface, my facade. She had reached the center and was now looking back at the distance she had traveled.

"Noah, I have always said that I want to be with you as long as I can be – and I meant that. Except, I might not have to explain it. I said it that way so you would take it as, 'as long as you will allow me to be', which was part of it. But it also meant as long as I wanted to be." She stops and searches her mind for a minute. "Phrasing it that way isn't quite right, but you understand, right?" I am not sure if this is a rhetorical question or not, so I don't answer. "I am not going to recite a handful of clichés. I think we need to break up."

Her words reach me in slow motion.

"I would ask for penance for my sins, but there hasn't been too many with you." I tell her.

"I know that. It isn't because of that. I am not Lily. I started thinking of what it would mean if you met my parents. You would be my first boyfriend to have dinner with them. Then I started to think about what it would mean if I went to Connecticut with you and met your family. Your extended family. And was introduced as your girlfriend to all these strangers. I wanted to do all of it. I wanted to be there for you. I wanted to show you off to my parents but that is something heavy to go through, and we only have a week left of school."

"So?" I ask.

"I am not your high school girlfriend. We have been together for three months. It ends when you go off to college. I don't want to see you every other weekend."

I didn't want to convince her and I didn't want to pull out some pretty words that would keep her with me. I believed the truth of what she said. I kissed her goodbye and left. I wasn't leaving a burden, I was leaving someone who relieved me of my burdens. She was everything I needed when I needed a lot. A rebound girl in name only.

I put a lot of bullshit on our relationship. I accept that. But I had thought we were about to reach beyond all of it, I did. It is not something I wanted but it is something I understand. I could start to debate it. To say you will miss someone is admitting you need them. I have always thought that, and I still do. But there might be different meaning to it as well. I will miss Rachel. I will miss the way she looked at me. How she touched me. Her innocence, which always had more strength and resilience than my jadedness. I was someone she wanted but I never had anything she needed. Yet she made me feel needed. Well, maybe it was desire I mistook for need. We had talked about taking her to visit Jessica. She inched along those in roads. I was never against the idea. There was always a separation between her knowing about Jessica and being able to trust what she would think if she met her.

The thought of asking Rachel to come down to Connecticut was a debate I couldn't sway either way. She was my girlfriend, it would have been logical. Maybe after I had processed everything more I would have thought about it, except that wouldn't have happened until after graduation. Everything Rachel had said is true. I would have seen it eventually. I wanted a few more tastes before quitting. I wanted a better space for the words to exist in. It takes a dying star a long time before burning out. She saw it was ending and ended it. I don't trust myself to make that call.

Lily and Shay avoid me every time I appear in their line of sight at school. I don't approach them either. I have to allow it not to matter anymore. Josh is flying to Tulsa for a visit to Oral Roberts and wasn't going to make it down to Connecticut this time. He said if he had any choice he would bail and be there for me. I believe he would be. But he needed to go and start that part of his life, I understood that. Truth is, I think I need to do this alone anyway.

Everything seems exactly the same at the hotel as before. Even down to the cars in the parking. Which makes sense being the same people are inside. I didn't feel as though I really belonged here last time. I was a fringe player weaving his way toward the center. For the most part, I was treated this way as well – an outsider allowed in because of his name. This time it is different. They are gathered because of my sister. By someone who has been pulling out of me for the last seven years. I am not here to pay my respects or to honor her. I am here to say goodbye. I am here to try and understand what her absence makes of me.

I walk into the function hall with its vaulted ceilings and dangling chandeliers to a room full of people that seemed to be frozen, only to start moving when I enter. It is an eerie time-freeze. I sort of drift in at first, slowly surveying the room. This was so much easier with Josh. With him, it didn't matter where in the room I was; I wasn't alone. Now, I wanted to find my parents as quickly as possible and duck in the shadows of them. I find them to the far right and start heading that way. I am stopped on my way and greeted. I don't know these people, but they all assume I do. I am hugged by the women with tears in their eyes. I am told how sorry for me they are. The men give me a firm, somber handshake, and tell me to 'hang in there'. I am unsure of the look on my face, but am able to get by with head nods. My mood is an increasing anxiety and confusion.

I finally have a straight path to my parents when I see my grandfather walking toward me. I stop. I don't know if I would call it weakness or vulnerability, but the emotions I have turned to stone begin to find life again. He embraces me without words. He looks at me as though he is judging my condition, puts his arm around me, and leads me over to my parents. There is weariness in their faces but they seem to brighten when they see me. They both hug me. I settle into my space and find myself surrounded by family. I feel comfort but cannot allow the feeling to hold. I think all my life this is what I wanted: to be surrounded by family. I soaked it up as a kid and walked around lost when I didn't have it, until acceptance that the option no longer existed for me fully took over. But now it does exist. Today, I am warmed by its embrace. Except, it exists because my sister is not here, and I would give up everything to have my sister back the way she used to be. To have myself back the way I use to be. I am surrounded by family and I am completely unformed. I offer nothing but a breathing body in a fancy shirt. That seems to be enough for my company, but I do not accept that for myself. I owe myself more than that. I owe my family more than that. I owe Jessica more than that. I can choose how the pieces fit. I never got that until now.

I spend over an hour here. Talking and glad-handing. I even smile a few times. In between this, I sneak in a few glasses of wine. I forget the heaviness in me for a while. When it hits ten o'clock, I say my goodnights and head for the door. Sleep is rarely easy and I know I will need a while to decompress myself before even attempting it. As I reach the doorway, I hear someone behind me. "Hey,"

I turn around and see Emily. She wears a dark green dress that could appear black in the right light. With ease, she walks through the walls in me.

"Hey, Emily." I pause. "I don't know what to say here. Should I thank you for coming?" Emily gives a short laugh.

"No. I just wanted to say hi."

"Well, hi." I go silent again. I look out to all the people in the room. "Isn't it strange that a gathering for someone becomes about everyone that attends except the person it was meant for?"

Emily follows my gaze out across the room. "Tonight is about everyone here. It is mutual support and love. Tomorrow is for her." Emily explains.

"You are wise in the way of funerals, huh?"

"I have been to too many."

"So have I." This is only my second, but it feels like too many. "Josh isn't here, if you are wondering."

"I wasn't really, but it's good to know." She tells me.

"After last time, I thought you might be."

"He is your friend and we had a good time. That is all I can say about it." She says.

"Fair enough."

"What about you? Girlfriend couldn't make it down again?" Emily asks.

"That is a hella long story."

"Want to get a drink and talk about it?" She asks.

It is an innocent invitation by a girl who is anything but. By a girl who can dirty your mind in the holiest of places. I try to decode her intention but can't see anything hidden.

"I need to try and sleep." I tell her.

"Okay."

"If you want, we can meet up for breakfast in the morning?"

"That sounds nice. I know a good spot five minutes from here. Pick you up at eight?" She asks.

"Yeah. Goodnight."

I start to leave and she tries to give me a hug when I am half turned. She retreats before touching me. I notice in mid-hesitation as she sees she doesn't have an angle to hug me. I turn my body to face her. She laughs at the silliness of it, not from any awkwardness.

"Goodnight." She says, hugging me.

I disappear into the hallway and up to my room. I put the TV on to a baseball game, strip my clothes off and collapse in bed. My mind wanders from Lily to Shay to Rachel. I think of all the happy memories and the memories that sting. I think of all the choices I made that have led me here, alone. I think of all my failures. I have left a lot behind, but as the memories cycle through me, I realize I have so much to find ahead of me. High school has built up a world for me and I thought I was satisfied there. But I was hiding. It was safe. When it broke, I was scattered. I collected enough to form something with Rachel, but when she needed more, all I had was scraps of paper with 'incomplete' scribbled on them. They will all be fine without me. And there is sadness in that for me. I am beginning to believe I will be okay without them, and that doesn't lessen the sadness.

I wake up at six the next morning and go out to my car to get my duffle bag of clothes. The sun had risen just enough for me to see how its light changes my perception the stronger it gets. Back in my room, I lay out a pair of jeans and a mostly wrinkled black t-shirt. I attempt to smooth the wrinkles out with my hand but that has no effect. I am not sure why I even did it. I have rarely cared if my shirt is wrinkled or not. I guess I don't really care now either, there is just some instinct that draws me to try to get the wrinkles out. I pull out a towel from my bag and take a shower. Afterwards, I dry myself off and put my boxers and jeans on, then stop. I stare at my black t-shirt. I pick it up and give it a few strong shakes and lay it back on the bed; it is still wrinkled. I again smooth it out with my hand which, as I knew it would, did nothing. I pause and begin to become angry at myself at this debate. I finally reach into my duffle bag and pull out a button-down shirt that I had the foresight to fold before throwing it into the bag. I put the button-down shirt on, socks and shoes and take a look at the time. It is almost seven-thirty. I grab my keys and wallet, take one last look at the t-shirt and head out.

When I reach the lobby, I see my dad holding a tray of coffee, heading toward me. He notices me a few steps after I had seen him, and his reaction is an abrupt stop. He looks at me with some mix of embarrassment and shame. "Noah, hi. I am sorry I didn't ask if you wanted a coffee. I wasn't sure if you were up or not."
"It's cool, Dad. I don't drink coffee. Unless it has a little Bailey's in it." I tell him. He laughs.
"Okay then. Mom, your grandfather and I are heading to breakfast soon if you would like to join us?"
"Thanks. I have breakfast plans."
"You do? Is Josh coming down? Or your girlfriend, what is her name? Michelle?"
"It was Rachel. We broke up. We broke up yesterday, actually." I tell him. He looks at me for a minute. I can't tell if he is trying to tell if I am joking or if this is a place for

some fatherly intervention. "Josh is in Tulsa. It is that girl, Emily." His eyes widen a bit. "Don't give me that look."
"I don't mean to give you a look." He tells me. "I am glad there is someone your age here. My brother's kids didn't come." He tells me.
"They didn't when grandma died either, so I am not surprised they aren't here. They didn't know Jessica. It wouldn't mean anything even if they were here." I say.

He looks at me for a hard minute.
"Maybe you are right. The service is at 11am." He tells me. "I won't be late."

He nods his head, walks to the elevator and pushes the button for his floor. I watch him for a moment but he doesn't turn back to me. I wait until the elevator takes him away before walking outside.

It is bright now and already pretty hot. I walk to the end of the walkway and stand in the middle of the sidewalk. No cars pass me and I don't see any movement in either direction. I stand there with no point or purpose other than an act of waiting. When a car turns toward where I stand, it can only be Emily. She drives an old bright red Neon. She drives slower than the speed limit leading up to me, and stops a good five feet from where I stand. I see her through the windshield. Her hair is pulled back in a ponytail, giving a clear view of her neck and collarbone. She tilts her head in a way that makes me believe she is not moving the car any closer to me. I don't allow a staring contest to begin – I walk to the car.
"Good morning," She says as I slide in.
"Hey," I say. She looks at me, not for long enough to be called a stare, but long enough to unnerve me.
"Lead the way." I tell her. She puts the car in drive and we head to her breakfast spot.

She takes me to a place called "Early Bird" a few left turns from the hotel. It is part of a strip mall, but at a little past seven, it's the only place open. Inside, the word 'kitschy' comes to mind, but as we sit down, I give the place a minute to settle in on me. It is filled with a collection of random items and pictures. A three-foot-high plastic egg sits on a throne in the corner. There are words scribbled on the walls all around. I have an urge to get up and read it, but don't. Emily places her menu down and I realize I haven't even picked mine up. She glares at me as though looking to make sure the measuring cup was at the correct line.

"This is your spot, and I am the one who doesn't need a menu. Interesting. No favorites?" I ask.

"Of course I have a favorite. I was trying to be polite and give you a minute." Her tone indicates her understanding I am teasing, but doesn't have a grip on quite how to read me.

We order and sit looking around each other for a moment.

"So, tell me about this mysterious girlfriend of yours. Why the no-show?"

How do I frame this answer? What is the summary of Lily and me? Of Rachel and me? I have battered it around in my head; I have analyzed it through multiple algorithms. I have never thought how to translate it all so someone else would be able to understand.

"It is a long, crazy story." I tell her.

"Good. Long and crazy stories are my favorite kind." She looks at me unrelenting. She isn't trying to unburden me. I don't think she even understands that having to explain it to her might do that. There are many options of what her intentions are, which is what compels me to answer her question.

"I had this girlfriend, Lily, for most of high school. She was my girlfriend when my grandmother died. She didn't come because I was halfway here when she found out."

"You didn't tell her?" Emily asks.

"No."

"Why?"

Why? Lily wanted to know the same thing. And the answer I had then…

"Because I was a shitty boyfriend. I don't handle things well sometimes and I disappear from people, even from the people who would notice that I disappeared." I say.

Emily doesn't shy away from my honesty. I didn't know how I would answer it, so I know she couldn't have had an idea. The words I say hold meaning, yes, but my mind is filled with hurt, regret, shame and I know my voice must be emoting that. We are eating breakfast with the sun brightening and heating us even through darkened shades. I don't want to undermine how that should make us feel. "So, it is on me. She would have come. She wanted to be here."

"But you didn't want her here?" She asks.

"I think that is how she took it."

"Was that how it was?"

"No. I had just gotten back from seeing my sister and my head wasn't right." I tell her.

"Did she go with you to see your sister?"

"No. She didn't know I had a sister."

"Oh." She says.

This seems to explain something that she doesn't have enough pieces to put together. Does that one piece of information give enough to form an opinion on my entire relationship?

"What about this time?"

"Different girlfriend. We broke up yesterday."

"That's rough."

"She was right. If she came down here, it would take us a level that would only complicate things. I graduate next week. College soon."

"She isn't going to the same school next year?"

I look at her for a minute. I go through all the ways to spin my answer. All the half-truths that would not quite be lies. The omissions I could make that would lead her to the conclusions I wanted her to reach.

"She is going to be a sophomore in high school next year." I tell her.

There is a moment of bewilderment in her before crossing over to acceptance of what I said. I can't find disagreement or judgement in her, even though I am looking hard for it. She piles the information inside her and waits for more.

"What about you? Where is your boyfriend?" I ask.

She straightens herself a bit. Her demeanor changes in a quick shedding. Her eyes now hold an easy in them that is almost fake enough for me to believe it.

"My last boyfriend cheated on me. Since then, I have been unavailable."

"Was this before or after Josh?"

I pull out the brief bit of history we have, and I can tell this unnerves her.

"Before Josh. He was the exception." Emily tells me.

My instinct is to be snide. I wouldn't mean it, but I would usually say it. Those around me would understand or screw off. I couldn't do that here. I didn't want to do that here. That isn't who I am here.

Our food is served and our conversation goes to college and plans beyond that. She is going to study sports medicine and continue to play tennis. She is attending Southern Connecticut State, a less than forty-minute drive from here. I listen and ask questions, but don't have anything to add. I tell her I had a few options, about Albany State, and how that didn't make sense anymore. How that was the last school I wanted to go to now. I tell her that my only friend was going to a school I couldn't get into, and if I could, it would be the second to last school I wanted to go to.

"Why not go to Southern?" She asks. "It's near your family and you will have a friend there."

I want to pinpoint her intentions. Am I experiencing a lack of faith in other people or a lack of faith in myself? My ego is not in a state that would allow me to believe she is hitting on me, even though I can admit the girl has mastered a way of flirting to ease your nerves and feel comfortable with her. It frightens me that I don't know how to respond here. My mind flutters with all the tricks and ways I have kept people at arm's length. But that was to protect Jessica. That's not right. I was protecting myself. I could not allow anyone to know about her so I could keep her as a still-life from before she got sick. But that secret has been spoken, echoed, and etched in stone. Outside of it, I realize how damning it was to me.

"Is there still time to apply?" I ask.

Emily drops me back at the hotel and I change for the funeral service. I wear a black suit with a forest green tie. Forest green was always Jessica's favorite color. I get to the funeral home and find my parents and grandfather standing at the end of a line. People are shaking their hands, giving them hugs. I want to condemn everyone else's sadness. They are choosing to be sad just to feel the emotion. There is nothing real behind it. There couldn't be.

None of them knew Jessica and none of them were crippled by losing her seven years ago. It is only stated on a certificate now. The wind has chosen to release what was left hanging on the fence. And maybe they are here to offer support and comfort. Except, none of them know me. They didn't offer support and comfort before when it would actually have made some sort of difference. I am not sad, I am relieved. I spent years being depressed as hell. This gave me some resolution, some closure, some sense of peace. I don't need people to misinterpret it. I don't need people telling me how I should feel.

I stay in the back and am happily left alone. When people start to take their seats, and the service is about to start, I walk down the aisle and sit in the empty chair behind my father and grandfather. I think I hear scattered whispers about who I am.

The service lasts close to twenty minutes. My mom and dad both speak. I close my eyes and imagine they are speaking only to me. That these are the words they have been working on since I was eleven. All the silence, all the time I was ignored, their words now are there to fill in the spaces when it became unbearable. I feel tears on my cheeks, but I don't care. I want to cry. My eyes are closed. I can make myself believe no else can see me.

At the end of the service, there is one last parade. My parents, grandfather and I are the first to leave, and have to walk past everyone. My hand is grabbed and squeezed as I pass, and I hear people say they will pray for me. I do my best to withdraw. As we approach the exit, I see Emily. She stands there as part of the crowd and, at first, doesn't look at me. I slow my pace and keep my eyes on her until she looks up. She blushes a smile. I can see water glaze her eyes. She blinks them but no water is washed away. I step out of the line my family has formed and go to her. I wrap my arms around her. I know I have become the center of attention. I don't care. I stay there and allow myself a moment to grieve, then another to compose myself. When my embrace with Emily ends, I look at her, her cheeks are stained with tears as I can feel mine are as well.

"I guess I am not all sand." I say to her. She smiles an understanding of what I mean. I lower my head and walk out.

The burial is a small affair. Maybe ten people. My grandfather leads things. He doesn't quote scripture. He reads a part of a poem by Lord Byron called, "The Dream". We stand in a semi-circle when he is finished, as the casket is lowered into the ground. We each take turns shoveling dirt and saying a few words. Everyone retreats to their cars from there and the small group becomes my parents, grandfather and me. I go over to my parents and they each hug me. Their eyes are stricken in a heaviness of emotion pulsating them. We talk a little and agree to meet to have dinner together. We were to spend one more night at the hotel before returning home. As they leave, I turn and find my grandfather waiting for me by my car. I walk to him. "This is a lot to process. For me as well. And I have been here too many times." He tells me.

"Are you telling me it gets easier?" I ask.

"No. I am telling you it is hard every time. I want you to remember that there is still joy for you out there. This doesn't void you from that."

"I know." I look at him and can sense his sincerity. I guess you don't have to know all the details to understand the overview. "I have a lot to work through. I will be fine, though."

"I know you will." He pauses. "I talked to your parents and have invited them to move here. I have found a great new job for your father, and your mom would only have to work part-time. I know you are off to college in a few months and they will talk to you about it. I just wanted to let you know and hear what you think."

I have no idea what I think. The thought of me leaving for college, and my parents moving, had never been parallel. I did get the fact that they could use a new beginning, and it makes sense to come here to do it.

"I might be too late, but I had thoughts about applying to Southern Connecticut State. I have already been accepted to a few schools, but it would be nice to be close to family."

My grandfather is noticeably surprised.

"I think that is a fine idea. If I can do anything to help, please let me know."

"I will."

He pats me on the shoulder, walks to his car and drives away. I watch his car until it exits the cemetery and drives out of view. I reach into my pockets for my keys when I notice the gravedigger filling in my sister's grave. The pile of dirt was more than half gone, and I could not make myself move until her grave was completely filled. The gravedigger takes his shovel and walks to his golf cart no more than thirty feet away.

I wait a few minutes to make sure he is gone before walking back to where my sister's casket was lowered. I move right up to the edge, where grass becomes dirt. I push some dirt treading on the grass over into the dirt side with my foot. I become acutely aware of the texture and the nuisance of the dirt. These surroundings were now my sister's company. I wanted to know it too. I wanted it to know me. To be able to distinguish me from everyone else. From everything else. All the conversations I had with Jessica over the last five years, I wanted to believe she heard. That she understood. That there was some tiny cell that stored a memory of them. Even in her most lucid states, I never had any indication that this was the case.

Now, I look to her grave and then up to the sky. If there is a heaven, I don't know the requirements, and therefore, don't know what their response will be if Jessica knocks on the gates. I think of her soul being turned away and left to wander. She was lost to this world and denied a place in the next. But maybe when you die it simply ends. The stardust inside you gives pieces to the creation of something else. That would mean I would never see her again. There would be nothing to keep the memories current. I tell myself if that is the way of it, I needed to take this time to say goodbye. Before she is completely part of the ether.

"Jessica." I start. "This is your brother, Noah. This is probably stupid, meaningless to talk to you now. I know I can't reach you. I have not been able to reach you for a while, and that has done something to me. I thought it was just a weight in me, a secret I couldn't explain. But I never thought of the consequences of that. I stopped. I found a space I knew how to move around in, and stayed there. And when people I cared about began to change, I had no answer for it. I was stopped. And now I am here. A distance with too many burned bridges to retrace my steps. I had stopped. But now I think I can begin again. Always know I love you. Please forgive anything that was my fault; that caused this. You always took care of me and I failed when you needed me to take care of you. Please know I love you. Maybe you needed me to keep going when you got sick. Maybe mom and dad needed me to keep going too. I didn't know how. I wasn't strong enough. I am not confident that I am now, but it is time to start. Goodbye, Jessica."

I stay, in the silence, looking down at the fresh dirt, almost in meditation. I wait for some kind of change to take hold of me. For some seal of closure. The feeling doesn't come. Maybe that is the point.